PROTECTING MR. FINE

LUCY LENNOX

PROTECTING MR. FINE

I'm a lucky man and I know it.

Kids from backwoods Georgia don't land scholarships to Yale, but I did, and striking it rich–like, *billions of dollars* rich–with my best friends after graduation should have used up my luck for a lifetime.

But luck struck again when I followed my passion into music. My career exploded, and now I get to travel the world, performing for thousands of raving fans every night.

When you get this lucky, you don't get to want more, and you definitely don't get to complain about the little things. My family, my crew, and my label are counting on me and I refuse to let them down. I pretend I'm fine, totally fine, Mr. freaking Fine... even when someone starts targeting me with a strange series of threats.

The only one who sees beneath the pretense is my gorgeous, strictly-professional bodyguard. Ryan keeps me safe and calm. He holds me when I'm terrified.

But even Ryan doesn't see everything. He doesn't know I want him. That I crave him. The man who keeps me together has no idea how much I want him to take me apart.

And I'll never tell. Because there's no way someone as strong and confident as Ryan could have feelings for someone as chaotic as me.

Nobody's *that* lucky... not even *Mr. Fine*.

PROLOGUE

RYAN

Don't let a bear's aloofness fool you—they feel emotions deeply.
They may act tough, wandering solo through the wilderness,
but inside? They've got hearts as big as their appetite for honey.
—Bear Facts for Insomniacs, Episode 13

The moment I truly learned what hubris meant was the moment I first met Zane Hendley.

Correction, it was the day I first met *Zee Barlo*, Grammy Award–winning rock star, headliner of sold-out arenas around the globe, and one of the Sexiest Men Alive... according to *People* magazine. I didn't catch a glimpse of the real man behind the public persona until later.

"He's the new Taylor Swift, if Taylor Swift was a beautiful man instead of a beautiful woman," Violet explained as we made our way into the record label's Los Angeles recording studio for our first client meeting. I was still getting used to seeing my new boss in person instead of on a Zoom screen, and I noticed a sparkle in her eyes when she referred to her newest client. "And this is a super-cush assignment. You're welcome."

"You mean there are no actual threats to his safety?"

Her heels made a clip-clip sound on the marble floor of the large corporate lobby as we crossed to the elevator bank. "No, no. There definitely are. But they're from rabid fans wanting a piece of him more than sociopolitical agents hell-bent on his destruction."

I must have winced because Violet immediately apologized. "Shit, Ryan. I'm sorry."

After a deep, calming inhale through my nostrils, I attempted a reassuring smile. "It's okay."

"It's not. Here I am discussing assassinations when your previous employer is still lying in state. Are you sure you don't want to go back to Ventdestine for the funeral?"

My memories of Asger Salling and the rest of the Ventdestinian royal family were a mixed bag. While I'd deeply respected the king for the entire twelve years I'd worked on his security detail as a member of the royal guard, and we'd shared plenty of friendly moments, I hadn't truly been his friend. I'd been more like very friendly wallpaper.

I'd also been skeptical of the king's prediction that he'd be a target for assassination because he'd sensed "the winds of fate whispering ill tidings around the palace"—the kind of claim that only someone in the tiny, superstitious nation of Ventdestine could make with a straight face—but as it turned out, I'd been wrong.

My decision to leave the royal guard and return to the US had happened well in advance of his assassination, and the security failure hadn't had anything to do with me. In fact, I'd already been comfortably ensconced at my sister's place in Montana when I'd gotten the news along with everyone else that the king of Ventdestine had been shot and killed during a PR visit to the royal naval yard.

I still felt partially responsible for it, though. Maybe if I'd taken Asger's concerns more seriously, if I hadn't let my feelings about his superstitions affect my assessments, I could have better prepared my replacement.

In my new assignment, I'd make sure there were no feelings involved whatsoever.

"I'm sure," I said, clearing my throat as I followed her into the elevator.

Violet grinned as she jabbed the button. "Good. Because I can't lie, I feel like if you went back for a visit, you might end up staying. The new king is so eager to have you back his head of security reached out to ask if I'd subcontract you to them. And the salary the guy offered was... substantial."

"I know," I said gruffly. "Kasper contacted me directly, too. But as I told him, I'm not interested in going back to Ventdestine. I'm ready for a new assignment, and like you said, this one sounds great."

Protecting a popular rock star from overeager fans when no one would be trying to take him out with sniper fire from across the red carpet... presumably? This would be a walk in the park compared to my previous assignment.

I was supremely confident about this. Perhaps, one might say, excessively confident. So confident I momentarily forgot that old expression about hubris leading to downfall.

Then I stepped out of the elevator and saw the most beautiful man I'd ever laid eyes on... and hubris literally knocked the breath out of me.

Gorgeous face. Long, sun-kissed hair. Honey-brown eyes that regarded me curiously. A mouth so soft and sensual my gut went painfully tight in an instant.

I needed no Ventdestinian mystical woo-woo to know "the winds of fate were blowing ill" in regard to my ability to do this job without complications.

In fact, the real reason I'd quit my job in Ventdestine and moved back to the United States was even clearer than before.

I wanted to have sex with men.

Ventdestine was a beautiful country, full of wonderful people and charming traditions, but their laws and cultural expectations regarding LGBTQ issues remained locked in an earlier, intolerant era. I'd spent twelve years closeted and practically celibate because I couldn't afford to get caught breaking the ancient law. The scandal it would have caused to the royal family would have been devastating.

I'd known what I was getting into when Asger bestowed the royal guard position on me. At that time, the opportunity to travel and make more money than I'd ever imagined had been worth the personal sacrifice. But now... now I was ready to have a life outside of work. To live a little and fuck a lot.

A thought that should not have been at the forefront of my brain the moment I met my new client.

Violet performed the introduction. "Zee, this is Ryan Galloway. Ryan, Zee Barlo."

"Hi, I'm Zane," he said with a polite smile, surprising me since I hadn't known Zee was short for anything. "I hear you're my new close protection officer. Welcome to the team."

We were standing in the reception area of the recording studio, and the morning sun had slanted in through one of the high windows, lighting up the golden strands in his long brown hair. The air-conditioning had even kicked on, making the strands blow in an artificial breeze.

Winds of fate, indeed.

"H-hi," I stammered before reminding myself I was a professional. I cleared my throat and tried again. "Nice to meet you. I know you have a recording session today. Anything else you have planned?"

He shook his head. "No. The session will take most of the day, and they'll order in lunch for us. Ready?"

I nodded and followed him toward a hallway while he walked and typed messages in his phone at the same time. Clearly, he didn't take any personal responsibility for situational awareness, but maybe that was simply due to feeling safe in such a familiar space. Or maybe he was an entitled ass who left the pesky security shit to the hired help.

You can ignore a pretty face if it comes attached to a self-important celebrity, I told myself. *There's nothing sexy about that.*

Zane pointed me to a chair against the wall between the sound booth's door and the door to the editing suite. After glancing around both spaces to get a sense of who was in the room with us and what other exits there were and determining there were no active threats, I sat.

Violet had prepared me for how tedious a day in the studio could be, but I'd spent years keeping watch over a king whose favorite activity was watching the news on TV. This couldn't be much different.

Then Zane began singing.

I sat up straight in my chair like I'd been jolted by a live wire.

That voice. Sweet fucking god. It was phenomenal.

It was also, I realized, familiar. Several younger members of the Ventdestinian royal family—Asger's grandchildren—had been obsessed with Zee and had played his music nonstop out by the pool last summer.

Song after song, take after take, I let that glorious voice wash over me. For some reason, it felt like he was singing right to me, even though his eyes were closed in concentration most of the time.

When we broke for lunch, he was inundated with people who needed to talk to him. An assistant asking him questions, his manager, Micki, informing him of schedule changes, and a member of his band telling him a long, detailed story of how he'd spent his weekend. Throughout all of it, Zane listened as if the person he was talking to was the only person in the room.

He had the patience of a saint and the kindness of a damned Disney princess.

And that was when I came to a couple of mortifying realizations.

First, that Zane wasn't just a gorgeous face and a captivating voice. He was a decent person.

And second, that I might possibly have a little bit of trouble maintaining my professional distance... though I *would*. I obviously would.

Hubris whispered, *Don't be so sure*, but I ignored it.

I spent the next few days escorting Zane from his home in Malibu to the recording studio while he worked long hours performing music for a new album. Each day, I expected the music to get old, for the songs to begin to sound the same, or for me to wish for silence.

None of those things happened.

I found myself falling into a strange and easy obsession with him. Somehow, in the span of three days, I turned into one of the singer's rabid fans, only I had to hide it as my own horrifying and dirty secret.

Zee Barlo became my idol. He had the voice of a fallen angel and eyes that melted my fucking heart.

Okay, I told myself. *So I like his music and think he's one of the few people in the world who truly deserves to be as famous as he is. I maybe even have a small crush on him. So what?*

It was a *good* thing I was pleasantly obsessed with his voice since I'd be hearing a nauseating amount of it as long as he was my principal. And my crush simply meant that I was more aware of him. Better able to do my job. It didn't have to be a big deal.

Hubris said, *Hold my beer*.

On the fourth day of my "super-cushy" assignment, I realized Zane wasn't just a good person... he was maybe the best person I'd ever met.

Zane didn't have a full-time PA because it was "stressful" and made him feel like a diva. Instead, he had a house manager who kept his fridge stocked and his laundry done, and he had an assistant named Kenji, who was based in New York and seemed to run Zane's financial and legal life. On this particular day, Kenji flew out in the corporate jet, seemingly for the sole purpose of getting Zane's undivided attention while Zane traveled to Toronto for a meet and greet.

We were the only three people in the cabin with the exception of the flight attendant, who was busy doing something in the galley at the front of the jet. Since I was sitting behind the pair, I wondered if maybe they'd forgotten I was there because they began discussing financials using very specific and very large numbers.

Kenji's voice was low and calm. "The original education fund in Barlo is growing faster than the fund manager expected. She wants you to consider splitting in two and possibly designating the second one as merit-based."

"Instead of increasing the amount of need-based scholarships? I'm not sure, Kenji..."

"I told her you'd say that," he said with a chuckle. "She said that the need-based applicants are fully covered at this time. But if you want to continue focusing on need-based kids, you can expand into the neighboring counties, or her team can research—"

"Can't we do both?" Zane asked. "I mean, didn't we already talk about expanding into Terrell and Mitchell counties?"

Kenji's dark hair flashed between the seats as he nodded. "Those funds have already been established, and the one in south Fulton is still running strong, especially with the corporate matching programs we have there."

As they continued to discuss the scholarship funds, I learned that these were scholarships for kids in his home state of Georgia who were living in poverty. Instead of college scholarships, they were scholarships that fully funded elementary through high school projects, helping teachers with supplies, learning assessments, technology, field trips, and even additional teaching staff. His funds covered hot meals for all kids in those schools regardless of need, and he even made plans to visit each school once a year for a quick meet and greet to give the kids bragging rights.

Once he and Kenji had gotten through the topic of his education projects, Kenji went over contributions to local foster care systems in the cities where he was playing concerts.

Chest tight, I remembered the intel in Violet's client file. Zane had lost both his parents to addiction. His father had been convicted of drug-related violence before dying in prison when Zane was in elementary school, and his mother had died of an overdose only a few months later. After that, he'd been raised by his grandmother and various other extended family members in a tiny town in Georgia.

I'd also learned that the town of Barlo, Georgia, had been dirt-poor until only a couple of years ago when Zane had begun funneling serious money into the town to revitalize it and bring much-needed jobs to the people there. Even his choice to use Barlo in his stage name had contributed to the town getting an influx of tourism money.

I'd had a pang of sympathy when I'd first read his story, as anyone would. Admiration, too, for what Zane had made of himself.

But that afternoon on the flight from LA to Toronto, listening to Kenji review what had to be millions of dollars in charity funds, I learned just how selfless and generous Zane Hendley was, and I...

I realized I didn't just have a minor crush on Zee Barlow, the nice guy, killer performer, kick-ass singer, and hot single gay man who seemed to hook up with someone in every town he played.

I also genuinely *liked* and respected Zane Hendley.

Which was kind of a problem since I'd resolved to keep my professional distance and not allow any feelings to sway me whatsoever.

Hubris cackled, *I told you so.*

Zane was the kind of man who would pay to fix a backstage crew member's flat tire when he overheard the guy couldn't fix it till payday. Who'd stay up all night making sure his closest friends heard his voice first thing on their birthday. Who fell asleep every day listening to an animal facts podcast because his hairstylist's brother produced it. Who'd stop halfway through a perfect take to encourage his drummer to take a call from his kid. And who asked me—*me*, the guy who was supposed to be worried about *him*—before every single concert if I had a comfortable place to sit while he performed.

Was it any wonder I wanted to be around him all the time, to soak up his presence, to protect him for reasons that had nothing to do with my job?

And Zane Hendley needed my protection.

The man bordered on *too* nice. Sometimes he was late taking the stage because he couldn't walk away from someone whose feelings might be hurt if he ended a conversation abruptly, so I became the heavy, growling at him to get a move on before he disappointed his fans.

He also refused to be treated like the VIP he was. He insisted on rolling with any punches. He didn't want his actions to negatively affect anyone, which meant he pretended to be fine when he wasn't.

Hundred-degree fever and chills? He'd say he was *fine* to perform the final long set in Detroit.

Suspected sprained ankle after slipping down a wet ramp? He was *fine* to do that night's choreography in Anaheim.

Giggling teenager tried to turn a selfie into a make-out session by kissing Zane's cheek just before she snapped the pic? He was *fine* to keep the meet and greet going and even dubbed me *Bear*—a nickname that stuck and managed to hit me in the solar plexus every time he used it—when I snarled at the girl and confiscated her phone to delete the picture.

Learning that his grandmother needed an urgent heart cath procedure right before taking the stage in Munich? He was *fine* to do the show... but could someone please arrange a quick flight home to be with her before the Zurich show in four days?

No matter what obstacles landed in his path, Zee Barlo made sure to tell everyone on his team he was fine.

But over time, I began to see that *Zane Hendley* was not fine. Zane Hendley was bending over backwards to look out for everyone except himself. Zane Hendley was killing himself to make sure to *be* fine so that everyone else around him thrived. Zane Hendley was terrified of letting anyone down.

Zane Hendley was the walking definition of a person who set himself on fire to keep everyone around him warm.

And it began to make me angry. So angry, in fact, that I could no longer keep it to myself.

About six months after I started the job, hubris finally won.

I lost the ability to remain calm and professional with my principal.

We were in Tulsa, Oklahoma, for an appearance at a fundraiser to benefit the victims of recent tornadoes in the area. Zane was joining a group of five local bands as the concert headliner. Not only were the ticket and concession sales going to the cause, but the streaming rights would also produce significant income to help those families and communities devastated by the storms.

It was a last-minute idea pitched to him as we'd finished up a performance in Oklahoma City. He'd immediately insisted on helping any way he could, even though it meant scrambling to fit the event into his already crushing tour schedule.

Halfway from the airport to the concert venue, the SUV we were in was sideswiped on the interstate and sent careening into two other cars in the next lane. The accident happened so fast it was over before my brain caught up with what was happening.

I'd been through simulated vehicle attack training many times during my years with the royal guard, so I immediately went into response mode with my principal, checking his breathing and pulse.

"B-bear?" he asked weakly. "What happened?"

My heart gave a crazy leap at hearing that name on his lips. I loved all the things it represented—the teasing, the familiarity, the trust we'd built, the knowledge that I'd do anything to keep him safe —and I hated it, too. Because I wanted it to mean even more.

I forced myself to focus on my training.

Breathing good. Pulse strong. But there was a trickle of blood streaming down the side of his face. "Car accident." I stabilized his neck and ignored my own pain. "Stay still and tell me what hurts."

Suddenly, he let out a heart-wrenching keening noise, and my heart rate went into full panic mode, wondering what possible life-threatening injury I'd overlooked. I scrambled to pat him down gently, trying desperately to figure out what I was missing. "Zane!

What hurts? Tell me what it is." I couldn't see any blood other than what was on his face.

"All the people hit by the storms," he said, tears starting to fall and mix with the blood on one side. "The fundraiser, Bear. We won't get there in time to help them."

I stared at him. We were lucky to be alive—in fact, I wasn't sure yet if everyone involved *was* alive—and this man was worried about raising money for people in need.

"Who gives a fuck about that right now?" I barked at him. "We need to get out of this vehicle. Can you move? Are you hurt?"

"What? No. I'm fine."

Fine.

The man had blood down his face and into the collar of his shirt. I didn't know it at the time, but he also had serious thoracic contusions from the seat belt that made him breathe shallowly for several days and a severely bruised elbow from where it had been smashed between his body and the door, and he ended up getting six stitches in a cut by his hairline.

"You're not fucking fine!" I shouted as I hustled him out of the crushed vehicle and onto the side of the highway. "Why do you always say you're fine when you're not? You drive me absolutely fucking batshit with your 'I'm fines'! Why can't you allow yourself to be hurt for once when you're... oh, I don't know... actually hurt?"

He was pale and shaky, eyes white in shock and fear. I wanted —*needed*—nothing more than to take him into my arms and comfort him... but I couldn't.

Zane was my principal. This was my *job*. And the man deserved to know there were people in his life who would put his wants and needs before their own.

Cars sped past us despite the angled presence of the three scattered vehicles that had been involved in the accident. Thankfully, emergency vehicles were almost to us, and their lights and sirens began slowing down traffic approaching the site of the accident.

After insisting he be transported in an ambulance to the nearest emergency room where he was treated for his injuries, I watched him ensure everyone else involved was okay, too.

When we finally got to a hotel in the early hours of the morning and they asked for a name for the reservation, I was so filled with frustrated need, so angry and outraged on Zane's behalf, I couldn't remember the fake name we always used for Zane's hotel reservations.

"Last name?" the receptionist asked, blinking at Zane in disbelief. Even with a bandage on his forehead, blood on his shirt, and a tangled nest of hair, he was the most beautiful man within several city blocks.

"He's fine," I snapped, wishing I could burn the world to make it so. "He's Mr. fucking Fine."

And the horrifying truth hit me in that moment—a truth I could never tell Zane without losing my right to stay by his side and protect him.

Somehow—through my own hubris, or chance, or the fucking Ventdestinian winds of fortune—Zane Hendley had crawled under my impenetrable professional walls... and burrowed himself claws-deep in my heart.

ONE

ZANE - SIX MONTHS LATER

Bears are bottomless pits when it comes to food, gobbling up honey every chance they get. And when their favorite snack is in danger, they'll be the fiercest bodyguard in the wild. Nothing will stand between them and their most cherished bite!

    —Bear Facts for Insomniacs, Episode 17

I hadn't even felt the stamp this time. The best I could tell, it had happened when I'd been jostled to the side by a stage tech rushing past during the set break. Immediately afterward, Carlo and Kim, the makeup and hair duo, had stepped forward for a quick touch-up, and Kim had quirked her head and asked why I had red ink under the collar of my shirt.

There hadn't been time for the words to even sink in until I'd taken the stage. But there, in front of the hometown Atlanta crowd at the Shaky Knees festival, I'd realized what she meant.

I'd been marked with another red bull's-eye.

Another target.

Another time someone had proven they could get to me by pressing a tiny rubber stamp onto my skin with permanent ink.

As soon as I'd realized what had happened, I hadn't been able to help glancing over at the wings. My tall, heavily muscled bodyguard —the man I'd begun calling *Bear* a few months ago to tease him and even started *thinking* of as Bear for... other reasons—had been waylaid by my petite former publicist. Noelle had tried several times to speak to me, but Bear had made it his personal mission to keep her away, especially since I was due onstage.

When he'd seen my face, he'd known immediately that something serious had happened. Bear always had the ability to see through my attempts at hiding my emotions... and it drove me up a wall.

He'd already taken a large stride in my direction before someone stopped him, gesturing wildly to the tape on the ground indicating the sight line for the backstage area. Bear's square jaw had flexed, his brown eyes had darkened, and he'd practically bared his teeth at the poor stage manager. I'd forced myself to look ahead into the tens of thousands of screaming fans. The crowd here in the park was pumped, the weather was unseasonably warm, and the sun had been setting in golden peaches and pinks across the concert venue.

It would have been glorious...

If only I hadn't been ice-cold inside.

Thankfully, the set had gone by fast with all of that energy. I'd allowed myself to get lost in the music, to let it comfort me and help me forget my troubles, as it always did.

At least until I came off the stage and Bear yanked me past everyone into the dressing room before demanding, "What."

It wasn't a question but a command, and it cracked the icy, calm blanket I'd pulled around myself to get through my set. My hands shook, and my skin began to tingle as the reality of the situation sank in. How ridiculous was it that I hadn't started trembling until Bear was with me and I'd known I was safe?

"It's fine," I said automatically. "Really, Bear. F-fine."

His eyes narrowed, but he didn't speak.

I tried to keep my voice steady. "I think..." I gestured to the collar of my shirt. "Um... behind... over my..."

He stepped behind me and pulled at my collar. When he sucked in an outraged breath, it made it all real. My legs wobbled, and his arm banded around my front. The strong warmth of his touch never failed to make my breath catch, which caused my head to feel even floatier.

I hated feeling weak, hated causing concern and more work for others. And I especially hated the idea of Bear thinking I was some kind of fragile diva who needed protecting from the big, scary world.

So I shoved him away and took a breath. "I told you, it's fine."

"Say that word to me again," he said in a low voice. "I dare you."

I closed my eyes and tried to focus. "I mean to say, I'm not hurt."

Bear made a grumbling noise that suggested he'd be the judge of that. "Take off your shirt."

A huff of humorless laughter came out of my nose. I'd fantasized about Bear saying that many, many times in the past year. Fantasies in which he'd growled exactly that phrase, among many others, with the same ferocity.

Never had I imagined it would carry so little lust.

Instead of arguing with him—which I knew would be pointless—I yanked off my sweaty tee and dropped it over a nearby chair. I kept my back to him so he could investigate the stamp, but I watched him in the dressing room mirror.

His face was a full storm. A hurricane band swirling around and around, picking up strength as it circled. His large hands came up to hold my shoulders, one thumb smoothing the patch of skin just over my shoulder and out of my own sight range.

"Is it the same?" I asked softly, trying to ignore my prickling awareness of his gentle touch.

He grunted confirmation.

Silence filled the room with jagged tension before he spoke.

"This is the third time, Zane. We can't keep ignoring this. We need to get back to LA and call in reinforcements—"

"No," I said emphatically. "No way. We're due in Barlo tomorrow morning to see my family for a few days. I *promised* them. And I'm not canceling it."

"You're not canceling it. I am. This is the third time some psycho has gotten their hands on you, Zane, and I'm not allowing you to—"

I whipped around, shaking his hands off me in the process. "Not allowing? I'm not your child, *Ryan*. I'm your principal, as you remind me on a regular basis. You work for me, remember?"

His eyebrow winged up, possibly at my use of his real name, and there was the barest hint of a smirk at the edge of his mouth. "I actually don't work for you." He paused before casting my own word back at me. "Remember?"

I pressed my lips together in frustration. "Fine. You work for the label. But you're here for me, for my protection. And the label doesn't get to decide that I can't visit my family. I've been looking forward to this trip for months, and you know it."

"I do know, and I'm sorry. Genuinely. But it's not safe. We don't know what the stamps mean. We don't know who's doing this. We don't know how they keep getting to you. And we don't know what they might do next. We need to regroup. To come up with a new personal protection strategy to—"

I held up my hand. "No. I know what you're going to say. You want the label to bump up the detail and put a fucking army of people on me. That's not happening, not when there's no proof the person or people doing this mean me any harm."

He shot me another look. The man had an innate ability to read my mind, but I did my best to keep my emotions locked down anyway. If he realized just how freaked-out I was by this situation, he'd burn the whole world to get me home to LA and shut me up tight in my Malibu home.

He'd threatened to suspend the tour to "reassess our security strategy" more than once, but thus far, I'd always managed to convince him to do the reassessing while keeping the tour going. Canceling shows meant costing the venues revenue and costing their workers jobs, not to mention costing the fans lost time and money.

Bear knew how committed I was to following through on my promises, to providing jobs and bonuses to the people on the team who busted their asses to make these performances the best they could be. He knew how devastated I'd be if our team's decision caused even one penny-pinching preteen to be disappointed.

But this time... this time, I was almost tempted to let him take over. To curl up in a ball and ask him to ferry me away from the crowds and the fear of the unknown. The only thing stopping me was the thought of missing a long-awaited visit with my gran.

There was no place I felt safer or more loved than in Barlo, Georgia. In Barlo, nothing would be able to reach me. There, everyone knew me and loved me. Everyone would gather round and keep me safe. For at least a little while, I'd be able to forget about Zee Barlo and simply be...

"Zane." Bear's voice was like whiskey poured over gravel. "Someone *touched* you. They stamped a literal target onto your fucking skin—"

I sucked in a breath. "Yes, a stylized target. The same target as the one on my first album cover," I reminded him. "It's not a threat. Necessarily. It's probably a... a... I don't know. A prank. A dare, maybe. Or they have a weird obsession with the album. Or the target icon. Or they think they'll seem cool if they can get close enough to me to..." I didn't have the words to describe what I was trying to say, and I could tell that my arguments were only making Bear more angry. I added hastily, "My point is, there's no proof they intend harm. So we're not going to overreact. You and Lou can handle things in Barlo. It's a tiny town, for god's sake. *Then* we'll head back to LA and figure out if there's anything to be concerned about. But I can already tell you there won't be."

"Need I remind you there is a contract stipulation about your safety that indicates..."

I stopped paying attention to the lecture since it was nothing new and instead focused on Bear's face as he spoke—on his intense, broody eyes and chiseled jaw, on his strong hands that always touched me so gently, on the broad shoulders and barrel chest that made me feel safe and nervous all at once.

"Zane? Are you even listening?" he demanded.

I winced. "Uh. Yes?"

"Jesus Christ," he muttered, storming out of the room. He paused and turned when he got to the hall.

"I'm done trying to reason with you, Zane," he barked. "We're doing this my way, and that means wheels up in sixty minutes. Do you understand?"

I firmed my jaw and forced myself to sound unaffected. "No. I told my family I was coming in time for Sunday supper tomorrow. We're not leaving Georgia until after I've had my aunt Rinny's tomato corn pie and cheese grits. I've waited months to see my family, and I'm not letting some bullshit prank take that away from me."

Bear was usually an island of calm sanity in the midst of my chaotic life, and seeing him upset—especially when I knew it was out of fear for my safety—brought home exactly how serious he perceived this threat to be.

It wasn't a prank.

He knew it. So did I.

But while I loved how much he worried about me—seriously *loved* it—I hated seeing him this way. Hated knowing that I caused him stress and worry. I swallowed and tried to get us back to normal, to the way things were supposed to be.

"Bears are supposed to be *very* food-motivated. They'll eat anything and everything, according to the podcast episode I listened to last week," I managed to tease, though my voice came out wobbly and an entire octave higher than usual, which probably ruined the effect. "So I'll remind you that last time we were at Gran's, you ate three helpings of those cheese grits—"

"Are you fucking kidding me?" he demanded. "I don't give a shit about your podcast, Zane. This is about your safety. It's not a joke—"

"I know it's not," I soothed. "I do know. I promise. It's just... how many times do I have to tell you... I'm fine!"

"Sure you are, Zane. You're Mr. fucking Fine. Keep telling yourself that."

As soon as Bear—*Ryan*—stormed off, I closed the dressing room door behind him and locked it before leaning my back against it and sliding down.

The tears came instantly. I'd been holding them off for hours to get through the final set, and now here I was, on the floor, face swamped with tears of exhaustion, fear, and a desperate, bone-deep need to go home and see my family.

To forget that someone had touched me without my knowledge.

Had managed to pull aside my shirt and ink my skin.

Had tried sending me a message of some kind without explaining what the fucking point was.

I let out a shaky breath and tried to get control of my emotions.

I was the king of good fortune, I knew that.

In the grand scheme of things, my current hardships were small potatoes, and I had no right to complain.

Not only was I a megastar—one of the rare unicorns who'd dreamed of being a successful rock musician and had actually made it happen—I was also part of a priceless brotherhood of lifelong friends and, although hardly anyone outside of my brotherhood knew it, a rags-to-riches story even before I'd started my music career.

Bash, Silas, Landry, Dev, and I had met while attending Yale and had worked together to invent ETC, an emergency response software. Selling our company had netted us each over a billion dollars. We'd also learned the hard way to keep our windfall a secret from everyone but our assistant, Kenji, and our life partners, for those brothers lucky enough to find one.

Obviously, the millions I made from my music career were impossible to hide, but that was no hardship. It just meant that I got to be crazy-generous with my wealth without risk of divulging my brothers' secrets. It meant that I could consult with property agents about which of several multi-acre spreads in Wyoming I'd like best and not have to factor the cost into my decision. It meant that I got to be selective about the music I recorded and the contracts I signed.

It was the kind of life I'd have been scared to even dream of, growing up in Barlo. A comfortable, easy life, where I'd gotten to make all—or at least *almost* all—of my dreams come true. And by living my own dream, I was able to help others reach theirs. That was a privilege as well as a responsibility.

So yeah, I was Mr. fucking Fine, as Bear called me. And I damn well should be.

I damn well *had* to be.

Too many people were counting on me for me to be anything else.

So even if I was scared, even if I was freaked-out and violated and outraged and wanted nothing more than to curl up in a ball under the covers, I was going to remind myself of how freaking lucky I was. Then, I was gonna smile and get on with the show.

And I did...

Until the emails started.

TWO

RYAN

---

*Everyone knows bears are fiercely protective of their territory
and their loved ones. When a bear claims something, it's theirs,
and they won't hesitate to defend it. It's a foolish bear indeed
who goes sniffing around another bear's honey.*
—Bear Facts for Insomniacs, Episode 21

No one tested my patience like Zane Hendley.

Before meeting Zane a little over a year ago, I hadn't known it was possible to be so annoyed by a genuinely good human. He was kind and generous, sweet and talented, and even after a year of being together almost twenty-four seven, I still had an enormous crush on him.

Possibly slightly more than a crush.

Yet I also fantasized about sedating him just to keep him from lying to my face about being "fine."

That wasn't the only thing I fantasized about doing to him, but the other things were even more unprofessional than the first. And I took my job way too seriously to consider wrecking it by—

"Fucking assholes!" Landry jabbed his phone screen to end a call. He paced Zane's Shaky Knees dressing room, where he and the other men Zane called his "brothers" had congregated after Zane's set ended.

The fact that Zane's friends had arrived not long after Zane and I had our dust-up and had managed to cheer him up and distract him the way I wished *I* could while I stood in the corner silently watching was neither here nor there.

I was a professional, damn it. Zane was my principal.

And maybe if I repeated those words to myself for *another* year or two, I might begin to believe them.

"What's up?" Zane grabbed Landry's arm in a friendly gesture and forced him to stop his pacing.

My eyes zeroed in on the spot where Zane's tan hand met Landry's slightly paler skin with a laser-like intensity.

I immediately looked away, afraid Landry might have noticed me looking, though Zane hadn't.

"Now they want me in Paris a full week before the shoot." Landry threw himself into a chair and pouted, which I had to admit was not a bad look on him.

I was sure Zane thought the same... and I told myself *that* was neither here nor there, either. Zane's friend was tall and beautiful, as most fashion models were, and my principal was an even more gorgeous, openly gay man. It was only natural that there was an attraction there.

Even if they hid it when they were in public or with their other friends, I'd heard what Zane and Landry got up to behind closed doors.

And it was none of my business.

If I currently wanted to grab Landry, drag him away from Zane, and buy him a one-way ticket to... someplace populated by actual bears... that had nothing to do with my crush on my principal and everything to do with wanting Zane to focus on the very real security threat rather than on his friend's modeling woes.

I inhaled a breath. "Folks, I'm going to need you to get the hell out of here. Zane needs to be moved now... and without an entourage."

Landry side-eyed me. "It seems to me he'd be better protected if we walked as a large unit circled around him to keep the riffraff at bay."

I could just imagine the janky-ass circle these fuckers would attempt. It bore absolutely no resemblance to anything taught in a close-protection skills course. "A ball cap disguise will do a better job of getting us out of here without drawing attention than a circle of hot rich men. No offense."

Landry flicked his long, blond hair over one shoulder and sniffed. "None taken, obvs."

Zane peered at me and tried to fake a grin as if he was super chill and not at all affected by the target stamp. "You think my friends are hot?"

I saw right through his "fine-ness" as I always did. Zane was terrified that someone had gotten close enough to ink that target on him, and I felt the twist of guilt deep in my gut.

I hadn't been there with him in that moment it had happened. I'd let myself get distracted by Noelle and her incessant attempts to reconcile with her former client.

"Hot like too much wasabi, hot," I grumbled. "The kind that makes you sweat and want to die at the same time. Let's go."

As I waited impatiently, Zane said goodbye to his friends.

I reached for Zane's arm and felt his muscles contract. Now was not the time to be distracted by his biceps and the feel of his warm skin on my fingers. There was *never* a good time for that.

I handed Zane the ball cap I kept as a makeshift "disguise" for him and spoke into the radio using our prearranged code. "Lou, coming out west-side door in three. All clear?"

"Copy. Clear to the vehicle. Echo Delta."

Zane moved a little closer to me as we headed for the door leading from the backstage area to the staging lot outside, where the SUVs would be idling. Ed Hilton always drove the second vehicle, so we would head straight for that one this time.

Zane finished stuffing his long hair into the cap and tilted his face down. He'd already changed out of his sweaty Majestic Rocks T-shirt and into a clean black T-shirt with no markings. I threw a plain black windbreaker over his shoulders and nudged him to put his arms in it. Not only would the windbreaker help hide his recognizable tattoos, but it would also cover more skin to keep any happy-stamper from getting easy access to him again tonight.

Lou's voice came over the radio. "West-side door still clear."

She and I had worked together long enough that we both knew this meant the east entrance.

"Coming out." I opened the east-side door and pressed my hand against the small of Zane's back as I guided him out. The staging lots were supposed to be free of any fans, but I'd learned long ago that there were always fans among the backstage crew and facility people who were authorized to be in these restricted areas.

"Straight to Ed," I murmured. "Second vehicle." Zane's nod was jerky and mostly covered by the ball cap. His chin was tucked down, and I felt the stress coming off him in waves. "Almost there."

"I'm fine," he muttered.

"Right."

I opened the SUV door just as someone off to our left shouted, "Zee! Can we get some autographs! Zee! Over here!"

Once he was identified by a fan on the far side of a chain-link barrier, others nearby began to scream and shake the fence, creating a cacophony. Facility security personnel moved over to quiet the crowd and protect the fence's integrity while I basically shoved Zane into the vehicle and lunged in after him.

"Let's go, Ed," I called.

Lou finished closing the passenger door and reached for her seat belt while I reached over Zane to grab his.

"I can do it," he said, shoving me away. "I got it. I'm not a fucking kid."

You're my principal. I'm responsible for your safety. Let me fucking help you.

I bit back all the words I wanted to say to him and sat back to let him manage the buckle himself. I knew after the car accident in Tulsa I was still extra-vigilant... okay, fine, a little too vigilant... when it came to vehicle safety. I wanted Zane whole and, well, not stifled and caged.

Once buckled, Zane struggled out of the windbreaker and yanked the cap off. His hair tumbled down over his shoulders. Several strands by his face and neck were still damp with sweat, and I knew he was already craving a shower to wash it all off.

"We'll be at the hotel soon," I assured him.

"Why can't we go straight home? To Barlo, I mean. It's only a couple of hours down I-85. Then we could wake up to Gran's hot breakfast."

"You know the answer to that."

He turned to face out the window. When he spoke, there was no inflection. "Because the only way you agreed to keep the trip to Barlo was to ensure the advance team was properly set up."

Zane's slender hands smoothed nervously over his jean-clad thighs.

I wanted to reach out and stop the nervous gesture, run my own fingertips over the rough spots where years of playing guitar had hardened his skin into calluses. There'd been many silent moments in the past year when my eyes had imagined what those rough spots would feel like skating over my bare skin.

I blinked and shook the thoughts away before sending a quick text and then turning to look out the opposite window into Atlanta's darkening sky.

"I told your friends they could come to the suite," I admitted in a low voice.

I felt Zane turn to stare at me. "Really?"

I shrugged. "Figured you could use a distraction, and if Landry is leaving sooner than he thought for his next job, you'll want to see him before he goes."

How was that for maturity? I could even facilitate a hookup with the man Zane seemed to be having a secret affair with. Because I was a goddamned professional.

"Yeah. Yeah, I do," he agreed softly. Then, even more softly, he added, "Thank you."

I bit back all the things I wanted to say—that he didn't have to thank me, that I wanted him happy more than anything, that he hadn't called me by that stupid nickname in over an hour, and I was starting to miss it—and focused on what I was allowed to care about. His safety.

A hotel security team member stood ready to escort us into the building as Ed pulled up at the side door to the hotel.

Lou hopped out first, studied the area around the vehicle, and then opened the door for me to exit first. We stood on either side of the open door while Zane shoved his ball cap back on and climbed out. Lou took the front left position, and I took the back right as we followed hotel security inside and up to the suite.

Lou met a member of our team just inside the suite and got the all clear for us to enter. Zane beelined straight for the bedroom that had his stuff in it so he could close himself inside and take a long shower.

Once I heard the bathroom door snick closed, I released the team member to take his position in the hall and then arranged access with Lou for the rest of Zane's brotherhood.

"I'm not sure if any of them are spending the night, but I have to assume Landry is," I said tightly.

Lou rolled her eyes. "They're not fucking, Ryan. They're just friends."

"None of my business unless it impacts our security measures," I said firmly.

"You know him way better than I do, but I'd put money down on the just-friends thing."

I headed to the kitchen area to grab a bottle of cold water from the stocked fridge. "You weren't around last year. He and Landry were always together, always getting into trouble—"

"Yeah, I remember reading the details in the reports, but I thought that behavior ended when Zane got rid of his old publicist."

While taking a sip of water, I cursed his former publicist again for tonight's distraction. "It did. Noelle and her team encouraged Zane to get into some trouble. I guess she wanted him to have an edgier, bad-boy reputation." I fiddled with the bottle cap between my fingers. "And Landry was only too happy to comply. The man is not a good influence on Zane."

"Meh. I think the guy talks a big game, but he seems insecure deep down."

"Landry? The model with side-eye for days?" I gave her a skeptical look. "Must have that insecurity buried real deep."

She nodded. "Exactly. But just to say, he's incredibly sweet and respectful with the rest of us. If he's side-eyeing you, maybe you provoked him—"

"I didn't," I grumbled, conveniently ignoring that just today, Landry might have caught me looking too intently at the friend he was currently fucking.

"...and if you ask me," she went on, "the secret affair Landry's having *isn't* with Zane."

Before I could ask her who else Landry could be sleeping with, Zane's voice called out for me to come help him with something.

I moved quickly into the bedroom and toward the bathroom door before edging it open slowly. Inside, Zane was still flushed from the shower, wearing only a towel wrapped around his waist.

"Get it off," he said, turning to show me the target on his shoulder. Water droplets skated down his bare back and into the towel. His hair was a wet tangle pulled over the opposite shoulder, and tension radiated from every damp pore of his skin.

"It's permanent," I said gently. "You know I can't get it off. Remember last time?"

"I need it off, Bear. Get it off." His voice carried the horror I knew he'd been feeling deep down, underneath the "fine" he insisted on claiming. And the *Bear*, especially now, did things to me I didn't want to admit.

"Hey, hey, okay," I said softly. "Take a breath. I'll try. Dry off and put on some clothes while I go grab a few things."

If I remained close to him while his beautiful body was in nothing but a towel, I would embarrass both of us.

After leaving him to dry off, I went back out into the common area of the suite and found the first aid kit in my security bag. I opened the kit to pull out cotton balls and hand sanitizer. Lou lifted her eyebrow at me.

"Another target."

Her eyes shot wide. "Are you fucking kidding me? When? When were you going to tell me?"

"Just before going on stage. He's really upset. Gimme a few minutes," I said before disappearing back into Zane's bedroom and closing the door.

He sat on the edge of the bed, wearing pajama pants. His hair was twisted up in the towel piled on top of his head. Zane's entire body was curled in on himself, and when he saw me enter, he immediately turned his back to me and curled up even more to give me access.

I sat beside him and got to work wetting a cotton ball with hand sanitizer and swiping it gently across the mark over and over again.

Earlier in the dressing room, I'd captured a photo of it for my records, but I knew from experience the sanitizer would only fade the mark.

His shoulders lifted as he took a deep breath. "I'm sure it's just an overzealous fan," he began.

This was part of his coping process. The man couldn't imagine anyone having nefarious intentions toward him, so he needed to figure out another explanation.

"I hope it is," I said softly as I continued to go over the mark with the cotton ball.

"But... but the other times we were in..."

"San Diego and LA," I supplied, knowing what was bothering him so much about this.

"Yeah. So, I thought..." Zane swallowed. "I thought maybe it was a local fan. Someone who came to both shows. That first time was outside the venue in that VIP crowd, and then the San Diego one was when we got swarmed at the entrance to the hotel. Like... it could have been anyone. But now..."

"Now it means it's someone who can afford to follow you across the country," I said. "Or someone on the crew."

He shivered. I tried not to move my hands over his bare back and shoulder to warm and reassure him, but if wanting him could keep him warm, the man would have been on fire.

Zane's voice was unsteady. "It can't be someone on the crew."

I didn't say anything even though we both knew it could be.

"I treat the crew really well. Why would they want to scare me?"

At least he was finally able to admit this could be more than a well-meaning prank. He was right, though—Zane was uncommonly generous to everyone on his crew, handing out bonuses and remembering almost everyone's names and details about their families.

"Sometimes people aren't always in their right minds, Zane."

The mark had faded a little, but it was nowhere near coming off completely. I had another idea. "Stay here. I'll be right back."

I returned to the main room and found my own bags in the other bedroom. I pulled out a Sharpie from a catch-all pouch in my bag and returned to Zane's room. "Hold still."

"What are you doing?"

"Replacing the old mark with a new one."

I caught the edge of his mouth as it turned up. If I could take away his fear even for a moment, I'd consider that a win.

"What are you going to draw?" he asked.

"Wait and see," I said as I brainstormed what I could create that would cover the small circular target icon and not exceed my limited drawing ability.

"If only I knew what the person wanted," he mused. "Maybe I could help them."

I closed my eyes and dragged in a breath to keep from roaring at him to stop being so goddamned nice. After a beat, I opened my eyes and began to drag the marker across his skin.

"What did you decide on?"

"You're impatient."

"I won't be able to see it."

"That's probably for the best. I'm shit at drawing," I admitted.

When I was done, he asked again. I took his phone and snapped a picture of the drawing before handing the phone back.

Zane blinked at the screen. "A... saw blade?"

"It's a sun," I insisted. "I told you I sucked at drawing."

He tilted his head one way and then the other as he studied the photo. "Is it... an angry sun?"

I turned to leave when the magical sound of Zane's laughter hit the air between us.

"Don't go. I'm sorry, Bear. I'm teasing you. Thank you for doing this. I love it. And... you putting something—anything—there is so much better than what was there before."

I thought about all the ways I wished I could mark him...

I blew out a breath and glanced over my shoulder. "You need anything before your friends get here? Want me to order you a salad?"

He didn't like eating heavy this time of night, but if I could get him to eat a salad with protein on it, I'd call it a win. While tonight's show hadn't been a full set list like a solo concert, the stress of the situation had probably still taken a lot out of him. The guy had a hard time consuming enough calories to keep from a deficit on concert days.

Zane shook his head. "Maybe some carrot sticks or pretzels?"

"How about a protein drink?"

He shrugged. "I'll try."

I nodded and headed back out to fetch it from the stocked kitchenette, where Lou was busy on the phone with the team headed to Barlo. When I got back to Zane's bedroom, I noticed he had put on a hoodie and was dragging a brush through his hair while sitting in front of a mirror over a small vanity table.

"Hey, Bear? Don't, ah... don't tell the guys about the stamp, okay?"

I met his eyes in the mirror. "You know I don't tell anyone anything unless it's necessary to keep you safe."

"No, I know, I just... wanted to be sure. I don't want anyone to worry."

I nodded but kept my mouth shut. What I wanted to say was definitely inappropriate.

I wanted to tell him that it was a privilege to worry about him, that his friends loved him and would want to protect him as much as I did. Well... maybe not as much as I did. He couldn't possibly know just how much I wanted to keep him safe. Even though I hadn't known Zane as long as his friends had, I'd spent many hours, days, and months in close quarters with him, getting to know him under many circumstances.

I felt like I knew him better than anyone... though I probably didn't have a right to.

The sounds of Lou greeting Zane's friends filtered through to the bedroom, and I took it as my cue to leave. I made my way back out to the main part of the suite while Landry, Silas, Way, Dev, Tully, Bash, and Rowe all trooped past me on their way into Zane's bedroom.

Half an hour later, all but Landry trooped back out, giving Lou and me friendly "good night" waves and thanks for taking care of "our superstar."

I stared at the bedroom door as Landry pushed it closed with a cheeky wink and grin.

Yeah, the fucker definitely saw me looking at them earlier.

My stomach somersaulted as I sat back down at the dining table and pretended to check my email.

Sure enough, just like five other times in the past several months, soon there came the distinctive sounds of sex from inside the bedroom—loud moans and muffled cries I tried not to attribute to anyone in particular, squeaking mattress springs, and the rhythmic *bang bang bang* of a headboard whacking forcefully into a wall.

I tried to grit it out. Lou was scheduled to head to her own hotel room down the hall for a much-deserved night's sleep... but she knew better.

When I glanced over at her, she winced and gave me a look of complete pity. Somehow, she'd picked up a few months back that I was uncomfortable with Zane's hookups, and I tried not to wonder whether she thought I had a crush on my principal or was actually homophobic. Either way, I was grateful for what she said next.

"Go," she said in a low voice. "I'll stay."

I didn't argue, though maybe I should have. I bolted out of my chair, headed straight for the door to the suite, then down the hall and into the stairwell.

There, I did stairwell sprints for twenty full minutes until my legs shook with exertion and my head swam.

But try as I might, I couldn't outrun the fact that the man I had a crush on... okay, fine, the man I loved more than any other human on Earth... was having sex with the stupidest and second most beautiful man on the planet.

THREE

ZANE

Bears usually mind their business, but they can become dangerous if provoked. Sudden, loud noises and those who encroach on their dens or their food can trigger a defensive reaction. The best way to avoid danger is to keep your mouth shut... and stay away from their honey!
—*Bear Facts for Insomniacs, Episode 23*

Landry did what he always did when trying to cheer me up. He reenacted the most ridiculous hookups he'd ever had on his modeling circuit, including full-body shudders, full-volume moaning and shrieking, and full-of-shit exaggeration.

"Then, the guy was like, 'God, *mooooore*,'" he groaned, loud enough for people in Alabama to hear. "'Suck me harder! I can't get enough.'"

"Sure he was." I rolled my eyes and threw myself down on the side of the bed where he wasn't currently bouncing. "Quit. You're fucking up my sheets." I tried to smooth the bedding back to some semblance of normal.

Usually I found Landry's antics amusing as hell, but today, I was struggling. Between the stamp incident and the memory of Bear's hands on my skin in the bathroom, my system didn't know whether to be terrified or thrilled.

Landry scoffed. "Stop being a princess. Nobody needs their bedding pristine. Besides, I love fucking with your bodyguard."

"B—*Ryan's* not homophobic," I told Landry for the millionth time.

It was getting harder to hold back from using Bear's nickname in front of my friends, but I knew Landry, in particular, would tease me forever if he suspected how out-of-control-huge my crush on my bodyguard had gotten.

"Ryan wouldn't clutch his pearls at the two of us having sex," I went on. "Hell, he probably wouldn't even notice, unless he thought I was in some kind of mortal danger." This glum thought did nothing to help my mood. "And you shouldn't make assumptions about people's sexuality. We don't know that he's straight, do we?"

I liked to pretend he wasn't anyway, but Landry's assumption was probably right.

I'd never once heard Bear refer to his own love life, and the only clue I'd ever gotten was a Ventdestinian royal gossip blog post speculating about him and a woman in the royal public relations department several years ago.

"I'm not assuming Ryan's straight or homophobic. But he's *definitely* not happy at the idea of us having sex." Landry grinned mischievously, but before I could ask him to explain himself, he went on. "Wonder how he could have survived living in a backwoods place like Ventdestine all those years if he's not straight, though. You know you're not allowed to be gay there? It's like this little island in the North Sea that time forgot, and they're all still living like it's the Middle Ages. But, like, with internet." He crossed one slender ankle over his knee and bounced his foot in the air.

"Surely, he wouldn't have taken the job there if he was gay, though, right?"

Landry shrugged. "The way it all went down, maybe he didn't feel like he had much choice."

He had a point. A dozen or so years ago, Bear had made international news when he'd tackled one of his competitors in the middle of his Olympic biathlon competition. When the videos were replayed, it became clear that the man he'd taken down had been aiming into the VIP stands, where the king of Ventdestine was sitting to watch the event.

King Salling had been overwhelmed with gratitude. According to the internet, he'd made a speech saying, "The winds whispered fortune to us this day and have called Ryan Galloway to be a true protector of Ventdestine!" He'd then defied hundreds of years of tradition by offering a coveted spot in his royal guard to a foreigner.

I think for Bear, the choice to take the job had been less about fate and more about opportunity. He'd explained the difference between the annual pay for the head of security at the ski resort where he'd worked in Montana and the amount he made as a royal guard.

"The money was too good," I suggested.

"Understandable. I met a guy in Colorado once who said the ski resorts pay for shit, and I can't imagine there's a market for professional biathletes."

Landry was right. But that put us right back into speculating about Bear's sexuality without any actual information, a situation I'd been in for a full year already. More thinking on this topic would only drive me nuts.

I sighed, and Landry frowned as he levered himself up onto his elbows in the bed.

"You're upset tonight. Gonna tell me what's up, baby cakes?"

I thought about the spot on my shoulder, the faded target now hidden under what could only be described as a logo for a solar-powered anger management program. I found I didn't want to tell

Landry about it. Though there wasn't much non-Bear stuff I didn't share with my brotherhood, I knew if I told Landry about the targets, he'd quickly tell the others. They'd drop their modeling contracts and their business consulting plans, their charity work and their horse breeding programs—all the things they loved—to come to my aid.

They'd *worry*.

And there was no need for it. Not when we didn't know whether the stamps were really a threat. Not when I already had Bear keeping me safe.

"Stressed about going home," I said, because that was also kind of true.

Landry's perfect forehead creased in confusion. "You love going to Barlo and seeing your gran."

I shrugged and turned to face him, punching the pillow under my head until it was more comfortable. "I do. But it's different now. When I go back, everyone wants to see me, which is great. I love seeing everyone. But it's also..."

Hard to put into words.

"High pressure?" he suggested. When I nodded, he peered at me. "You know you can say no to things, right? You don't have to visit everyone's store downtown just because they ask you to."

"I know. But it brings in a ton of extra business when I do. Shop owners like to take photos and put them up and, like, post on social media and stuff. It makes a huge difference to their bottom line."

Landry reached out and straightened a lock of my hair. He was so careful about his own look it sometimes drove him nuts that I didn't give a shit about mine. "You're not responsible for the whole world, Zane. I know it feels like that sometimes, but it's okay to simply go home to visit Gran and hide away at her place. You're allowed to have privacy, you know."

"It's not that big a deal. I'm just... tired. I'm sure I'll rally in the morning."

He tugged the strand of hair he'd straightened. "You could always take Gran somewhere else. Get away from all the expectations on you when you go back to Barlo."

I laughed. "Like where? She hates to leave town, and she loves to show me off at home."

Landry grinned. "She's one proud granny. Her sweet baby boy is a Yale graduate and 'a big fancy star like if Travis Tritt and Elvis Presley had a baby,'" he teased, using an exaggerated old-lady Southern accent.

"You suck at accents," I said with a laugh. "You can't even do a proper English one right, and your dad's British. Which part of England are you from, again?"

He made a noncommittal noise. "You wouldn't have heard of it."

Landry didn't talk much about his childhood in England, and I figured it was because he was embarrassed to have grown up poor. I understood this better than anyone—I didn't much like talking about my early years, either.

Dev, Landry, and I had all gotten a free ride to Yale, but Dev at least had enjoyed a fairly middle-class stability. I, on the other hand, had grown up entirely dependent on government assistance. I'd been the kind of poor that meant special paperwork each year to get free lunch, help with internet access and computers so I could do my homework, and furtive trips to the "clothes closet" behind the teacher's lounge at school to shop from my classmates' old cast-offs.

Landry had shown up our first year wearing thrift-store clothes and using the same kind of laptop I'd gotten through the school store with my scholarship computer allowance. Like me, he hadn't gone home over the breaks, which made sense given the cost of flying back to England. And though we never discussed it outright, I'd always had a soft spot for Landry because of this. I assumed it was one of the reasons he seemed to look out for me, too.

Landry flopped back on the bed again with his hands on his chest. "My point is, you need a place of your own. Not your house in Malibu," he added before I could remind him of that very thing.

"That's nothing but a high-priced crash pad for when you're recording in LA, and you know it."

"I'm buying a place in Majestic," I reminded him. When our friend Silas had settled down with his rancher hubby in the weird, wonderful Wyoming town, the rest of our brotherhood followed. "I showed you the pictures. Now I just need to make a final decision and put in the paperwork."

I had to admit, I'd been dithering about it. There was a ginormous spread available just down the road from Silas's place, but I'd need to build a house there, and what would I do with all that space? I loved it, but it felt like a big responsibility. I was leaning toward a brand-new modern build a little farther from town, which was tiny but high-end and better suited to a life spent mostly on the road.

"That's great, Zane. But I wasn't talking about that... necessarily." Landry's eyes took on a faraway look as he stared at the ceiling. "I'm talking about a place that... that *calls* to you. A place that's *yours*. A place that makes you smile when you think of it because it feels good, and happy, and safe. A place that anchors you when you've been traveling around so much you start to forget who you are and where you belong. A place where you... where you bring the people who matter."

I gaped at him. That was the most genuine, un-Landry-like thing I'd ever heard him say... and it made me wonder how much more I didn't know about this man I considered a brother. "Do *you* have a place like that?"

"Hmm?" Landry blinked like he was coming out of a daze, and when he turned his head to look at me, the mischievous twinkle was back in his eyes. "Oh, of course. Several. And I have loads of good times in each of them." He raised his voice in a loud, protracted, keening moan. "So. *Fucking. Goooood. Baby!*"

Snickering, I slapped his arm lightly. "You're an ass."

"Thousands of men have said so," he agreed. He turned on his side to face me, squashing the pillow between his arm and his head.

"So. What are you looking forward to when we get to Barlo tomorrow?" he asked with a fond smile.

Even though Landry didn't know about the targets, he knew something had been bugging me lately. He'd even made a point of sleeping over in my hotel room whenever he joined me in tour cities. It was a kind gesture—a thoughtful, caring side of Landry he didn't show many people—and I loved him for it.

I yawned. "The usual. Gran's cooking and Aunt Rinny's teasing. I love that they still treat me like my old self no matter what they read about me on the internet. The two of them... well, they've been amazing."

The truth was, I looked forward to pretending, if only for two days, that I wasn't Zee Barlo anymore. That I was simply plain Zane Hendley—no one interesting enough to scream at, reach for, or sneak stamps onto. No one who owed anyone anything or had commitments to hundreds of thousands of people across the globe for months on end. Someone who could dare to ask his crush out on a date, just to see where things went, without it turning into a feature of viral social media posts or causing conflicts with someone's job.

I let out another loud yawn.

"Go on, then," Landry said, breaking me out of my thoughts. He waved a hand toward my phone. "Do your thing, boo."

I blinked at him sleepily. "My thing?"

He rolled his eyes. "You're clearly exhausted and ready for bed, so turn on that podcast you listen to every night, and let's sleep."

"It's not *every* night." I cradled my phone to my chest a bit defensively. "It's just... sometimes."

"*Mmhm.* That's what you say every time I stay over," Landry agreed. "Then you toss and turn until you think I'm asleep and finally turn it on. Tonight, let's cut to the chase." He rolled off the bed just long enough to strip the covers back and crawl beneath them and motioned for me to do the same. "Don't get me wrong, I don't understand the appeal *at all*. What's relaxing about learning that mindless, ferocious, territorial predators lurk in the woods around us waiting to attack?" He gave a mock shudder. "But we all have our strange comforts. Who am I to deny you yours?"

I plugged my phone into the charger on the nightstand and cued up the newest *Bear Facts for Insomniacs* episode, then curled back under the blankets. "You're wrong, you know," I said with a yawn. "Bears aren't mindless—they're scary-intelligent. They have the biggest relative brain size of any mammal. They know which creatures are their friends and which are their potential enemies, and their priority is protecting their territory. They only attack if they feel provoked."

"Well, good." Landry turned off his lamp with a satisfied huff. "One less thing to worry about. I can't recall provoking any bears lately."

I laughed sleepily. The man had no idea.

As I drifted off to the sounds of the podcast, though, I thought over Landry's advice to find a place that was mine... and about bears and their territories. Where was my place, my territory? Where did I feel safest and happiest? I wasn't sure it was Barlo anymore, though I loved the town and the people and always would. Was it in Majestic, where most of my brothers had made their homes? Maybe. Or maybe it was a place I hadn't seen yet. A place I needed to keep looking for.

Maybe once I found it, I wouldn't need podcasts to sleep.

I fell into slumber thinking about bears—specifically *my* Bear— curled up in a warm, cozy bed...

So it was a real shock when, a little while later, I found myself on the Scream Machine at Six Flags. The ancient wooden roller coaster squeaked and shuddered as the car I was on careened out of control. People crowded into the car with me, screaming and laughing maniacally. I kept dropping my phone over the side and leaning precariously over other people to reach for it. Someone's large hand always grabbed the back of my shirt to pull me back at the last minute, just as we fell into a large drop.

As soon as we began going up the next incline, I felt the familiar press of a rubber ink stamp against the back of my neck and a huff of laughter.

"This is fun, isn't it?" a stranger's voice asked. "This is fun. Isn't. It." The voice repeated the question over and over with increasing anger.

I looked around for Bear in hopes he would get me out of here, get me off the ride, or somehow tell me this was all a bad dream, but I couldn't make my voice call out for him.

I kept opening my mouth to scream his name, but it wouldn't come.

Bear. *Bear. Bear!*

I tried to climb out of the roller-coaster car the next time it dipped down, but someone tried to wrestle me away from the edge again.

Bear! Why couldn't I say his name? If he knew I was stuck here, he'd get me off this ride. Where was he? Why wasn't he watching me?

And why the fuck wasn't my voice working? If my voice wasn't working, what did that mean for my tour? My career? All of the people counting on me to do my job?

When I finally woke up from my stress dream, I realized my voice worked just fine. And it was screaming loud enough to wake the dead.

FOUR

RYAN

Bears may be solitary, but when they care about something—whether a mate, a close companion, or their precious honey—they remain alert to danger, even in sleep. In the wild, when a bear bonds, their loyalty runs as deep as their strength.

—*Bear Facts for Insomniacs, Episode 25*

By the time I got back to Zane's suite, dripping sweat and jelly-legged from the stair climbing, everything was blessedly quiet. I thanked Lou and released her for the night before making my way into my own room and into the shower.

I let the cold water cool me down before finally turning it warmer to work on my muscles. After brushing my teeth, I set out my clothes for the next day and cleaned my gun before doing another check of the main room of the suite and making sure the door from the suite to the hotel hallway was still secured by the floor wedge alarm. As usual, I left the door from my bedroom to the main room of the suite open in case anything happened. Then, I forced myself to close my eyes.

My brain helpfully provided graphic images of Landry fucking Zane in every single possible position until I felt like I was going to vomit. I gritted my teeth and ran through meditation scripts in an attempt to clear my mind.

Images of the inked target flashed behind my eyes, and the anger of someone daring to presume to touch my principal negated the little bit of work the meditation scripts had done.

I finally fell into a restless sleep over an hour later... only to be awakened sometime after that by Zane's terrified cries.

I was halfway across my bedroom before I realized I'd woken up. Zane was screaming my name, and my heart rocketed into my throat. As I raced across the suite, I noticed the security wedge was still under the door. How the fuck had someone gotten inside? I knew it couldn't be Landry, so did that mean someone had come in through a window despite our location on the twentieth floor?

Landry met me at the doorway to Zane's bedroom. "I can't calm him down. He keeps screaming about bears! I think he's having a nightmare. That stupid podcast—"

I ignored him and shot straight to the bed, where Zane was fighting against tangled sheets, fully dressed in the same pajama bottoms and hoodie he'd put on before his friends had arrived.

"Hey, hey," I said, reaching for him and holding his upper arms. "I'm here. B... *fuck*. I'm here, Zane."

I'd almost fucking called him *baby*. As if he were mine to comfort. Mine to care for with *love* instead of a professional close-protection strategy.

"Bear! Bear." He alternated between frantically crying and whimpering my name. The sound of his terror squeezed my fucking chest until I felt like I couldn't breathe. "I need you. *Bear*."

"I'm here." I pulled him into my arms and held him tightly. "Zane. I'm here. You're safe. Wake up."

His eyes, half-opened, looked around without focusing until his gaze landed on me. Then, his entire face crumpled as he began to cry in earnest. He lunged into my arms more fully, wrapping his arms around my neck and burying his face in my neck.

He smelled sleepy and warm. The faded scent of his shampoo mixed with faint traces of minty toothpaste. I held the back of his head and murmured soothing words into his ear.

"You're okay. It was just a bad dream. You're safe."

His lithe body hitched as he struggled to catch his breath, and I felt the warm damp of his tears against the skin of my neck. Movement out of the corner of my eye reminded me Landry was there.

Suddenly, I felt very awkward. "Landry's here," I murmured to Zane. "Do you want—"

His arms squeezed around me tighter. "No." It was barely audible. Only I could hear the word. But when he added, "Just you," Landry must have picked up on it.

"Should I go?" he asked hesitantly. I could see the worry in his eyes from the lamp he'd turned on in the corner of the room.

I shot him a look that hopefully expressed my own confusion over the situation, the eyeball version of a perplexed shrug. Landry nodded and tilted his head toward the outer room of the suite before exiting and closing the bedroom door behind him.

Leaving me alone with Zane.

"Want to talk about it?" I asked after a few more minutes.

I tried to pull away, but Zane wouldn't let me go. Instead, I moved over to lean back against the headboard and let Zane relax against my front.

This had happened before. Once. And neither one of us had ever spoken of it again.

We'd been in New Orleans for a show. Zane had wanted to walk around Bourbon Street late at night just to get a feel for the sights and sounds. We'd shoved his hair up in a ball cap, thrown some dummy eyeglasses on him, and headed out of the hotel. There'd been several suspicious people down a nearby alley, and it was obvious at least a couple of them were high on something. I hadn't paid particularly close attention to them, other than ensuring Zane's safety, but I discovered later, when Zane woke up screaming for me hours later, that seeing the junkies on the street had brought back terrible childhood memories from when he'd still been with his mom.

That night, I'd held him in my arms as he'd filled in some details about the way he'd grown up, with parents who cared more about their next fix than his next meal and being left alone in dark, empty buildings while they tried to score. Or worse, left him with people they shouldn't have.

Zane had admitted between sniffles that when he'd found himself in those situations, he'd closed his eyes, clapped his hands over his ears, and started singing to block out the fear.

"If Garth Brooks could stand outside the fire, then I could, too," he'd said, letting out a little laugh. "Any song I knew about being brave, I sang it. Pat Benatar's 'Hit Me With Your Best Shot,' Starship's 'Nothing's Gonna Stop Us Now,' and 'Don't Stop Thinking About Tomorrow' by Fleetwood Mac. You name it, I sang it to myself. Gran had this little plastic radio out on her porch, and it was always tuned to the same station that said they played hits 'from the seventies, eighties, and now!' Those songs were like my security blanket."

It had explained why he seemed to disappear onstage when he performed music. He went somewhere completely away in his mind, to a place safer and more welcoming than this cruel world. When he sang, his entire body relaxed into the music, and his face took on this dreamy expression that made me love him even more.

Zane Hendley was a precious treasure. He wasn't fragile, but fuck if I didn't want to wrap him up in bubble wrap anyway and protect him from any more cruelty in this life.

"It was a stupid nightmare about a roller coaster," Zane said now, shifting against my chest until his head rested under my chin. I ran my fingers through his hair, gently pulling out the tangles as I came to them.

"You know things in our dreams represent bigger things in our lives," I reminded him.

He let out a long breath. "Yeah. It doesn't take a PhD to interpret this one."

"I think you need a break, Zane." It wasn't the first or even fiftieth time I'd suggested it.

"I'm taking a break. I'm going home to see my family."

I closed my eyes and reminded myself to stay calm. "Visiting Barlo isn't a break. Not for you. Not anymore."

Surprisingly, he didn't argue this. "I'm supposed to be in New York for those interviews after the Georgia trip," he said, ignoring what I'd said. "And then we have the next European leg..."

"The interviews can be rescheduled. And I think being in the city right now is a spectacularly bad idea unless we significantly beef up the protection team, which we're going to have to do anyway before Amsterdam."

Even with a more robust team, I wouldn't feel comfortable moving him through Manhattan. There were too many places crowds would be able to push in or unvetted strangers would have easier access to him. What I really wanted was to take him somewhere secluded and take time to regroup while he had some much-needed decompression time.

"What about the Boundary Waters?" I suggested, naming an area in Minnesota he'd read about recently in an article. "You said you wanted to check it out one day. Kenji can probably find us a rental—"

He huffed out a laugh. "November in northern Minnesota? Have you forgotten I'm a Georgia boy?"

"You like the cold. Sweatshirts and pajama pants are your favorite outfit."

"I like the chilly. Not the frozen."

He had a point. Northern Minnesota was harsher than where I'd grown up in Montana. "Fine. We'll find a private island in the Caribbean—"

Zane made a noise of dismissal. "No. I don't want more time in the sun. Not after the burn I got playing in Miami."

"I still blame the makeup team," I muttered, remembering the homicidal rage I'd wanted to go into when I'd realized just how badly an oversight had been made. Poor Zane had been in agony for three nights in the hotel suite, and I'd finally insisted on bringing in medical professionals to treat him.

"What I really want is to do my job," he said, shifting off me as if he'd made a decision. "And that means going to New York for the interviews."

Don't say it, I thought. *For fuck's sake, don't—*

"And you don't need to worry about me. I'm fine."

I stared at him while my body began to tremble with the need to spew my opinions all over the fucking place. To tell him he was definitely the fuck not fine.

But... and here was my dirty little secret... I loved him too much to deny him anything.

Zane wanted to go to Barlo to see his family.

So we would go to Barlo.

Zane wanted to go to New York to do his job.

So we would go to New York.

I moved off the bed and tried to get myself under control, tried to keep my hands to myself instead of grabbing him and pulling him back against my body where he fucking belonged.

"Okay," I forced myself to say.

Zane looked awkward as he stood barefoot on the lush carpet and shifted from foot to foot. For some reason, he looked tiny in his oversized clothes. "Okay?"

I nodded and clenched my jaw. "It's fine, right? You said it's fine, so it'll be fine."

He frowned. I could tell he wanted to know why I was suddenly agreeing with him instead of arguing with him.

Too bad for him, because I could never tell him that if I stayed in that room with him for even three more seconds, I would do or say something both of us would regret.

So, instead of staying in that bedroom and playing with fire, I moved past him and opened the door to the main room of the suite.

Landry's head snapped up from where he'd been reading one of the style magazines from the coffee table. "Zane okay?"

"Oh, yeah," I growled. "He's totally *fine*. I'm sure he's waiting for you to get back there and calm him down."

Landry tilted his head thoughtfully. "I'm not sure he is, but okay. Hey, Ryan? I apologize if I've, ah… provoked you at all."

I scowled. "I have no idea what you're talking about." I strode past the supermodel to my bedroom and closed the door behind me, then stepped back to press my ass and shoulders against the cool wooden surface of the door while I focused on not having a stroke.

Breathe in for four… hold it for four… breathe out for four… hold it for four…

Box breathing. Apparently, Navy SEALs used it before missions. It did fuck all for calming me down, though, which left me wondering what the hell the SEALs did when their stupid breathing techniques failed to put them in the right frame of mind for a mission.

"Fuck," I breathed. "Fucking fuck."

My sweet principal, the man I loved more than anyone, was scared out of his fucking mind and determined to push through it. And there wasn't a damned thing I could do except be there for him and help keep him safe.

For the first time, I thought I might understand why the Ventdestinians relied so much on their damn winds "whispering fortune." The fear I felt for Zane—for his safety *and* for the emotional toll this was taking on him—was so huge I might have actually listened to superstitions if it meant keeping him whole and protecting his heart.

As I lay in bed that night, staring at my darkened ceiling, though, the winds weren't whispering a goddamn thing. All I knew for sure was that Zane was *not* fine…

But that I would make sure he was, as soon as possible.
Even if it fucking killed me.

FIVE
ZANE

"There he is, my sweet punkin." Gran stood proudly on the front porch of the house she'd lived in for as long as I could remember. Nowadays, it was practically unrecognizable since I'd bought up three vacant lots around it and forced a big renovation on her about five years ago. The only thing that hadn't changed was the upside-down horseshoe over the front door for luck and to ward off bad spirits.

As I got out of the dark SUV, I tried not to notice the eight other vehicles crowded in Gran's driveway. I knew from experience she didn't see any reason to say no when all of our extended family insisted on swinging by "just to say hey" to "good ole Zee."

"Fucking Christ," Bear muttered under his breath from where he stood holding the door open for me. He stretched his head from side to side before murmuring into his wireless earbud, "Lou, get Boomer to run those plates."

I sighed. "White truck with the Jesus stickers is my uncle Bart. Gray Malibu is my second cousin Pearl. Red Trans Am is my cousin JK. I think the yellow Jeep is my high school friend Carrie-Beth. Brown minivan with the Coexist sticker is Aunt Rinny. No clue who drives the motorcycle, but that's pretty sick."

"You will not be taking a ride on anyone's motorcycle," Bear warned too low for anyone to hear.

I ignored him and trotted up the three steps and into Gran's arms. "Hey," I said, inhaling her Jean Naté bath splash and the scent of french toast and syrup. "God, I missed you."

"Gosh," she corrected out of habit. "And I missed you, too, angel."

"Boy, when you gonna get a haircut?" The boisterous voice of my uncle Bart came from inside the open front door a split second before his wide body sauntered through it. He met my eyes over Gran's shoulder and winked at me. "Good to see ya, son."

I moved away from Gran to give Bart a quick hug, even though his use of the word "son" in reference to me had begun at exactly the same time my family began to realize I had money. It wasn't until my first recording deal that some of my extended family perked up and took notice of me.

I felt Bear's presence behind me as I backed out of the awkward hug with my uncle. Bart was definitely not Bear's favorite of my family members, and I couldn't blame him. Bart tended to drink too much beer and make pointed comments about people's "lifestyle choices" when the night was no longer young.

Even though, as I'd told Landry, Bear was (probably, almost definitely, despite my many fantasies) straight, he was a staunch ally. He'd never once side-eyed me or my friends when we talked about being with other guys, and he was completely accepting of the members of the brotherhood who had partners now.

I'd been the recipient of plenty of homophobic comments by the general public, and I could tell it got under Bear's skin. But then again, any threats against me got under his skin. He took it as a personal affront when one of his principals was under threat.

It was simply part of his job. And he took his job seriously.

Pearl's voice called from inside the house. "Zee's here! Quick, hide your abs!"

I let out a laugh as I walked through the door. "Ain't no abs in this place, girl. You should know that by now."

My cousin JK and several guys I didn't recognize but were clearly JK-adjacent glanced up from the big sectional sofa in the family room, where sports coverage was playing before today's football games started. JK made a point of stretching backward over the cushions and pulling up his faded red Bulldogs T-shirt to show he did, in fact, have abs. They were just hidden under a manscaping nightmare.

I rolled my eyes. "Put that fur pelt away. You're scaring people."

Pearl made her way through the maze of people and leaped at me with a squeal. "Finally," she said. "I told my friend Grace you were coming, and she didn't believe me. She wants you to sign her harmonica if that's okay."

I nodded while blowing a few strands of her hair out of my mouth as she hugged me. The barest brush of Bear's fingers across my lower back reminded me he was there and was more than happy to be the bad guy if and when I decided I'd had enough physical contact with people. All I needed to do was mention any word associated with *fish* —an inside joke I'd come up with after hearing how protective bears were of their salmon—and he'd step in.

It was a longtime understanding but one I rarely took advantage of when I was around my family.

I wasn't touch-starved, exactly, but it was rare for me to get as much physical contact as I craved. And after the target stamping happened the first time, when I'd thought it was simply an overzealous fan who'd stamped me, I'd realized just how scary it was to be touched by strangers. I'd quickly gone from being very willing to hug fans when they approached to being more hesitant and more likely to lead with a fist bump instead.

This meant I was touched even less than before. My closest friends, my brotherhood, were touchy-feely. We all hugged quickly and easily. But I didn't see them as often anymore, thanks to my hectic travel schedule.

So I appreciated it when Aunt Rinny came in and nudged Pearl away to give me a *real* hug. She held me tight and held on for a long time. "So freaking good to have you here," she said in a low voice. "I missed your good sense and sweet face. Gosh, I wish you weren't quite so successful. I'd like to have you around more."

I knew she didn't mean the part about my success. She was as proud of me as Gran was. But I also knew she meant what she'd said about wishing I was around more. And that made me feel truly loved and needed—for *myself*, not my cash or my clout—in a way I didn't get much of.

Gran and Rinny were the real deal in my life, and that was why I'd needed so badly to come to Barlo before getting back on the road.

"Missed you, too," I said, hearing the emotion in my own voice. "More than you can know."

She pulled back and held my upper arms, meeting my eyes with wet ones of her own. "You come home whenever you need, hear? We will always be here for you. Always."

I felt the tears come quickly, but I willed them to stay put in my eyeballs and not dare spill over in front of such a collection of random friends and family. My jaw tightened against the tremble in my chin, and I nodded firmly and quickly before clearing my throat to dispel the emotion.

"Need help in the kitchen?" If there was a crack in my voice, no one seemed to notice... except Bear, of course, who kept a close eye on me as I followed Rinny down the short hall and into Gran's favorite room of the house.

The expansive kitchen was the heart of this home, and I could see several more friends and family members clustered around the breakfast bar half of the large kitchen island. Gran had various people cutting fruit and veggies to contribute to the day's feast.

"Make yourself useful," Rinny said, pointing to a large colander full of green beans next to the sink. "Snap and string those."

I went to the sink first to wash my hands while several people called out greetings from the island. My friend Carrie-Beth suddenly started blinking fast, and I squinted at her to see if something was the matter with her eyes. Bear leaned in and lowered his voice until only I could hear it.

"Told you so."

I glanced at him in confusion until I remembered something he'd said after our last visit here. *That 'old friend' of yours has a crush on you.*

My cheeks heated as I turned my head to whisper in his ear. "She's barking up the wrong tree, but I did touch her boob once. It was nice. I can see why you'd be into it."

Now Bear's cheeks were turning pink, too. His eyes flared in surprise, and it seemed like they also held a little confusion. "Why *I'd* be into it?"

"Never mind," I muttered, waving a dismissive hand through the air when I caught several people watching me. It was inappropriate to put him on the spot about his sexuality. I was his principal, not his friend, no matter how close I sometimes felt to him. I needed to remember that.

There'd been plenty of times early on in our professional relationship when I'd tried to poke around about his sexuality, but he hadn't taken the bait. I'd told him about a friend of mine who'd come out to me as nonbinary and how "I hope I'm a safe person to come out to." He'd agreed politely that I probably was and wished my friend well, but that had been the end of that.

Rinny had returned to a spot on the other side of the island, filling halves of hard-boiled eggs with "devil," or whatever the gooey inside of the deviled egg was called, and she made a point of lifting an eyebrow at me to remind me I had work to do.

I immediately found my own spot at the island and began snapping beans. Carrie-Beth asked me how my Shaky Knees performance had gone and if I'd met Chet Hamer, who'd taken the stage after me. I answered with all of the gossipy details I knew she was hunting for, and the conversation quickly took its usual turns. Several of my cousins and their friends asked me about various aspects of touring and being famous, each of them obviously on different points of a spectrum between genuinely curious and downright mercenary.

This was the usual fare when I visited Barlo, so I did my best to feed the beast and give everyone the access they craved while also enjoying being surrounded by familiar faces from home.

Bear never wandered far. He used the downtime to check his email, and I was pretty sure he was also sounding the alarm with his boss about the target stamp. But he remained calmly and quietly in the background as usual. Two of Pearl's friends kept flashing him looks and then dissolving into blushing giggles periodically, but I could hardly blame them when I, too, had a ridiculous teenage crush on the man despite being more than a decade past my teens.

At one point, Bear leaned in to speak low into my ear again. "FYI, the motorcycle belongs to one of JK's friends who has an active warrant for a firearm-related charge. You know the drill. We leave, you get someone to ask him quietly to leave, or we call in an anonymous tip and he leaves here with local LEOs."

I closed my eyes and sighed before waving Rinny over.

"What is it, darlin'?"

"JK has a friend who came here on a motorcycle. He needs to leave, or he risks being arrested for an outstanding warrant."

She rolled her eyes. "John-Keith couldn't stay away from trouble if trouble was a snake with ten fangs, I swear to all that's holy. I told him not to bring that kid. I'll handle it."

Thankfully, it was handled without drama, but I noticed Bear stood directly behind me until he got the "All clear" message in his earpiece that the guy was gone.

The rest of the morning passed peacefully, and I was convinced to join the guys for the start of the Falcons–Ravens game in the family room after most of the supper prep work was done. The coffee table in front of the big sectional was overflowing with chips, dips, soda cans, and beer bottles, but I managed to find a corner where I could sit to enjoy the BLT Gran had put together to tide me over until supper.

JK made one of his friends switch places so he could take the spot closest to me. "Hey, so, ah... I was wondering if I could ask you about something."

"Sure," I said, wondering how Gran still had home-grown tomatoes this far into October. The sandwich was magical, just like always.

JK lowered his voice. "You know that building up on Clinton and Walnut that used to be a pawn shop?"

I tried to picture the corner he was talking about. "Green-striped metal awning? Next to the store that used to sell ceiling fans?"

"Yeah, yeah. That's the one. They're offering a killer deal on a lease, and a buddy and I were thinking about opening up a CBD store."

JK was about as responsible with money as my parents had been. "Oh. Yeah?"

"Yeah, so like... we've done a bunch of research and shit. Seems like we'll only need about fifty grand to get started. The building needs some fixing on the inside, and then we'd have to buy, like, shelves and stuff, you know? Display pieces, they're called. And then we'd need an iPad register thing, but someone said they can help us figure that out at the bank when we open our accounts."

The sandwich suddenly didn't taste quite as good as it had when I'd first sat down. "Sounds exciting."

He shrugged. "You can buy into a franchise for ninety thousand, but we figured we can do it on our own and not have to split the profits, you know? My friend's got a cousin who does something similar down in Dothan. Says he's raking it in."

I nodded and took another bite of the sandwich. JK looked at me expectantly. I looked back at him as cluelessly and naively as I possibly could.

If I hadn't been listening for it, I would have missed the nearly silent grunt of disgust from Bear standing somewhere behind the sofa. I bit back a laugh.

"So, uh… we were thinking this would be a sweet investment deal for you."

I blinked at him. "For me? Oh, no, thank you. I've got all my investments handled at the moment. A team up in New York manages everything for me. I try not to get involved."

This was a complete lie. With Kenji's help, I micromanaged the hell out of my money in an effort to give most of it away.

JK's face crinkled in frustration. "No, but like… this would be an *investment*. Like… it could *make* you money."

"How much?"

He frowned. "Like… you want numbers?"

I shrugged. "I mean, usually, when someone is asking you to invest in their business, they have a business plan and an estimated rate of return. Do you have that?"

The sound of Bear slowly blowing air out through his nose made me bite my upper lip to keep a straight face. I didn't dare turn to see his colossal eye roll.

"No, but like… I could. I could totally get that for you."

I knew I shouldn't have egged him on, but I hadn't been able to help myself. Now, it was time to crawl it back. "I don't think my public relations people would be okay with me getting involved in a CBD business. But good luck. Running your own business sounds like a *lot* of work, but I'm sure you'll be great at it."

Since JK was currently employed as a lawn care technician for a weed-killing chemical company, I'd put fifty-fifty odds on which environmental hazard would be more optimal for his health between the two options, and I wouldn't have put much money on his longevity in either one.

The crowd watching the game shouted in response to a play, and the sudden sound made me jump out of my skin and clutch my chest. I tried to hide my racing heart and shaking hands, but I was sure at least one person in the room had noticed my response and wasn't thrilled about it.

I turned away from JK to find someone else to talk to so I could avoid another attempt at a business investment. "So, ah, Pearl... tell me how things are going at the salon? Did you ever convince Ke'An to start using that new product line you were telling me about?"

"Omigosh, *yes*. And it's amazing. I was hoping while you're here, you'd let me style you up with it and post a few pics. Maybe just a blowout? It would mean a lot and could really get me some exposure with how great this stuff is. We could run up there right now, in fact, while the salon's closed, and you wouldn't even have to—"

I didn't even need to look at Bear to know he was growling silently in disapproval.

"I don't know... I was kind of hoping to just chill out here today..."

She started forking her fingers into my hair and moving it here and there. "Wait till you see how sleek it is after I use the smoothing infusion. It would just shine under the stage lights like you wouldn't believe. Zee... this stuff is amazing, and it's all paraben- and tetra-sodium-free. I would never put your beautiful hair at risk; you know I wouldn't. Your image is important, and this company takes its image just as seriously as you do. That's why I knew right away you'd be the perfect person to use it on. The conditioning serum will do wonders for these ends, too, and the cleansing system is exactly what you need to keep your color from fading out between visits."

I blinked at her. "I don't color my hair."

She snorted. "Right. Anyway, the cleansing system has these special nanotechnics that do some special stuff that's too complicated to explain right now. But the result speaks for itself."

Aunt Rinny walked up and grabbed my wrist and yanked me up. "Sorry, Pearl, Gran needs Zane in the kitchen. C'mon."

I nearly tripped over the corner of the coffee table as she yanked me away from all the people shouting at the television. When we got into the kitchen, Gran was nowhere to be found.

The familiar sound of Bear's quiet footsteps trailed behind me, and I caught a whiff of his scent, which had always been a strange mix of pine trees and Red Hots cinnamon candies. Some days, it was mostly pine, and some days, it was all Red Hots, but no matter when or where I caught a whiff of it, I always knew it wasn't anyone other than Ryan Galloway. My grumpy, protective Bear.

Instead of explaining where Gran was, Rinny glanced over my shoulder and spoke directly to Bear. "For the love of all that's holy, Ryan, take him upstairs before someone asks him for money again."

I let out a breath. "It's fine. I can handle it."

"It's not fine," she snapped, surprising me. "Gran and I wait for you to have time for a visit, and then what nonsense do you have to put up with? The nonsens-iest. I warned everyone to keep their cool, but did they listen? No. And I can tell you're doing your best to be polite, just like you've always been, but that's outside of enough. You're exhausted, Zane Michael, and I declare it's nap time for silly boys." She finished with a tease, using a phrase I hadn't heard in a million years. "Now, git. You can come back down when it's time for supper."

She shot a look at Bear again as if he was the decider of all things. Unfortunately, I was too tired to remind anyone that he *wasn't*, so I let him press a hand against my lower back and nudge me toward the back stairs. Before we disappeared through the doorway, Uncle Bart came in for another beer. "Oh, hey, I wanted to ask Zee a question about—"

"Nope," Rinny said. "He has a headache. Save your questions for later. Mark and Coot are coming over for a bonfire and bringing Coot's mandolin. If they don't monopolize Zane's time asking him to play with them, you can ask him your question then."

I smiled to myself. Rinny and Scooter "Coot" MacNamy had been sweet on each other for about a million years. He was a dedi-cated long-haul trucker, which was the only reason she'd never agreed to marry him. He was also the best damned mandolin player I'd ever come across in all my years playing with professional musicians. I'd offered him a job playing with me more than once, and he refused every time. "I'm not much of a people person, Zane," he'd said. "The thought of those crowds makes my stomach feel like it might sneak outta my ass without warning."

Knowing he was coming over later to play music out by the fire reminded me why I loved being here... and helped me forget about all the other bullshit.

As soon as I entered my old bedroom, I felt my shoulders drop. "You don't have to stay," I told Bear, knowing it was pointless to dismiss him.

He shot me a look. I tried not to notice how intense his dark eyes were when they landed on me. "You want me to sit in the hall?"

I groaned. *No*, I thought, *I want you to wrap your arms around me like you did last night and remind me that I'm an actual human being, not a walking ATM and sales tool. Make me feel like me again.*

I couldn't say any of that, obviously. I relied on Bear too much as it was.

"Fine," I said instead. "You can stay, but I'm actually going to nap, so you'll be bored to tears."

"I'm never bored when we're here. I get to snoop through all your shit while you sleep." Bear grinned and bounced his eyebrows.

I rolled my eyes and kicked off my shoes before pulling back the faded blue-and-yellow quilt to reveal yellow checkered sheets that were so wash-worn the checkers weren't even discernible anymore. "There's hardly much shit to snoop anymore."

"Pfft. You lived here in high school. I'm still holding out hope I'll find your porn stash."

I laughed as I yanked off my hoodie and unbuttoned my jeans. I made sure to set both items carefully on the edge of my bedside table so they wouldn't wrinkle, and then I slid between the sheets in my boxer briefs. The smell of Gran's discount laundry detergent was still the same as my head sank into the old pillow. "You're going to be disappointed when you learn my porn stash consisted of one signed photo of Cristiano Ronaldo without his shirt on, one newspaper clipping of Garrett Latimore making a big save during the Barlo vs Adams-Kearney High game junior year—he was the goalie on our team and gave me a giant woody in the locker room at least weekly during soccer season—and a movie poster of *Casino Royale* because on it, Daniel Craig's fingers are..."

I snapped my mouth closed before I actually blurted out all the ways I'd fantasized about James Bond using those fingers on me.

Bear met my eyes, a smirk at the edges of his lips. "Daniel Craig, huh? Seems an odd choice."

I shrugged. "Pierce Brosnan, Sean Connery, Daniel Craig... any of them could eat crackers in my bed and I wouldn't kick them out. What about you?"

"What about me?"

I settled down into my bed and closed my eyes. If I could get Ryan to talk to me for a little while with his soothing voice, I'd fall asleep so much faster. "Which Bond girl would you pick? Please say Rosamund Pike. I know she wasn't *technically* the Bond girl in *Die Another Day*, and I'll be totally happy if you pick Halle Berry, of course, but—"

"Pierce Brosnan. Hands down."

For a split second, I thought he was serious. I froze mid-inhale and almost choked on my own spit. But then I quickly realized he was joking. "Haha. But I applaud your taste."

"Wasn't Rosamund Pike the one in *Pride and Prejudice*? She's gorgeous."

I smiled into my pillow. At least the man had eyes. Even if they were straight ones. "Yes. She was also in *Gone Girl*. Now, Ben Affleck I might kick out of bed for eating crackers, but not Neil Patrick Harris or Tyler Perry. They were both in that, too, remember?"

"I never knew soccer was a big deal in Georgia," he said after a few moments.

I cracked an eye open and saw him peering at a photo collage on my bulletin board. On it was a stupid team shot where I was knock-kneed and covered in acne. "Don't look at that," I groaned. "I have a reputation to uphold."

"You're adorable. Look at those teeth."

"They're like elephant ears. I worked nights playing gigs in college just so I could get cosmetic dentistry."

He turned to gaze at me. "No shit? Why?"

I sighed. "I was kind of dating this guy named Bodhi—"

"Bodhi Sorrentino," he murmured. "Played drums with you for three years in school."

I cocked my head. "Yeah, how'd you know?"

"He's on the list," Bear said, referring to the "persons of interest in Zee's life" list my security team kept up to date. "He also comes to concerts from time to time to watch you play. I get a list of VIP pass holders for every show."

"Oh. Yeah, we keep in touch. He was supposed to be at Shaky Knees last night, I thought, but either he couldn't make it, or he showed up and we never connected. I'll see if he wants to meet for lunch in New York next week. He's a nice guy."

"I didn't realize you dated."

"No... it wasn't really... I mean. We kissed and stuff, but he had something going with this other guy that was on again, off again, so I bailed. Mostly, I was into him for the music. Oh! He helped me write 'Hard New Day.' The one with the killer drum solo? That was his idea."

I tried to remember why we were even talking about this. "So, yeah, Bodhi said I'd never get a big music deal with freakishly small ears and big elephant-ear teeth. He suggested I grow out my hair and do whatever I could to fix my mouth."

Bear's jaw dropped comically. "He said that?" he snarled.

As usual, when he learned of anyone disparaging me, my sweet, calm rock of a bodyguard looked like he wanted to moonlight as a feral assassin. I laughed. "Not exactly. *I* called them elephant ears.

He just said I needed braces. Bodhi was young and stupid like the rest of us in college. He's since apologized profusely, don't worry."

"Your teeth were *endearing,* and your ears are *a*-fucking-*dorable.* Fucking *Bodhi* can shove his opinions up his ass."

Before I could pack that sweet moment into my mental treasure box, my bedroom door slammed open, and several things happened at once.

Three teenage girls came in giggling with their cell phones up, my cousin Farrah shouted for them to stop being complete losers, and Ryan Galloway stepped between me and the doorway while drawing his weapon on all four of them.

SIX

RYAN

Bears are naturally protective of the things they value, and they're not known for giving up their territory or their honey without a fight. But if the reward is sweet enough, a bear might just learn to trust and share.
—Bear Facts for Insomniacs, Episode 10

What the fuck was wrong with me that I'd forgotten something as simple as pushing the button lock on Zane's bedroom door?

"Freeze," I barked before calling Lou to come help me deal with these fuckers. "Everyone set your phone camera down on the floor right now and step back."

Because they were stupid kids who didn't know better and I happened to have an effective commanding voice when I chose to use it, all four of them did as I said. I holstered my weapon and stepped forward to pick up the first phone. "Were you recording?"

I didn't wait for an answer, simply went into the girl's camera roll and deleted what I found that looked remotely like it had been taken since they'd come onto the Hendley property today. I narrowed my eyes at her before handing it back. "If you take any unauthorized photos or video of Zee Barlo, do you have any idea what his record label will do?"

"N-no, sir."

"I suggest you don't find out," I warned, mostly because she'd find out they'd do absolutely nothing to her.

I repeated the activity with all of the other phones, secretly appreciating the fact that Farrah hadn't taken any photos or video of her cousin. "Go downstairs and stop bothering Mr. Barlo. This is his private bedroom, for god's sake. How would you feel if a man had just barged into your bedroom uninvited?" I lifted an eyebrow and made eye contact with each of them, hopefully causing them to realize what a violation their actions had been.

As Lou arrived, the poor girls were shaking with fear. They muttered apologies as they backed away from the door and scattered down the hallway. Lou put her hands on her hips and glared at me. "Did you have to make them piss themselves? Jesus. They're just kids."

"They're kids who violated someone's most personal space. Would you react that way if it had been teen boys barging in on a young woman who was in her underwear in bed?"

Lou's cheeks flushed as she looked away. "Sorry, Zane. Didn't realize you were in your skivvies. And obviously it's a breach, Ryan, but I'm not sure it required pulling your weapon."

I met her eyes long enough for her to realize her mistake. She shook her head. "Sorry. I didn't mean to question your reaction. I know those decisions have to happen quickly, and you didn't know who was barging in."

"My finger never left the trigger guard," I said. "And we had someone here earlier with an outstanding weapons charge, Lou." I didn't expound on the fact Zane's extended family was full of questionable characters, and it was a constant challenge to keep an updated security profile on them because Lou knew all of that.

"You're right. I was wrong. I'm sorry. Zane, you okay?"

"Yeah, fine, no worries."

I glanced at him, wondering if Lou could hear the definite thread of "not fine" in his voice.

"Good," she said. "Although, good luck getting any rest now."

She closed us back in the bedroom, and I knew she would take a position outside the door for the rest of the time we spent in Zane's room.

Zane threw himself back onto the pillow with a groan. "She's right. My body's full of adrenaline now."

I stepped forward and clicked the button lock. "Sorry. That was my oversight."

"Not your fault. Farrah knew better than to bring them up here."

Zane got up and dragged on some clothing from his suitcase. While I hated that he felt uncomfortable being undressed—and, okay, slightly mourned the loss of all that smooth, tan skin on display—I had to smile when he turned around.

He'd chosen pajama bottoms and an oversized hoodie he'd bought years ago, the night he'd opened for Jude and the Saints. I'd overheard him telling an interviewer once that playing with Jude Marian had been one of the most surreal experiences of his life. Not many people knew that he'd since had Kenji scour the internet to buy up extras of the shirt—dozens of them, a lifetime supply—so he'd always be able to see his name appear in the same concert graphic as one of his idols.

When Zane's first song had gone platinum, Zane's brothers had tracked down the graphic designer, begged for a printable copy of the design to be made into a poster, and had gotten Jude Marian to sign it. The framed poster hung in his home studio in Malibu.

It was no wonder he'd pulled that shirt on now... and I loved that I knew him well enough to know this.

He flopped back down in the bed and curled his body around another pillow with his back to me. I wanted to move closer and rub his back, help him relax back into the drowsy state he'd been in before the girls had barged in, even turn on his stupid Bear Facts podcast to see if that would help him zone out.

Instead, I took a seat in the wooden desk chair and pulled out my phone. After a few minutes, Zane began to hum a tune under his breath the way he did when he was noodling through an idea for a song.

I could listen to him do that all day long. His voice was soothing and often soulful, depending on what he was working on. This melody was one I hadn't heard before. It was light and playful... which surprised me, considering how much stress he'd been under lately.

He reached for his phone and started making notes in his song-writing app as he continued to hum the new tune.

The sound of his voice wove in and out of the sound of people downstairs. Periodic shouts of victory interspersed with collective groans of defeat came from the group in the family room, while women's laughter came from the kitchen and a few shouts from younger kids accompanied the rhythmic, hollow-sounding *bapbap* of a basketball being dribbled on the driveway outside the bedroom window.

I understood why Zane craved being here. It made him feel as close to "normal" as he could get these days. But he was so desperate for that normalcy he refused to see how many of those "friends and family members" were mercenary users. Almost every single one of them, with the exceptions of his grandmother and one aunt, was desperate to trade on his celebrity image or take advantage of his wealth.

I hated it for him. The man wanted to be loved for who he was on the inside—as Zane Hendley—when all of the people downstairs only wanted to see Zee Barlo, the megastar.

"You're brooding," he teased without looking up from his phone. "A big, broody Bear."

"*Mpfh.* I do not brood."

Zane chuckled. "You hate it here."

"I don't," I insisted. "There are things I like here. And people."
Namely, Zane himself.

"You're itching to leave."

I hesitated. "I'm itching to boot most of those jackasses out," I
admitted. "Your gran and Rinny can stay."

Zane laughed again. "Generous of you."

"Sorry. That was unprofessional."

He flicked his eyes at me. "Bear, pretty sure we passed professional about ten months ago. We're friends, aren't we? Or do you
want to go back to the days when I called you Ryan and you tried
really hard not to swear in my presence because it was
unprofessional?"

My lips twitched. "No. I fucking don't."

He laughed lightly. "Good. Then don't censor yourself with me. I
have enough people in my life who only tell me what I want to hear."

I let out a huff. "None of them are downstairs."

Zane tossed his phone down and turned over to prop himself up
against the headboard. "Not true. Farrah's friends would be more
than happy to tell me what I want to hear." I could tell by his grin he
was enjoying arguing with me.

"Your cousin JK needs to take a long walk off a short pier."

"My cousin JK will never get out of Barlo, Georgia. And that
makes me feel sorry for him. I love that he's dreaming about starting
his own business. Growing up poor in a small town means you don't
have a whole lot *other* than dreams of something better, Bear.
Nothing wrong with him trying to make his dream a reality."

"You sound like an inspirational poster sold at the dollar store."

Zane barked out a laugh. "Since when have *you* been to a dollar
store?"

I couldn't hold back a matching grin. "Since King Asger wanted
the royal family and their entourage to experience, quote, 'the real
America' on their tour here six years ago. I took them to all kinds of
places. We even went bowling and had those upside-down ice creams
at Dairy Queen. The kids loved it. I think the king did, too. Crown

Prince Gerhard and the rest of the staff... less so. Distinct lack of formal protocol here, let alone Ventdestinian mysticism. When the 'winds of fate' don't blow as predicted, it ruffles their feathers." I gave him a half smile. "But I liked that the king tried."

Zane chuckled. "I can only imagine what the royal chef thought of a set of yellow-and-green-painted corn handles."

"And the bendy straws," I added.

"And the off-brand Tupperware whose lids never fit right, even from day one."

I shook my head. "The worst were the chip clips. He was fascinated by them, even though I'm not sure the man had ever seen a bag of chips in his life."

Zane's smile softened. "We always used wooden clothespins. You could get a pack of a hundred for five bucks at the Walmart over in Tipton. Gran used to share them with the neighbors like she was royalty. She would have done the Ventdestinian royal family proud."

I thought about the stark difference between the way the Ventdestinian princes and princess were raised compared to how Zane had been brought up here in Barlo. I'd joined the royal guard when Asger's oldest grandson was only ten, and I'd seen just how stifling his upbringing was.

Money didn't always solve everything, as Zane... and the royal children... well knew.

"You know, every time I see that horseshoe over the front door, I think how your gran would actually get a kick out of the superstitions in Ventdestine," I said. "The royal family in particular are a little over-the-top with certain things."

Zane lifted his eyebrows as if asking for an explanation, so I continued. Zane always loved hearing about Ventdestine. He said my stories seemed like fairy tales.

"Asger used to tap his toe on the rug every time he entered his bedroom. Apparently, there was a several-hundred-year-old superstition that had something to do with a previous king who had commissioned a tapestry for the royal chambers and then hadn't properly paid the artisan. So, the weaver had put a curse on the royal family. It took years for the curse to be reversed, and ever since then, the king has to pay homage to the weaver when he enters the royal chamber to ward off the curse."

"How exhausting," Zane said.

"They still burn a special combination of herbs in the palace every spring to clean out the evil spirits left from winter. And the winds are always whispering fortune, or ill, or love, or loss." I shook my head. "It was hard, when I first moved there, to reconcile myself to how deeply ingrained these ideas are in their culture. I'm curious if things will change now that Gerhard is on the throne. In some ways, he was as superstitious as his father."

"You said his wife is super modern, though. She's from…"

"The Netherlands. Yeah. Gisella. She's a good influence on him. She's a big fan of yours, actually. That's one of the reasons I knew your music. She and the kids used to play your stuff all the time."

Zane flicked his eyes to the ceiling and shook his head. "I think one of the reasons Violet assigned you to me was because you barely knew who I was. There was practically no chance you'd be weird around me. Sure enough, you acted like I was Joe Schmoe. It was kind of refreshing."

"It wasn't until I heard you sing the first time that I realized I knew your stuff; I'd just never seen you or really learned your name. It's funny, Gisella saw you in concert in Berlin once, but since the king was my principal and he wasn't there, I didn't go."

"Maybe they want to come to the concert in Amsterdam?" he asked. "You know I'm happy to arrange passes and stuff."

I nodded. "Already offered it. I'm sure they'll be there if they can get away."

Zane eventually drifted off to sleep. I watched him and wondered, not for the first time, how I would feel if he ever stopped hooking up with people and started dating someone for real. Whatever he had going with Landry wasn't serious—they were friends, but

Zane's busy tour lifestyle and Landry's hectic modeling schedule weren't compatible.

I thought back to last night. To Lou's observations about Landry hooking up with someone else. To racing into Zane's bedroom to find Zane wearing the same comfortable lounge clothes he'd put on before his friends arrived. I wasn't the most sexually experienced person in the world—far, far from it—but I assumed if they'd had the kind of sex I'd heard through the door, they would have fallen asleep together naked. Or at least only dressed in underwear.

Now that I had time to think back, I realized Landry had been fully dressed also. Had they even had sex? If not, then what the hell had I heard? And what had Landry's weird comments been about after the fact?

Last night hadn't been the first time I'd had to sit outside of a hotel room door while Zane hooked up with someone, though, and Landry wasn't the only person he'd been with. He'd had plenty of hookups since I'd been on his detail, and he'd had a reputation for having had even more of them under his previous publicist. Noelle had encouraged Zane to create a bad-boy reputation by indulging in hookup culture as much as he wanted and going out drinking after shows. It wasn't until he'd gotten rid of her and hired Micki that he'd stopped making such bad decisions.

If only he'd stop hooking up with people altogether. At this rate, I was going to start losing weight from the number of times I'd had to escape and run the stairs at random hotels.

Maybe it was because of the sheer amount of time I spent that afternoon ruminating about Zane's sexual exploits that my ears tuned in to what happened later that night around the bonfire.

Regardless of the reason for it, I was shocked by what I heard.

SEVEN
ZANE

It's a little-known fact that bears can end up in some tricky situations. Their relentless pursuit of honey sometimes results in a sticky mess. But bears never get hung up on these awkward moments. They know a little embarrassment is worthwhile when they end up with something sweet.
—Bear Facts for Insomniacs, Episode 11

I felt much better after a nap, and Gran's big Sunday supper was exactly as amazing as I'd anticipated. The long dining table sagged under the weight of all my favorite dishes, and the sounds of friends and family happily chatting around the table reminded me of countless Sunday suppers when I was growing up.

Not everyone from the brotherhood was able to make it to Barlo, but Landry, Silas, Way, Dev, and Tully showed up that evening for the meal and joined us around the fire pit afterward.

Camp chairs and string lights were scattered around the large patio, and Uncle Bart had lit a circle of tiki torches all around to provide extra light.

Sure enough, Coot showed up and asked me to join him in playing some favorites out by the fire. I grabbed my acoustic guitar from where someone had stashed it in my room with the rest of my personal bags and took a seat on one of the cut tree stumps in the center of the group.

Pearl's friend had brought her harmonica, an old friend from high school had brought his elementary recorder and could actually play the damned thing, and there turned out to be several good vocalists among the group. All of them joined in when they wanted to, and we had ourselves a good old-fashioned jam session.

Bear—who, I'd noted with satisfaction, had eaten at least two helpings of cheesy grits and a huge plate of peach cobbler—reminded me to keep drinking water between songs and sent Boomer to bring me a fresh bottle. But even with all of that effort, the smoke eventually caused me to stop singing for a bit. I enjoyed having downtime to ask Dev and Tully about their new house in Majestic and how things were going with their daughter.

People wandered in and out of the house for bathroom visits and to grab a fresh bottle of beer or soda. Old stories from high school resurfaced, and people shared what they'd been up to more recently. More than once, someone asked me to invest in their business endeavors or give them some kind of access to my time, but my closest friends used old tried-and-true distraction methods if I started looking uncomfortable.

I'd gotten used to giving polite refusals, but it still took a lot out of me. I hated letting people down, especially people who'd been important to me at one time.

So I did what I always did and tried to make it up to them by being present with them in the moment and creating a good memory we could share. And maybe that's why later, when everyone except my brotherhood, my closest cousins, and a couple of their friends had left, I ended up sharing more than I should have.

"I'll bet you get so much ass," JK said with a laugh after taking a swig of his millionth beer.

I felt my face heat even more than what the fire had already accomplished. Thank god the older generation had already gone to bed. "No, actually. I don't," I said truthfully. I didn't want to pretend to be someone I wasn't around my own family.

Pearl's friend Grace, the one who played killer harmonica and had stayed later to ask me to sign it, looked disbelieving. "I've read about you online. You've hooked up with tons of guys. I heard you and Isaiah Harbin were a thing for a while—"

I frowned. "Who?"

"Football player," Way explained. "One of the few out gay players in the NFL."

"Ah." I shook my head. "Sorry. Never met the man. Definitely not 'a thing.'"

Grace shrugged. "I bet the scheduling would've been a nightmare anyway. And there are plenty of other fish in the sea. Speaking of which, my friend Jay from work is frantically checking Grindr all weekend in case you get on it."

I felt Silas's eyes on me. He and the others were fiercely protective, and I knew he'd step in and take over if I was too uncomfortable to speak. I shook my head again. "He can stop checking. I don't, uh... I don't use Grindr."

Pearl was the only one of my cousins who seemed to take me seriously. She frowned and asked why not.

I shrugged and let out a nervous laugh. "My old publicist warned me never to put myself in a situation where I could accidentally wind up in a sex tape scandal. She told me horror stories about hidden cameras and stuff like that. So I don't, uh... do the kind of stuff that would land me in a sex scandal."

Landry muttered, "Noelle was good for one thing, I guess."

Silas reached over and clinked Solo cups with him.

"Sure," JK said, rolling his eyes. "You're the hottest rock star on the planet right now next to Taylor Swift, and you're not out there fucking roadies? No freaking way that's true."

"I swear," I insisted before trying to laugh it off with a joke. "Believe me, I've thought about it. But I also don't want people I've hooked up with posting online about me about my scrawny body and how shit I am at sex."

Bear shifted behind me, but Grace distracted me with another question before I could think too much about it. "But you have a reputation for hookups."

"Hookups can include heavy make-out sessions," I reminded her. "I'm not saying I've never messed around with a guy. I just don't... get naked, basically. With other people."

Pearl blinked at me. "You... don't have sex? Like... you've never had sex, or you have to really know and trust a guy before you do?"

I ground my back teeth together while I tried to figure out how honest to be. "I told you, I never put myself in a situation where someone could film me having sex."

Now, JK looked confused. "So, who've you had sex with?"

I inhaled slowly through my nose and decided to be honest. There were impressionable people here, including Grace's younger brother, who I'd caught blushing at me and my gay friends several times from across the fire. "No one. And if you tell that to the media or post it online, I will say I've never met you in my life, and I will absolutely sue you until you're dead-ass broke and begging me to stop."

Impressionable teens were one thing. Messing with my reputation and causing a public relations situation was another.

Landry sat up straighter. "And I'll hire someone to beat the shit out of you because I'm not that nice."

JK's jaw dropped open. "No one? Bro. We need to get you laid. You can do it at my place. There's no cameras or nothin'."

I could only imagine the state of JK and his roommate's bachelor apartment at the edge of town. "Um, no, thanks."

Pearl smacked him on the chest. "With who? You think he's

suddenly going to give it up for the one good-looking gay guy in Barlo?" She glanced at Grace's brother. "No offense, Hayden, but you're jailbait."

"N-no," the poor kid stammered. "I-I didn't say anything. H-he... I..."

I mouthed the word *sorry* at him, but it only made him blush harder and mutter something about the heat and smoke from the fire.

I tried to change the subject. "Can we stop talking about my sex life, please?"

JK wasn't ready to let it go. He jabbed a thumb over his shoulder at Landry. "What about these guys? Your friends from Yale? Surely you all..."

"Ew," Silas said, exaggerating.

"Hook up with these guys? Nooo." Landry pretended to gag before flicking his hair over his shoulder. "They're all leg-shackled now. Monogamous as fuck, like the straights. Besides, hookups are a surefire way to complicate a... a friendship."

I looked at Landry curiously. He spoke like he knew this from experience, and by process of elimination, there was only one person he could be talking about. More than once over the past couple of years, he'd let something slip that made me think he and Kenji had slept together, but I'd never asked either of them directly. Kenji wouldn't answer, and Landry would only turn it into a joke. Besides, it was infamous among the brotherhood that Landry annoyed the fuck out of Kenji.

But then again, I'd worked hard to hide my crush on Bear, and all that strong emotion Kenji displayed might be less about dislike and more about fighting an inconvenient attraction.

"Okay, but... why not just do it once?" Grace said, turning toward Landry. "You're both single. You could pop his cherry, right?"

Landry squinted at me as if assessing the possibility.

I glared at him. "You wish."

He shrugged. "I mean, I'd do ya. And JK so generously offered us a camera-free zone, which sounds romantic as all heckity."

"Don't fake a Southern accent," I said with a laugh. "You'll make someone choke on their beer."

Landry winked at me. Pearl sighed. "The more I think about it, the more I think it's kind of nice. You're saving yourself for someone special."

I barked out a laugh. "I'm definitely not. I'd have sex tomorrow if I could ensure it wouldn't end up on the internet."

Landry made a big production about looking at his watch. "I do have some free time in the morning."

I felt more than heard Bear shift his weight behind me again. Suddenly, I felt light-headed and vaguely sick. Ryan Galloway—my Bear—the man I had a secret and all-consuming crush on, had just found out my most embarrassing secret.

I was a world-famous rock star.

And a complete and total virgin.

I felt my eyes drift closed as I tried to decide whether to take off running and attempt to lose myself in the scraggly woods at the end of Gran's street.

Landry must have caught the look on my face because he turned to Pearl. "You said there was one good-looking gay guy in Barlo. Were you talking about me, or do I need to get someone's number? Because, like I said, I do have a few hours free in the morning..."

Silas immediately began giving him hell for his playboy ways and rolled right into a story from Yale about the time Landry had decided to try being straight for a month.

"It was Lent," Landry said with a sniff. "You're supposed to give up something good."

"You're not Catholic," Silas pointed out.

I tried to let my embarrassing moment go, but I couldn't. My entire face prickled as I tried not to make eye contact with anyone. Revealing personal information wasn't something I was used to doing without careful consideration, but I didn't want my cousins to have a false impression of me and think my life was a stereotypical rock star bang-fest. I worked my ass off, and I spent more time worrying about getting a full eight hours of sleep and staying hydrated than I did trying to get laid.

After a few more minutes and more topic changes, I took the opportunity to go into the house to use the bathroom. I ignored Bear as he trailed me silently. When I came out of the hall bathroom, I was surprised to see Grace's little brother waiting outside.

"It's all yours," I said, gesturing toward the powder room door.

"No, I... I was wondering if... I could ask you a question about... what you talked about earlier."

This guy was a high schooler, which made me leery. I was glad Bear was here so I wasn't alone with the kid. "What's your question?"

"Yeah, so like... how did you get so good at sweeping?" He made a guitar-strumming gesture to go along with his words.

I tilted my head as my brain tried to make sense of his question. I'd thought for sure he was going to ask me about being gay. Or about being the world's lamest virgin. But he was asking about... a guitar-picking technique?

"Uh. Sweep picking. Well... let's see..." I tried to think back to how I learned. It seemed a million years ago. "Padge has some YouTube stuff. Search for one I think called solo? I think honestly... slowing the videos down and then just repeating. Start with your left hand first, and then bring in the pick."

His blush continued as he stammered out a few more polite questions and then thanked me before going into the bathroom.

I took a deep breath and pointed myself back in the direction of the patio door to rejoin everyone by the fire.

Bear did what he always did and followed me silently, remaining in my blind spot so I didn't even catch sight of him out of the corner of my eye.

When I took my seat again by the fire, my cousins rattled off all the plans they had for taking me into town the next day to see and be seen. I knew I would enjoy seeing everyone and visiting some of my old haunts and some of the newer places that had cropped up with the infusion of investment capital that I'd helped bring in, but right now, I was bone-tired.

"I think I'm going to head in so I'll be fresh for our big day tomorrow," I said after a while, standing and wriggling my fingers in a little wave. "See you all in the morning."

I heard Bear murmur an update to Lou and Boomer into his earpiece as he followed me into the house and up to my room. Thankfully, there was a guest room across the hall from my bedroom that Bear would stay in. Boomer had most likely taken a long nap in it earlier and would stay up while Bear got some sleep and Lou headed to a nearby hotel.

Before I could disappear into my room, Bear handed me a fresh water bottle. "Do you want me to make you some hot lemon water for your throat?"

I blinked up at him. "Oh, ah, no? No, thanks. I just want to go to sleep."

He started to reach out with his hand but then dropped it by his side. Then he shifted on his feet. "Did you get enough to eat?"

"Bear, I ate enough to sustain a small Viking community. Did *you* get enough to eat?"

His eyebrows furrowed in an incredibly bearlike, impossibly adorable way that made my heart squeeze. "Of course."

I wanted to laugh, but I was too tired. "Good night, Bear," I said softly.

As I turned to close the door to my bedroom, I caught one last glimpse of him watching me.

Always watching me.

I got ready for bed quickly and hoped like hell there would be no more nightmares tonight.

EIGHT

RYAN

Bears are clever and resourceful... and sometimes really sneaky. They'll move their den locations if they sense a threat and disguise their trails to throw off curious onlookers. For a bear, staying hidden and unpredictable is the best way to ensure that no one can get at the honey that was meant for them and them alone.

—Bear Facts for Insomniacs, Episode 48

Was it terrible for me to wish Zane had another nightmare? I couldn't deny that I loved it when he needed me, and I especially appreciated any excuse to hold him close.

But thankfully for Zane, the night went smoothly, and Boomer reported that the bonfire crowd had gone to bed shortly after we'd left.

It had taken me a long time to fall asleep because I couldn't stop replaying the shocking news I'd heard about Zane's love life. I happened to be able to tell when Zane Hendley was lying—a slight hesitation in the way he spoke, an inability to meet someone's eyes that usually preceded the words "I'm fine"—and he hadn't been lying when he'd admitted to being a virgin.

But I also knew that I'd stood outside many a hotel room while he was inside making out with men... and I had racked up the stair work-outs to prove it. So, did that mean they'd only done kissing and heavy petting? A few under-the-clothes handies or over-the-clothes dry-humping?

I was desperate to find out more, but it was definitely not a topic I could ask him about.

The idea that Zane had never fully shared his body with another man made something inside of me tip off-center and thump around wildly like a washing machine with a broken belt.

I'd fantasized about being naked with him innumerable times, and I'd been in a green rage each time another man had the privilege.

Was it truly possible *no* man had actually had that privilege? And if so, what did that mean for Zane? Was he going to deny himself that kind of sexual pleasure until sometime in the distant future when he retired? Surely he could find someone he trusted enough to sleep with?

Why not Landry? And... if not Landry, what had all those moans coming from Zane's room been about?

I fell asleep without any answers.

The next morning's visit into the small town of Barlo took enough arranging to fully distract me. My boss, Violet, had put a logistics coordinator on it, who'd brought in additional help in the form of off-duty Barlo law enforcement officers and other security personnel.

It was a bit of a production, but I appreciated that the people hired to help us seemed professional and were willing to try to keep the situation as low-key as possible.

Our first stop was a place called the Neatnik, a breakfast diner where Zane had worked as a busser in middle school. I'd secretly developed a mini-obsession with their breakfast potatoes, so I didn't mind this stop one bit.

"Please tell me we're not going to Bart's place again," I muttered before taking a sip of coffee.

We weren't alone at the large round booth. But Zane's great-aunt Shell was busy gossiping with every local who entered the place, and her granddaughter was busy taking selfies with Zane in the background while pretending to check her hair.

"No. I was trying to figure out how to tell him we didn't have time when he told me that he's being sent on a job up in Cordelle. But I did tell Jordy Crowder we'd stop by his print shop." Zane flashed me an apologetic wince. "Sorry, but after he didn't charge me for the printing on all those field day shirts last year, I felt like I owed him a solid."

He was right. Even though the good old boy was a talker, he was a good guy, and he helped Zane out with plenty of local charity projects. "We already have that one on the schedule. I'm trying to figure out which unexpected ones are going to pop up while we're out and about. Bart's is usually the one that pops up."

Bart was an ass, and he never hesitated to drag Zane to the HVAC service center where he worked to impress his boss and sucker Zane into a photo op.

Zane pressed his lips together in thought before his eyes brightened and his cheeks turned a little pink. "Oh, Carrie-Beth said I might run into Sully Bynam and, if so, to be sure and ask to see his tulip poplars."

Shell overheard and snapped her head around. "Sully's tulip poplars are a sight to behold. You've never seen golden beauties like those. A whole driveway full of 'em. It's like... like something on TV."

I couldn't remember why that name sounded familiar... until I remembered Pearl talking around the bonfire about the *one* hot gay guy in Barlo.

"We might not have time for any of that," I said gruffly.

Zane shrugged. "We probably won't see him anyway."

Right. Zane seemed to forget that when he was in Barlo, everyone and their hot gay uncle flocked to the tiny downtown area to catch sight of him.

The rest of the day was a nightmare. Several times, I'd thought someone was trying to get close enough to Zane to sneak a stamp onto his skin, and I'd roughly interjected myself between the stranger and my principal. Each time, it had turned out to simply be a friend or fan with innocent intentions.

Several months ago, Zane had laughingly sent me an Instagram video of Lionel Messi's bodyguard comically cutting off zealous fans before they could get to the famous soccer star. That was what my day in Barlo ended up looking like.

Thankfully, Zane politely declined the (admittedly gorgeous) Sully Bynam's offer to see his poplars, and we ended up back at Gran's before dinner. Zane threw himself down in the corner of the large sectional sofa and pulled out his phone while I went to the kitchen to grab him a fresh water bottle and some carrot sticks out of the fridge.

As I was walking back into the family room, I caught sight of his face as his jaw dropped and his complexion paled. His eyes flicked from his phone screen up to me, and I saw him hesitate for a split second before sighing and handing me the phone. I handed him the water and carrots before sitting on the edge of the coffee table across from him and looking at his screen.

The email on the screen was from a junk Gmail address and had been sent to Zane's private, personal email account—the one that only the brotherhood, his agent, his manager, and a few other select people had access to.

To Zee,
Do you like wearing my mark? I can get to you whenever I
want. You're not his to protect. Cut him loose.
See you in New York.
Semper in scopum.

The Stamper.

My rage was a feral beast clawing at my skin from the inside. How fucking dare they find another way to get at Zane? How dare they cause him another single moment of fear and worry? How dare they insinuate that I couldn't protect him when there was nothing I wouldn't do to keep him safe?

I forced myself to read the words over and over, partly in hopes of discovering new information and partly in an attempt to calm myself down since I knew my anger would only upset Zane further. When nothing new revealed itself, I forwarded it to myself and Violet, closed it in his email app, and then made a folder in his email account to put it into so I could preserve it without him having to see it every time he opened his personal email.

Always on target.

The Latin galled me, but I was grateful for it since it at least offered us a little bit of insight into the sender. Violet's technical guys could try to trace the email, but I didn't hold out much hope. If the perp was smart enough to use Latin, they were probably smart enough to mask their virtual identity.

I glanced up at Zane, who'd pulled his legs up to wrap his arms around his knees. "We have to go," I said softly.

He nodded, dislodging a piece of brown hair to fall over one eyebrow. I reached out to brush it behind his ear without fully realizing what I was doing. "We have to cancel New York."

"I know."

I glanced around to make sure no one was close enough to overhear me.

"Where do you want to go?"

Zane's eyebrows winged up. "I assumed we'd go to LA. Isn't that what you said you wanted? To meet up with Violet, call in reinforcements, and strategize?"

I pressed my lips together and inhaled. "No. I think it makes more sense to go somewhere unexpected, where we'll know you're safe while Violet and the team assess the risks of continuing the tour."

"I'm not canceling the tour," he said with a slight flare of his nostrils. "Tell Violet to figure it out because we're going to the rest of the European stops and the fundraiser in Berlin as planned. The fans freaked out when we added those dates, and I'm supposed to be debuting my new song with Jude Marian in Berlin. We're going to raise a ton of money for LGBTQ programs. I'm not reneging because some asshole is trying to scare me."

His passionate response didn't surprise me. Zane would rather throw himself across train tracks than disappoint his fans or, worse, contribute to the loss of income for his employees and all of the contractors who depended on him for their livelihoods.

"I'll let her know," I said, trying to remain calm when what I really wanted to do was put my foot down and demand he cancel every show from here until the end of time.

That wouldn't be fair to him. It was bad enough that the Stamper had taken his peace of mind. I wouldn't let them take away the things Zane loved most.

He let out a breath and stewed for a few minutes before finally reaching for a carrot stick. He snapped off the end and crunched before turning to me. "We could go to Majestic."

I looked up from where I'd been texting with Violet. "We're not going anywhere connected to you."

"It's tiny and in the middle of nowhere. People there notice and comment when their neighbors got a haircut. They'd notice if a stranger came to town—"

"They'll also definitely notice *you're* there, and word will get out," I countered.

Zane's face fell.

I was trying to remain calm and not let it show, but the email had ignited a strong need in me to grab Zane and bolt this minute. My rational brain knew that with Lou, Boomer, and me here, guarding a vetted and controlled property like his gran's house, Zane was most likely safe in the short term. But my rational brain was trying very hard to fuck off to parts unknown, leaving my irrational caveman gut in charge.

And the caveman wanted to grab Zane and run far, far away, right the hell now, to a place where no one could find him.

So, I made a concession to the caveman.

"I'm going to rent a place in a random location. You, Lou, and I will be the only ones who know where it is. Boomer will continue to the first tour city as planned and be Violet's local liaison."

I messaged the pilot to let her know about the change of plans and ask about filing flight plans to White Plains and being prepared to continue straight on from there to a Northern European destination. Then, I started searching for a place to hole up.

I immediately knew where I wanted to bring Zane, if the house was available on such short notice.

The front door banged open, and someone's shouted greeting made us both jump. I glared at JK and ground my teeth together to keep from snapping at him.

He approached Zane with a fist bump. "Hey, bro. I told Kenny and them we'd hit up Peaches tonight and maybe you'd play a set with the house band. What do you say?"

Zane tried to fake being chill, but he was definitely not. "Yeah, so... no. We have to go. Duty calls, you know?"

JK frowned. "I thought you were staying till Wednesday? Gran has a whole thing planned for Rinny's birthday tomorrow."

Zane's shoulders fell. I half expected him to shoot me a pleading look before promising to stay. He adored his aunt, and she was the only one besides his grandmother I actually liked enough to feel guilty about ditching.

Instead of agreeing to stay, though, he surprised me. "I hate to miss it, but something's come up."

"Aww, man. Okay. I'll text Kenny and tell him they all need to come here if they want to see you." He pulled out his phone and wandered away as he began to type.

After texting Lou and Boomer that we might have an influx of

JK's friends showing up again, I went back to booking the place I'd found for us and making sure we'd have access to everything we needed when we got there without having to leave the property.

After a few minutes, I felt Zane's eyes on me. I glanced up from my phone to see him scraping his top lip with his bottom teeth, looking so uncertain I wanted to take him in my arms.

"What's up, b—Zane?" I asked. *Not my baby. Not my baby. Not my baby. No matter how much I wish he could be.*

"Can we leave now? I don't... I don't want to talk to a lot of people."

Thank fuck.

"Of course," I said softly. "Go pack your stuff and start making your goodbyes. I'll get Lou and Boomer on board and make sure the driver's ready to head to the airport."

Zane hopped up and made his way upstairs while I made the arrangements and packed my own things. Within half an hour, we were on the road, and a half hour after that, we were in the air.

"Why White Plains?" Zane asked when the pilot mentioned our destination.

"I didn't want anyone in Barlo to know we were changing our plans to go to New York, but I didn't want to land at Teterboro since that's where we're expected."

"Okay." Zane accepted this easily, and as it always did, the trust he placed in me soothed something deep in my chest. "Where are we going after that?" he asked, snuggling under the soft blanket he often used on flights.

"Northern Europe." I showed him a photo of the fjord in Norway where a small luxury home had stunning views of the water. Zane was a sucker for an inspirational view. Hopefully, he could distract himself with songwriting while I worked remotely to make sure the European stops were adequately protected.

His eyes widened, and I felt his body relax. "Gorgeous."

Within moments, he was asleep in the wide leather chair next to mine. I opened up my laptop and connected to the plane's Wi-Fi so I could get to work.

Halfway to New York, Zane's head had slid over to the side. I shifted in my seat so that when his head slid farther, it would land on my shoulder. It took an excruciating several minutes before the warmth of him landed on me, and the faint scent of his hair wafted into my nose.

I let out a breath and felt some of my tension fall away. As long as I was touching Zane Hendley, I could relax a little.

Because Zane was okay...

And finally right where he was supposed to be.

NINE

ZANE

Bears don't take betrayal lightly. They have an uncanny sense of loyalty, and if you cross them, you're done. In the wild, respect is a two-way street, honey is earned, not stolen, and a bear will make sure a betrayer doesn't stick around for long. Mess with the honey and you'll feel the claws.
—Bear Facts for Insomniacs, Episode 34

The string of flights from Barlo, Georgia, to Ørsta, Norway, was long, but the more distance we put between the site of the stamping incident and myself, the more relaxed I became.

Bear was right. I would have been a nervous wreck if we'd continued on to New York as planned, knowing there was someone out there trying to prove they could get to me.

By the time we pulled through the gates to the secluded property Bear had rented, I was ready to get outside and move my body.

"I'm going for a walk," I said, inhaling the fresh cold air. "Is that okay? It looks like there's a fence around the property."

Bear and Lou exchanged a look I was very familiar with. Before they could tell me no, I added, "Let me be clear. I am going for a walk. If you'd like me to wait a few minutes or take one of you along, that's fine. But I can't spend another moment sitting down."

Bear stretched his arms up and leaned his muscled torso from side to side, looking a little sleepy and disgruntled... exactly like the animal I'd named him for. His crumpled button-down shirt was half-untucked, and the motion exposed a glimpse of a furry happy trail leading down into royal blue underwear behind the low waistband of his jeans. My eyes locked onto the sight like a starving cub who's just spotted a salmon.

"I'm very happy to take a walk," he said. He dropped his arms, cutting off the stellar view of his happy trail, and I blinked and looked around. "Lou?"

"Nah." Lou tilted her head toward the gatehouse we'd passed as we'd entered the property. Two men in dark trousers and sweaters had let us in while actively monitoring a bank of monitors showing security camera feeds. "I'm going to touch base with those guys and get settled in."

On the plane, Bear had explained that he'd selected this property because of its built-in security staff. Apparently, it had been built originally by a minor Norwegian royal who'd upgraded to a newer place farther north. I couldn't imagine an upgrade nicer than this.

The property was incredible, perched above a fjord with jaw-dropping views in every direction. The house itself sat on a peninsula. Its clapboard siding was painted red, set off by a dark roof. Giant windows looked out from three sides, and a large deck jutted out from the side facing the water, providing the perfect view of the mountain peaks across the fjord.

Behind the house was an open, grassy field leading to tree-covered hills I was eager to explore. I waited impatiently for Bear to tighten the laces on one of his shoes, and then we set off.

Within five minutes, I was already feeling more settled in my skin. The sky was a light, steely blue, and the silence around us was broken only by the sound of the wind through the trees and across the water. The leaves seemed to be in their peak autumnal splendor, and the air felt just shy of bracing. It was the kind of day I'd only seen in Hallmark movies growing up, when the air was cold enough to turn your nose and cheeks pink and fresh enough to brighten your eyes. The leaves floated on the wind in reds and oranges.

"You picked the right place," I admitted. "How did you find it?"

"I came here once with King Asger and Prince Gerhard's oldest son, Auden, years ago on a grandfather-grandson trip. Auden had been caught cheating in school, and Asger was convinced it was because he and Gerhard hadn't been present enough in the boy's life. The trip was his attempt to correct that."

"Did it work?"

"Surprisingly, yes. They spent a lot of time talking about tradition and reputation, about the burden of being born into the royal family and the privileges that helped balance out the responsibilities. Asger was a good man, and that trip was one of the first times I got to see that part of him. Auden always looked up to his grandfather, but that trip really made an impact on him, too. He seemed to grow up a little and start to embrace his role. He began to emulate Asger and aspire to be just like him."

"Auden must have been devastated when the king died. Both of them, really. Gerhard and Auden."

"Mm. I can't even imagine. I'm glad they have Gisella. She's very fun-loving. A great mom and wife. Hopefully, she'll balance out Gerhard's strict stodginess and remind Auden not to take himself too seriously."

We reached the tree line and continued into the small forest on a path that looked well traveled by the property's summer visitors.

"I had a friend like that in college," I said. "Bodhi, actually."

"Asshole," Bear coughed.

A laugh bubbled up unexpectedly. "He's not an asshole."

"Remind me again what he said about your teeth."

Bear's growly, instinctive protectiveness surrounded me like a warm blanket and made things in the vicinity of my heart get tight... to say nothing of the situation in my jeans.

Instead of luxuriating in the warmth, though, I forced myself to wave his words away. I concentrated on walking faster and the rhythmic *crunch, swish* of my feet on the leaf-strewn ground.

"Bodhi was young and stupid," I said. "That was one of the things I liked about him. I took myself incredibly seriously at Yale. Felt like I had something to prove. Bodhi convinced me to live a little. Have some fun. Make time for music in the midst of all the academics. He taught me about balance." I thought about it for a moment and added with a smile, "And my teeth *were* genuinely awful."

"I think he sounds like a shithead. A jealous, immature shithead who wanted to make you feel bad," Bear grumbled.

I snickered. "Hardly. I helped him get seen in the music world. Bodhi always wanted to play drums professionally, and now he does."

Bear glanced at me. "That's rare."

I nodded. "It's not easy to make a living as a musician."

"No, I mean it's rare for you to take credit for helping someone."

My face heated, but I hoped I could pass it off as exertion from walking uphill. "Bodhi was grateful, and he's very supportive. When I stopped using Noelle as my publicist, he did the same—"

"Zane, Noelle was incompetent. Any idiot would have left her after learning how she and her PR team almost 'publicized' you right into state prison."

He wasn't wrong. "Still. Bodhi is good people. I got an email from him this morning, actually. I asked him why he never showed at Shaky Knees, and he said he *did*—he actually really wanted to talk to me—but security wouldn't give him access to my dressing room after the show."

I wrinkled my nose. Bear had locked everything down after hearing about the Stamper, and I didn't blame him one bit, but I hated that Bodhi might have felt unwanted after making an effort to see me.

"Anyway," I went on, "he's playing a few gigs somewhere in

Ireland, I think, so he'll be at the Amsterdam show. He asked if I could arrange another VIP pass for him. Kinda cool that the two of us will both be playing in Europe at the same time, huh?"

"Do you think it's interesting that he's picked now to 'really want to talk to you'?"

"Nope. He does this every few years. It usually coincides with him breaking up with a guy. Bodhi doesn't do solo very well, in music or in his personal life. He probably just needs a shoulder to cry on."

"Hmm."

I'd gotten to know Bear well enough in the past year to recognize when he was holding himself back from stating his opinions.

I'd also gotten to know him well enough to know exactly what those opinions were.

First, Bear thought Bodhi was a hanger-on, like certain members of my family. He thought our friendship was mostly one-sided. He'd almost definitely put Bodhi on a short list of possible stampers and was having him investigated by Violet's team. I knew Bear was wrong about this part, at least—Bodhi might be a little self-absorbed, but he wasn't dangerous—but I knew better than to waste my breath explaining. Especially not when Bear's protectiveness felt so damn nice.

More importantly, though, it was Bear's opinion that I should cancel the remaining tour dates.

"I know you're over there perseverating on my insistence to still do these shows," I began.

"Yale grads sure do like their big words," he said, not for the first time. I glanced away to keep from staring at the edge of his lip that was turned up from teasing me.

"Articulating your vitriol is superfluous," I said with a sniff. "You imply I'm loquacious, which is a definitive juxtaposition with your previous implication I'm cautious and perspicacious. And totes adorbs."

Bear's brown eyes lightened and crinkled at the corners when he laughed out loud. My heart leapt into my throat at the sight. "I don't remember saying totes adorbs, and we both know it doesn't sound like something I'd say at all."

I flicked my hair over my shoulder. "But I am, though. Right?"

He stopped and turned to face me. All traces of his smile were gone. "*People* magazine named you the Sexiest Man Alive," he said, reaching out to untangle the hoodie cords at the front of my throat. "It's too bad they don't have a Totes-iest Adorbs-iest contest." The words sounded comical in his deep and steady voice. His eyes flicked up to meet mine. "You'd nail it every time."

My breath came in short, insufficient bursts like air dragged through a broken straw. "So... not sexy, then?"

What in the world had gotten into me? My question was inappropriate and provoking. Almost... flirty. *What the hell was I thinking?*

"No..." he said, and my stomach dropped.

But then he continued softly. "*People* got it right." He turned back to the trail to continue walking. "They just failed to add you're the sweetest, too."

I stared after him. My stomach was a tumble of rabid snakes, all lifting their heads up to ask what the fuck had just happened.

Had Ryan Galloway—my stoic, professional, grumpy Bear—just called me sexy and sweet?

"You done stretching your legs?" he called back over his shoulder.

"N-no," I admitted.

"Then quit standing around, and let's go."

We spent the rest of the walk in silence as I replayed the exchange in my mind. Was it possible Bear was just trying to be nice because he knew I'd been thrown by the threatening email?

Or was he simply stating a fact that didn't much matter to him—like "Yeah, Zane's a nice guy, and I guess I can see why people call him sexy, even though he definitely doesn't do it for me"—kind of like the way I found Gal Gadot objectively sexy with her deep voice, even though I didn't want to sleep with her?

Surely this was like that. Just because Bear could see why I'd been voted Sexiest Man Alive didn't mean *he* found me sexy *himself*.

He wouldn't.

Of course he wouldn't.

Not if he was straight like I assumed he was—like *everyone* except possibly Landry assumed he was.

But... what if he wasn't?

That night, I fell asleep fantasizing about what it would be like if he wasn't straight. I imagined the two of us on a secluded beach with Bear in nothing but a tiny scrap of a swimsuit and the sun lovingly lighting up all of the hard planes of his body. I imagined rubbing sunscreen into his warm skin, fingers skating over firm, muscled bumps and the dark fur of his happy trail...

But somehow, the scene turned strange and dark. An old, rusted fishing vessel bobbed offshore, and the screech of metal on metal split the air every time the captain lowered the booms with the nets into the water.

"They'll catch something alright," an old woman said from down the beach. A cigarillo bobbed between her lips as she spoke. "Mark my words. They'll catch him. String him up like a trophy in town."

Did they mean a trophy fish? I tried to ask, but the words wouldn't come. Suddenly, I was in a crowded train station, and I couldn't remember where I was going or which train I needed. I frantically searched the large board overhead in hopes something would jog my memory. People jostled me as they sped past on their way to various platforms. I looked around to find Bear because he would know which train we needed.

"Bear?" I called for him, but no noise came out of my mouth. "Bear!" I tried again and again, but nothing happened. Floods of people moved past me, knocking me first one way and then the other. Someone over a loudspeaker announced the final boarding call for a flight to White Plains. Another voice came on to announce a correction that the flight was actually to Scottsdale. I glanced around to see if anyone else was wondering why they were announcing flights instead of trains, but no one seemed to notice or care.

Was I at an airport? Wasn't I supposed to be at a train station?

Surely my train was here, and I was going to miss it. I looked around for Bear again and spotted Landry across the station. He waved and pointed to the board over my head.

You're going to be late, he mouthed. *Hurry.*

"I'm lost!" I shouted, no longer worried about what people would think of me making a scene. "I don't know where I'm supposed to go!"

This time, the sound came out, but all I heard was my voice shouting, "Bear!" over and over again until I could barely breathe.

"Shhh. I'm here, baby. Shhh. I've got you."

Strong arms grabbed me and pulled me close. Bear's familiar scent surrounded me. I felt safe. I was no longer alone. Bear would figure out where I needed to go. Bear would take charge and make sure everything was okay. I let myself relax into his embrace.

A vague embarrassment tried to slither into my subconscious, but I was too relieved to feel it.

"Bear," I breathed. "I don't know which train. Which platform. Which city."

His fingers brushed through my hair. "You don't need to take the train right now. Just sleep."

I slowed my breathing down. "Are you sure? Everyone is catching a train... or-or a plane. We're going to be late. For the show?" It was probably a show. We were always on our way to another show.

"No show right now. Just rest time. Maybe you can work on that new song you've been humming."

Faint traces of chords replayed in my memory, a tune I'd been working on but hadn't had the words to yet. "I'd like that. Need to write it down."

"Not right now. Right now... will you sing 'The Solo Hour' for me?"

Bear loved that one. I'd caught sight of him once backstage, singing along with his eyes closed. I would have teased him about it, but then he might have realized he'd had his eyes closed, and he would have felt like he'd fallen down on the job.

Since there wasn't much I wouldn't do for him if he asked me, I began singing softly.

> After the lights and the cheers
> Even after all these years
> No one walks with me
> Across the deep wide sea
> Of empty seats.
> I sing to you,
> You,
> You,
> And you...
> But when it ends,
> I walk home to me.
> After the final bow,
> After the lights go out
> I turn around
> And glide into the solo hour...

I hummed the guitar riff, my fingers ghosting over invisible strings.

> I'm coming home,
> Home to me.
> Alone with me.
> A place to be,
> A place to breathe.
> Alone with me.
> In the solo hour.

The slow tempo and soft tone did its magic and soothed me deeper into sleep. I felt the ghost of Bear's arms around me. Smelled traces of him on my pillow. Heard the soft caress of his voice calling me *baby*.

The dream ended, but the sense of him didn't. It carried through until I awoke, remembering.

Thankfully, I was alone. Bear had been part of my dream. If I'd woken up in Bear's arms again, like I had in Atlanta, I would have been mortified. Twice in the span of a week? He would have called a therapist and canceled the next leg of the tour for sure.

I let out a breath and remembered one of the moments from the dream. The fleeting thought that I could spend time working on new music. It was true that I'd had a song on my mind. The tune was almost there, but the words were still elusive.

After showering and dressing in comfortable clothes, I had to admit to being a little relieved we weren't in New York preparing for a bunch of interviews. Instead, it was another beautiful clear day at the edge of the world.

I breezed out of my bedroom and made my way through the open main room to the kitchen, where Bear was already standing, his hip propped against the counter while he sipped coffee from a mug.

"Morning!"

He glanced at me over the rim of the thick ceramic. "*Mpfh.*"

"Sleep okay?"

He peered at me while I walked past him to take in the view through the wide windows. The sun glinted on the water across the fjord.

I didn't wait for an answer before exclaiming. "This place is amazing! Look at the views. Was it like this when you were here before?"

When he didn't answer, I glanced back over my shoulder to see him shaking his head. "It was full summer. Very green and warm. Still gorgeous, though."

Bear's voice was rough with sleep. I noticed he was barefoot. The denim of his jeans brushed across the arched tops of his long feet on the hardwood floors. There was something vulnerable about seeing him barefoot and drinking coffee while the morning sun lay shimmering stripes across the kitchen around him.

I turned back to the view outside to keep from staring at him. Or jumping him. "I'd ask if you miss Ventdestine, but I'm sure you do, even if just for the winter weather. Hard to biathlon in Southern California."

"I miss the skiing, sure, but I don't wish I was still there."

I glanced over my shoulder again. "You like living in LA?"

He shook his head and took his time swallowing another sip of coffee before explaining. "I like my principal."

I blinked.

He grinned. "You're a hundred percent less high-maintenance than Asger Salling and the rest of the royal family."

"Oh." I resisted rolling my eyes as I moved over to the coffeepot. For a minute, I'd thought he'd meant something more. That he'd, like, *liked* me-liked me. Which was ridiculous.

"They probably set a low bar," I said, imagining that protecting one musician paled in comparison to the challenge of protecting a king.

"They do."

"And I'm probably way less likely to be shot at," I said, remembering how he'd come to work for them in the first place and how King Asger had been killed after Bear had left.

Bear's eyes darkened. "You'd better be."

He was obviously worried about the threatening email and the target stamp, so I tried to reassure him. "Bear... if they wanted to hurt me, they could have done it already. If they got close enough to stamp me, they were close enough to hurt me. And they chose not to."

He didn't say anything, so I scrambled to fill the silence as I poured coffee into a mug. "They're just trying to scare me. Maybe they're trying to make me beef up security. Do you think?"

"I don't know what to think."

I busied myself adding cream and sugar when a thought came to me. "Maybe it's a security company who wants my business. What better way than to show they can infiltrate my current security detail?"

Bear made another grumbling noise under his breath. I knew he thought the mysterious Stamper was right, that my own bodyguard hadn't been able to protect me, but I also knew I wouldn't feel nearly as safe with anyone else in charge of my security.

"You should tell Violet my theory," I said before taking my first sip of coffee.

"I will. It's not a bad theory." I could tell he was serious, but I also knew that he would treat the current threat like a harbinger of the apocalypse until he got to the bottom of it.

My pride at contributing in some small way to the investigation carried me through the creation of the world's best avocado toast breakfast and into the sun-filled glass-enclosed room at the end of the house facing the fjord. There was an overstuffed sofa perfect for curling up on to noodle over my music ideas while Bear prepared for a day full of making sure my European tour was planned with royal precision and a military defense to match.

I expected the two weeks we would spend here would be mostly this: me writing new music in the peaceful and inspiring sunroom and Bear grumbling and pulling his hair out in front of his laptop on the kitchen counter.

But that afternoon, everything changed.

Bear stuck his head into the sunroom. "Lou said you wanted to take another walk?"

I looked up from the scribbled notes I was making on the pad next to me. "Oh, I didn't mean for her to bother you. I just texted to ask if she could maybe watch me from the cameras if I stay on the path so I could stretch my legs and get some fresh air."

"I could use a break, and it would be better to go now before the sun goes down. The cameras only cover the fence line."

I put my guitar down and stood up, stretching my arms up and rolling my shoulders. "You don't need to babysit me. I can always walk on the treadmill downstairs."

"Yeah, Zane, it's a real hardship. Let's go."

I couldn't tell if he was being gruff because he was put out about the walk or stressed from his workday. I knew that my insistence on not canceling the tour dates was adding worry to his life, but I was caught between a rock and a hard place. Canceling the dates to spare Bear and the team meant I'd disappoint thousands of fans and hundreds of event workers. It would become a global news story, and who knew what would happen to my personal security then? Disappointed fans were often dangerous enough, especially if they thought I was being a diva.

As long as my manager, Micki, wasn't recommending it and the security team wasn't expressly forbidding it, we would move forward. Too many people were relying on these shows for us to cancel them.

I followed Bear to the entryway and toed my running shoes on. He always had his black boots on, as if he needed to be ready to bolt at a moment's notice.

"You sure you don't mind?" I asked, feeling guilty.

"Zane. It's my job."

While his words were true, they still stung a little. After my dream last night in which he'd been kind and comforting, his distance and gruffness in real life felt cold in comparison.

We made our way out to the same trail behind the house we'd explored yesterday. I kept quiet in case he wanted time to himself. He seemed annoyed with me, and I could hardly blame him.

Our entire schedule had been thrown off by this situation, and now we were in the middle of nowhere for a couple of weeks while he doubled his workload, trying to both keep me safe and plan a higher-intensity protection scheme for the remainder of the tour.

I felt guilty for all of the additional work he and the rest of Violet's team were having to do because of me, like maybe I'd done something to provoke this person—the Stamper—into whatever they were trying to do.

The cold air felt refreshing and invigorating. I drew in a long pull as I felt my muscles warm up and loosen. The scenery was beautiful, and I was grateful to be here instead of the crowded and chaotic city.

Bear pulled ahead of me as the trail narrowed, and my eyes

immediately flicked down to his ass. He had an amazing ass. No matter how busy our travel schedule was, he always found time to work out in the gym. I'd even seen him doing squats and stair sprints in hotels when we were on the road. Was it any wonder he had such a perfect muscular butt?

I pulled out my phone for a little distraction, to give myself something else to look at. The phone had been in Focus mode all day as I'd been working, so as soon as I turned off the Focus, messages came streaming in. I clicked into a text from Aunt Rinny right away in case something had happened.

It had.

RINNY

Might need to alert your PR team about John-Keith. That boy's cornbread ain't done in the middle. I'm sorry, sweetheart. I tried warning him.

I felt a sense of dread as I clicked through the other notifications. When I got to JK's social media post, I sucked in a breath.

Is it even possible to be a virgin in your thirties? #CousinConfessions Not saying which one, so don't ask.

As if the world didn't know whose cousin he was. The fucker's profile pic was one of him and me together, and he took every opportunity to post about me. And what other thirties-aged cousin could it be? Pearl was twenty-eight, Horace was forty-one, and while Jayden and Jordyn were thirty-two, both of them were married with kids.

I must have made a noise when I saw the horrendous flood of comments because Bear stopped and demanded to know what was going on. "What is it?"

"Nothing. It's fine," I said, not taking my eyes off the shitshow on my screen. My PR team had to already know, but I needed to get back to the house anyway and prepare for a flood of messages and calls.

"'Course it is," he ground out. "Give me the phone. Is it another threatening email?"

My fingers began to feel numb. I wasn't sure if it was from the bite in the air or a combination of nerves and embarrassment from being exposed to the world. I'd been through tons of stuff like this before, so you'd think it would get easier.

It never did.

Bear snatched it out of my hand and barked out a curse as soon as he saw what had happened. "That *motherfucker*."

Heat flooded my face. Bear probably thought I was an idiot for confessing my virginal secret to someone completely untrustworthy. Hell, *I* thought I was an idiot for doing it. But at the same time, I hated not being able to connect with people authentically, especially people I was supposed to be able to trust.

"At least he didn't mention my name," I said lamely.

"Zane, everyone knows who he's talking about. I knew this would happen. That motherfucker. He cannot be allowed to do this."

"He shouldn't have done it, I know. But... I feel sorry for him."

Bear turned to me with an almost comical expression of incredulity on his face. "Sorry for him? *Him?*"

I pulled in another breath of cold air. "He's a little bit jealous... or maybe a *lot* bit. Doing stuff like this makes him feel like he's not the loser in the family... by making *me* seem like a loser instead."

Bear's face was a dark storm, his eyes like lightning bolts aimed right at me. "You are not a loser. You are the opposite of a loser, Zane."

I felt the intensity in my chest and tried to deflect it with a joke. "So, that makes me a winner?"

Bear refused to be distracted. "That man does not get to use you as currency," he said, pointing his arm back down the hill as if Barlo, Georgia, was in that direction. For all I knew, it was. "He doesn't get to sell his connection with you to the highest bidder."

I knew what he meant. JK had been trying to build up a social media presence in order to make bank from it. The guy was desperate for money, which meant Violet's security team kept an eye on him, knowing he'd be susceptible to bribes for personal information about me. Fortunately, he hadn't had much personal information about me that I hadn't already shared freely with the world...

Until now.

"I'll offer him money to sign an NDA," I suggested.

"I'll offer him something else," he snapped, punching his fist into his palm with a smack. "And you're not rewarding him for this behavior. No fucking way."

"Ryan," I said firmly. "No. It has to be hard for him. He grew up just like me, and yet I lucked into this big—"

"Lucked? *Lucked*? No. And don't you dare *Ryan* me." Those brown eyes I could usually curl up in were practically on fire now with anger on my behalf. "Zane, tell me you don't actually believe that. You work your ass off. Despite your shitty upbringing, you worked hard enough to get a full ride to a great school. You took advantage of it by working harder still and learning as much as you could so you could pursue your music dream. John-Keith couldn't even keep the job your uncle got him as an HVAC tech. He didn't want to wake up on time and do the work."

I was kind of surprised at the level of detail Bear had picked up from bits and pieces of things said in his presence over the past year. He was right, though. JK had been given many opportunities, including several I'd offered him directly. None of them had interested him.

"He has a job. He's a lawn care tech," I said.

Bear closed his eyes and took in a breath before responding. "Yes. Correct. And he's been doing that work for about five minutes, earning much less than he could if he followed in Bart's footsteps. We all know where his lucrative weed-killer career is going."

He was right. But I still tried to give JK the benefit of the doubt because if I agreed with Bear and acknowledged even to myself that my cousin was using me... where did that leave me? With one less person I could count on. With one less person who loved me and who

I could consider a true friend. Thousands of screaming fans every night, but in the end... it was just me in the Solo Hour.

I started to walk again, hoping to at least wear out my muscles before having to go inside and face the PR disaster. Bear kept up with me, silently simmering with rage.

"It's fine," I said after I realized he wasn't calming down.

He shot me a look. I'd said the dreaded word.

"But it is," I insisted. "I warned John-Keith there'd be conse-quences if this got out. And now... now I'll cut contact."

My stomach soured at the idea. JK and I had spent a lot of good times together over the years. Yes, he'd always been a bit shallow and competitive with me, but there'd also been moments of kindness. Like when he'd given me some of his clothes after I came to live with Gran. Or when he snuck me a copy of Mr. Casey's fourth-period biology quiz so I wouldn't fail it when I got it in sixth period. It wasn't his fault I'd already memorized the entire list of terms the night before.

"He's not a bad guy," I said softly as I remembered all the times he'd tried looking out for me.

"He's not a good one, Zane," he said, still obviously angry as hell. "And you deserve good people in your life. Who the hell exposes someone like that publicly? Who does that to *anyone*, let alone to his own cousin, the person who's tried to help him over and over again? You're such a nice person, and JK just can't handle it."

I let out a nervous laugh, feeling suddenly awkward receiving his compliment. "It's not like that—"

"It is. He has the privilege of having access to someone as kind and talented and smart and generous as you. He has the privilege of having grown up with you and having memories with you. He has the privilege of having Zane Hendley in his goddamn life... and all he can see is Zee fucking Barlo. When was the last time he asked how you were and meant it? When was the last time he tried to help *you*? When was the last time he tried to spend time with you without trying to spin it into an Instagram post? Having you—

you, *Zane*—in his life is a fucking blessing, and he just shits all over it."

His impassioned rant was unexpected and... really, really nice. But it made me feel flustered.

"You're taking this too seriously," I explained. "I'm not that big a deal."

"You are," he said without turning to look at me.

"It's fine," I assured him. "I promise."

"Stop saying shit's fine when it's not! The moments he gets to spend with you, like that night around the bonfire, are special. His relationship isn't something he should get to capitalize on. You're not a fucking commodity!"

"JK doesn't know better. And I've been given so much, I feel bad for him—"

"You've been given nothing you didn't work for. And your cousin exposed the details of your sex life to the entire world." The words were low and dangerous.

I swallowed. He was right, but I didn't want to face it. "I'm okay, though. I am. I promise it's—"

He turned to look at me, the storm crashing in his expression. "Say it again. I dare you. Watch what happens."

"Fine," I whispered, not sounding like I meant it at all.

Bear grabbed my shoulders and pressed forward into my personal space. I backed up instinctively until I felt the rough bark of a tree at my back.

"*Fine* is not acceptable for you. Not anymore. Not ever. You can be happy. You can be sad. You can be pissed off or confused, angry or betrayed." His cheeks flushed as he spoke, and his eyes implored me as they flicked between my own. "Zane, your music connects with people because you're so fucking *honest*. Where is that honesty when you're talking with the people in your real life?"

The shock of his emotional outburst kept me pinned, but with his body nearly pressed up against mine, I would never complain about it. My eyes strayed to his lips and lingered as I tried to process his question.

"Well... I..." The only thought in my head was about how his lips would taste and why my dream had been of Bear in a busy train station instead of Bear in my bed. Was that the kind of honesty he was looking for? I didn't think so.

"Tell me," Bear pleaded. "Tell me exactly what you're feeling right now."

My heart pounded as his much larger body leaned over me. I couldn't tell him the truth—that I wanted to know what it felt like to be touched intimately and possibly devoured violently by my personal protection specialist.

"I'm feeling like I've never seen this part of you before," I admitted in a quiet voice. Part of me was afraid if I spoke too loudly, I'd scare him off. He'd realize how close he was and back away. That was the last thing I wanted.

He narrowed his eyes at me. "You deserve better than your asshole cousin. At least I can be honest about it. I'm angry. I'm fucking *enraged*. And I'm so damned confused as to how someone who's supposed to love and care for you can treat that like... like... like it's nothing."

"You're more upset about this than I am. I promise I'm—"

Bear lurched forward and crushed his mouth against mine, stopping the dreaded word before it could pass my lips.

I must have made an embarrassing sound, had a humiliatingly shocked look on my face, but I didn't care.

Because it seemed to me I'd angered my bodyguard into kissing the hell out of me.

And if I said I was fine with that... this time, I'd really mean it.

TEN

RYAN

Being around Zane without kissing him had been hard enough, but watching him try to be brave when facing the loss of yet another person he should have been able to count on—someone who was stupid enough to throw away their relationship with the world's kindest man—was too much.

Zane needed to know he was loved. He needed to know there were people in this world who wanted him.

Desperately.

And if I heard him lie to me and say he was fine one more time...

As soon as my lips touched his, I knew I'd made a terrible mistake. Not only was I putting my job in jeopardy—which I only cared about because I could lose access to Zane—but I'd also opened up a Pandora's box by learning just how soft and pliable his lips were. Just how incredible he tasted. How sweet the sounds he made were.

How much I needed more.

Instead of pulling away like my brain was begging me to do, I stepped even closer. My hands drifted up to cup his jaw, to hold him in place while I discovered what it was like to worship him with kisses.

Zane's fingers twisted in my shirtfront and pulled me even closer while he straightened up to kiss me more deeply.

His skin was cold from the nip in the air. The soft prickle of his short whiskers against my palms contrasted with the silky touch of several loose strands of hair caught between my fingers. The hushed sound of the trees around us made me feel like I was in a surreal time-out of time.

A time in which it was possible to kiss this man without dire consequences.

Zane tilted his head and tangled his tongue with mine. He moved a hand up to sneak his fingers into the front of my collar like he was trying to get a tighter grip. The touch of his cold fingertips on my hot skin made me suck in a breath. I moved my arms around him to keep him from pulling away.

The feel of Zane Hendley in my arms was indescribable. My head swam with a heady mixture of disbelief, pleasure, relief... and maybe a little fear. Fear of being fired. Fear of offending him. Fear of being rejected by the one person who had the ability to crush me.

Little details of that moment came back to me later. The short, staccato sound of his shallow breaths. The feel of his tongue twisting around mine. The soft and shy caress of his fingertip in the dip of my throat. The sharp sweetness of Scots pine mingling with Zane's familiar scent. The fleeting brush of his erection against my thigh.

"Ryan, you need help? You two haven't moved in a while. Everything okay?"

It took a beat before I processed Lou's voice in my ear. I jumped back as reality came crashing in, and I scrambled to press the button on my radio's earpiece. "Uh, yeah. All good."

Holy fuck. Holy *fuck*, what had I just done?

I could barely meet Zane's shocked eyes. "I'm sorry." It was a lame apology because I didn't mean a single bit of it. Or maybe I did because I *was* sorry I'd put pressure on him, that I'd backed him against a tree and basically forced my attentions on him.

When he didn't respond, I forced myself to meet his eyes. Angry eyes. Eyes filled with an annoyance Zane rarely showed.

"Are you?" he challenged.

I firmed my jaw and decided to do the right thing.

To protect him.

"Yes. I'm very sorry I crossed a line. It won't happen again."

Should I have offered him my resignation on the spot? Yes. Absolutely. Was I man enough to do it? Absolutely not.

Zane's gaze searched mine. Whatever he did or didn't find there seemed to give him some relief I'd meant what I'd said. He dropped his shoulders and blew out a breath. "I believe you. We should probably head back to the house."

I nodded and looked away so I wouldn't have to see his disappointment in me. Instead of watching his slender body as he stepped back onto the trail, I looked around us to make sure the area was clear of any looming threats. Considering this was an isolated, fenced property, monitored by boundary cameras and round-the-clock guards, it wasn't completely necessary. But at least it gave me something to look at while I berated myself soundly.

We moved down the trail in silence, only the soft sounds of our footfalls breaking the awkward tension in the air. As soon as we got back to the house, Zane disappeared into his bedroom, and I busied myself with work on my laptop.

Eventually, hunger drove the man out of his bedroom. Lou had delivered pizza from a local restaurant and ended up staying to eat with us. There was plenty to talk about since we now had the JK debacle to deal with.

"According to Micki, the PR team has your cousin well in hand. The social media post has been removed. The team helped him make an additional post about how a friend dared him to post something ridiculous to see how many likes he could get and that thanks to 'all y'all,' he was one case of beer richer," Lou explained.

Zane nodded half-heartedly. I could tell from his hunched-over posture and the way he was picking at one of his favorite foods he wasn't as reassured as Lou had hoped.

"He needs to be banned from Zane's future visits home," I grumbled.

I felt the heat of Zane's anger on me as he spoke. "Easy for you to say when you have parents, a sister, two brothers, and four niblings back in Montana you can visit anytime. And let's not even get started on all the extended Galloway and Hager families."

I glanced at him in surprise. For the sake of professionalism, I tried not to share too much of my personal life. Zane knew my background, of course, but I'd had no idea he'd kept track of the details so well.

"Sorry," I murmured.

He let out a huff. "Yeah. You're good at sorries."

I stared at him in time to see his cheeks flame. He buried his chin in his hoodie and kept his eyes on his plate. Lou shot me a questioning look, but I shook my head in dismissal. There was no way I could explain why our principal was angry at me without opening up a whole can of worms.

Lou cleared her throat and tried to dispel the tension she couldn't have understood. "Niblings?" she asked.

"Nieces and nephews," Zane muttered to his plate.

The rest of the evening was just as excruciating. As soon as politely possible, Zane disappeared into his room again. Lou asked me what was going on, but I fudged and said he was upset by the JK thing... which wasn't exactly a lie. Zane *was* upset about that and should be.

But his cousin wasn't the only one who'd taken advantage of him that day.

As soon as Lou disappeared back to the gatehouse, I closed my computer and locked up the main house. I lingered in the main gathering room of the house in hopes Zane would reappear, but he never did.

The following day, after grabbing coffee and a premade smoothie, he disappeared back into the sunroom to work on his music. I might have followed him if I didn't already have at least three urgent messages from Violet requiring my attention.

I hopped on a Zoom call with the European logistics team that lasted most of the morning. I passed on the information Zane had given me about Bodhi—that he *had* been in the crowd at Shaky Knees, that he knew Zane's private email address, and that he was conveniently playing gigs in Dublin and planned to meet up with Zane in Amsterdam. Violet agreed that he was our strongest suspect to date and tasked Boomer with finding and shadowing Bodhi. He agreed enthusiastically. "Trust me, boss. If that guy is the one messing with Zee he's gonna be sorry."

At least that one aspect of my day was going right.

At noon, Lou came into the house to spell me so I could take a long run on the roads. I needed some air. Some space. Some time to fucking think. My whole life, I'd leaned toward physicality. Whenever I was angry or frustrated or confused, I'd go outside and work it out by moving or pushing my body until all I could do was feel and not think.

It was how I'd become good at sports, how I'd ended up with the kind of discipline, strength, and focus to become an Olympic athlete.

Even now, when most of my time at work was spent standing or, god forbid, sitting, I made sure I had time to move and sweat. My job demanded peak physical performance. I had to be able to run and lift, hold off attackers or grab my principal and get them out of a bad situation. Lou, of all people, knew I needed time to keep up with my workouts, and that included at least one long run per week.

So I ran.

And ran. And ran.

I made my way down to the water's edge and found the gravel footpath that wound its way along the shoreline. Only a few people were on it, and I pounded my way past them, arms swinging and muscles working. Eminem pumped through my earbuds. My workouts were the rare times each week I allowed myself to sacrifice situational awareness for the sake of indulging in fast-paced music. The lyrics from "Lose Yourself" mocked me. If my opportunity to shoot my shot only came once, then I was fucked.

Because I'd blown it.

I'd kissed him out of the blue. With no buildup or romance first. No way of determining whether he would accept my interest or not.

And clearly, he did not.

Zane's reaction was exactly what I should have expected.

He'd seemed to be into it while it was happening, sure, but that might have been him getting caught up in the moment more than actual desire. In my worst imaginings, he'd simply been going along with it while telling himself it was "fine" that his bodyguard was basically assaulting him.

He hadn't argued with me when I'd stopped the kiss, and that said a lot.

He hadn't asked for more, or apologized himself, or even waved away my apology and told me it was no big deal that I'd crossed all kinds of professional boundaries.

Clearly, for him, it *was* a big deal.

He'd been angry. And Zane Hendley was rarely angry at anyone. Ever.

Self-recrimination dogged me as my body pushed harder. Blood pumped through my muscles, and sweat poured from my skin. The worst part was, despite how guilty I felt, I wanted nothing more than to kiss Zane again. Now that I'd had a taste of him, now that I'd felt what it was like to cradle the back of his head in my palm while pressing my lips to his, I couldn't even fathom the idea of never having it again.

But that way lay madness. I had to find a way to set aside my desire for him so I could do my job.

By the time I got to the spot on the gravel path where I needed to turn around, my head was clearer. What I needed was a plan. A plan to keep from fucking things up even more. A plan to keep from kissing Zane again.

But also a plan to get things back on track between us because… I missed him, damn it. I missed seeing his sweet smile. I missed his gorgeous voice as he hummed distractedly to himself while he waited for the toaster to pop. And I really, *really* missed the way it felt when he'd curl up beside me on the sofa at night and let himself relax.

I might never be able to have Zane's lips against mine again, and I would surely never have him in my bed, and that sucked. But the idea that he might be so upset he'd no longer want me in his life, that I might have lost his trust and, with it, the privilege of keeping him safe, that I was no better than his cousin—yet another person he should have been able to count on but *couldn't*—was fucking intolerable.

It took the duration of the cool-off walk back to the house before I came up with an idea that could work. It would take a miracle to create the kind of conditions that would make kissing Zane unattractive, but I just might have come up with one.

ELEVEN

ZANE

It's hard to stay mad at a bear. Underneath that ursine stub-bornness, bears are surprisingly charming creatures, constantly playing and testing themselves. This play isn't just for fun; it's how they learn to survive in the wild. But it also makes it nearly impossible to hold a grudge against them for long.
—Bear Facts for Insomniacs, Episode 27

I was still in shock. It had been twenty-four hours, and I couldn't stop replaying the kiss.

Ryan Galloway had kissed me.

He'd more than kissed me—he'd *devoured* me.

And I'd loved every minute of it.

My heart thundered as I remembered the details. The way Bear's large body had blocked the wind. The feel of his warm hand on the back of my head. The fact that he didn't pull away when I kissed him back but instead stepped closer, had put his arm around me and pulled me tighter. The thick length of the hard bulge in his pants nudging my lower belly before pulling away.

The dizzying moment when I realized none of it was in my imagination.

Guitar in hand, I exhaled and stared out at the sun setting across the water. The sunroom was warm and silent. Only the echoes of the G major 7 chord filled the space around me as I tried to piece together the fragments of melody that had been tumbling around my brain since Barlo. But though the house was mostly silent, my mind was in turmoil.

I'm sorry, Bear had said.

Are you? I'd challenged, hoping against hope he'd say he hadn't been—that, in fact, he'd wanted to do it again.

He hadn't taken it back, though. Instead, he'd doubled down and reiterated just how sorry he was.

Apparently, kissing me was a regrettable activity.

Well, he could take that apology and shove it up his ass. Bear didn't get to lecture me about people like my cousin using me for their own gains and then try to pretend the sexiest fucking kiss in recorded history hadn't happened, as if my feelings didn't matter one bit.

He wanted my honest emotions? He wanted me to be real with him and not *fine?*

Then he needed to know I was angry. That I was mad as a fucking wasp. That I was a whole nest of wasps, in fact, and they buzzed with restless intensity under my skin.

What was I supposed to do with this feeling? Of wanting him, getting a single taste of him, and then learning there were no more tastes coming?

And how was I supposed to act normal and pretend it hadn't happened?

I tried to be reasonable and calm myself down. Was Bear even gay? I still didn't know for sure. Had the kiss been some kind of failed experiment for him? Or was he so wonderfully and annoyingly dedicated to his job that he thought kissing me might somehow compromise my safety?

If so, he was dead wrong. I couldn't be in the same room with my bodyguard anymore without feeling nervous and hot. Without feeling like my face and ears were going to melt off from the humiliation of wanting someone who didn't want me back.

Without wondering if kissing me had been like getting a free sample of something that looked and smelled amazing at the grocery store and realizing it tasted like dog shit.

That was me. I was the dog shit.

And yes, my brain could argue against that conclusion perfectly well. Millions of fans around the world found me way more attractive than dog shit. I knew that, objectively. But there was nothing objective about this feeling of rejection from the man I was most attracted to. From the man I most wanted to like me back.

I was like a pathetic emo teenager, sitting alone in the darkening room, strumming my feelings out on a guitar.

I needed a distraction.

Better yet, I needed things to go back to normal with my close protection officer.

Which was why, when Bear poked his head into the sunroom after the sun finished slipping behind the mountains across the water, his eyes serious and wary and tentatively hopeful, and said, "Hey, I, ah... had an idea for dinner." I set my guitar on the stand and stood.

"Yeah, okay. I'm easy." Hopefully, he didn't notice me wince at the embarrassing word choice.

"Hope you like horseradish." Bear turned and moved toward the kitchen. My eyes flicked down to his ass out of habit.

He had clearly just showered because his hair was wet, and he was wearing different clothes than he'd had on earlier. Now, he was dressed in soft sweatpants—the kind that were loose at the hem and so thin from washing that the fabric draped over... everything... in a way that highlighted his assets rather than concealing them.

Goddamn.

I blinked and followed the lines of his body up to his broad shoulders, which pulled the smooth cotton of his T-shirt taut across his back. The shirt was new with a still-bright list of tour cities on it.

Halifax
Montreal
Toronto
Milwaukee
Detroit
Chicago
Minneapolis...

I remembered each city we'd visited late last year. Memories of shows came flooding through my mind, moments when Bear had pressed his large hand against my lower back to usher me through tunnels and down hallways. It had been during that portion of the tour that we'd truly broken the ice between us. Once someone had seen the ugly, backstage side of you, it was hard to keep them at arm's length.

It had started with a few small moments.

In Halifax, he'd accidentally walked in on me while my voice coach was making me sing a silly song that repeated the line "Rubber Baby Buggy Bumpers" over and over at ascending scale and speed. In addition to sounding ridiculous, I was also shirtless with a giant orange warming muff around my throat.

Somehow, he'd managed to say, "Micki is limiting the VIP meet and greet to fifteen minutes," with a neutral expression.

In Toronto, I'd tripped in front of hundreds of people. Thankfully, Bear—or had I still called him Ryan then? He'd been "Bear" to me so long I couldn't remember anymore—had been holding my elbow, so he kept me from face-planting. Then he'd immediately said in a voice loud enough to carry, "Sorry, Mr. Barlo. Didn't mean to bump you."

In Detroit, I'd been so tired I'd forgotten the name of my own hometown. "Where are you from in Georgia?" the hairstylist had asked, making friendly conversation. I'd stared at her in the mirror. "I have family in Valdosta. Anywhere near there?" she'd prodded.

"Barlo," Bear had answered. I'd turned to face him with a look of confusion. Why was he calling me by my last name? "Georgia," he added. "Barlo, Georgia. It's northwest of Valdosta."

"Oh, right," I'd said stupidly. "Yes. Barlo. Like my name."

The stylist had tilted her head. "Is the town named after your people? They must have been there for generations."

I couldn't for the life of me process what she was asking. "Other way around," Bear had explained. "He picked his stage name to honor his hometown. Hey, ah... Sylvie. Would you mind giving us a minute? I need to go over some security details and need privacy."

"Sure thing, hon."

She'd stepped out, and Bear had come over, crouched down in front of me, and put his hands on the arms of my chair. "Hey. You okay?"

"Yeah. I'm fine."

He frowned and reached up to press the back of his fingers against my forehead. "You don't seem fine. You seem out of it."

I brushed his hand away and shook my head, feeling it swim a little. "Totally fine. Promise. I'll be glad to get to Chicago and catch up on sleep before the next show."

And then, after one of the Chicago shows, I'd finally succumbed to the full-blown version of whatever virus I'd been trying to fight off, and Bear had found me vomiting in the hotel bathroom at four in the morning. He'd rubbed my back and washed my face with a cold washcloth for two hours while I humiliated myself in front of him.

"Fine, huh? You still fine?" he'd teased.

"It's not that bad," I'd insisted weakly.

"No, 'course not. Being un-fine would be so off-brand for you."

"You don't have to stay. Maybe we can call someone like a visiting nurse or something. You don't have to—"

"Shut it, Zane," he'd said firmly. "No one takes care of you but me."

At the time, I'd known he was protecting me, looking out for my reputation and making sure no one else saw me in such a moment of vulnerability. Protecting my reputation was part of his job, after all. But after that, I'd had fantasies about him looking out for me because he wanted to.

Because he cared for me.

And I knew he did care... just not in the way I wanted him to. Not in the way I fantasized about.

"Zane?" he prompted now.

I blinked away my memories and tried to replay the last thing he'd asked me. "Uh... horseradish? Yeah. I like it fine. Every year on Rinny's birthday, Gran would take us all out for shrimp cocktail at Ruby's. I'd ask for extra horseradish to mix in my cocktail sauce and ate it till my nose ran."

"Go get comfortable, then, and I'll set everything out."

I was already dressed fairly comfortably, but I was wearing jeans that would show if I got a Bear-boner... which was definitely going to happen since Lou didn't seem to be joining us and since that kiss was still seared directly into my brain.

I detoured to my room and rifled through my clothes until I found the most shapeless full-coverage outfit I owned. The giant fleece onesie would not only be good for a cold autumn evening in Norway, but it would also cover up as much skin as humanly possible and hopefully keep Bear from discovering how often his inadvertent touches gave me goose bumps.

When I got to the dining table between the kitchen and gathering room, I noticed a platter in the center with several dishes of dips I didn't recognize, surrounded by stacks of cut vegetables, meats, and breads.

"What is this?" I wondered.

Bear gestured for me to take a seat. "Did I ever tell you that horseradish is one of the primary condiments in Ventdestinian cuisine?"

I shook my head as I sat.

"Ventdestine is a hodgepodge country," he explained. "Lots of French influence, a little German, and plenty of British—which makes sense, considering English is the most commonly spoken language there. But there's also a huge Scandinavian influence, and horseradish is common there, just like it is here in Norway. I guess it grows well here."

I took a cautious sniff in the direction of the platter. "Okay. So... we're eating horseradish?"

"Yup. In Ventdestine, the royal family used to play a game called Hemmret Sovets... Secret Sauce, and I think it would be fun for us to play it, too... if you wanted?"

I could hear the words Bear wasn't saying—that he was as desperate to get our relationship back to normal as I was—and that went a long way to dissolving my anger.

"Secret Sauce," I repeated. It sounded sketchy but also intriguing. "Are you making this up?"

"Definitely not. The game started back when Asger's father was king. A tabloid teased a story about a secret scandal involving an unnamed member of the royal family, which they'd reveal in the coming week's issue. Asger's father lost his royal mind. He called the whole family together—his own siblings, his wife, even little Asger himself, who was only eight at the time—and ranted at all of them, demanding to know what the scandal was so that the palace could get ahead of it." Bear's eyes twinkled. "Can you imagine what happened?"

I blinked, distracted by how gorgeous Bear was when he smiled. "Uh... no?"

"One of Asger's sisters broke down and admitted she'd been engaged in a serious flirtation with a foreign prince who was already promised in marriage to someone else."

"Oh. Wow. That's kinda—" I began.

"And another of Asger's siblings confessed that he'd fallen in love with a local schoolteacher—a commoner."

"Wait, what?" I frowned. "There were two scandals?"

"Annnnd—" Bear grinned openly. "His other sister admitted she'd been writing some pretty well-received racy books under a pen name. And his cousin confessed that he'd been paying a kid to do his homework. And the queen admitted she was pregnant again—"

"No way!"

"Yup. And little Asger himself admitted he'd adopted a stray cat and was keeping it hidden in the barn."

Against my will, I laughed out loud. "So which was the real 'secret scandal'?"

"Who knows? Eventually, all of them might have come to light since the truth has an annoying habit of doing that. But Asger's father consulted the winds of fortune..." Bear rolled his eyes at this. "...and determined that the best way to deal with multiple potential scandals was to let them all blow free at once. The palace released five simultaneous statements, effectively overloading the Ventdestinian gossip networks. With so many salacious revelations to ponder, nobody got too excited about any one story... and soon, *all* the scandals were old news."

"Oh my god." I clapped a hand to my mouth. "Perfect."

"It was pretty smart, actually," Bear admitted. "But while that was an effective strategy for dealing with tabloids, privately, the family realized just how much they'd been keeping from one another, so they came up with a way to share their private truths while keeping them in the family. Hence... Secret Sauce. It's kind of like Truth or Dare. Or maybe more like... Truth or Horseradish."

I shook my head. "This might be the wildest thing you've ever told me about Ventdestine... and that's saying something, given the story about the weaver and the possessed carpet. How do we play?"

Bear quickly explained the game. Each bowl on the table held a different sauce Lou had ordered from a local place—some mild, some that might make your sinuses weep—all of which had their labels hidden under the bowl.

We'd take turns asking each other questions, and if we answered truthfully, we got to choose which sauce we'd eat, with the only caveat being that you couldn't choose the same sauce twice in a row.

If we avoided the question or lied, as judged by the other player, we had to eat a sauce of the other person's choosing *and* had to answer a second question.

After explaining, Bear moved over to the fridge. "What drink do you want to go with it? I'm having water, but you can have beer or soda or—"

"Beer," I said quickly. I needed my shoulders to come down away from my ears, but I didn't want to get drunk and say something stupid. Hopefully, beer would split the difference.

He brought our drinks to the table and sat down while I perused the sauces. A white sauce that looked like ranch dressing seemed safe. A violent red one looked like it might blow my head off, and I planned to avoid that one... at least until Bear tried it first so I could gauge his reaction.

"Okay," Bear said. "Since you're a newbie, you decide whether you'd rather ask or answer first."

"Answer," I said promptly. "Go ahead. Do your worst."

He smiled softly. "Why do you have long hair? I noticed it was short in your old pictures."

His question surprised me. I didn't think anyone had ever asked me that. "My cousin Pearl had always cut my hair in high school, so it was military-short. But when I got to Yale, I didn't have anyone to cut it, and I couldn't fathom paying fifteen bucks for a quick-cut place, so it got shaggy. I couldn't afford to go home for Thanksgiving or Christmas that first year, and by the time I got home the next summer, my hair was wild. But I liked it. Liked running my fingers through it when I studied. So I decided to keep it."

"Good choice," Bear said gruffly. He pointed at the platter of sauces. "Take your pick."

I dunked a carrot stick in the white sauce and found that I'd been correct—the horseradish was mild and mixed with a lemon-and-dill flavor that was delicious.

I took a sip of beer to wash down the food while I tried to think of a question for Bear as he grabbed a pita triangle and waited.

"What's the scariest situation you've ever been in?" I asked, choosing something related to his job.

He wrinkled his forehead. "Got stuck in an unexpected blizzard on a training run one time. I was alone overnight in dangerous temperatures. If I hadn't read an article a few days before that mentioned winter survival gear, I wouldn't have had a survival blanket in my pocket that day, and I might not have made it. I was so grateful I tracked down the guy who wrote the article and emailed him my thanks. Never done a run without one since."

I'd never heard that story before, and I wanted to ask follow-up questions, but I figured that wasn't part of the game. Instead, I nodded toward the sauces.

Bear dragged his pita through a thicker dip that was light green in color. His face remained impassive as he chewed, so I assumed the green one was safe also.

"My turn." He gave me a teasing grin. "Who's 'Sugar Time Easy' written about?"

That was easy. "Jude Marian."

Bear's eyebrows shot up. "No shit? Why don't you ever tell people that? Everyone knows how much you love him."

"We allowed to ask follow-up questions?" I teased. But I answered him anyway. "My relationship with music growing up was... it was like that winter survival blanket of yours. It saved my life. When I had Jude's warm, easy voice in my ears..." I let out a breath. "I could relax for a little while. It made me happy. His voice is like butter."

"And now you've opened for him and written a song with him, and you're performing with him at the fundraiser in Berlin," Bear said softly.

"I know. I still can't fathom it. Can you imagine having the person you think is the coolest, kindest, most talented human on the planet actually know your name and consider you kind of a... a friend? It's crazy."

"Yeah." Bear's smile warmed a fraction. "It's crazy alright." Before I could ask what he meant by that, he pushed the sauce platter toward me. "Go for it."

I cautiously chose a dip that had an orangish tinge. This time, I wasn't so lucky with the horseradish. Hot fire seared my mouth, and my eyes watered slightly.

Bear chuckled at my reaction. "Note to self: avoid the orange."

I gulped the cold beer greedily, trying to wash off Satan's own taint from my tongue, and narrowed my eyes. This time, I wasn't going easy on him.

"Biggest crush?"

"Ooof." He winced. "Uh... Jude Marian?"

He was clearly parroting my earlier answer, and the twinkle in his eye said he wasn't even trying to hide it.

"Liar." I tossed a carrot stick at him and pointed to the red sauce that looked like actual lava. "Dip deep, my friend. Dip deep."

While Bear loaded sauce on the carrot stick, I thought of a second question. I had so many things I wanted to know that weren't appropriate, like whether he was gay, and whether he'd liked our kiss, and why he wouldn't answer about his crush.

Instead, as he put his penalty carrot in his mouth, I asked a bigger question. "If you could have any dream in the future, what would it be?"

Bear's nostrils flared, and his eyes looked pained as they flashed to me. He made a big production out of chewing and swallowing before answering, and I mentally patted myself on the back for avoiding the red sauce myself. Clearly, it was *awful*.

"I, um..." Bear coughed slightly. "I have a lot of dreams. That's a pretty broad question..."

"Are you hedging? What's the penalty for hedging?" I demanded, pretending to reach for my phone. "Please give me King Gerhard's phone number so I can call him and—"

"Hush." He put one large hand on mine, halting my movement... and the flow of oxygen to my lungs. "I didn't say I wouldn't answer. I just need to think about it."

I raised one eyebrow but waited patiently with my hand still trapped under his while he grabbed a shrimp from the platter and chewed, probably hoping to cleanse the last of the fire sauce from his tongue.

"I... I always daydreamed about saving up to buy a piece of property somewhere like this. Not Norway," he said quickly. "I mean a big open piece of land in a place where winter brings plenty of snow for playing outside. I'd like to open a winter sports camp. For kids."

I blinked. I wasn't sure what I'd expected him to say, but it hadn't been that. "Tell me more."

"You know I love biathlon. It set me on a good path and gave structure to my life at a time when I didn't have any. But winter sports require some pretty extensive equipment—skis, rifles, clothing, shooting ranges, synthetic tracks... *snow*, which is really hard to come by in lots of places. I'd love to be able to give kids the opportunity to experience that, the way I did." His eyes met mine before he quickly looked away. "I'm sure that sounds silly. The world has much larger problems to solve than winter sports—"

"Actually..." I leaned forward. "I think that sounds amazing. Not everybody has gobs of money to throw at problems, Bear. I sure didn't, for most of my life. I think figuring out how each of us can use our own skills and passions to make the world a better, more equitable place is... maybe the best and most important idea I've ever heard."

He exhaled softly, tension bleeding from his shoulders. "Yeah?"

"Oh yeah." I nodded, only noticing at the last minute just how close our faces had gotten.

This was not getting us back on track.

I pulled back slightly. "Uh. Good job with the... with the

honesty." I waved a hand at the dips. "May the odds be ever in your favor."

"Right. Yeah." To my surprise, Bear dunked another pita triangle in the lava sauce and popped it in his mouth like a champ. Because I was hyperaware of him, I noticed his hairline had begun to dampen with sweat, but I couldn't tell if that was from the dip or the temperature in the room... or because of our proximity and our questions.

I was overly warm, too, for all the same reasons.

And I only got warmer when Bear tilted his head and said, "My turn to ask. You and your brotherhood... What secret are the five of you hiding?"

Shit. It wasn't that I didn't want to answer—I trusted Ryan Galloway implicitly—but my brothers and I had a rule. No one outside of our friend group was to know about our billion-dollar windfall, except for Kenji and our life partners. Revealing the truth for one of us would reveal it for all of us, and it wasn't my place to do that.

I sighed. "Dip me."

Bear laughed like he hadn't expected any different and loaded up another pita with a huge gob of orange dip.

"Oh, god. The first dunk of that one almost killed me. I'm definitely going to die now. Remember me fondly," I said as I put the bite in my mouth.

Bear snorted. "Baby."

He said the word as a tease. Obviously. He was saying *Zane, you're acting like an infant.* I understood that. But hearing the word on his lips had me imagining all kinds of other ways he could say it, and that made me suck in a gasp at the same moment the horseradish hit my tongue.

I stared at him as I began to choke. The dip clung to my throat like an abusive esophageal koala.

Way to get things back on track, I warned myself.

"Shit," Bear said. "Here. Take a sip of your beer. Good. Now, breathe... there you go."

Once I regained my equanimity several sips later—though I could still feel the dip leaving fiery traces down the inside of my chest—Bear sat back, folded his arms in front of him, and stroked his lower lip with his thumb.

"Wow. That was unexpectedly dramatic. Now I'm a little hesitant to ask my next question."

"I'm fine," I assured him in a croak.

His lips twitched up in a smile. "Of course you are. Okay, then, Mr. Fine, tell me why, aside from adding onto your gran's house, you haven't showered your family in lavish gifts. Don't get me wrong, I don't think you should," he added quickly. "Not at all. But knowing how generous you are and how hard it is for you to say no to them, it's surprising that your aunt still drives an old minivan and your cousin doesn't simply ask you for money outright rather than asking you to invest in his businesses."

I watched Bear steadily for a moment. The answer to this question was actually related to the last, though Bear couldn't possibly know that. I wasn't sure what the penalty was for dodging two questions in a row, though, and I wasn't sure my digestive system could handle it. More than that, I found I wanted to tell Bear. I wanted him to understand.

"When I first... got money," I said carefully, "I planned to share it with my family, exactly like you said. But someone else I knew—another Yalie—had a... a sort of similar experience to me. He came into a lot of money all at once, also. And he bought his brother a sports car." I remembered Dev's pride in being able to take care of his little brother that way. "Unfortunately, my friend's brother was a reckless, irresponsible idiot. Not unlike my cousin JK."

Bear winced. "Didn't go well?"

"Went tragically," I corrected. "He crashed the car and died instantly."

"Fuck," Bear said softly.

I nodded. "My friend's parents blamed him and his money for his brother's death. So I decided instead of giving away cash and fancy cars, I wanted to give my family opportunities to make something of their own. I wanted to truly help them rather than throw cash at them."

Bear shook his head. "Smart. I like that, Z."

I sucked in a breath and girded my loins, trying not to enjoy the way that nickname sounded coming from him. Unlike the earlier *baby*, I knew this one was meant exactly the way I heard it, and that warmed me all the way through even more than the horseradish had. It was the first time Z had ever sounded like a shortened version of my own name instead of a reference to someone completely separate, my rock star alter ego.

I took another gulp of the beer and set the empty bottle down. "Your turn again."

"Hang on." Bear moved to the fridge to get me another drink.

I noticed he'd decided to join me by bringing one back to the table for himself, too. I didn't make a comment about it, but secretly, I was happy to see him take advantage of the extra security outside to relax a little.

"Okay," he said as he resumed his seat. "Go."

I bit my lip, thinking. As I considered, Bear studied the bowls of dip, clearly trying to determine heat level by sight like I'd done earlier. It seemed like on his next turn he was planning to take a chance on a dip neither of us had tried before that looked to be made out of chopped-up mangoes, slivers of almonds, and mayonnaise. I nearly laughed out loud. I hoped for his sake none of those things had been combined with horseradish.

Sometimes in quiet moments like this, when Bear wasn't doing anything particularly amazing—not growling at someone to back off, or comforting me in the middle of the night, or even kissing me sense-less up against a tree, but just being his own, sweet, intelligent self—the overwhelming *like* I felt for him swamped me.

How freaking great was he, just as a person? How freaking lucky was I, that I got to have him in my life?

I wasn't sure if some part of what I was feeling showed on my face, but I decided it didn't matter. I cared about him and appreciated him, and I hoped that showed.

Which was why when he looked at me expectantly, I found myself asking something I hadn't intended to ask. Something that was more about me and the trust I felt for him than anything else.

"If you suddenly had a billion dollars, would you tell anyone?"

TWELVE

RYAN

Bears are famously solitary most of the time, sticking to their own paths in the wild, but when they find the right match, they'll show their interest with a kind of single-minded devotion and charm that's hard to ignore. When a bear finally decides he wants something, he's impossible to resist.
—Bear Facts for Insomniacs, Episode 20

I stared at him with my hand poised over the bowl of mango almond dip.

"Jesus fuck, what kind of question is that? How the hell should I know?" I sputtered. "And that doesn't count as a deflection. I literally don't know the answer."

I expected to see Zane's eyes bright with teasing, but instead, I saw a strange kind of vulnerability in them.

"I want to know," he said. "Think about it for a minute. On the one hand, yay! You can splurge and buy half the town. On the other..."

"On the other, everybody you knew would want a piece of it," I finished.

He nodded.

Everyone knew Zane was richer than any god. Hell, he was most likely wealthier than the royal family of Ventdestine. But because his money came from massive global fame, there would have been no way of keeping his wealth a secret. So why was he acting like it would have been a choice?

Zane looked so earnest, like he really wanted to hear my opinion on this topic, that I couldn't help but give it serious consideration. I took a sip of beer while I thought about it.

"I don't trust people by default," I said carefully. "I've seen too much in my job, too many people trying to use others for wealth and status. So I think... if I had the choice, I'd probably try to keep it under wraps. I might do what you do and try to help people instead."

He nodded, as if something I'd said had validated his own feelings.

"Except there'd be signs," I added with a wink. "I wouldn't be able to hide my Madshus Redline skis and my sudden retirement so I could enjoy them."

The teasing returned to his eyes. "At your winter sports camp?"

"Eventually," I agreed.

"You'd leave me just like that, Bear? All it would take is a cool bil?"

My grin dropped. I wanted to bark out a laugh at just how ridiculous that was. I would leave Zane Hendley when the last breath whistled out of my carcass and not a minute sooner. But then I realized I couldn't even joke about the topic without wanting to hit something or being tempted to blurt out all the things I was trying to hold back.

I shoved the mango almond dip in my mouth... which was a little kicky but surprisingly tasty.

"On the same topic," I said when it was Zane's turn to answer again. "What would be the hardest luxury to give up if you lost it all?"

Zane didn't hesitate. "I should say the ability to help others, but I'm too selfish. It would be my couture clothing."

He said it with such a straight face, smoothing a hand down his front, it took me a minute to notice what he was wearing.

His unicorn fleece onesie.

The most god-awful monstrosity of a pajama concept ever created. It had started out as a gag gift from Landry but had quickly become the only way Zane could stay warm last winter when we toured through Minnesota and Wisconsin. The poor guy had been sick in addition to being saddled with having to visit the frozen Midwest during January and February, and Landry's gift had been just the thing.

Now, it was definitely not the thing. The man was sweating from the horseradish like I was, and the unicorn onesie wasn't doing him any favors.

I imagined peeling it off him for a split second before I shook my head.

I needed to stop this fantasy. Whose turn was it? Shouldn't somebody be asking a question? I needed to say something, anything, to snap myself out of it.

"Why the fuck have you never had sex before?" I blurted.

My words slipped out like the notes of a song played off-key, each discordant syllable tumbling over the last as we listened in horror.

Zane's eyes flashed to me and widened in surprise. My own words replayed in my mind as I realized the depth of my mistake.

My *career-ruining* mistake.

"Oh fuck. I'm sorry, Zane. Please." My face was on fire and not from the kick of the horseradish. Panic rushed through my veins.

The kiss had been bad enough, but not letting it lie after he'd clearly wanted to pretend it hadn't happened? *Worse. Way worse.*

"That is absolutely none of my business and highly inappropriate. I beg your pardon." I stood up quickly and reached for the dishes. I would clean up our dinner mess and disappear into my room to give him the privacy he probably craved. At least I hadn't made such a grievous mistake in front of others.

How could I have been so stupid? Should I offer my resignation now or wait until the morning? Should I tell him or tell Violet first? Was I even strong enough to bring myself to do it when it would mean leaving him more vulnerable?

No. Definitely not. Then maybe I needed to—

Zane's long fingers closed around my wrist, directly over my hammering pulse. "Stop, Bear. Sit down."

I looked over at him without fully turning to face him. "I'm sorry," I said again softly. "Zane—"

"*Ryan.* Will you stop acting like you just stabbed me by accident? Sit back down."

The sound of my real name on his lips caught my attention as it usually did. I slowly lowered myself back into my seat next to him at the table, and once he knew I wasn't going to bolt, he let go of me.

The air outside had gotten cold enough later in the day to justify turning on the gas fireplace, and full darkness had descended a while ago, leaving us feeling isolated and hunkered down.

I clasped my hands together in my lap and focused on them.

After an awkward moment, Zane spoke. "I'm actually glad you finally said something. I knew you heard me talking about it the other night, and I was so embarrassed."

I glanced up. "Embarrassed? Why?"

His own cheeks were pink, but there was no way he was as mortified as I was.

"Because I'm a thirty-three-year-old virgin? Is there even such a thing? I know I'm not supposed to care about virginity because it's a social construct... but tell that to every other man on Earth, will you?"

I took a deep breath. "Don't ever feel pressured to do something you don't want to do because of what other people think—"

"I *do* want to do it!" Zane snapped, throwing his arms up. "That's the problem. I want to do it badly. Very, *very* badly. But I..." He blew out a noisy breath. "I'm so twisted up about it now I'd only embarrass myself. And what if Noelle was right? What if the first time I have sex, someone captures it on film, and everyone sees me come in one point five seconds?"

My body thrummed with a toxic mix of embarrassment, second-hand embarrassment, greed, and lust.

So. Much. Lust.

"Don't do it with someone you can't trust." As much as I wanted to encourage him to stop worrying and just do it, I couldn't help but give him at least that one warning. He was mine to protect, and I'd be damned if I was going to let him get taken advantage of.

Zane glanced up at me and then looked back down at where he was running his thumbnail over a callus on the inside edge of his ring finger. Those guitar-player hands never failed to make my heart skip a beat. I wanted them on me, always. "That makes for a very short list."

"The brotherhood?" I suggested, even though my gut roiled at the idea.

He grimaced. "Ew. I call them my brothers for a reason, Bear. Besides, the only one who's single is Landry, and if he's not hate-fucking Kenji, he's at least thinking about it."

I reached out and grabbed his hand to stop his fiddling. "Zane."

Honey-brown eyes peeked at me through his eyelashes. "You probably think I'm the world's biggest loser."

"Fuck no. I was proud of you confessing your truth in front of that kid the other night when it clearly made you uncomfortable around your cousins."

"I didn't want him to think all rock stars are out there sleeping with tons of people."

I let go of his hand but turned more fully to face him, nudging his chair back so I could see him better. "Second of all," I continued carefully, "any man would be lucky to be with you."

Including me, I added in my head, but the air between us immediately began buzzing like I'd spoken the words out loud.

Zane twisted his lips and took a breath. "*Any* man?"

"Hell yes. Every man," I insisted, not fully realizing the road I was going down.

"I mean... I'm sitting right here, Bear."

Caution signs sprang up, and warning lights flashed.

"Wanting it very badly?" I teased, trying to break the tension and failing utterly. "Very, very badly?"

The edge of his mouth quirked. "Very."

I felt my heart rate kick up. "Except now we're stuck on an isolated peninsula on a Norwegian fjord."

Zane's cheeks rounded with a big grin. "With a hundred percent too few sex opportunities..."

I opened my mouth to make a joke about there still being one, but I quickly snapped it closed. It was bad enough I'd introduced this topic with my principal, *kissed* my principal. I wasn't going to joke about sleeping with him, too.

He glanced at me through his dark lashes again. "But a hundred percent too many temptations," he murmured before looking away.

His words sat between us, still and dangerous as an undetonated bomb.

"Zane," I said in a low voice.

"No, sorry. Forget I said that. I don't want to put you in an awkward position. The only thing worse than a sex video would be an actual sexual harassment lawsuit." He didn't look at me but let out an awkward laugh. His cheeks were mottled red, and the tips of his ears were crimson.

"Zane," I said again. I was unsure what I wanted to say, but I knew I didn't want him to feel awkward or uncomfortable. Not around me. Not ever.

He glanced at me and then away again.

I took a breath. "I would never, *ever* consider sleeping with you—"

"I get it!" he cut in. "Christ, Bear, I know you wouldn't. I... I don't even know if you're into guys, and even if you might be, that doesn't mean you're into *me*. I'm sorry I said anything—"

I reached out and grabbed his hand again. It was warm and clammy and shook a little bit. "*Let. Me. Finish.*"

Zane's eyes widened.

"I would never consider sleeping with you... as anything other than a dream and a goddamn *privilege.* I certainly wouldn't consider it harassment of any kind."

He blinked, his breath coming in fast, choppy little pants. "You... you're joking?"

"No," I said firmly. "That's the furthest thing from a joke."

"You'd have sex with me?" His voice squeaked on the last word.

I closed my eyes and inhaled to keep from laughing. "If I wasn't in charge of protecting you? If I didn't think you'd regret it? In a skinny minute. I'm definitely into guys, and I'm very definitely into you."

"Oh, god," he breathed like Christmas had come early. Then he blurted, "I wouldn't regret it. Are you kidding? Who could sleep with you and regret it?"

My brain scrambled to do the calculations, which was exponentially harder with his hand in mine.

Technically, I didn't work for him. Violet's contract was with Zane's record label.

But what if things became awkward? Would I still be able to do my job properly?

And what if things didn't become awkward? Would I be able to keep a level head?

Who was I kidding? I wasn't able to keep a level head *now.* I'd been in love with the man for longer than I cared to admit... which meant I would get my heart smashed to pieces.

Because there was no way a man like Zane Hendley—talented, kind, and open-hearted—would ever want to settle down with someone whose talents were skiing and shooting targets with bullets. I'd never been described as kind. I certainly wasn't open-hearted. I was guarded and gruff, suspicious and easily annoyed.

A bear, exactly as Zane called me... and bears were solitary animals.

Zane deserved better.

"It's not a good idea," I said, desperate for him to accept my weak attempt at stopping this before it became unstoppable.

"Yeah, no. You're probably right." He sighed and reached for the front of his onesie, pulling it in and out to fan himself. "Is it hot in here, or is it just you?" he murmured.

"Open it up," I said with a laugh, reaching out to yank the zipper down an inch. "You're obviously roasting."

I'd assumed he had on a T-shirt and shorts or something underneath, but instead of a shirt, I only saw a small tuft of soft brown chest hair peeking up into the hollow of his throat.

"Oh," I said, reaching out to yank it back up. The zipper caught a hair, making Zane yelp. I tried pulling the zip back down right as Zane reached up to do the same. I attempted to yank my hand away and let him deal with it, but instead, I somehow managed to knock him under his chin. He was so surprised, he lost his balance, which was when I realized he'd been leaning his chair partway back on only two feet. "Fuck!"

I lurched forward and grabbed for his chair, pulling it down until Zane himself spilled into my lap.

I was horrified. I'd tried to keep my distance, to do the right thing, and instead, I'd tried undressing him, punching him, and then nearly knocking him to the floor.

He must have seen my panic. "I'm fine," Zane said quickly.

"Zane, fuck!" I drew in a jagged breath. My arms came around him to keep him from tumbling off my lap.

"*Bear*. I'm fine. I promise."

"You're not. I knocked you in the chin." I reached out to tilt his chin up carefully so I could see the damage. Thankfully, there wasn't any blood on his mouth, so he didn't seem to have bitten his lip.

Zane's hair spilled over my hand as I tilted his head. "I'm *fine*."

The word reverberated between us, tweaking me like a discordant note, but worse. Like clock hands forcibly moved the wrong direction and then left out of rhythm, always a step out of time from then on.

His eyes flicked to mine as he realized what he'd said. As he remembered my warning about saying those words to me yesterday... and what had happened after that.

Zane dragged his tongue across his lower lip. "I'm fine," he said again, this time speaking slowly and softly, like a caress.

Like a *dare*.

I watched his brown eyes heat with challenge. He was a matador, and I was helpless against the flare of a red cape.

My thumb grazed his bottom lip, my eyes riveted on how plump it was. I remembered how it felt against mine. Even now, knowing his mouth was probably a toxic cauldron of horseradish like mine, I wanted another taste.

"Zane," I warned, desperate for someone—anyone but me—to be mature enough to stop us from making a colossal mistake.

"Totally and completely *fine*," he said softly, eyes now on my own mouth.

He felt like perfection in my arms. Like he was made to sit pressed up against me like this, where I could hold him and feel him and gaze into his beautiful face.

"This is a mistake," I pleaded.

"Probably." He leaned in until the tip of his nose barely brushed against my cheek.

"I reek of horseradish."

The edge of his lip quirked up. "Misery loves company."

"Zane," I breathed, turning my face just enough to feel the prickle of his whiskers against the tender skin of my lips.

"Please, Bear." The broken words were so soft I barely heard them. But his plea carried years of need, the kind he'd never felt safe enough to reveal.

His need was nothing to mine because I needed Zane Hendley like I needed the Earth to keep spinning around the sun. Like I needed plants to keep producing oxygen. Like I needed winter's snow to melt and fill the rivers and lakes so I could drink my fill.

"Tell me to stop," I finally begged before pressing my lips against his cheek, his jaw, the tender skin under his ear.

He sucked in a breath. "No."

That might have been the first time I'd ever heard Zane say the word.

I hid a grin against his ear. "You'll tell me if you stop being fine."

"I'll always be fine with you."

I closed my eyes and imagined that to be possible. "Zane. You will tell me if you stop being fine."

He made a little growling sound in his throat. "*Fine.*"

I sucked his earlobe into my mouth. "I hope you still like horseradish," I said while bubbles of happy nerves popped haphazardly in my stomach.

He pulled in a shaky breath. "Who knew you were the world's worst tease?"

I kissed him then, full on the lips. Blood roared in my ears and thundered in my veins. He *wanted* me. He wanted *me. He* wanted me.

We kissed for a long time, Zane happily straddling my lap while I held on to him with one arm and explored his face and neck with my other hand.

My cock filled as I imagined all the things I wanted to do with him. I shifted a little, and Zane let out a noise of protest. Instead of stopping kissing him long enough to explain, I reached for his hand and brought it down between us. The next sound out of him was a low groan as he explored the ridge of my hard cock through my sweatpants.

I unzipped his onesie to his navel and brushed it off his shoulders and down his tattooed arms. His skin was on fire. My hands turned warm from exploring.

He was small but toned from professional workouts with a personal trainer and hours-long performances that included choreography and demanded stamina. I took advantage of the opportunity to touch all of the curves and dips that had been off-limits before now.

When I got to the lower part of his belly, I reached around to his back and snuck my fingers down beneath the soft elastic waistband of his boxer briefs. I was hyperaware of his reaction, poised and ready to stop at any indication I was crossing a line.

He didn't stop me.

I cupped the bare skin of his ass and squeezed.

"Bear." His voice was a muffled whimper.

"I want to make you come," I admitted, moving to whisper against his ear.

His dick pressed against my stomach as he arched into me. "Touch me."

My gut twisted with need, but I didn't make a move to touch his cock. It was a line I wouldn't be able to uncross. I wanted to give him time to change his mind because one thing was clear: I wouldn't be the one stopping this from progressing.

I was in control of many, many things, but stopping myself from touching Zane wasn't one of them. Not unless he asked me to.

He didn't wait for me to make a move. Zane grabbed my arm and moved my hand down the front of his onesie. "Touch me," he said again, nearly panting with desire. His face was flushed, and his eyes glittered.

I didn't even need to ask because he volunteered, "Yes, I'm sure," he groaned. "*Please.*"

I reached into his underwear and pulled his cock out. It was hot and hard in my palm. Zane didn't make a sound, but his eyes widened, and his lips opened in an O shape before his eyes fluttered closed, and he let out a low, jagged sound that went straight to my own cock.

Making him feel that good was like catching air when going over a rise on a cross-country ski run. My stomach swooped, and the breath caught in my lungs. I quickly licked my palm before grasping him again and tugging gently, watching his reaction to learn what he liked and what felt good. I experimented with different pressure and speed until his eyes rolled back, and he let out a jagged exhale.

"Gonna come." His words were breathy, and his lips were wet from my kisses. He was so hot I wondered if just jacking him while seeing him this way was going to make me come, too.

His hands clenched around my shoulders, and his hips canted into my grip as I murmured encouragement in his ear.

When he came, Zane let out a strangled sound and shuddered. He hid his face in my neck as the orgasm ripped through him.

I couldn't believe I'd gotten to see him like this, to share this moment of complete vulnerability with him, to make him feel good.

Even though my dick was throbbing painfully in my pants, it was enough.

"You," he said.

I turned my face to press a kiss to his hair and ear. Thankfully, he couldn't see what had to be a satisfied smile on my face.

He shuddered again. "Want to make you feel good, too."

I opened my mouth to tell him he already did when he shocked me by sliding to the floor between my legs. When his warm brown eyes met mine, still hot with desire but also hesitant with insecurity, the saliva dried up in my mouth and throat.

Zane Hendley was on his knees for me with a look so fucking eager to please, the breath punched out of me in a *huh* sound.

He reached for the tie on my sweatpants while my brain computed the variables of the current situation at record speed. Should I stop him? *Could* I, even if I wanted to? Why would I want to? But maybe he was doing this out of obligation to reciprocate. Should I tell him he didn't need to reciprocate? What if he stopped?

"Is this okay?"

My eyes shot from his hands to his face. Zane's expression was even more unsure.

"Do you want this?" I asked, my voice sounding ragged and raw.

His jaw shifted, and his lips tightened, as if holding back more than he said. "Don't make me beg."

I slid my hips forward on the wooden chair, widening my legs to make room. When he reached for the tie on my pants again, I helped him slide them down and completely off.

Zane's eyes zeroed in on my hard cock, making it jerk. I reached out to stroke it, which seemed to wake him from a trance. He knee-walked closer and pressed one hand on my thigh while he reached for my cock with the other. I released it to him and moved my hand to caress his cheek.

"You're so fucking sexy," I murmured. My only hope was that this was happening in some kind of fever dream, and when it was all over, he would forget the admissions I couldn't help but make.

When his warm, wet tongue stroked up my shaft, I let out a low groan and let my head fall back. Zane cradled my balls with one hand, and just as I'd always imagined, those rough, callused, guitar-playing fingers felt fucking amazing. One fingertip accidentally brushed against the skin behind them, and I clenched with a sudden image of him finger-fucking me, invading my body in search of just the right spot to make me see fucking stars. I'd never had anyone touch me there before, but with Zane, I wanted it.

Wanted *everything*.

"Zane." I groaned again, unable to come up with any other words that weren't humiliating pleas for him to take me in any way he pleased.

He closed his mouth over my tip, bathing the sensitive part under the head with the tip of his tongue. His movements were tentative but hungry. I could tell he'd spent plenty of time imagining how he'd do this, how he'd give another man pleasure with his mouth.

"So good," I urged. My fingers threaded into his hair. "Just like that."

He reached down to touch himself, even though he'd just come. The idea that sucking my cock made him hard again was enough to bring on my orgasm. The pleasure was white-hot, contracting my lower half and shooting pleasure along my spine until I was shuddering and gasping. Zane choked as I came in his mouth.

I opened my eyes in time to see the last bit of my release hit his lips as he pulled off. My dick gave another feeble spurt at the sight of Zane Hendley with my spunk on his face.

My fingers were still tangled in his hair, so I pulled him close to kiss him hungrily, tasting my own salty release on his lips and tongue.

He stood up and embraced me while we continued to kiss. I pulled him onto my lap, suddenly fearful that this was it. One and done. I needed to take as much of him as I could before reality came crashing down on us and rational heads prevailed.

His body was so warm, skin like silk under my hands as I roamed them up and down his back and down to his ass.

Zane finally slowed down and tucked his face into my neck, leaning his head against my chest with his arms pulled in between us. It took me a moment to realize he was cold.

"Hey. You should hop in a hot shower," I said, chafing up and down his back more rapidly in hopes of warming him.

"With you?" Soft brown eyes twinkling with humor met mine...

And I froze. Ninety percent of my brain (not to mention my dick) screamed a resounding yes. But that other ten percent played an insistent slideshow of all the ways this was wrong and dangerous... for both of us.

Attuned to each other as we were, Zane noticed my hesitation immediately. He sat up straight and nodded. "Or alone. That's... yeah, I get it. Okay."

Shit. This was suddenly even more awkward than I feared. "Zane," I said as he stood up and turned away from me, yanking up his onesie and jamming his arms into the sleeves. He ignored me and headed toward his room. "Zane, wait—"

He waved a hand dismissively over his shoulder without looking back. "Don't worry about it, B-bear..." He took a shuddering breath before adding...

"I'm fine."

THIRTEEN
ZANE

Bears might seem straightforward, but they can be surprisingly conflicted when it comes to relationships. After mating, a bear's protective drive might urge him to push his mate away when he most wants to hold them close. Fortunately, their survival instincts always lead them in the right direction. A bear knows what he can't live without.
—Bear Facts for Insomniacs, Episode 89

Any idiot would know I was anything but fine, and Bear *especially* would know. There was no one more attuned to my moods than he was and no one less likely to believe my "fines."

But I also wasn't about to let him know just how much that interlude had affected me.

I stayed strong until I got into the hot shower, and then I pressed my face into my hands and let out a long breath.

Holy fuck. Holy *fuck.*

I just had sex with Ryan Galloway.

I just blew my bodyguard.

I just sucked Bear's dick.

I shuddered at the delicious memory. The feel of his heavy cock on my tongue. The musky scent of him in my nose. The sounds he made from deep in his chest.

"Zane, open the door."

I jumped and nearly slipped on the wet tile. "Can't. Showering," I blurted without thinking.

"Tell me I can come in."

I hesitated, wondering if I wanted to face him when I was feeling this vulnerable. But ultimately, I wanted to see him. I wanted to be with him. I wanted any excuse to have his eyes and hands on me.

"You can come in," I said.

Bear opened the door and strode in, yanking off his clothes and throwing them down. Within seconds, his big, beautiful body was pushing into the shower stall and cornering me up against the wall. His hand came up to tilt my head, so I was forced to meet his eyes.

His eyes flicked frantically between my eyes and mouth before he leaned in to kiss me firmly but quickly. "I need to know what you're thinking."

"I... I'm... I'm thinking you're, like, even hotter naked than I imagined?"

Bear closed his eyes briefly as if in relief. "Thank you. But that's not what I meant."

"I'm just... processing, okay? That was really fucking amazing. I enjoyed it and want to do it again. The fact you don't want a repeat is taking me a moment to get my head around—"

He pressed his thick cock against my hip. "Who said I didn't want a repeat?"

His presence was affecting me, making me dizzy again with hot want. "You acted like..." I closed my eyes and swallowed after catching him glancing at my mouth. "Stop doing that. I can't fucking think."

"I want a repeat, Zane."

Wait, what?

I blinked my eyes open and met his.

"I want you so fucking much," he continued. "And it would kill me if you doubted that even for an instant. I never want you to feel bad because of me. Understand?"

Water from the spray made his eyelashes even darker and spiky, setting off the intensity of his irises, and I could only nod helplessly.

"But you're my protectee. And that makes this complicated," Bear said softly. He caressed my back with one large hand. "I'll try to explain, if you'll let me."

Still not quite able to believe I was allowed to do it, I ran my hands around his waist to his back, reveling in the feel of his hard muscles under my fingers. "Why didn't I know you liked men? You never said anything."

"I promise, I'll answer all your questions. But first..." He moved his hand to the side of my face, sliding his fingers into my hair despite the hair tie keeping it piled on top of my head. Then he leaned down to kiss me. It was soft and precious, gentle and sweet. For someone who resembled a grumpy bear half the time, Ryan Galloway was heart-achingly tender with me. Always had been.

I bit my lip to keep from asking even more questions. For the past twenty-four hours, I'd been brimming with them, but I'd concluded Bear's sex life was none of my business. Things were different now—he was rubbing his business all over my business—but I still didn't want to pressure him. He didn't owe me details.

Bear reached for the soap and began to rub it all over me as if washing me was something normal and expected. For the record, it wasn't. I wasn't sure anyone had washed anything other than my face in thirty years.

He finished washing and rinsing himself off before reaching for the towels.

As we stepped out of the shower to dry off, my mind spun while I considered what I truly wanted to know. How invasive could my questions be? Would he be offended if I was too curious?

After drying off, I found a clean pair of pajama pants while Bear pulled his sweatpants back on. Then, he led me to the bed and nudged me onto it until we lay side by side, facing each other with the duvet draped over us.

The sky outside was pitch-black, and the house was quiet. Bear reached for the elastic band in my hair, offering me a sheepish raised eyebrow as if seeking permission.

I nodded and helped him pull it out. As soon as my hair was down, he began playing with it. And like he'd turned a key in a lock, all of my questions came bubbling out.

"So... is your sexuality a secret? Because of Ventdestine? Or your family?"

"Not my family. They'd probably be fine with it," he said softly. "I figured I'd tell them when I had someone to introduce them to. I've never said anything one way or the other, so maybe they know. I don't shy away from commenting that certain men are attractive."

This was true. I remembered him agreeing once when Micki had mentioned how attractive Omar Rudberg was. *"I've met him,"* he'd said. *"He's as nice as he is good-looking."*

I hadn't thought much of it at the time. The *Young Royals* actor was objectively pretty. You didn't have to be into men to think so. But now, I rifled back through my memories as if searching for corroborating evidence.

There was that whole Daniel Craig thing back in Barlo, which took on a whole new meaning in light of recent evidence. And that made me remember my conversation with Landry the other night.

"Were you out in Ventdestine?"

Bear didn't answer right away.

"I'm sorry. Tell me if I'm being too nosy," I said quickly. "It's just... I really thought you were straight. There was a story online that you dated a woman on the same security team in Ventdestine—"

"You're not nosy. I'm just not used to being open about it." He made a face. "The story about the woman was something the PR office did. There was a rumor that a guard had been spotted at a gay club while on holiday in London, so the royal PR office arranged for all of the high-profile male guards to be seen around town with women. And *no*, to answer your other question, I was not out in Ventdestine. I couldn't be. It's illegal there."

"Who was the guy? The guard, I mean. What happened to him?"

"It blew over. Those rumors were always happening since actual gay people exist, and guys in the guard were probably actually fucking while on leave… and at any other time, for that matter." Bear sighed.

I felt a sliver of discomfort at the idea of Bear fucking someone while on leave… or ever. "Did you ever hook up with him?"

Bear found my hand and twined his fingers through mine. "I told you, it's illegal in Ventdestine."

"No, I know, but… surely people still do it."

"Surely they do. But *I* didn't."

"You didn't? Like… ever? I mean, if you were both in the guards, the stakes would have been just as high for him as you. Seems ideal for keeping it secret."

Bear squeezed my hand. "When Asger Salling offered me the job to come to Ventdestine, I knew what I was getting into. I knew I was sacrificing my personal life for professional gain. It was an honor to be asked, to be recognized for saving him, and I was proud of it. And even if he claimed the winds of fortune had commanded it, I also knew his choice to elevate a foreigner to his personal guard earned Asger a lot of side-eye, at least until I proved myself. I understood that I'd been given an opportunity, and I didn't want to fuck it up."

Bear paused again, so I moved a little closer and kissed him softly. He smiled against my lips. "This isn't helping me tell the story," he murmured. I kissed him through it.

Finally, Bear pulled back. And he was no longer smiling. "So I took the oath. And then proceeded to spend twelve years upholding it."

I tried to figure out what that meant. "You… didn't hook up with anyone for *twelve* years?"

He pressed his lips together and shook his head. "I remember asking one of the other guards about the law once. We'd just coordinated a visit with the head of the Norwegian royal family's security, and Kasper had politely asked after the woman's wife like it was no big deal. So I said, since Kasper seemed fairly accepting of gay marriage, did he think the Ventdestinian laws about homosexuality should be changed? You should have seen the look on his face. 'The winds of fate don't look kindly on change.'"

I shook my head. As confining as my career sometimes was, I realized how privileged I was that I'd never had to hide my sexuality. But mostly, I was still stuck back on... "*Twelve years?*"

Bear chuckled. "Yes. I've hooked up with men in the past. But I haven't been with one in a very, very long time."

I stared at Bear as the image I had of him was shaken like a snow globe in the hands of a toddler on a sugar high... which was maybe why I sounded like one when I voiced my reaction.

"B-but... *why?* You've been back in the States for over a year! You could have been sleeping with tons of guys!"

He glanced away before shrugging. "I didn't want to jump into anything."

"Okay, but like... you *could*. You could jump into... *me*, for example." My face burned with pre-embarrassment, but I wasn't about to lose my shot at getting Ryan Galloway's hands on me again.

I'd developed a crush on my bodyguard pretty much the moment we'd met. When the tall, muscled man with dark brown hair, darker brown eyes, shadowy beard, and the sexiest broody expression I'd ever seen walked into the reception area of the recording studio, I'd nearly swallowed my tongue.

And apparently, my deepest fantasy—that Bear was into men and found me physically attractive—was also coming true. My heart felt like it was attached to electrodes set to shock over and over with an unpredictable irregularity.

Bear looked hesitant. "I want to. I want a repeat more than anything..."

"But?" I cocked my head.

He blew out a breath. "*But* I worry that it's not a good idea to cross a professional line—"

"No one would need to know. And you could... finally get..." I didn't know how to say what I was thinking because my thoughts were like multicolored bumper cars being driven by hamsters on speed.

Very horny hamsters.

"Laid?" he finished, eyes bright with teasing.

I closed my eyes and nodded maniacally. "So much laid. The laid-iest."

The soft huff of his laugh made me grin.

"Zane..."

"Unless... unless you don't want to. Sleep with me, I mean," I added after seeing his hesitation.

He tilted his chin down and looked up at me through his lashes like I was being obtuse. "I told you already, there's no gay man on Earth who doesn't want to sleep with you." Bear reached out to brush a strand of hair off my forehead with the back of a finger.

I wanted to close my eyes and revel in the moment like a cat in the sun, but I didn't. I needed to focus. I'd never been in Debate Club in high school, but I imagined this was the kind of high-stakes pressure those kids had felt during competition. What could I say to convince him I was right?

I swallowed. "Okay. So you're in... ah... need. After a very long dry spell. And I'm in... well, you could say I am also in need after a very long dry spell. Thirty-three years, as a matter of fact. So, I propose we take advantage of this isolated, secure location and the downtime we have here to, uh, douse the spell."

"Douse the spell."

"Wet it. Make it not dry anymore. Quench it? Whatever."

Bear's eyes continued to dance. "I know what douse means. I've never heard it used like that."

I winced. "There's a distinct blood supply shortage to my brain right now."

He reached out again and ran his thumb across my cheek and down the side of my face. "You're doing fine," he murmured with a smile.

"Bear," I breathed. "Please."

He sighed. "Are you sure you don't want to save yourself for someone special?"

You are special, I wanted to scream. But I knew better than to scare him off with the implication I would expect more of him than simple physical release.

"I honestly just want to do it. I want to have sex. With you. Again. Right now. Very much."

It was the most selfish and forthright thing I'd said in as long as I could remember. But I was too far gone to care. I wanted him enough to throw out the truth and hope for the best.

Bear met my eyes and leaned in. My breathing picked up, turning shallow and jagged at the same time.

"You're really hard to say no to," he said, no longer smiling.

I could still see signs of hesitation in his eyes... but it didn't stop him from leaning in and kissing me.

FOURTEEN

RYAN

Kissing Zane was the least likely way in the entire universe of maintaining my sanity.

I sounded breathless—and my brain felt severely oxygen deprived—when he pulled back a moment later.

Zane scooted closer to me and touched the tip of his index finger to one of the collarbone bumps at the base of my throat. His eyes stayed riveted there so he didn't have to look at me. "What if... what if we just, um, *practiced* here. A little. In Norway. We're on our own, mostly. You're horny. I'm horny. You want practice. I want practice.

This is like..." He traced my collarbone, which was proving to be an erogenous zone I hadn't known existed. "The perfect practice scenario."

His point was well-made.

Frankly, he could have said, *"Me want,"* and I would have thought it was a point well-made.

But Zane continued making a very strong case to my neck. "B-besides, I don't get opportunities like this, a-and this was really special to me, what we did. Earlier. Because I know I can trust you—I trust you more than anyone—and that made it amazing. And you're closer to me than anyone in the world, other than my brothers. And it really, it really sucks if that's going to be, like, the only time we get to do that because I feel like I just finally got this opportunity, and also, I don't know about you, but that... what we did. Earlier. That's not enough for me. So it's going to be really hard for me not to want that every time I'm with you from now on. And we're going to be stuck together here in the house, so, like, what if we... just temporarily! It doesn't have to go past Norway..."

He stopped, cleared his throat, and peeked up at me from beneath his lashes... which was quickly becoming my favorite Zane look. "You're not saying anything. Does that mean no? Because... okay. That's cool. I mean, I guess I could try to find someone else. I could ask—"

I leaned in again and kissed the words out of his mouth. His nervous babbling was my Kryptonite, and if he thought he was going to "find someone else," he had another think coming.

I was done fighting this. If this interlude was my only chance to have him, I was going to take it with both hands, both feet, and all the fucking rest of me. How could I say no when it was exactly what I wanted? He was dangling my dream right in front of me and telling me it was what he needed.

Was it unprofessional? Yes. Hell, yes. But he was right. No one was around to witness it.

Would it distract me from protecting him? Maybe... although I'd craved him desperately for a year already, and I felt like I was doing okay. Besides which, Lou and the rest of the perimeter team had us covered, and we were in the wilds of a Norwegian fjord, so far off the beaten path there was no possible way a random stalker from America could find us.

So I would give him what he wanted. What *I* wanted. And then I would let him go when we left this little sanctuary, even if it meant watching him fall for someone else one day. Because that was what you fucking did for the people you loved. You took a bullet for them, literally or figuratively.

Zane's slender fingers curled into my chest hair and tugged. The time had come to stop stressing and allow myself to enjoy this.

I rolled him over onto his back and deepened the kiss, arching my hips to press my cock against the inside of his thigh. He made a sound of surrender in his throat that tweaked my need to take care of him. Zane deserved the best, and while I was nowhere near the best, I'd try my hardest to make this good for him.

My hands explored every inch of his exposed skin, caressing sensitive spots and squeezing firm muscles, tweaking his nipples and finally reaching down to pull off his pajama pants.

The duvet was long gone, tossed off the bed when heat from our bodies had made it an inferno.

"Bear," Zane said on a groan as I tugged on his earlobe with my teeth and growled.

He wasn't wrong. I felt semi-feral, overcome with the need to take and have, maul and conquer.

I moved down his body, teasing his chest, stomach, and lower belly with my tongue, eager to suck him. This wasn't my first time, but it was definitely my *best* time.

Zane sucked in an audible breath. As I finally put my mouth on his cock, his hands moved into my hair and held on. "Oh god. Fuck. *Ryan.*"

Hearing the sound of my name in his lust-graveled voice made my cock even harder. Knowing he'd never had the pleasure of receiving oral sex before incited my desire to make this one the best damned blow job in history.

I licked and sucked and tormented him until his nails dug into my scalp and his breathing stuttered. My hands moved beneath him to grab his ass. Zane's ass cheeks flexed under my fingers as he couldn't help but gently thrust forward, seeking more.

My brain was a kaleidoscope of images of things we could do—positions I could put him in and parts of his body I could taste and touch. I reveled in the privilege of giving him pleasure. He was mine to enjoy, mine to guide, mine to relish.

"Let me," he gasped. "God, let... me... *nnnghh!*"

The warm, salty taste of his release hit my tongue as he choked out intelligible sounds and arched into me. His hair fell forward as he sat up and leaned over me, cupping the back of my head while his body continued to shudder.

I ran my hands down over his ass to the back of his thighs and calves before moving them back up to his sides and abs as I pulled away from him and met his eyes.

Zane's face was flushed, and his eyes were bright. I reached up to brush his hair back and cup his face. "Good?"

He tackled me full-body, pushing me back and kissing me soundly. I laughed into his mouth and held on tightly as I kept us from falling off the bed. I flipped him so he was pinned beneath me, trapped and wriggling like a fish.

"Was supposed to be..." He pushed half-heartedly at my hips. "... *my* turn. Please."

Even when he was brainless and loose from an orgasm, the man still had manners.

I leaned in and pressed another drugging kiss to his mouth until his eyes rolled up and closed. I didn't need another orgasm from him—though god knew I would always appreciate the fuck out of one—but I needed *this*. The chance to hold him. Tease him. Kiss him and watch him go limp with satisfaction and contentment.

After a while, our kissing slowed, and we settled ourselves with me on my back and Zane's head on my shoulder.

"I was going to blow you again," he said, making my slowly deflating dick reflate painfully fast.

I ran fingertips up and down his back. "I was going to let you."

"Oh."

I peered down at him, wondering why he sounded surprised. "But there's no pressure, Zane. I'm happy with this also."

"I thought for some reason you weren't interested in that. Like maybe I didn't do great the first time or something."

I couldn't help but bark out a laugh. "You're joking."

"Maybe I sucked," he said in a small voice.

I reached up to run my thumb across his lower lip. "You did. And it was fucking amazing."

Zane batted my hand away, flushing a delightful pink. "What if that was beginner's luck? What if I'm terrible the second time, and then it's sitting there between us like this horrifying thing neither of us can forget?"

I stared at him. "You're acting like you're completely inexperienced, but I've heard you with other guys. Hell, I thought you and Landry—"

"Me and Landry?" He seemed to remember the sex noises from the hotel room. His eyes filled with glee, and he snickered. "Ohhh. So many things are clear suddenly. No. That was Landry recounting a hookup... and, um, poking the bear, so to speak." He grinned. "I did tell him bears attack when provoked."

I snorted. "And... the other guys?"

Zane moved to sit up, crossing his legs in front of him and pulling a pillow over his lap. "You remember me telling you about my former publicist, Noelle, and how she tried to get me to create a bad-boy persona?"

I grumbled acknowledgment. Noelle could fuck off for all she'd had him do. The woman had made him feel like he was nothing; all the while, she'd gotten rich off his "nothingness."

Zane continued. "It worked for me because they started encouraging me to bring guys back to my hotel room from time to time. We'd kiss. Do a little heavy petting. Under-the-clothes mutual jerk-offs. That's it. I'd always make up an excuse—I didn't have time for more, or I was tired and had to be up early for something, or I couldn't suck them off because I had to protect my vocal cords."

I secretly thanked the maker of delicate vocal cords. "Is that true?"

Zane's breathing quickened. "Maybe if I had a show tomorrow, I'd be concerned about it. But I don't... I mean..." He swallowed. "I don't have enough experience to know if it's even an issue," he finished, searching my eyes as if anticipating my reaction.

I reached out to run my thumb across his full bottom lip again. My cock was aching to feel the soft press of his lips, the wet swipe of his tongue.

"I'm willing to be your guinea pig," I said with a smile. "When you're ready to experiment further, I mean. There's no rush—"

Zane tackled me again, kissing my mouth hungrily before moving quickly down the bed and yanking at the tie on my sweatpants. This time, I was no longer wearing underwear, so when the pants came down, my dick came up.

His eyes heated. "Bear-sized," he murmured before sticking out his tongue to caress the tip. I let out a broken sound as the reality of the situation continued to sink in.

The man I loved, the man I wanted more than anyone or anything I'd ever wanted, had his mouth on me again. Wanted to please me. Was nervous he was going to let me down.

"That's so good," I said, reaching out to run my fingers through his hair as he continued to experiment, licking and sucking, wrapping his tongue around me. "God, Zane. Just like that."

He blinked up at me as he continued to wet my dick. His lips were full and moist, his cheeks flushed. His honey-brown eyes were a little glazed, and the tip of his nose was pink from my beard stubble.

My balls tightened. If Zane had any idea how strongly I felt about him—how much this did *not* feel casual or practice or temporary—he'd run in the other direction. He'd definitely request a new personal security lead... and, knowing him, probably offer me a generous severance package through Violet.

But that was a problem for a different day because right now, I was too giddy to care, too turned on to worry about anything other than the man in front of me.

There had to be a rule against being this turned on, this happy. He was so gorgeous, so enthusiastic, he never failed to spike my heart rate.

"You're so fucking beautiful," I said.

He kept his eyes on me but continued to run his wet lips and tongue everywhere until I could barely see straight. If I hadn't already come once tonight, I would have popped off immediately, and I took a moment to glory in the fact I was able to last long enough to enjoy this.

When he sucked me deep into his mouth, I moved my hand around to cup the back of his head, trying my hardest not to yank him onto my dick.

He took me in too deep and gagged, pulling off for a moment to catch his breath and then lowering himself again. The warm, wet clasp of his mouth and throat sent me soaring until I choked out his name and came down his throat.

Breaths heaved in my chest as my legs quivered. Zane crawled up my body and kissed my chest, neck, and cheek. "S'okay?"

I grabbed the back of his head and kissed him again, even though the skin of my lips was tender from all the kissing we'd already done. "Better than okay. It was *fine*."

He pulled back and glared, which only made me laugh.

"Now you know how it feels to hear that word."

He let out a *mpfh* and settled down to lie on my chest. His fingers played in my chest hair as we both calmed down from the excitement.

I wasn't sure when I'd ever been this relaxed, this content and ebullient all at the same time. It was blissful...

For about ten minutes.

Zane moved off me with a sigh. "I'd better go clean up." He took a step toward the bathroom, then paused and shifted his weight from foot to foot. "Er... thank you, Bear. I'll see you in the morning?"

I blinked at him. Was he giving me the brush-off?

I sat up and moved to the edge of the bed to watch him go. The pale globes of his ass flared out slightly below his slender waist and back.

He paused at the doorway to the bathroom as if waiting for my response, and I pulled myself out of my daze.

"Oh. Uh, sure. I'll just... go."

Zane nodded and continued into the bathroom, closing the door behind him.

I stared at the closed door for a beat, feeling off-balance and unsure. Was he having regrets? Was this a simple desire not to share a bed while sleeping? Was he scared I was going to expect more from him than he was willing to give?

Was he rejecting me? Or was he worried that I would reject him, and he was trying to beat me to the punch?

What the hell was that?

I wanted to stay and ask him, to press him for an explanation and assure him that I would respect whatever wishes he had, but then I realized he'd already made his wishes clear.

And he wished to see me in the morning. Not tonight.

Not right now.

I stood up and gathered my clothes before making my way to my own bedroom.

It took me hours to fall asleep. For as many years as I'd spent on hyper-alert, I'd never been so tuned in to trying to hear something as I was when I listened for Zane that night.

But he didn't call.

FIFTEEN

ZANE

---

*When brown bears flash an open-mouth grin, it usually means,
"Let's play!" But if they happen to spot a tasty snack—for
example, a camper's sausage—that playful expression is just as
likely to mean, 'Get in my mouth!' Bears are ravenous creatures, and their appetites for their favorite treats are never
satisfied.*
    —Bear Facts for Insomniacs, Episode 7

My hands shook as I turned on the water in the sink and attempted to
brush my teeth. I was feeling completely topsy-turvy and out of sorts.
We'd agreed to hook up for *practice*. Temporarily. But when I'd lain
there with my head on Bear's chest, enjoying the aftermath of our
first practice session, suddenly, a tidal wave of doubts had washed
over me.

I'd realized he hadn't said much about what he wanted and what
he was okay with. He'd *kissed* me after I'd suggested the agreement,

but he hadn't actually *said* much of anything. What if... what if he hadn't felt like he was in a position to say no?

I shook my head at myself in the mirror. No. He definitely wanted it. There was no doubt in my mind he'd been turned on and totally down for the hookup... er, *practice*. He'd said he wanted a repeat. He'd said... he'd said I was beautiful.

And I'd taken those kind words and run with them. I'd erected beautiful imaginary castles in the air in my mind—happily ever afters in which I had a big grumpy bear looking out for me and I was the center of Ryan Galloway's world. I'd done the stupid thing where I'd jumped from a one-night hookup to... well, everything dreamy and rainbow-colored.

A fairy tale.

But that wasn't the way the real world was. In the real world, hookups didn't have to mean anything. Guys fucked, exchanged happy orgasms, and went their separate ways. They didn't... necessarily... demand cuddles and beg the other guy to stay all night.

Did they?

Certainly not when they'd just agreed to a temporary agreement of sorts.

So I'd been an adult. I'd done the mature, expected thing. "See you in the morning!" I'd chirped while sauntering off to...

I spit out a mouthful of paste in the sink and closed my eyes with a groan.

Second-guess. Perseverate. Worry. Obsess.

No wonder Bear didn't push back when I ended the night. No wonder he didn't beg to stay. I was a child. I had no idea what I was doing.

I was the very definition of awkward, acting like I'd never freaking kissed a man before.

But the reality was, when Bear's lips brushed against mine, I'd felt like maybe I hadn't ever *truly* kissed a man before. Because this was different. Ryan Galloway's kiss put everyone else's to shame.

I let out an embarrassing sound, something between a whimper and a frustrated sigh. For a man coming out of a very long dry spell, Bear kissed like a master of seduction.

After rinsing my mouth and washing my face, I opened the bathroom door, half hoping—okay, full hoping—he'd still be waiting in my bed, ready to laugh with me about my silly behavior.

He wasn't.

I crawled onto the bed and hurled the big duvet back up to cover me. The scent of Bear lingered on the sheets, and I inhaled like a dental junkie on laughing gas.

My phone buzzed on the side table, and I rolled over to grab it.

Unfortunately, it wasn't Bear.

LANDRY

Do I want Don Angie's Chrysanthemum Salad or the Peanut Chicken Salad from American Bar?

Just get the Pinwheel Lasagne and be done with it. We both know that's what you really want.

LANDRY

Can't. Runway show in Paris next week.

Wait. I thought you were already in Paris?

LANDRY

No. They changed it again. Fucking assholes. I leave day after tomorrow.

Then those salads aren't your friend either. Get the Sesame Chicken Salad from Little Beet.

My mouth watered, remembering some of our favorite places in New York. I hated that I'd missed visiting there.

The reminder of the target stamp and subsequent email threat was enough to seriously harsh my post-double-orgasm vibe.

LANDRY

> You slammed with work? You want to meet up for salad? If you get the lasagne, I can have a bite or twelve.

I stared at the screen as I realized I'd never told the guys I was skipping New York.

> I'm not in the city. Change of plans. Sorry.

LANDRY

> Are you still in Barlo? Everything okay with Gran?

> All is well. I'm in a tiny town in Europe. Long story. But also, I forgot to ask if we're going to Majestic for Christmas. You still good with that? Dev said we can all stay with them and start settling into our own rooms in his and Tully's place.

LANDRY

> Europe? How very unspecific. Why?

> I'm thinking about getting an extra guitar to leave in Majestic so I can have one there in case I ever visit unannounced.

LANDRY

> Mr. Fine is being Mr. Mysterious. What's going on?

> No mystery. The team is being extra cautious before the next leg of the tour by parking me in the middle of nowhere to rest.

It wasn't the truth, but it also wasn't *un*true.

LANDRY

> Hmm, mysterious vacation with Grumpy Bear in… Europe.

My stomach tightened at the mention of Bear, but I ignored

Landry's reference to him.

I'm working on a new song. Enjoying the peace and quiet. It's nice.

Or it had been. Until a literal year's worth of frustrated longing for my bodyguard had exploded into a giant forest fire of need and want... and overthinking.

LANDRY

Nice.

I closed my eyes and let out a breath. Leave it to fucking Landry to be provoking.

It's late here. I'm going to sleep. Get the lasagne. You can afford to enjoy yourself, even if you're a little bloated on the runway.

I still had no idea why Landry killed himself to stay runway ready when he was already a billionaire, but then again, people would say the same about me if they knew about the money I'd made with the brotherhood.

LANDRY

Kiss that big, beautiful bodyguard for me.

His message was nothing but a tease. He'd have no way of knowing I'd actually done it and that I hoped (and planned and dreamed) of doing it again as soon as possible.

But still, my cheeks lit on fire, and I scrambled to think of a way to respond that wouldn't tip my hand.

"You can just... not respond," I warned myself before forcing myself to toss the phone back on the nightstand.

I blew out a breath and tried to calm down, but memories of Bear —of his possessive mouth, his talented tongue, and his gorgeous bear-sized cock—flooded my brain.

The bed was simultaneously too hot and too cold. Too hard and too soft. Too smooth and also itchy. I'd become freaking Goldilocks... except I was actually wishing for a Bear to come and share my bed.

Even after I turned on my podcast, it took forever for sleep to come, but when it did, it was deep and peaceful.

Until I awoke the next morning to the sound of something metal being thrown against the side of the house. I froze in place, suddenly demanding my sleep-fogged brain make sense of the noise. When I heard a muttered curse, I called out.

"B-bear?"

The rule was for me to stay in place or hide if I ever thought I was in danger. Bear or someone else on my team would come. Was that what this was?

"Zane? You awake?"

I moved to the edge of the bed and started to climb out. "Yeah? Did something happen?"

"You okay?" This time, his voice was close, just on the other side of my door. "Can I come in?"

I stood up and opened the door for him. He was dressed in workout clothes, his cheeks pink and his hair wind-blown like he'd just come back from a run. He didn't look concerned, so I forced myself to chill. "What happened? It sounded like someone threw something at the house."

The air was cold outside of my duvet cocoon, so I reached for a nearby sweatshirt to pull on over my pajama bottoms.

"No, shit. Sorry. That was me. I dropped a pan on the floor. I was..." He looked a little sheepish. "I was going to cook you that spinach breakfast casserole you like."

I stared at him. "Gran's breakfast casserole?"

He pressed his lips together and nodded before looking down at my bare feet. "I read an article last night that said spinach is good for your voice. It's rich in nutrients like magnesium and potassium, which fosters healthy mucous membranes."

That was what he'd been doing after he left me last night? My stomach filled with sassy little butterflies. "You worried about my voice, Bear?"

His eyes flicked up to mine and back down to the ground. "Sure. I mean, always. So, anyway, I got out the pan to brown the sausage, but then I remembered I... uh... don't know how to cook."

I swallowed the laughter that wanted to come barreling out.

This guy.

He was so freaking nice. He liked to act like a grumpy bear, but he wasn't. Not at all.

I reached out and grabbed the hem of his shirt, yanking it so he had to stumble closer to me or risk ripping the shirt. "That's the nicest thing anyone's done for me in a long time."

He stumbled toward me and put his hands on my hips to keep from knocking me over. I let out a breath of relief at having his hands on me again. "I didn't actually do anything, though," he admitted. "Maybe it's the thought that counts?"

I nodded and stepped even closer until my chest brushed his. "Definitely. Besides, there's still time for you to do it. I can show you how."

His eyes came up to stare at my lips. "How's your voice today? Sounds... okay?"

I grinned at him, borrowing confidence from the knowledge he would have never offered to make one of my favorite breakfasts if he didn't still think well of me. "Dunno. Have a look and tell me if you see anything off." I opened my mouth and stuck my tongue out, leaning back to expose my throat to him as provocatively as I could.

Just as I noticed his eyes widening in surprise, the horrifying thought occurred to me that, despite a thorough toothbrushing job last night, I might have post-horseradish death mouth.

I snapped my teeth closed without remembering to pull my tongue back in first and then yelped and clapped my hands in front of my face. Tears sprang to my eyes as the pain registered. Poor Bear's face fell as he realized what had happened.

"Zane!"

"I'm okay," I tried to say. "Not that bad."

He shuffled me into the bathroom and sat me down on the back of the toilet seat while he filled a cup with cold water from the tap. I couldn't help but stare at the bulge in his running tights since it was right there at eye level.

"Here. Let the cold water sit on your tongue and see if it helps."

It did. But so did the eye candy. When I finally recovered, I tried to act like the incident was no big deal. "You ready for your cooking lesson?"

Bear tried to hide a smile but failed. "Nice try. Show me your tongue."

I glared at him. "Unnecessary. I'm fine."

His eyes narrowed at the word. "*Fine*. You? Seems unusual. Tongue. Now."

I ran my tongue along my teeth to check for tender spots. Thankfully, the damage was minimal, but I wasn't about to open my mouth at him, just in case I'd also be unleashing morning-after Secret Sauce dragon breath. "Back away," I said with one hand covering my mouth and the other making a "shoo" motion.

He put his hands up and backed away a few paces. I moved to the sink and brushed my teeth for a solid five minutes before wiping my mouth and presenting him with my tongue. "Fee? Fime," I said around my tongue.

His eyes twinkled as he peered into my mouth. "Yes. It looks quite fime. Fime indeed."

Bear shifted his weight, accidentally drawing my attention to the front of his running tights again. I tried not to stare as I cleared my throat. "I should, ah, get dressed. So... so we can eat. Sausage. So we can *cook*. Sausage. And then, um. Eat it. With the other stuff. Mixed in."

He tilted his head at me, his lips now smirking to match the twinkle in his eyes. At least one of us was enjoying ourselves.

"What's happening right now?" he asked.

I want to suck your cock again.

"Nothing," I said in a high-pitched voice, shaking my head to dispel the intrusive thought. "Nothing at all. I'm fine."

"Yes. *Fine*. Excellent," he said drily. "Then I'll wait for you in the kitchen while you get dressed. Sorry about the noise earlier."

"No problem," I said with excessive cheer as I escorted him out of the room and closed the door behind him.

I turned my back to the door and sank to the floor. "Jesus fuck."

Maybe the reason I'd never had a boyfriend in all these years wasn't really because of Noelle's strictures. Maybe Noelle's scary advice had actually saved me from making a colossal fool out of myself in front of men.

Because if this was the way I was around men I liked, I was in a heap ton of trouble.

I took my time getting dressed, mostly because halfway through, I gave up the fight and jerked off in the bathroom to images of Bear's junk crammed in running tights. When I finally emerged from my room, I was much more relaxed and ready to face the day, even though I knew I was sporting a beet-red face.

"So, I chopped everything up," Bear said as I came into the kitchen. "But I didn't trust myself to brown the meat without your help."

The scent of coffee filled the air, and warm sunlight slanted in through the large number of windows in the open space. As I approached the coffee maker, he pointed to a mug already poured and ready for me. "Get a few sips down, but then I need you to help me get this going. It says it has to go in the oven for twenty minutes, and I'm starving."

I did as he said, secretly giddy that he'd made my coffee exactly the way I liked it. It wasn't the first time he'd done it, but the thrill of being cared for never went away. My life hadn't been the kind that had included pampering or spoiling of any kind. Yes, my gran loved me, always had. But she'd also worked hard raising or half raising grandkids, supporting her own kids when they went through stages of high need, and holding down various jobs to keep food on the table.

There hadn't been time, money, or energy left at the end of the day to pamper anyone.

Which was why this simple gesture meant the world to me.

I took the first sip as I began talking him through the process of browning the sausage. He'd already preheated the oven and had everything else prepped on the counter.

"How do you know how to do this stuff?" he asked as I moved around him to hand him various spices and instruct him on how much to add.

"Gran made all of us learn. We had to do our share growing up. She was especially diligent with me and JK since she insisted men needed to be helpful to their wives."

We shared a snicker over that. "Your poor nonexistent wife," he teased. "Doesn't know what she's missing."

"I would have been a hell of a husband," I joked. "Always gone."

"Making millions," he added.

"Always exhausted."

"Beloved by the world," Bear pointed out.

I made a joke to cover my discomfort. "Always dreaming about sucking dick."

He laughed. "Ah, therein lies the rub."

"Poor wife."

"I believe you mean poor Carrie-Beth," he tossed back with a smirk before adding the drained sausage to the rest of the ingredients.

I rolled my eyes. "No."

Bear bounced his eyebrows at me. "You touched her boob once. She's clearly never forgotten. It must have been epic. She's fantasized about becoming Mrs. Hendley and having mini Hendleys ever since."

"Barlos, more like," I tossed out, not really meaning much by it. But the correction erased Bear's teasing grin.

"Yeah, probably. Sorry. I hate that for you."

I shrugged. "I'm used to it. It's fine."

He slid the casserole dish into the oven and set a timer on his phone before walking up to me and putting his hands on my sides. He lifted me up and set me on the counter before pushing between my legs and wrapping his arms around my back. "Why do you do that?"

Bear was so close. So tempting. I wanted to do so many things. Kiss him wildly. Bury my face in his chest and simply breathe him in. Ask him if we could get naked in bed and spend the rest of the day fucking.

Confess that I had a crush on him and fantasized about him being more than my bodyguard.

"Do what?" I asked nervously. Did any of those thoughts show on my face?

"Say you're fine all the fucking time," he growled. "Fucking drives me fucking crazy."

"That's a lot of fucks," I said, hearing the breathy sound in my voice. He was so close. So hot. So incredibly open to kissing and touching me. Why were we talking right now?

His big hand came up to hold my face so he could peer into it. "I said this the other day, but in case you've forgotten: I don't want your *fines*, Zane. I want your real feelings. But here's the thing... I don't think you tell *yourself* your real feelings. I don't think you let yourself have any."

I inhaled a shaky breath. "That's... a lot for first thing in the morning."

And it was the opposite of sexy.

Bear studied me for a moment. "Want me to back off?" He started to pull away, but I grabbed his shirt and held him close.

"No."

He studied me again but didn't say anything. I smoothed his shirt over his chest and stomach as an excuse to feel the ridges of muscles beneath it.

"I, ah..." I looked down at my hand and the smooth performance fabric. For some reason, a trivia factoid hit my brain. "This fabric is called Elustre. It's, um. Environmentally friendly or something. I read an article on it once."

"Zane. If you don't want to talk about it..."

I kept studying the fabric. "I have to be fine, Bear. A lot of people are counting on me."

His hand came up to toy with my hair. I loved how obsessed he was with running his fingers through it. "It's okay to not be fine, Z."

"But I am fine. I *am*."

He stepped closer and kissed the top of my head. "Okay." He started to turn around as if letting it go, but I realized I didn't want to.

I grabbed his shirt again. "Wait."

For as grumpy and commanding as Bear sometimes was, he was also incredibly gentle and patient with me. He exuded a calm I didn't often feel these days.

He stepped close again and ran his hands up my thighs. "Talk to me... and not like I'm someone with expectations of you."

"I just..." I took a breath and exhaled. "I just feel like I've been given this gift. This chance to help people. Help kids in situations like I was in. Help adults like my parents and my grandmother. Because of this job, I get to employ lots of people. Pay them good wages and offer good benefits. I get to give a ton of money away to charity and..." I let out another breath. "How the hell am I allowed to complain or stress or... or want things to be different... when I have everything?"

My throat tightened in fear that he wouldn't understand. That he would think I was entitled. That I was making a mountain out of a molehill.

"And really," I continued nervously, "in the grand scheme of things, I don't have anything to complain or stress about, and I don't really want things to be different... much. Saying I'm fine is about keeping things in perspective. No matter how bad things are for me, they're seriously so much better than they are for almost everyone else in that world. You know?"

He made a sound of disapproval in his throat. "No, I don't know. You're allowed to feel sad and scared and upset. You're allowed to put your own needs first. You're allowed to admit you're tired. Remember that you're a role model to millions, Z. You can show people it's okay to take a break."

"I am taking a break!" I squawked. "I'm going to Majestic for Christmas."

"Good. But it will also be the first vacation you've taken in a year, with the exception of a few days here and there."

"Same with you," I snapped back like a petulant child. "Your holiday visit to Montana will be your first break since you came to work for me."

He nodded. "Not quite the same thing, but okay."

"You work hard, too," I pointed out.

"I sit around and shoot people evil looks while bossing around a diva celebrity," he said, a grin teasing the edge of his mouth. "It's not that hard."

I knew he didn't actually believe I was a diva celebrity, but since being perceived as one was a big fear of mine, my face must have fallen.

"Zane, Jesus Christ," he said, moving a hand up to clasp gently around the front of my throat. Blood shot straight to my dick so fast I almost swooned. "You're the *opposite* of a diva. You never make demands."

My brain went spinning. *I want to demand you bend me over and put your cock in me.*

"Right," I breathed. Sexy images flashed through my mind like paparazzi lights.

"Hell, you hardly even make requests."

I request for you to kiss me. Touch me. Suck me. I request it now. This very minute.

"Uh-huh."

Bear tilted his head. "What are you thinking?"

I blinked at him and pushed the sexy thoughts away. "I'm thinking I would like to eat that sausage," I said.

As soon as my own words penetrated, my mouth dropped open,

and I began trying to explain.

Mistake. Big mistake.

"Not *your* sausage," I clarified. "The casserole sausage."

Bear's eyebrows shot up, and I realized that might have sounded offensive.

"I mean, your sausage also. I definitely want to taste that again. Nothing wrong with that sausage. But that's not the sausage I meant."

His eyebrows got even higher. Did he still have enough forehead real estate for that?

Can I say sausage more than I already have?

I licked my lips before pressing them closed and wishing with all my might that saliva was, just for this one tiny moment, Super Glue.

"You want to taste my sausage, Zane?" His hand was still around the front of my throat, and I felt every fingertip making contact with my skin.

"I don't even know why we got on this subject. I'd rather talk about me being a diva." I locked eyes with him. "About me, uh... giving commands."

He let out a little laugh. "You want to give commands, Z?"

I shook my head, feeling the press of his warm fingers as they took the opportunity to slide up into my hair. Bear stepped closer until his bulge pressed against mine. "No," I breathed. "Not really."

"Didn't think so."

He leaned in so slowly I stopped breathing, turning my face slightly so our lips would brush. But he bypassed my lips and moved his mouth to my ear. "Be patient, little one," he murmured before pressing a kiss under my ear and another behind my ear. "God, you taste so good. Sweet, like honey."

"B-bears like honey," I pointed out as he ran more open-mouthed kisses down the side of my neck.

"More than you know."

I swallowed. "I want..."

My thoughts and words scattered as he sucked on a patch of skin at the base of my throat.

"You want...?"

"You're the worst," I moaned. I moved my hands into Bear's dark hair. "I don't know what I was even saying. You're distracting me."

"Want me to stop?" he offered insincerely.

"You fucking crazy?" I asked, voice hoarse.

"We back to our deal, Zane?"

"Deal?" It was impossible to focus when his hands and mouth were on me.

"You and me, practicing in Norway?"

My brain was officially offline. There was no man on Earth who'd be able to focus with this giant, gorgeous man marking a delicious trail along the collar of their shirt. "Uh-huh."

"Excellent." Bear pulled away. "But not right now."

Just as I was about to snap out a curse at him for teasing me with such cruelty, the timer on his phone went off. I shot it a death glare, which only made Bear laugh as he moved away to check the casserole. My only satisfaction was noticing him adjust himself in his running tights.

As soon as he turned away from me to lean over the oven, I drank my fill of his ass.

He started talking to me about nonsense. Another article he'd read on vocal exercises for professional opera singers. A podcast he'd come across on using steam to pamper your vocal cords before demanding performances. These were all things I'd already heard before from my vocal coaches, but I was touched he'd spent so much time going down a rabbit hole with me in mind.

By the time he served the food onto plates and moved us over to the dining table, I'd calmed down a little.

After all, we had time. This Norway trip was scheduled to last another week—seven glorious days and nights of touching and kissing and experimenting with my very own Bear—and maybe for once, I *would* go all diva. Maybe I'd demand we spend pretty much the entire time naked in bed...

But that wasn't what happened.

SIXTEEN

RYAN

Bears have an eye for natural beauty, pausing to take in the scenery while they search for snacks, but when they get their sights set on honey, all bets are off. They'll climb, claw, and bulldoze right through obstacles for that perfect treat, completely ignoring the view if it means they can get their paws on something sweet. Nature's nice and all, but there's no time for sightseeing when there's honey in the air.
—Bear Facts for Insomniacs, Episode 30

I was pretty sure Zane had been hoping we'd spend the entire next week naked and in bed, and if it had been up to me, I would have gladly indulged him.

But whether the man wanted to acknowledge it or not, he did actually have a multimillion-dollar set of vocal cords. I couldn't, in good conscience, keep him away from his job while also potentially dehydrating and damaging his voice box.

"I want to take you skiing," I said a few mornings later. Yes, we'd spent the bulk of those few days in bed, sucking, jacking, and frotting until we were both hollowed-out shells with more desire than stamina remaining. But being the voice of reason still wasn't easy.

Zane stood in front of the bathroom mirror with a towel around his slim waist, getting ready to shave his face. He'd just gotten out of the shower, and I knew he had plans to lure me back into bed as soon as he downed his first cup of coffee.

The man was insatiable, and I couldn't blame him for wanting to make up for lost time when god knew I wanted the same. If our hands and mouths weren't exploring each other's bodies, we were pretending to work in separate rooms. In reality, I carried my laptop into the sunroom several times with the lamest excuses of "needing more light" or "keeping an eye on him" while he worked on his song-writing.

More often than not, we'd end up making out on the sofa until finally orgasming and forcing ourselves back to work for a little while. It had been amazing... but exhausting.

And then Lou had texted to ask what the fuck we were doing—

> **LOU**
> You've missed your long run for three days.
> You okay?

—and I'd panicked.

> Zane wanted to try cross-country skiing, so we've been training in the home gym. Can you help me arrange for an outing?

Thank fuck the first heavy snow had fallen the day before. Both of us needed some fresh air... and I needed to cool my fucking jets.

It wasn't that I was falling too hard and too fast for my principal. No, that had already happened months ago.

It was that I'd fallen into the silly daydream that we were meant to be together. That Zane reciprocated my feelings and would be open to turning our physical "practice" sessions into an actual emotional connection.

Just last night, as I'd carried a sleeping Zane from the sofa, where we'd fallen asleep in front of the fire after a heavy make-out session, into his bedroom, I'd imagined slipping into bed with him and pulling him right back into my arms.

Instead, he'd done what he'd done each night since our first kiss.

See you in the morning, Bear.

And I'd left him there. Alone.

Which was probably for the best. I'd needed the reminder this wasn't an actual relationship. And he seemed to be sleeping well without me in there. I'd kept an ear out for any cries of distress, but I hadn't heard any. It seemed I was at least tiring him out enough to sleep through any nightmare disruptions.

So that was good.

"Skiing?" he asked, staring at me in the bathroom mirror.

"Yes. Lou and the locals have arranged for us to go to a local trail. A guy just came by and dropped off some rental equipment. You up for it? Let me show you a few things?"

"I've never been on skis before."

"Lie. I happen to know you went one time in college with your friends."

"Skiing in Connecticut doesn't count. Everything was so numb from the cold I bailed out to the avant ski lodge as soon as the other guys hit the lift."

I let out a huff of laughter. "*Après* ski, not avant."

"When you go before you ever hit the slopes, it's probably called avant."

"This isn't downhill," I reminded him. "It's very different."

Zane's phone dinged with a notification, and he grabbed it off the counter and unlocked it. "Yes," he said distractedly. "Much more like running... which isn't my favorite."

I took his phone from his hand and turned him back toward the mirror to finish getting ready. "You love running."

He pulled a face. "I love *having* run. Not the same thing."

"Imagine how beautiful it will be. The sun is shining, and the sky is an impossible blue..."

Zane's semi-bare body was a thousand percent more beautiful, though, and if I stayed here drooling over it, we'd never get out the door. "Dress warmly and meet me in the kitchen. I'll fix your coffee."

I walked out of the bathroom...

And only then did I look down at Zane's phone.

I instantly recognized that the new email had come from the same dummy account as the last creepy message Zane had received, and the subject line? *Missed You.*

Skin crawling, I clicked into it.

To Zee,
I waited for you in New York. Are you scared? If you're
thinking you're safe with him, you're wrong. He's not meant to
protect you. You'll be in my sights again soon enough.
See you soon.
Semper in scopum.

I cast a glance at the bathroom, where Zane had begun humming happily as he resumed shaving, and my stomach churned.

I should tell him about the email... probably. He had a right to know, definitely.

But damn it, the man also had a right to a few days of rest and relaxation. A few days when the world would stop stealing fragments of his peace. A few days without someone using him as a pawn in their schemes.

If I told him about this now, his nightmares would almost definitely return, and his quiet slumber would be a thing of the past.

That thought was enough to make me act. I quickly forwarded the email to Violet with a note asking her to send it on to our cyber people, then moved it into the folder with the Stamper's last message. Without hesitating, I set up a filter that would move any new emails from that address directly into the folder and also forward them to Violet and to me.

I would eventually tell Zane about the emails. Of course I would. But in the meantime, I'd protect his peace and his sweet heart as passionately as I protected his body.

"If you loved me, you'd have brought the coffee in here and delivered it with the bad news about the skiing!" Zane called from the bathroom.

I squeezed my eyes shut and clicked his phone off. *If only you knew*, I thought.

"If you loved me, you'd be excited to try my favorite sport," I called back instead.

———

"I don't love you," Zane grumbled an hour later.

The soft sound of snow sliding under our skis accompanied us as we moved down the trail past several chalets with gingerbread trim and fresh-painted shutters tucked back in the trees. It was a dreamland covered in new powder and set off by the sun and deep blue sky.

I was having an amazing time. My body felt warm and invigorated by the exercise—it had been about a year since I'd been on skis, and I'd missed it. It was a gorgeous day to be out. And I loved that I got to share this with Zane.

Zane had been enjoying it, too... until the poor man had sunk knee-deep in powder after stepping off the trail to take a piss and falling into a low spot. The thermal exercise tights that lovingly cradled his ass were now coated with snow. Wisps of brown hair escaped his yellow wool beanie and tangled in the arms of his sunglasses, and his cheeks were red from cold and exertion.

Zane was always bright and magnetic, but seeing him like this, beautiful and fit, while experiencing one of my favorite things was pretty damned satisfying. He looked disgruntled... and adorable.

It was practically impossible to keep from grinning, but I managed it. "I tried to warn you to use your pole to test before taking a step. You never know what the ground is like off the trail."

Zane glared at me, a pair of laser eyeballs that shone even through his sunglasses. "Yeah, well, some of us aren't professional skiers, *Ryan*. Some of us are meant to be more... *aesthetic* than athletic."

This time, I couldn't hold back my laughter. "Is that right, *Zane Michael*?" When his mouth pursed, I shrugged. "You calling me Ryan is the equivalent of middle-naming me."

He snorted but didn't disagree.

"Besides," I teased, "a true artist could write songs just as easily out here as in the sunroom, especially with all this gorgeous scenery to get your imagination going."

This was patently untrue since Zane had no guitar or notebook, and his hands were occupied with his poles, but I wasn't worried about accuracy when my teasing tone had the desired effect of making him sputter with outraged laughter.

"You know, you're right," Zane shot back breathlessly. "In fact, I'm writing a song in my head right now. I'm just trying to get the lyrics down. What rhymes with *my fingers are frozen stiff*? Ooh, I know!" he went on before I could reply. "*I threw my bodyguard off a wintry cliff!* Perfect. That one's gonna be a banger. Double platinum. Wait and see."

I laughed harder. "There are no cliffs here—"

"It's symbolism, Bear. Look it up. What rhymes with *I left my dignity back there?*" He tapped his lip thoughtfully and gave an exaggerated, mournful sigh. "Probably something, something, *devoured by a polar bear.*"

This playful side of Zane wasn't one I saw often, and Jesus Christ, I loved it. Loved that he finally felt comfortable and relaxed enough to let loose.

I grabbed his arm, pulling him to a stop, and wrapped one gloved hand around his waist. "You know I'd never let that happen. You're safe with me, always." The words came out more serious than I'd intended. Like a promise. Like a vow.

Zane shivered slightly, and his smile softened. "Of course I know. Being here, with you..." He looked around at the trees, the snow, the endless skies. At this moment, it felt like we were the only people in the world. "It's a sanctuary, isn't it? And there's only one *bear* you'd let devour me." He bounced his eyebrows suggestively.

"Damn straight." I grinned. "Thank you for coming out with me. You're doing great, you know."

He returned my smile, and it felt like the fucking trees even stretched and sighed in response. "I'm loathe to admit it, but... I do like it. It's peaceful, and it's a great workout but also... fun? Kind of. Arguably too much snow, but I like the little hops. And you were right about the scenery. It's beautiful."

It was an excellent trail—a long, winding loop recommended by a local ski shop, not too hard and not too boring. Zane was in excellent shape and was able to get up enough momentum on the flats to carry him over the small hills. He'd learned the stride motions well and was his usual eager achiever when taking on something new. There'd only been a few times we'd had to step aside to let others pass, but thankfully, no one had given us a second look.

"I've been enjoying the view myself," I agreed.

Chuckling, Zane twisted at the waist so he could twine his arms around my neck. "Is that so? Because my booty's been feeling the heat of your stare for the last mile or more. You're not fooling anyone with those mirrored shades."

"I'm not trying to."

"It's a good thing you can't see my actual thighs, though. I think they're purple from the chill." He laughed again, and this time, I heard the tremor in it.

"Shit, Zane. Are you that cold?" It wasn't particularly cold *out*, so I hadn't expected our lack of ideal gear to be much of a problem, even after Zane's tumble. But then again, I was a much bigger guy than he was. I hated that I'd been having so much fun I might have over-looked his tendency to get cold quicker.

"A little, but only when we go through the trees."

"We're almost back around to the vehicle. Give me half an hour, and we'll get you warmed up and back home."

He rolled his eyes and pulled away. "Bear, I'm not a delicate flower. I can handle a little cold."

"Take my jacket. I'm a little overheated anyway." It was a lie, but I wasn't about to let him know that. "Wear it or tie it around your waist to keep the wind off of your thighs."

"Bro." Zane stuck his pole in the ground and began striding forward. "If you wanna warm me up, keep your eyes on my ass and help me think of a rhyme for *gonna make you come so hard you see stars.*"

My jaw dropped.

In all my years of practice and training, I didn't think I'd ever enjoyed a morning of skiing so much...

And I suddenly couldn't wait for it to be done.

As soon as we got back to the house, I low-key rushed him inside and straight to the shower, where I turned on the water from the multiple jets before peeling the clothes off him. Sure enough, his thighs were still red, and he was covered in goose bumps despite the heated drive back.

"If you get sick, I'm not taking the fall with Micki," I muttered, rubbing up and down his legs with my hands.

His manager was a wonderful woman, and it was killing her not to be with him right now to make sure he took care of himself, but Violet had decided that the only people allowed to know Zane's exact location were her, me, Lou, and Zane himself.

"P-poor Bear," Zane mocked, despite his shivers. "Scared of Micki?"

"Hell yes. She'd kick my ass."

"She would," he admitted. "Because she'd know the only reason

I'd have willingly strapped on skis was because you convinced me to try it."

I pinched his ass before shoving him into the shower. "Get in there and stop running your mouth, Z. If you aren't fully warmed up in the next five minutes, I'm going to break out that immune-support tea Kenji sent. We'll see who's laughing then."

Zane hated tea, and Kenji knew it. But that didn't stop the guy from forcing it on us every time Zane went on tour.

"There's a very easy way to warm a man up, Bear," he said matter-of-factly. He turned away from me and shook his pert little ass. "What rhymes with '*Getting my pick plucked*'? Hm."

"I cannot wait to hear this song," I teased, secretly thrilled he was giving me unspoken permission to join him in the shower. I began pulling off my clothes. "This must be the lyrical brilliance that made the *Rolling Stone* guy say your songs 'weave a tapestry of raw emotion and inspiring imagery.'"

Zane laughed as hot water streamed down over his hair and shoulders. "I can't believe you can quote my reviews."

I stepped into the shower and closed the door behind me. "Why don't you put your hands on the wall and let me show you just how inspiring you are?"

As soon as he pressed his palms to the tile, I tilted a couple of the water jets to make sure he was still plenty covered by the warm spray.

And then I knelt behind him and spread his cheeks. His hole flexed automatically in response to my touch. "H-hey, what are you... *ohh.*"

My tongue came out to get a taste of him, just the inside of his ass cheek at first, but he could obviously see where I was going with it. I teased and licked and sucked until moving closer in to the whorl of sparse hair around his hole. Fantasies of fucking him, fingering him, stretching him out to ride my cock made my dick hard as fuck. I wanted to stand up and press him into the cold tile, impale him with my cock, and slam into him until he screamed for more.

But he hadn't asked for that. Hadn't implied anal was something he was ready for. I'd been content with hand jobs and blow jobs, but after staring at his ass out on the trail all day, I wanted to finally get a taste of it.

"You okay, Z?"

"Fuck yes," he whimpered. "Don't stop."

I doubled down, sucking on his hole and stretching him with my tongue. His whimpered curses turned into mewling-like sounds of pleasure and surrender. My name in breathy pants as his legs began to wobble.

"Make me come," he begged. "Please, Bear. Make me... oh fuck."

I reached for his dick and slid my hand around it, gripping and sliding it while continuing to eat his ass. His hand came around to clutch at my hair as he came with a broken groan that echoed around the enclosed space.

I stood up and whirled him around, boosting him up in my arms and pressing his back against the wall so I could hold him while he came down from his orgasm. My dick brushed against his hole, making me shudder.

I was tempted to press inside and let him sink down onto me, just a little, but I knew better than to suggest it while he wasn't clearheaded. Instead, I reached around his leg to grasp my cock and shuttled my hand over it quickly while Zane clung to me for dear life.

It didn't take much when the taste of him was still on my tongue and his sweet body was plastered against me.

"Fuck, Zane, fuck!" I cried when the orgasm hit.

"Oh god," he breathed, face tucked into my neck. "That's so hot. I want you to fuck me next. I want it so badly."

I kissed the side of his face, his wet hair, his ear. Anything I could get my mouth on.

"Never done that before," I admitted. "You'd be my first."

His whole body shuddered. "I'm at your service for anything you might need to practice."

I let out a laugh and cradled him in my arms, wanting to hold him close enough to meld our two souls together in a way that wouldn't unravel when we left here in a few days.

After a few minutes, he moved to drop down and stand up. "I really *did* have an idea for a song while we were out there today. If it's okay with you, I want to take some time to work on it tonight."

"Of course. Sure. I'd love to hear it."

His eyes flicked up to me, then away. "Alone. If... if that's okay."

"Oh." I tried not to feel stung. "No problem. I understand. I need to touch base with the office anyway about the... uh..." *The fucking email I hadn't told him about.* "...the updated Amsterdam protocol."

They were also supposed to have an update on Noelle's alibis for the three stamping events, and an update from Boomer about what he'd learned from trailing Bodhi around Dublin.

I began washing quickly so I could leave him in peace, but Zane reached out to stop me. "I didn't mean to hurry you. And it's not like... it's not... I just want to work on this song without feeling like anyone's listening. It's not because I don't want to share it with you. I just don't want to share it with you until it's right."

"I understand. Zane, it's fine."

The word echoed in the enclosed space. Zane's eyes widened. "It really does suck when someone uses that word, doesn't it?"

I tamped down my hurt feelings and plastered a smile on my face. "Artists need time and space to create. I get that. As the Ventdestinians would say, 'May the winds whisper fortune,' and the song you write become your next mega hit." I pressed a quick kiss to his lips.

But as I finished washing and made my way to my own room to find clean clothes, a niggle of worry took root in my chest, and I wished I hadn't brought up superstitious Ventdestine or their winds.

In only a few more days, my time here with Zane in our sex-filled little bubble would be over. I would have to share him with the rest of the world again.

I'd have to relearn how to exist in his space without touching him. Without pleasuring him.

Without being able to ensure his complete safety in a perfectly isolated place.

Giving up a few of my precious hours with him, even for something he enjoyed as much as his music, made me selfishly annoyed. I wanted to spend every minute of this time with him that I could.

Because I had a feeling when winds whispered fortune onto him, they would blow my own happiness to smithereens.

SEVENTEEN
ZANE

Bears are sometimes portrayed as dangerous villains, but nothing could be further from the truth. They have always been curious, playful, protective, gentle, and trustworthy creatures when left to their own devices. Someone needs to get bears a better PR person and demand that those old fairy tales get a rewrite.

—*Bear Facts for Insomniacs, Episode 37*

I'd lied to Bear in the shower. The song hadn't first come to me on the snowy trail. It had been percolating in my head for a while—ever since Barlo. But when I was in his arms in the shower, suddenly, the words had started coming, too, like popcorn kernels over a hot flame.

Pop pop pop.

They filled my head until all I could do was repeat them to myself over and over so I wouldn't forget them.

As soon as I was dressed in comfy clothes, I made my way to the sunroom and closed the door behind me.

My notebook and pen were still next to the guitar stand, so I grabbed them before sitting down on the sofa. I scribbled and plucked chords, playing around with the music until I began to feel it come together. The cheerful melody I'd been humming for days rolled like warm honey over me, melding with the lyrics, easy as breathing. And by the time the song was finished, I was giddy with the secret knowledge I'd written it about my bodyguard.

No one would ever know who the song was about, but suddenly, I wanted to sing it in front of a crowd of tens of thousands of people. I wanted to belt it out and feel the power of the music match the power of my feelings for him, especially after this week.

Part of me wanted the world to know that something inside me had been reborn because of Bear—that tiny shoots of happiness were sprouting up on once-barren stretches of my heart, unfurling like fern fronds in the sunshine, filling the places that had been parched and cracked from years of drought.

At the same time, though, part of me never wanted to share this gift, these feelings, with anyone but him. *That* part remembered my mother telling me that fairy tales were lies.

I'd worked on a song about that this week, too, as a way to exorcise my thoughts and make sense of my feelings—a song I was loosely calling "Broken Fairytale"—but ironically enough, the happy ending I'd envisioned just wasn't coming together.

"Fairy tales promise something that doesn't exist in the real world, Zanie," she used to say. "They make you think good things like that are possible, and so you keep looking for them until... well, let's just say I would have been smarter if I hadn't been looking for the fairy tale."

I'd known at the time she'd meant my father. He'd been handsome and exciting, always showing up with a wad of cash from payday and the offer to go out and "paint the town red." But by Monday... sometimes Tuesday at the latest, the cash would be gone, and so would he.

And she'd be back to working whatever jobs she could find.

Nights at Waffle House. Afternoons at McDonald's. One time, she had a job as a server at our local pizza place. They served beer and had a bar with sports on TVs hung over it. Enough guys from town would hold down the bar to make for decent tips. That year had been my favorite. She'd let me sneak into bed with her in the morning, and we'd sing songs I'd heard on the radio at Gran's house.

She'd told me I had the voice of an angel and a heart two sizes too big. "That heart's going to break into pieces one day, Zanie," she'd say.

And that deep-down scared part of me now worried she'd been right.

This time with Bear was maybe the happiest of my life. But in my experience, happy things didn't last.

In this case, the expiration date was coming in a matter of days.

By the time my stomach started demanding dinner, I'd grown melancholy. The excitement and joy I'd had at figuring out my cheerful song about Bear had drained away like fizzy pop in a broken bottle.

I made my way to the kitchen and began poking around in the fridge, not realizing Bear was sitting right there at the table. When he spoke, I jumped.

"Shit, sorry, what?" I said, clutching my chest.

"I said I was kind of in the mood for a big salad to go with that bread Lou brought over from the local bakery. That sound good to you? I can't cook, but I can chop ingredients for a salad, and there's grilled chicken in there."

"Yeah, good. I can help."

I felt Bear's eyes on me as he joined me in the kitchen and began pulling out ingredients. I washed my hands and busied myself cutting vegetables.

He didn't push me to talk even though it was clear he was concerned, and I appreciated that. But then I wondered if he wasn't asking because he didn't much care—not that he didn't care about *me*.

I knew he did. But because he might not have wanted to get involved in whatever emotional crap I had going on.

He might want to keep things professional... to the extent you can do that with someone's whose ass you ate earlier.

My cheeks flamed as usual as those memories replayed in my mind.

"Did your song go okay?" he asked gently without looking up from the giant bowl he was tearing lettuce into.

"Oh. Yeah. I'm, ah... I'm working on a couple of them right now, actually. The one that came to me today is done. It's a happy song, and I'm really pleased with it. The other..." I shook my head. "Something's not quite right yet. The subject is a little more serious, and the bridge and the final verse need work. Too bad, really. I was thinking about playing that one in Amsterdam, if it was ready."

"That'd be exciting," he said. "Your fans would go nuts if you debuted a new song onstage. But only if it feels right."

Silence fell again. I tossed the bell peppers into the salad and began to slice the red onion. "Tell me about your parents," I said, realizing he didn't talk about his family all that much. "You said the other day that they didn't necessarily know you were gay, and it made me wonder about your relationship with them. I thought you were close."

"We are. I know it seems strange I haven't told them, considering we are close, but..." He shrugged. "I didn't want it to be a thing, you know? A topic of conversation they might bring up at any time. I didn't want awkward moments of my mother casually mentioning every gay kid she knew or my dad showing up wearing a Montanan Pride shirt."

I snickered. "Yeah, they sound terrible."

"They're the opposite of terrible. They're the type to love your face off. They're aggressively supportive."

It made sense. "That's how you became an Olympic-level athlete."

"Exactly. They supported the shit out of me and did everything they could to help me pursue it. To this day I think my brothers and sister are prouder of my medals than I am. My sister has them on display in her house."

That surprised me. "They're not at your place in LA?"

I knew he had a small apartment in Santa Monica, but I'd never been there.

"God no. My apartment is a shit heap," he said with a laugh. "I haven't even finished unpacking the things I do have."

I stared at him. "Why? Is it because you spend too many hours at work? Because I could talk to Violet—"

"No. God, no. And don't you dare talk to Violet. No. I just... I like to explore. I don't hang around my apartment much. When we're in town and I'm not with you, I usually hike the canyon or go for long runs. I go to Topanga. Sometimes I'll try a new restaurant or find someplace with live music. That kind of thing."

"What kind of music?" I asked eagerly. I'd asked him about music before, but he'd always seemed to imply that he liked mine. Maybe he felt disloyal by telling me what he really liked.

"Zee Barlo cover bands," he said with a straight face.

I stared at him. "You are a complete and utter asshole. Tell me the truth."

"There's this place, Pips on La Brea, that does jazz and amazing cocktails. It's the vibe more than the music."

I deflated a little, remembering I was too high-profile to go to places like that anymore. If Bear and I ever had a real relationship, he'd miss out on some of the things he liked.

I sucked in a breath. "What else? Tell me about your sister. It sounds like she rules the roost. You always talk about her like she's the one in charge."

We talked about his family for a while as we continued fixing the meal. I moved around him to pull out ingredients to make a home-made dressing I liked while he chopped up garlic the way I asked.

There were upsides to not going out anymore, and one of them was learning to cook healthier and being able to afford fresh ingredients that made healthy eating taste way better.

And the other upside of doing it was that Ryan Galloway loved my salad dressings and acted like I'd walked on water every time I made one from scratch.

"This is fucking amazing," he said on a groan when we sat down and started eating. "I wish you could move in with me and cook for me all the time."

He didn't stop to hear his own words. If he had, he might have spluttered a clarification he didn't actually want me to move in with him. But since he didn't take the words back, I decided to tease him a little. "We'd have to live in my house, though, because I doubt you have a steam shower or a Vitamix."

He grinned at me. "You're right about the steam shower, but I do have a Vitamix. I got it six months ago thinking I'd copy what you did and make salad dressing."

"You're kidding? Why didn't you ask me for the recipes?"

"Because a guy at the gym convinced me to try making a spinach smoothie first, and once I perfected it, I never wanted to make anything else. Besides"—he shot me a wink that made my stomach tighten—"I can get homemade salad dressing at your place anytime I want. I have connections to the rich and famous."

Now I was jealous of a rando at his gym. "Smoothies can be high in calories."

He looked up at me in confusion, but something in my expression made him smile. "That right?"

I dug into my salad, poking it with more force than was necessary. "I'm just saying. Random gym bros don't always know everything about how to balance your nutrition."

"I dunno, Z. The guy looked *really* fit. Seemed like he knew what he was doing, nutrition-wise."

I crunched the big bite of salad, grateful we'd added jicama so I could attack the harder texture with my teeth. "Yeah, well. Looks can be deceiving. Imagine if I was sitting here telling you about getting self-defense advice from one of the guys at the recording studio. You'd have to wonder whether they were qualified, wouldn't you?"

This was ridiculous, and it was obvious to everyone. I scrambled to change the subject. "Do you believe in fairy tales?"

The record scratch might as well have been audible.

I let out a *heh* sound and tried to change course. "Not... that's not really what I meant." I shook my head. If I couldn't talk to Bear about this, who could I talk to about it? He was literally paid to keep my secrets, paid to keep me from harm. I knew with utter certainty that included emotional harm. "Yes it is. I want to know if you think..."

I hesitated, trying to get my thoughts in order.

"Hey," he said softly, putting his hand on my shoulder. "Take your time. Whatever you're asking, just ask."

I began slowly, explaining what my mom had always told me. "But I think that was her way of trying to temper her expectations," I said. "I don't think she actually believed it. I think she believed the opposite. But maybe she shouldn't have. Maybe if she'd been more pragmatic, more realistic, she wouldn't have fallen for my dad's charm every time he rolled back into town."

Bear's hand smoothed across my shoulder to the back of my neck and cupped it gently. "I think there's a difference between believing there's a better life out there and tossing your responsibilities aside in an effort to win it like it's a lottery or something. Falling for the same false promises over and over again isn't how you get your fairy tale, Z. Hard work, helping others, putting kindness into the world... those are good things. And that's who you are. You're living the fairy tale, Zane. Not because you won it, but because you busted your ass—and continue to bust your ass—for it. And you bring a ton of people with you, but not with lottery wins. You give them opportunities to pursue their own goals and reach their own dreams. And I think that's an important part of this. Everyone's fairy tale looks different."

"And yours looks like opening a winter sports camp, right? Get the kids to like the snow early so they won't become thirty-something delicate-flower musicians who freeze their tails off on the trail?"

"Not at all." Bear smiled softly. "But I'd definitely hammer home the part about using their poles to check depth before taking a leak."

I snorted. "Where did that dream come from? You said biathlon gave you structure... but it sounds like you already had a pretty great family."

He smiled and shook his head. "If I tell you this story, you'll think less of me."

"Not possible," I said.

His smile dropped, and I realized how that could've been interpreted. I shoved his shoulder gently. "Bear. You know what I mean. Tell your story."

"When I was in middle school, I was into gaming. Obsessed. I was that asshole kid who ignored everything else to game. It wasn't just me. My brothers and I played against each other, and one of my older brothers had a friend from school that played, too. We were complete losers, staying up all night, drinking too much soda, and eating too much sugar. Not getting any sleep. Being jerks to everyone around us. Not doing homework. All of that. So my parents decided to send us to this winter sports program. It was after school every day and then all day Saturday—or at least it seemed like it was all day. I fucking hated it."

He exhaled. "Until we got to try the biathlon. The program rotated around a bunch of different sports. One week, we did hockey, one week snowboarding, one week downhill skiing. We even did curling. But when we did target shooting, I learned that all those hours playing first-person shooter games didn't have shit to do with hitting a real target. I became obsessed with learning how to *actually* shoot, but the teacher wouldn't let us do it without the skiing part. As soon as you finished the ski run, you got to shoot. Well, I got real fast at skiing because I wanted to get my hands on that gun."

"You became a gold medalist because you're a homicidal maniac at heart?" I asked with a laugh.

"Pretty much... although now the shooting is pretty boring. Once you learn how to do it fast, it's less exciting. The exciting part becomes mastering your heart rate and concentration to be able to switch from the hard physical effort of skiing to the intense mental effort of calming down and focusing."

He continued to tell me more about his experience and how that program changed his life for the better. "It was a change-maker," he said. "Kind of like the way you talk about your time at Yale. Something you can look back on and say, 'There but for that one thing, my life would be completely different and probably not as rewarding.'"

I nodded. "I could see you doing that one day, you know. You're good with kids." I remembered him drawing his weapon on my cousin and her friends. "Sometimes," I added.

Thankfully, he laughed, most likely realizing what I was thinking about.

We spent the rest of the meal talking more about our experiences growing up. Rather, he told me about his while I expertly ducked any mention of mine outside of a few funny stories from the time after I'd gone to live with Gran full-time.

Thankfully, we were interrupted by a call from Landry. Bear took it as an excuse to go out to the gatehouse to check on Lou while I wandered back into my bedroom to talk in private.

"How's the honeymoon?" Landry teased.

Unfortunately, it was a video call, and I felt my cheeks already heating. "How was your pinwheel lasagne?"

He rolled his eyes. "I've been eating nothing but plants and water. I might as well go on the bottoming tour of Hell's Kitchen. All this prep for nothing."

"Not true. I'm sure you'll get to wear some beautiful clothes. Remember the Jon Stein show two years ago?"

"We had an agreement, Zane."

"Red inflatable codpieces," I continued, trying not to laugh. "They never did catch on, did they?"

"Had they been crafted out of anything other than vinyl, maybe they would have," he muttered. "Stop trying to change the subject. How is your surly bear of a bodyguard?"

I couldn't help but grin. "He taught me how to cross-country ski."

Landry gave me an unimpressed stare. "I can think of way better things he could have taught you, sweetness. Skiing is a waste of all that... brawn."

"He, uh... he..."

I wanted to tell someone what we'd done. What *I*'d finally done. But I wasn't sure what the protocol was for our current situation.

Landry's eyes popped open wider. "Girl. Spill the tea. Spill all the fucking tea right this minute. Tell mama what that big growly bear did to you, boo."

"Who said he did anything?" I squeaked.

Landry fluttered a hand in front of his long throat. "Oh my merciful heavens. That man touched you. Tell me every sordid detail, or I will find the two of you, and then I will ask him to account for his actions."

"It's not like that," I said quickly. "You make it sound like he did something inappropriate or unwanted. I assure you it was very... wanted."

"But certainly not appropriate," he stated drily. "That man is your employee, Zane. Have you ever heard of the Me Too movement? I'm surprised at you."

"Me?" I squawked. "First of all, he doesn't work for me. Secondly, you act like I pressured him into something. Does Ryan Galloway seem like the kind of guy who can get pressured into anything? Give me a break."

I huffed and added, "Besides. He wanted it. Trust me. He wanted it plenty."

Landry burst out laughing. "And what did you do to slake his want, hmm?"

"Okay, but I need your advice. And you can't tell anyone, especially Bash or Silas because they'll lecture me."

"Not true. They're true love converts now. They'd support you in your efforts."

I squawked again. "True love? Who said anyth—"

"Fine, skip the love part and tell me the nasty part. I'm listening."

I let out a breath and tried to calm down. "Kenji's right. You're a provoking shit."

Landry's teasing grin fell. "Kenji can fuck right off. I provoke him because he begs for it. The man needs to get the stick out of his ass."

Yeah, those two were *definitely* involved, and I desperately wanted to know the details... but not right then. "Sorry, my bad," I soothed. "Besides, now that Kenji got accepted into that retreat, I'm sure he'll come back refreshed and relaxed. Maybe it'll help him realign his chakras or whatever."

Landry's forehead crinkled. "What retreat?"

This was so not the point. "The one hosted by that guy Kenji's obsessed with. You know the one I'm talking about. Kenji listens to all his podcasts and reads his books for mindfulness and focus. I think he's an acharya—a guiding light—but I can't remember his name..."

"Chaska Inira," Landry muttered. "Fucking know-it-all."

"Uh-huh. I'm sure. Can we move on? Advice? Please?"

Landry flicked his hair over his shoulder. "Of course. I don't care about Kenji or his Peruvian healer. Like, at all."

"Right. Anyway, here's the situation with B-*Ryan*." I cleared my throat. "We hooked up."

Landry blinked sarcastically, if such a thing was possible. "You don't say. The way he ran to comfort you during your nightmare and looks like he wants to rip my hands off with his meaty paws anytime I happen to touch you gave me *zero* clue this might happen." He held his hands up to the camera and turned them back and forth. "If I didn't like you so much, Zane, I'd never risk these beauties in the presence of your growly lover boy."

"Okay, but like... it isn't actually... There are no feelings. No... no *love* with the lover boy. It's just sex. Temporarily. While we're here in No—nowheresville. And when we leave here, it'll be over. That was what we agreed. Back to normal. Bodyguard, principal. That's it."

"*Right.*"

I cleared my throat again. "But like... what if we didn't? What if I told him I wanted it to continue after No-nowheresville? What if I wanted to... keep, um..."

"Fucking the big, beautiful man who practically lives with you?"

My heart rate skyrocketed. "Yeah. That. But, like... it would be wrong. Right? And it wouldn't go anywhere, so what would the purpose be?"

"Well, some could argue the purpose was for fucking *fun*, Zane. Some people simply fuck for physical release and pleasure. Take me, for example. I fuck without feelings. It's the easiest way to stay free. Keep your options open. Not be tied down."

Something about his words seemed overly nonchalant, but maybe he was just exaggerating to make a point.

"What... what if I wanted to be tied down?"

Landry's lips quirked up. "Tell the big growly bear that's what you want, and I'm sure he'll whip out a book on knots, sweetheart. If he needs recommendations, let me know."

I rolled my eyes. "Can you be serious, please? I really..." I exhaled. "I really want to keep messing around with him. I... I can keep it casual. I can... stay free."

His smile dropped. "You? Not a chance. You'll end up having feelings. I mean, I'm able to keep that shit locked down. But you're a softie. And when feelings start getting involved, things get complicated. You'll find you try to get his attention all the time, doing crazy shit. You'll worry constantly that he's not as into you as you are to him. Maybe he'll be too laser focused on his job or... or focused on some random Peruvian faith healer. Or maybe he'll just lose patience with your bullshit after a while. And then where do you find yourself? Not in a good place, my friend. Not in a good place." He sucked in a breath. "That's why Uncle Landry's mantra is fuck only for fun. F-OFF."

I opened my mouth to ask about the Peruvian thing, but he continued talking.

"And the money is a complication. I mean, look at Bash and

Rowe, and Silas and Way, and even Dev and Tully. It's not easy explaining that you have a billion dollars to someone who's had to work his ass off all his life. And *secrets*. Christ, the *secrets*. How do you tell him you've been keeping a huge secret from him without him thinking you don't trust him? You can't. And if you don't tell the secret, it will continue to keep you apart. But that's probably a good thing, which is why... F-OFF. Less complicated." He ended with a shrug.

This was confusing because I was ninety-nine percent sure he was talking about Kenji... but Kenji already knew our financial situations intimately. What other secrets was he talking about?

I refocused on my own problem... which was more than enough to deal with.

"B-*Ryan* already knows about my money. I mean, not the money from ETC, but the money from my music career. It's not really that different. And as for the secret of founding and selling ETC..." I shrugged. "He wouldn't expect to have known before now. We haven't shared that kind of personal information. So... you think it's fine if I keep messing around with him, even after we leave No-nowheresville? We just... F-OFF indefinitely?"

My stomach twisted at the idea that what I did with Bear was fucking only for fun, that it wasn't serious and didn't carry any emotional connection. That didn't feel right. It didn't feel accurate, but it also didn't feel *enough*.

"You and Ryan?" Landry snorted. "Definitely not. You're incapable of not caring about someone, Zane. You're like... a giant squishy heart walking around unprotected in the world without even a rib cage to protect it."

I clenched my jaw. "Everyone seems to think I'm a tiny newborn baby who needs to be protected from the world. It's annoying as fuck, Landry. There's a difference between being weak and being kind."

"That's not what I meant."

"Then what did you mean?" I recognized I was being snappish, but I hated the idea that I couldn't look out for myself.

Landry had witnessed the night I'd woken up from a nightmare screaming for Bear, and that was humiliating. But I didn't like being perceived as someone who needed coddling... and what was worse was worrying it was actually true.

Ryan Galloway was someone who valued strength, endurance, perseverance under pressure. I didn't want to be the opposite of that. Someone who was weak. Who ran screaming at the slightest fear. Who wanted to hide away from danger.

"I meant that you love with your whole self, Zane," he said hesitantly. I could tell he was trying to choose his words carefully without sounding condescending. "That's one of the things we all love about you. You have a giant heart. You want to believe the best of everyone. But it also leaves you vulnerable to being taken advantage of. Of being hurt."

"I'm going to tell B-*Ryan* about the money. About ETC."

I expected him to argue. At the very least, I expected a reminder that only life partners were privy to that information and that Bear was no such thing to me.

His actual response surprised me.

"Can we talk about your new speech impediment? Or is the man's name *Bryan* all of a sudden?"

I paused, unable to admit the truth even though we both knew it.

"Babe," Landry said gently. "You already have feelings for your bear. You have for a long time."

I sighed. "I do," I groaned. "It's so ridiculous, but I like him so much."

"Then why don't you tell him?"

"Because! If he knew I had real feelings for him, he'd stop our deal. Things would get awkward because he'd know that I wanted more. We'd never be able to go back to bodyguard and principal. And then he'd leave. He'd ask to get put on someone else's detail, and I'd never see him again. I can't... I won't risk that."

"What makes you think he wouldn't want more, too? He cares about you."

I let out a frustrated sound. "He cares about keeping me safe. It's his job, Landry."

Landry's laugh startled me. "You're not wrong. He does care about keeping you safe, and it is *technically* his job. But, Zane... when that man looks at you, he's not seeing a job. You're more than a job to him. You have to know that."

Yes, I did know he cared about me as more than his principal. We'd become friends, at the very least. But was it possible he could think of me as more than friends? If not now, then maybe someday?

"Talk to him. Tell him how you feel. But use small words and a sharp tone. According to that silly podcast of yours, bears respond well to commanding tones. If he rubs his scent on you, you'll know he's agreed to keep you—"

I shook my head. "Goodbye, Landry."

He grinned. "Good night, Zane. And genuinely, baby... good luck."

I made a sound of agreement before ending the call... but the truth was, there was no way I'd be brave enough to talk to Bear about real feelings.

The very idea stressed me out so much that I hid in my room to avoid being weird and awkward around him.

But while I was lying in bed, staring at the ceiling, I started thinking about what Bear had said earlier. About how I was living a fairy tale not because it had just *happened* but because I'd *worked* for it. Everyone's fairy tale looked different, he'd said. But I knew exactly what my own fairy tale might look like, if I were brave enough to reach for it.

I reached for the pad of paper in my nightstand and scribbled some notes about the bridge of "Broken Fairytale"—the section of the song that provided the emotional shift from the beginning of the song. I was pretty sure I'd gotten that part down, but even after my eyelids began drooping, I wasn't entirely sure how the song should end.

I fell asleep worried about being the exact thing I feared: being someone weak and anxious who preferred to hide rather than stand up for himself and what he wanted. Who lived in a broken fairy tale because he wasn't brave enough to mend it.

And maybe that's why I ended up having nightmares again.

EIGHTEEN

RYAN

In many Native American cultures, bears are celebrated as spiritual guides that walk with you in your dreams. For tribes like the Lakota Sioux and Ojibwe, bears symbolize strength, wisdom, and healing. Dreaming of a bear? It might mean you're being offered a bit of bear-level protection or a little nudge to connect with your grizzly inner strength. In short, if a bear strolls through your dreams, embrace him!
—Bear Facts for Insomniacs, Episode 42

Zane never came back out of his room, so I took it as a signal that he wasn't up for more "practice" that night.

Maybe that was a good thing. Maybe we needed a break from spending so much time naked together.

I busied myself in my room with several sets of crunches and push-ups before moving to lunges and squats. This was a mistake because once I was done with the impromptu workout, my heart rate was up, and I was nowhere near being able to settle down to sleep.

I returned a phone call to my sister about Christmas at her place and shot a text back to the family chain, letting them know that Zane had confirmed his appearance at a music festival in Bozeman next summer, and I'd be able to get them passes to it if they found places to stay.

Violet had sent me a message regarding the email I'd forwarded earlier, but only to tell me she had no additional information yet. She'd also provided some more detail on the alibi information from Noelle she'd relayed earlier. I found it very suspect that Noelle had been out of town during both the LA and San Diego stamping events, but then again, Bodhi hadn't been at his home in New York, either. Since both of them traveled for their jobs, eliminating them from any suspect pool was damned near impossible.

Boomer reported that Bodhi had "almost definitely" been playing a gig during the San Diego incident, and he was waiting for confirmation. He'd also said Bodhi was "Really nice. Like, *really* nice. I just don't like this guy for the Stamper." Needless to say, this was not the facts-based report I'd expected from serious, stone-faced Boomer, who'd been in the protection business nearly as long as I had.

I wondered what the fuck had gotten into him... and hoped it would get the fuck *out* of him since I really needed him to focus on this.

One of Zane's over-the-top super fans had posted all over social media about being at the three stamping locations, so Violet's team was also looking into her. The only other suspect we'd been able to come up with was Isaiah Harbin, but it was hard to believe an NFL player would go that far for a PR stunt.

The man had also posted about Zane on social media, but it was in response to the various attempts to ship the most famous out gay NFL player and out gay rock star. There were entire forums, chat servers, and social media accounts dedicated to speculation about the two of them and how hot it would be if they got together.

Thankfully, Zane had no interest in the guy, and Harbin himself seemed more interested in chirping at the media about it than actually following up on it.

I tried to avoid looking at the social media sites, but I couldn't resist it. Zane himself had been warned against posting anything because of our location, but I noticed Micki had posted generic promo graphics on his account to keep it active.

When my scrolling turned into its usual time-suck, I forced myself to put my phone down and try to get some sleep. The house was quiet with the exception of the dishwasher running in the other room. Snowflakes caught the moonlight outside my window since I'd forgotten to close the blinds. I watched them fall lazily and thought back to our time on the trail together.

The memories of Zane's earnest efforts and his willingness to try new things made me smile. It was a good memory to think back on as I drifted to sleep...

I awoke with a start to the sound of Zane crying out my name.

I was on my feet and flying across the floorboards in seconds.

"Bear!"

"Shh, I'm here." I quickly moved to the bed and felt around for him in the dark until my eyes adjusted. Unlike in my room, the shades were closed in here, blocking out the moonlight. "Baby, I'm right here."

I slid onto the bed and pulled him into my arms, making sure he was still well covered by the duvet so he didn't get cold. He was shaking, and while I was pretty sure it was from fear, I wasn't taking any chances. The house was chilly, and Zane tended to run cold on his best day.

He heaved in a big, desperate gulp of air. "I got another email. It was bad. About you."

For a moment, I thought he meant he'd somehow found the Stamper's message from earlier and cursed myself for leaving it in an email folder where he could find it.

"Or maybe they said something about my mom," Zane went on.

His voice was muffled against my T-shirt, and he sounded groggy. "I don't remember."

I realized with a pang that he was probably referring to his bad dream. "Baby, are you awake? Was this in a dream or in real life?"

His breath hitched. "I don't know. It was... real, I think? They said I missed the deadline. I missed the show. And they were going to make sure my mom wasn't there, and you weren't there, either."

He was definitely still half-asleep, but just to be sure, I reached for his phone on the bedside table and got him to open it for me before scrolling to his email app.

Just like this morning, my conscience warred with my need to protect him. Technically, Zane knew Violet had someone monitoring his email remotely, and he'd already consented for the security team to have access to it, but I still felt a little uncomfortable invading his privacy.

"Can I look at your email, Z?" I murmured.

"'Course. Nothing you can't see. You can look at all of it. Tell you everything anyway. 'Cept about the money, but I told Landry I was going to tell you. I can't F-OFF," he said sadly. "Don't wanna keep secrets. I'd hate if you got a Peruvian healer just 'cause I had a billion dollars."

He was making less than zero sense, but his mention of a billion dollars reminded me of his odd question when we were playing the horseradish game. Did he have more money than people speculated? Did it matter? There came a point with obscene wealth where the zeroes no longer seemed to make much difference.

There was nothing new in his email other than the typical work messages, several photos from the trip to Barlo from his gran, and an email from Bodhi about meeting up for lunch before the Amsterdam show.

The email from Bodhi was friendly enough. Definitely nothing in it about his mom. And the email from Gran didn't mention his mother, either.

I set the phone back down on the nightstand and wrapped my arms around him. "It was just a dream."

"Thank god you're here," he said, sounding relieved. "I'm sorry for being scared."

My heart lurched. "Never be sorry for being scared. What does that even mean? You can't help it if you're scared, Z. Bad dreams are scary."

He sucked in a shaky breath. "I wish I could tape my mouth closed. Or that you'd sleep with a white noise machine so you couldn't hear me."

I brushed his hair back so I could try to see his face. He tucked his chin to keep from looking at me.

"Z," I said softly. "If I called out for help in the night because of a bad dream, would you expect me to apologize for being scared?"

He shook his head but didn't say anything.

"And if I felt comforted by your arms, would you think less of me?"

He lifted his face up to glare at me. "Of course not."

I lifted my eyebrows. "The prosecution rests, Your Honor."

He settled back down against my chest. "I don't want to be the guy you have to protect."

I wanted to laugh, but I sensed that would be the worst possible reaction. "That's upsetting, considering I enjoy protecting you."

"I'm not talking about your job. I want you to... to care for me."

His words hit me with a jolt, filling me with a kind of vulnerable hope I wasn't prepared for.

"I'm not talking about my job, either, Z," I confessed to the top of his head. "I do care about you. As a friend. As a good human. As a... as a man." I swallowed, backing away from any further verbalization of my feelings. "And keeping you safe is something I have a vested interest in. I want you safe because I want you to be happy. And, self-ishly, I want you to continue to be in my life for a very long time."

His arms tightened around me. "That's... nice."

I let out a soft laugh. "At least you didn't say *fine* this time."

"I care about you, too." His words were quiet, but I felt the truth in them, and it warmed me from the inside out.

I pressed a kiss to the top of his head. "Are we going to talk about how the nightmares started after the Stamper showed up?"

"No, thank you," he said in an attempt to make it sound light and singsongy.

"I think you need to see someone, Zane."

"Been there."

I ran my fingers through his hair. "Micki can find you a therapist who's good and discreet. The legal team can get all the NDAs in place—"

"It's not that."

I waited for him to explain.

"It'll bring up a bunch of other shit I don't want to talk about."

I wanted to push, to convince him it would be a healthy choice, and even if it got worse before it got better, it would get better. But I knew this time of night wasn't the time for making that argument. I'd give him time to think about it, but I'd bring it up again with him and soon.

"Tell me about the money," I said instead, hoping to throw him a softball. "You said you were going to tell me about the money."

"Oh." His fingers caressed the neck of my shirt. "I'm... I'm rich."

"You don't say."

"You sound like Landry," he said with a smile before pushing up to sit cross-legged in front of me. Light from the hallway was just enough to illuminate the outline of his head in the dark, but I wanted to see him. I reached over and turned on the light after warning him I was doing it.

"Really rich," he elaborated. "And not just from music."

Zane had sponsorships like most celebrities did. That was no surprise. Confusion must have shown on my face.

He hesitated. "I... I earned my first billion before I signed my first recording deal."

I blinked at him. "How?"

And had he said *billion* with a *B*?

His face lit up. "We did this amazing project at Yale," he said excitedly. "Me and the brotherhood. That's how we became so close. We came up with this technology we called the ETC that communicates between emergency vehicles and stoplights to cut down on accidents and assist the response rate. It's saving lives, Bear. It's incredible what it's been able to do. Other students are studying it now. The results, I mean."

"Holy shit," I said, shocked at his story. "Ventdestine implemented it while I lived there."

"Yeah, so that was us. Me and the guys. Bash, Silas, Dev, Landry, and me. We came up with it and then created an incubator company called Sterling Chase to represent ETC in its development and sale. We sort of hid our involvement by having Sterling Chase handle the transaction, and then the five of us agreed to keep the secret because... well, it's kind of a long story, but Dev's brother died and—"

"I know that part," I cut in. "You told me the other night. He's the friend who bought his brother a sports car, and the kid wrecked it."

"Yeah. It made us realize that the money kind of brought with it a lot of pressure to..." His shoulders slumped. "To help others and spend it in certain ways. So we realized it would be easier if no one knew exactly how much we had or where it had come from. Everyone just assumed we were making big money as corporate consultants in the city."

I couldn't even imagine him trying to pretend to be a corporate consultant. Zane without his music would be like a painter without a colorful palette.

"But now you're in that situation anyway," I said.

"Yeah, but at least the guys aren't. I can handle it."

I wanted to roll my eyes at his typical way of looking at things selflessly. Instead, I grasped his chin and met his eyes. "It's okay to resent it. It's okay to feel like the money is a burden. It's okay to get angry when people put pressure on you." I leaned in and kissed him on the cheek. He was so fucking sweet and kind and selfless. I wanted to burn the world down if it would make it easier for him to live in it. "It's okay to be selfish sometimes, Z."

He looked at me out of the corner of his eyes and then looked away. And then his eyes flicked over to me again. "What if I want... what if I want to keep sleeping with you after we leave Norway?"

My chest felt simultaneously too small and too big. The air didn't know where to go when I inhaled. "You're not *sleeping* with me *now*."

Where the fuck did that come from?

Zane's eyes widened. "Because I didn't want to wake you up with my nightmares! I was embarrassed, and I knew if you shared a bed with me, you'd notice if I had bad dreams. I was trying to... I mean, we said it was *practice*, right? I don't want you to think I'm... I'm needier than I already am."

"Are you kidding? Zane, Jesus fuck. You're not *needy*. I care about you. I want to know when you're having bad dreams! I would never want you to suffer through them on your own. How can you think I'd rather be in my own room if you were having bad dreams?"

"I don't want you to have to be a nightwatchman! I want you to be in my bed because you want to be there for me, not because you need to keep me safe."

I grabbed his face and kissed the fuck out of him. How else could I get him to understand how badly I wanted him?

"I want to be in your bed because I want to kiss your fucking face," I bit out between hungry kisses. "Touch you everywhere. Fuck you. Hold you. Watch you come undone. And, yes. I want to keep you safe, too, damn it. I want to comfort you when you wake up scared. That's what people do when they lo-*like* someone."

I was confessing too much, but I couldn't hold back. I didn't want him to second-guess my motivation or doubt for one minute that I truly wanted as much of him as I could get.

Within moments, the conversation was forgotten as we lost ourselves in each other's kisses and exploring hands. I pulled off his clothes and shucked my own until I was lying half on top of him, rutting against his leg like an animal.

"I want to fuck you," I confessed, moving my fingers down to his hole to tease it.

"Yes," he breathed. "I want that, too. So much."

We'd already made liberal use of the lube in his nightstand drawer, so I leaned over and fumbled for it. We'd already had a conversation about STI protection, but I stopped anyway and asked him if he was comfortable going bare, although I didn't have a condom, and I had to assume he didn't, either.

"Yes, god yes."

My slick fingers sank into his tight heat while I watched his face to make sure he wasn't uncomfortable.

"You like me," he said, meeting my eyes. He acted like it was a surprise.

I opened my mouth to tease him, to tell him he was alright, but then I realized he was having a moment of vulnerability and insecurity. I took a breath. "I more than like you, Zane. And I'm not ready for this to end."

His smile was a mix of relief and happiness. "Same."

He reached out to caress my face, tracing my eyebrows and cheekbones while I continued to stretch him. "You're going to tell me if it's too much," I warned. "If I need to slow down or stop."

His eyes narrowed. "I'm not a child."

"I should fucking hope not," I growled, pressing farther inside his body and making him gasp. "Do you want me to stop giving a shit about your comfort?"

"No." His expression softened. "I like that you care about me."

I brushed the messy hair back from his face and leaned in to kiss him while finally lining myself up with his hole. He pulled his legs back and held himself behind the knees, but his insecurity reared its head again. "Tell me what to do."

His tight channel strangled my cock as I began to push inside. Instead of answering him, I groaned and closed my eyes as he finally relaxed enough to let me in. "Fuck, Z. Fuck, you feel so good."

"Bear," he whimpered, squeezing around me. "Oh god. You're fucking huge."

I opened my eyes and watched him while pulling back and pushing forward and encouraging him to relax and keep breathing. "That's it, baby. Just like that."

I'd never done this before. Never felt the tight clasp of a hot body around my cock. The fact that it was Zane, that it was the man I loved more than anyone else in the world, overwhelmed me. I clenched my jaw against the onslaught of emotions.

"You're doing great," I said, barely hanging on to my self-control. Belatedly, I realized his own cock had wilted a bit with the intrusion. I reached for the lube and managed to slick my hand up again before shuttling my fist over his cock. It hardened in my hand, causing him to gasp. His breathing stuttered. He let go of his legs and wrapped them around my back, reaching down to grip my hand and move it the way he needed.

Heat buffeted the space between us. Sounds of shallow pants and muffled grunts and cries filled the air. Zane's face was flushed and his eyes glazed. How was it possible he could be even more attractive to me? How was it possible for me to love him more than I already did?

"Want you to come, baby," I begged. "Need you to come. I can't..."

His grip jerked over mine, and I felt the warmth of his release on my fingers. The tang of it filled the air and mixed with the scent of our combined sweat.

Being like this with him was intoxicating, overwhelming.

"Baby, fuck." Now, I was the one whimpering as my orgasm grabbed hold of me and took over, sending pleasure rolling through me as I thrust deep inside him. I groaned and shuddered, trying not to fall on top of him and almost failing.

Zane's hands moved to my back, my neck, my shoulders as he pressed kisses into my upper chest and throat.

I opened my eyes and stared down at him, only seeing the tangled mess of hair on top of his head and the reddened tip of his nose as he nuzzled into me.

My voice came out scratchy and gruff when I spoke. "Tell me I can stay."

He looked up at me. "You're not weirded out by all the things I told you?"

"Maybe I like being weirded out," I teased, moving off him so I didn't squash him. "Maybe I want more of it."

He grinned up at the ceiling before turning his megawatt smile on me. "Maybe that makes you the weird one and not me."

The lucky one, I thought. *I'm the lucky one.*

We eventually moved off the bed to clean up. His sheets were a tangled, sweaty mess, so we moved into my room and settled back into a clean bed.

Zane snuggled into me, resting his head on my shoulder and teasing my chest hair with his fingertips.

After a while I confessed to overhearing him talking to Kenji about charitable contributions early in my time with him. "I knew you had lots of money, but I also knew you were generous. Since then, I see it everywhere, even though you try to hide some of it. At the time, I worried because you seemed to be giving it all away."

"I do give it all away," he said. "All the ETC money anyway. The Zee Barlo money I'm more selfish about."

"Selfish," I said on a laugh. "Yes, that's you. You give away hundreds of millions of dollars, and you're selfish. Zane, *fuck*."

He flicked my nipple. Hard. "Hush. You know what I mean."

"No. I don't. I truly believe you think of yourself as selfish. I can see the way it bothers you to say no to people like JK and your uncle."

He paused for a moment. "I just... I feel like it's not fair. Lightning struck twice for me, Bear. How is that possible? It was like winning the lottery twice. And I don't need all of this money. I could give more of it away, and I don't. I saw a thing on Instagram about how childhood poverty can make you hold on to wealth. It can actually fuck up your money management stuff because you become too risk-averse."

He glanced at me before looking back at his hand on my chest. His voice was quieter when he spoke. "I stashed fifty million dollars away in a bunch of different cash accounts no one but me has access to. I won't let my money managers touch it, and it drives them up a wall. They keep telling me I'm losing money every day that cash isn't invested. I know they're right, but I just can't... I can't let someone else control all of my money. What if something happened? What if I lost everything and couldn't afford to help Gran anymore?"

I thought about his rich friends, the fact his music would continue to bring in significant royalties for the rest of his life, the reality of his existing talent and determination to make more. But I didn't say any of those things. He was right. This wasn't about reality. It was about fear.

I tilted his chin up. "You have enough money to be able to afford to spend some on a security blanket, Z. No one else gets to decide what you do with that money, and there are worse things to do with fifty million dollars."

"There are better things to do with it, too," he said with a self-deprecating smile.

"Maybe, but peace of mind is worth something."

I stroked his hair while I thought about an aspect of this subject that was bothering me. "I want you to consider reframing this in your mind. You talk about lightning striking. I get that there was luck involved. There's a little bit of that, maybe, especially in terms of being in the right place at the right time. But, Zane... You worked your ass off in both cases. You and your friends came up with an idea and actually followed it up. You researched a need and filled it. You developed it and got it to market. That wasn't lightning striking. And in your music career, you work incredibly hard. You dedicate all of your time and energy to your music and your fans."

"I know I work hard. But I wouldn't have been able to afford to pursue music full-time without having the ETC money. I was lucky.

People like Bodhi aren't. They have to work a full-time job while trying to get traction. It's different."

"I get that, I do. But the way you talk about it reminds me of the Ventdestinian superstition. There was a faction in the royal guard that blamed me for Asger's death. Since fortune had selected me to protect him, I'd messed with fate by leaving. It made me feel guilty. Like his death was, at least a little bit, my fault."

Zane looked up at me. "That's not fair. You weren't even there. It was the fault of the assassin. And maybe the existing security detail or conditions at the naval yard. It sure as hell wasn't the fault of someone who was thousands of miles away in another country!"

I nodded. "That's what I'm saying. We all have agency. We're not at the mercy of the winds. Not completely, anyway. Bodhi has been on the professional circuit for years now. He's had just as much opportunity in the past few years to make it big as you did in the beginning. He doesn't have the same skill, the same drive—hell, maybe it's just the combination of charisma, talent, and looks, who knows? My point is, if lightning struck, Zane, you were there to harness it."

Zane settled back on my chest with a *hmph*. "You don't feel guilty about the king's death, do you?"

"Not really. Not enough to consider going back. I was ready for a change. And now, here I am, naked in bed with the world's hottest rock star. So I can honestly say, no regrets. Ten out of ten, would do again."

He huffed out a laugh, his breath warm on my skin. After a few minutes of comfortable silence, Zane spoke again. "I don't want our time in Norway to end."

I kissed the top of his head. "Same."

He looked up at me with wide, warm eyes. "Tell me things won't change when we leave here, Bear."

My stomach tightened with anxiety. We both knew I couldn't make that false promise, so instead of speaking, I kissed him.

And tried to make real promises without saying a word.

NINETEEN

ZANE

Bears are masters of picking up on danger and know when they're being hunted. With their incredible sense of smell, they can detect humans—or predators—from miles away. When a bear gets even a hint that something's off, it moves with remarkable speed and strategy, ready to defend its life or its den. It's a foolish creature indeed that gets between a bear and his home... or his honey.
—*Bear Facts for Insomniacs, Episode 19*

By the time we left Norway, I'd almost forgotten about the Stamper threat. There hadn't been any new emails, and Violet's team had spent two solid weeks ensuring there was increased security at each event.

The first two cities went by in a blur. All extra VIP fan access had been curtailed to viewing me from more than arm's length away, and backstage access had been severely limited to only essential crew who'd passed stringent background checks. They were also required to wear double-sided ID badges at all times that tracked access in various areas so Bear's crew had a record of who was where and when.

The final verse to "Broken Fairytale" had come to me the morning after Bear and I made love for the first time—a sweetly perfect and poignant coda that gave the whole song new meaning and inspired me to change the name entirely—and I'd found time to practice it and my other new song with the band before possibly debuting them at one of the shows.

And every night, we went back to a hotel suite, where Bear made a point of messing up the bed in his bedroom before sneaking into mine. Several nights, I'd been too tired to do more than cuddle, so Bear had frog-marched me into the shower, hand scrubbed me while I swayed on my feet, and then poured me between crisp sheets before curling around me protectively.

I'd even slept like a baby, too deep for dreams good or bad, which was enough to convince me that regardless of my romantic future with Bear, I'd need to hire him as a bedmate for the rest of my life.

All in all, things were going well. Really well.

So well that as Bear and I sat across from one another in the limo as we made our way to the venue in Amsterdam, I had the sudden fear they were about to go terribly wrong.

Fairy tales happen, I reminded myself. *Be brave enough to believe it.*

"Zane? Are you listening?"

I snapped my eyes open and found Bear watching me closely. "Sorry. What was that?"

"I said, no touching anyone. If someone gets close, press the button on your watch. It will record a time stamp and buzz me."

His face was serious, and I could tell he was in full-on grizzly mode. If I made light of his warning right now, I would not be rewarded with a smile. I would be growled at, and he'd only start the lecture again.

"Aren't you going to be with me?" I asked.

"I'll be in the room, but Lou is taking point so I can make sure the royal family and their security people have everything they need. I won't be beside you the whole time. That's why I need you to listen to me right now, okay?"

"Yeah, fine. I'm f—"

Bear's eyes darkened at the word, so I quickly corrected myself. "I mean, yes. I understand. This is the same protocol we've been doing all week."

"But this is the first VIP event where people will be interacting with you," he said in a way that made me think he'd said it already while I'd been lost in thought. "People will want to shake your hand. They will forget the no-touching rule and do it out of habit."

"Right." I nodded. "Okay."

"You need to keep your hands in your pocket and shrug. Give them that cute, innocent look and say you're not allowed to shake hands as part of your health protocol, to stop the spread of germs and keep you healthy for the tour. That's the excuse we're using. All of the VIPs have been briefed about it, but like I said, they'll forget." Bear rubbed at the back of his neck, a sure sign that he was more agitated than he let on. "Lou is more permissive than I am."

I knew exactly what Bear wasn't saying—that it was killing him to know he wouldn't be hovering over me, ready to throw down at the slightest provocation. I didn't like it, either, to be honest. But I hated seeing Bear so worried even more.

"Got it," I assured him. Then I added, "I can hug people like Bodhi, though, right?" My voice trailed off as I saw the fierce look on his face.

"Bodhi is on the suspect list, Zane," he snarled. "Fuck, no. No touching anyone, *especially* Bodhi."

I wasn't sure if it was jealousy or fear for my well-being making his eyes so wild, but I couldn't deny how good it made me feel.

"Can I touch *you*?" I asked in a voice low enough not to be overheard by the driver and Boomer up front.

Bear's eyes heated, but he stayed on task. "You stay within arm's reach of me, Lou, Boomer, or Dennis. If you need to take a leak, one of us goes with you and clears the room first. You need to accept a gift or something, keep your hands in your pocket and nod at one of us to accept it on your behalf."

I stifled a sigh. "These are mostly people we know. It's an already vetted group. Can't we just...?" I swallowed and looked out the window when I noticed his glare.

He was right. I knew that. I just didn't want to look like a prima donna at this event.

"Do you know if the whole royal family is coming?"

His face finally softened. "Yes. Gerhard and Gisella are bringing the kids. They're desperate to meet you."

"I'm excited to meet them, too." I leaned toward him. "Can I eat the food?" I asked as a way of breaking the ice further. "I'm kind of hungry."

He rolled his eyes. "Yes. You can eat the food. The security around the catering is plenty strict, thanks to the royal guard."

I hadn't thought of that. "With the royal family there, I'll be doubly protected. Those are your people, right?"

"*You're* my people. They'll be busy protecting King Gerhard, not you."

"You know what I mean. It'll be a safe space. Even safer than usual. The safest."

He moved his foot until it pressed against mine. "Please don't let your guard down, Zane."

Bear's voice was less gruff, almost pleading.

There was nothing I could say to that but "Okay."

He nodded before looking back down at his phone and typing a message to someone. "Lou's at the entrance. She's going to walk with you while I greet and escort the royal family in." He rolled his eyes again. "Ventdestinian protocol. I'm the highest-ranking member of Violet's team here, so naturally, I'm the one who has to escort them."

I personally thought it had more to do with the royal delegation knowing and trusting Bear… and the fact that it was impossible not to feel safer with Ryan Galloway around.

When we arrived, a crowd of screaming fans greeted us and pressed in from the sides of the street. My nerves resurfaced since Bear had insisted on reminding me that there was an actual threat against me.

I hated that. Hated thinking one of my fans wanted to scare me.

So I pushed down the fear and waved through the closed window in case they could see through the tinted surface.

The limo slowed to pull into an alleyway blocked off by security personnel and orange barrels. Once we were past them, the crowd disappeared behind us, and we approached a roped-off side entrance to the arena.

Lou and several other people met us, escorting me inside and down a long hallway to the room reserved for the VIP reception.

Several musician friends were already there, and I quickly approached them to say hello. Bear had been right—it wasn't just their habit to shake hands or hug; it was mine, too. I tried to remember but failed in several instances. Buck Olson was there, and we hadn't seen each other since playing a festival together a couple of years ago. He'd brought his new wife, who I was eager to meet. Alana Vasa was also there with her wife. She had agreed to play the violin at the show tonight, and I couldn't help but give her a big hug in thanks since she was interrupting her solo tour to play with us.

There were several familiar faces—big-name politicians, celebrities, and friends—and I immediately felt more at ease. VIP receptions like this were well vetted ahead of time since access was limited. Thankfully, I'd remembered Bear's rules and had stepped back to a respectable distance with my hands in my pockets before he came in with the royal family.

The king was a tall, robust man in his late forties with a ruddy complexion and salt-and-pepper hair. Trailing after him was a veritable entourage, which shouldn't have surprised me. Bear was busy talking to the king himself, but another tall man walked on the other side of him. He was closer to the king's age and wore the all-black uniform of a member of the royal guard. I recognized the same kind of simple medal insignia on his sweater that Bear had worn in old pictures.

Bear stood taller as he made the introductions. "Your Highness, I'd like you to meet Zee Barlo. Zee, this is His Royal Highness, King Gerhard of Ventdestine."

The king held out his hand. I glanced quickly at Bear, whose nostrils flared but who gave me a subtle nod. I shook the man's hand and expressed my pleasure at meeting him. "I'm honored to have you here at one of our shows."

His smile was polite but formal. "Thank you for having us, and thank you for keeping Ryan out of harm's way. May the winds continue to whisper fortune upon you."

I was startled by the tone of his greeting. Bear had told me many times about Ventdestine's mystical beliefs, but hearing it from the horse's mouth was strangely off-putting. "Er, thank you. And you as well." I suddenly remembered the somewhat recent loss of his father and scrambled to correct myself. "I'm very sorry for the loss of your father. Ryan speaks very highly of him."

King Gerhard nodded. "Thank you. He was a good man and a great leader. We are lost without him."

A lovely woman in a butter-soft pink pantsuit stepped up next to him and placed her hand on Bear's shoulder. "Ryan, my apologies for allowing myself to be detained. Would you mind continuing the introductions?"

"Of course, Your Highness. This is Zee Barlo. Zee, this is Her Royal Highness, Queen Gisella of Ventdestine. And these are their children. Prince Auden, Prince Isak, and Princess Carina."

The three faces that popped out from behind their parents were almost comically starstruck.

The oldest teen, Auden, who seemed high-school-aged, stared and flushed a deep, mottled red. The middle one, Isak, grinned like a kid who'd stolen some candy. And the royal daughter blinked rapidly like she had something in her eye.

I glanced at Bear, who was busy trying to hide a smirk.

Queen Gisella grinned. "Maybe the three of you would like to say hello to Mr. Barlo?"

The younger two began speaking at once, thanking me rapidly for allowing them to come to the show. Auden only continued to stare. The king turned to speak with Bear and the royal guardsman while Gisella asked me questions about the tour and mentioned their plans for a large-scale royal tour of America next summer.

"The children were so little last time we were there," she mused. "Now that they're growing up, I want them to have a deeper understanding of other cultures." She reached up to run a fond hand over Auden's head. Though the prince didn't pull away, his eyes flashed with typical teenage annoyance at the insinuation that he was still "growing."

I stifled a smile and turned to him directly. "So, Auden, do you have any song requests for the show tonight? I always save a couple spots later in the set list for last-minute additions."

"Oh! *Oh.* Um..." His eyes shot over to his father before glancing at his mother. She gave him an encouraging smile. "If I could hear you play anything, it would be 'Very Much Myself,'" he said softly. "And anything new, of course, but I don't know if that's something you ever do?"

Ooof. I'd written that song about my coming out. I had a momentary flare of empathy for this young princeling from the country where the winds of fate didn't look kindly on change. "I'll definitely be playing that one and also at least one new one. You'll have to let me know what you think afterward."

Auden gave me a shy smile. "I can do that. I think Kasper has Ryan's email address?"

The royal guard standing with the king and Ryan turned his head. "Did you call me, Prince Auden?"

"No, sir. Only, I thought maybe you could help me get in touch with Mr. Barlo after this. He said I could let him know what I thought about the music."

The man glanced at me with the same detached politeness as the king and nodded. "Certainly. I'd be happy to put you in touch with Ryan, and he can pass your message along to Mr. Barlo."

I smiled. "Awesome. Thank you. When you guys come to the States next year, maybe you can come to a show again. I'd hook you up."

"Really?" Carina grabbed her mother's arm and squeezed. "Mama, can we?"

Gisella laughed. "I'll talk to your father, and maybe we can add it to the list. It's already fairly extensive." To me, she added with a wink, "Disneyland, you know?"

"Yes," Carina agreed. "When Papa went to California and I begged and begged him to bring me so we could go to Disneyland! Have you been, Zee?"

"I can answer that," a familiar voice cut in.

I turned to find Bodhi standing beside us, flashing a knowing grin. He looked so good, so familiar, I opened my arms to hug him without thinking. As soon as the hug was over, I quickly pressed the button on my watch and glanced at Boomer, who'd appeared at Bodhi's elbow. He was glaring at Bodhi with a death stare not unlike the ones Bear gave me when he'd warned me not to do something, which was kind of interesting.

At least this glare wasn't aimed at me, and Bear hadn't seen our hug.

"Better let me tell the Disneyland story," I said to Bodhi with a laugh, remembering the night in question. "You never get it right."

"You just don't like how accurate I am, man," he teased. He clapped me on the shoulder in a friendly gesture before stepping back. Within seconds, Lou had appeared between us, glaring at Boomer for letting Bodhi touch me. She made a show out of handing me a small plate of appetizers. Where the food had materialized from on short notice, I had no idea, but using it as an excuse to put some distance between us had been genius.

Bodhi didn't seem to notice. I could still feel the imprint of his hand on my shoulder, but thankfully, it had been over my clothes. Bear was clearly keeping an eye on him, and I even thought I'd noticed him say something to the royal guardsman, Kasper, before tilting his head at Bodhi.

As if I needed the entire security force of Ventdestine looking out for me in addition to Lou, Boomer, and my own grumpy Bear.

"Zee and I played this gig the summer after our junior year at Yale," Bodhi continued. "It was at a tavern not far from Disneyland. We'd gone to LA that summer to try and get discovered, you know? And we ended up getting some really great gigs. So at the tavern, we met this super-chill bass player who also worked as a cast member in the park. He got us tickets one night and let us stay for this extra hour thing..." He continued to tell the story about how I'd been fine on every thrill ride, but my stomach had revolted on the spinning tea cups. The Ventdestinian kids were riveted to his every word.

A few moments later, the event hostess pulled me away to greet the mayor of Amsterdam and her husband. I gave Bodhi an apologetic glance, but he waved me away good-naturedly. Boomer got called away for some reason, but Lou stayed with me as I was led from person to person around the room. It was a little exhausting, but the compliments not only on my music but on my charity efforts were really uplifting.

"We're looking forward to the fundraiser in Berlin," someone said. "It's quite a lineup."

I nodded politely. "I'm very excited for it. The LGBTQ Youth Coalition is working together with the Marian Foundation on some exciting projects. It's an organization I've worked with in the past, and I'm thrilled to be included in this benefit show."

The room was more crowded than I'd expected. "Lou," I muttered, "I thought this was supposed to be pretty small."

She nodded but didn't look concerned. "Apparently, the royal family invited some additional dignitaries. Don't worry, they were fully vetted by the royal guard. Boomer's making sure no one else gets past security."

"If you guys are okay with it, I'm okay with it," I said, even though the crowd was getting large enough to make it nearly impossible to avoid being touched. People brushed past me here and there, and it became difficult to keep my eye on Bear. The king seemed to be monopolizing his attention by introducing him to the prime minister, the mayor, and a few other people I didn't recognize.

Throughout it all, though, I felt his eyes on me. I knew he was making sure I was okay. And because I wanted him to be okay, too, whenever I caught him looking, I offered him a reassuring smile.

After that, everything happened in a blink.

Someone bumped me from behind and gasped a feminine apology. I turned to see Queen Gisella glaring down at her shoes in disgust. "Zee, I'm so sorry. I'm wearing impossible heels today. But I wanted to get a photograph of you with the children before you leave, if that's okay?" Her own security officer, a quiet but attentive woman, was murmuring into an earpiece for someone to arrange different footwear for the queen before the concert. While she was distracted, Gisella grabbed my arm and pulled me toward the side of the room where the royal teens were. I glanced back to make sure Lou was with me but saw someone had stepped between us, blocking her way.

"It's fine," Gisella said, "Hedda is..." She looked over her shoulder and realized her own protection officer was also separated from us. Several people had filled in the gap in the crowd we'd come through and were now standing between us and our security detail. Gisella sighed. "She'll catch up. She always does. I'm sorry my husband has taken Ryan away. He and Kasper are probably trying to lure him back to the royal guard for an obscene amount of money again. I told them no amount they offer will be enough. When Ryan left, he said he wanted to be in the US, closer to his family. That's important."

Before I could process what she was saying, Noelle appeared out of nowhere and reached for my hand. "There you are, Zee! Ryan asked me to find you and escort you to him."

I was so surprised to see her there I didn't know what to say. "Noelle? What are you doing in Amsterdam? How did you get in here?"

She marched through the crowd, keeping one hand on my back while shooing people out of the way with the other. "Sorry for the lie. I haven't actually talked to Ryan. I'm here consulting with the Ventdestinian team about some upcoming PR stuff, but I saw you without your protection and wanted to help." She took a breath. "I also wanted to thank you for releasing me as your publicist... but that's not important right now. Here's Lou." She pulled me even with her until I was standing beside Lou again.

My head spun with Noelle's words as Lou reached for her earpiece to signal Bear. Bodhi approached and put his hand on the back of my neck to pull my head out of the way of the high tray a server rushing by was carrying behind me. "Hey, you okay? Boomer sent me over to keep an eye on you, but it looks like Noelle rescued you first."

He and Noelle exchanged polite smiles.

I shook Bodhi off and pressed the button on my watch. Suddenly, it felt like everyone was touching me, and Lou was distracted, talking to Ryan on her ear mic. "I'm fine," I told Bodhi. "It just got a little chaotic there for a second."

"I know. It's super crowded, and everyone wants a piece of you. Boomer's too nice to say so, but I think he's been really stressed about this." He gave a little sigh. "Anyway, I'm glad I found you again. I wanted to grab a minute to talk to you about this girl I met in Dublin. I think you need to hear her music, Zane."

I glanced at him in confusion. "I don't understand."

"I know. And I'll email you the information, if you want, so you can check it out in peace, but she reminds me a lot of you. Grew up like you did, has incredible talent on mandolin, and her voice is like fucking *wine,* you know? I was hoping you could talk to her. Encourage her to pursue it."

Bodhi knew me well enough to know I appreciated discovering new voices, but I was too overwhelmed right now to consider what he was saying. "I'll... I... you can..."

Noelle seemed to pick up on my stress and asked Bodhi to go get me a glass of water. As soon as he walked away, she put her arm around me and murmured reassurances. "Where's Ryan?" she asked, patting my back gently as she looked around. "Isn't he your primary?"

I pressed the button on my watch again. I wanted everyone to stop touching me. Bear was right. This was too much.

Where was Bear? How the heck had Noelle gotten approved to be here? Why had Boomer asked *Bodhi,* of all people, to keep an eye on me? Why was the queen of Ventdestine acting like I was her new best friend?

Lou nudged Noelle away and put her hand on my lower back to steer me toward the door. "I've got this. Mr. Barlo needs to get ready for the concert now. Please excuse us."

"The princes and princess wanted to take a picture," I said, feeling overwhelmed. "I don't want to disappoint them."

Suddenly, I saw Bear hurry into the room, looking around frantically until he spotted me. He was followed by Kasper and the king, who were both talking as if nothing in particular was wrong.

And nothing *was* wrong. I reminded myself I was at a VIP reception in a room full of well-vetted people. There were cameras everywhere and security personnel from my team and the Ventdestinian royal guard.

It was fine. I was fine.

Bear finally arrived at our small group and slid his arm around me protectively. "Lou, go find Boomer and lock down the route so we're clear to get to the dressing room." As Lou left, he turned to me. "We need to go."

"I want to take a picture with the royal teens first," I said, forcing myself to seem unaffected. If he knew how not-fine I was, he'd whisk me out of there embarrassingly fast, possibly even causing a scene. "And then we can go. Okay?"

He studied my face. "Did you eat the fish?"

It took me a minute to remember our code word. "No. I didn't want any. I'm fi—uh, full. I'm *full*."

As usual, when I was lying, Bear didn't look convinced. In fact, he looked like he was two seconds away from spiriting me out of the room, and damn the consequences.

"Oh, Ryan," King Gerhard said. "One other thing I wanted to mention to you, if you have a minute?"

Bear hesitated, glancing from me to Gerhard and back, clearly torn.

"Please," I said in a soft voice hopefully only Bear could hear. "Let me take the picture, you talk to the king, then we'll go."

Bear nodded reluctantly. He exchanged a wordless look with Kasper, who seemed to immediately understand what Bear was asking. With the slightest of nods to Bear and a friendly smile for me, Kasper smoothly stepped in and set a hand on my back to guide me over to the queen.

Gisella apologized again for bumping me *and* for pulling me over without waiting for security to escort us. "You'd think at my age, after twenty years in a public role, I'd have learned to look before I leap, but no." She shook her head at herself. "No better than my children sometimes. Thank you for agreeing to take the photo. I remember when I was their age and went to see the Spice Girls. I would have completely lost it if I'd had a chance to take a photo with them."

I posed with the kids while Carina chattered happily about all the American things she wanted to see next summer. "We're going to America next month, too." She pouted. "But no Disneyland."

Gisella rolled her eyes. "We have a brief visit to America in early December since we'll be official guests at the tree lighting in Washington. We're also going to New York—"

"To skate at Rockefeller Center," Auden chimed in.

"And shop at all the toy stores," Isak added.

"You could come with us, Zee!" Carina begged. "We can go ice-skating together and see the big tree."

I smiled at her and shook my head. "I'll be with my friends in Wyoming then. The tiny town where they live has a Festival of the Bells a couple of weeks before Christmas. I'll be playing there and then staying there for the holiday."

Carina turned to her father, who'd walked up to join his family, and grabbed his hand in both her own. "Papa? Can we go to Wyoming for the Festival of the Bells after New York? I'd like to see Zee play."

When the king glanced at me, I shrugged and smiled. "Majestic would love to have you, I'm sure. It's a welcoming town with beautiful scenery and Christmas decorations, and there are plenty of large homes to rent."

King Gerhard pulled Carina into his side affectionately and wrapped an arm around her shoulders. "We will see."

All three of the kids started begging him, but I barely paid attention because Bear had slid up beside me. Just being in his presence, being able to smell his clean scent and feel his warmth, made my tense shoulders drop several inches.

I offered the royals a friendly wave goodbye and thanked them for coming before allowing Bear to lead me out of the room. Just before we reached the door, little Carina came barreling into the back of me, throwing her arms around my middle. "Thank you so much for everything! This is amazing. I can't wait to tell all my friends I met you in person. Can we take a picture just you and me?"

I smiled and put my arm around her. Her little arm came around my waist as we posed for a silly-faced selfie and then a smiling one. I handed her phone back before saying goodbye again and letting Bear lead me out. Lou stepped into place beside us once we reached the door

As soon as we were down the long hallway and on the elevator to another level, I let out a long exhale. "That was hectic."

Bear's jaw flexed, but the only sound he made was a deep grumble in his chest.

I wanted to lean against him, wanted to bury my face in his chest and inhale deeply to center myself, but I couldn't. Lou was busy typing something into her phone, and Bear... Bear seemed to be busy trying to keep from murdering me for all the unnecessary touching I'd done.

As soon as the elevator stopped, Boomer was waiting to escort us to the dressing room so I could prepare for the concert.

"Hey, Boomer? Why did you ask Bodhi to keep an eye on me?" I wondered. "I mean, it was no big deal. He's a sweet guy, and I... I don't actually think he has anything to do with the stamping, but—"

Bear shot Boomer an incredulous look. "You did what?"

Boomer shot Bear a guilty look. "He's clear, Ryan. I told you, he almost definitely had an alibi for San Diego—"

"And I told you, I don't care about *almost* definitely—"

"I got a callback tonight from the owner of the bar where he was playing. The guy has Bodhi on security cameras. He was in Reno that night. A hundred percent."

Bear fumed, clearly not ready to let it go. "He could have paid someone—"

Boomer shook his head insistently. "He didn't. I checked Bodhi's financials, and he's not in a position to be paying anyone for anything. Besides which, he's not the type. I told you—"

"That he's nice? Yeah, I got that. Would you stake your career on it?" Bear demanded.

"I'd stake my life on it," Boomer shot back. His cheeks went pink. "I mean, yeah, I'd definitely stake my career on it. You get to know somebody when you're tailing them like I've been doing, and Bodhi's like... he's like Snow White with the animals in the forest. He's not just a pretty face and a great musician. He's like... pure all the way down in his core. He's earnest and kind. He finds musicians who need a hand up, and he gets them contacts and stuff. And he's not obsessed with Zee. If anything, he's trying to help people like Zee does."

I blinked. I wasn't sure I'd heard Boomer string that many words together in all the months I'd known him... and definitely not that soulfully.

I bit my lip to hold back a laugh. I wondered if Bear noticed the heart-eyes bugging out of Boomer's face as he talked about my old friend or if that was just something I was attuned to, given my feelings for Bear himself.

"Told you," I said to Bear, relieved to know for sure. "Bodhi's a nice guy. One less person on the suspect list."

We got to the door of the dressing room, and Boomer went in first. Once the space was clear, he came back out and nodded to Bear. Bear gave Boomer a look that said he wasn't ready to forgive him for trusting Bodhi with my safety, then ushered me in and closed the door behind us, leaving Lou and Boomer out in the hall, guarding the door.

I immediately stepped into Bear's body and mashed my face into his chest. His arms came around me and banded tight.

"You're shaking," he said, moving his hands to the collar of my shirt. He pulled it open just enough to peek on my neck and shoulders and let out a grunt of satisfaction at finding it free of marks.

"I was." I shook my head. "I'm okay now. Truly."

"Did something happen? Gerhard and Kasper pulled me aside to give me some, ah... paperwork. When I came back, you were surrounded by people."

Even though I didn't want to pull out of his embrace, I wanted to see his expression when I asked the question I couldn't stop thinking about. "Are you going back to Ventdestine?"

"What?" His eyes narrowed. "Who told you that?"

My stomach twisted, and my heart gave a little lurch. I pulled completely out of his embrace and moved over to sit in a chair in front of the dressing table mirror. Bear put his hands on his hips and waited.

"Gisella mentioned the king and his security guy were offering you a lot of money to go back to them. Obscene amounts, she said."

"Oh." His posture relaxed. "Yes, they did. And no, I'm not."

I knew he'd taken the job in Ventdestine originally because they'd offered him a good salary. I also knew the label wasn't paying him enough for all the hours he spent guarding me, and I wasn't allowed to supplement it. All I could do was request he be compensated at their highest established level.

"I would understand," I began haltingly, "if—"

"Zane. Are you saying you *want* me to go back to Ventdestine?"

"What? No! Hell no. Of course not. I just..." *Feel nauseous. Want to chain you to the wall. Want to tell you how I really feel.* "Wanted you to know I would support you. I..." *Say it, Zane.* "I want you to be happy."

He crossed his big arms in front of his chest, eyes narrowed. "And you think my happiness lies in Ventdestine."

"No! I... I don't know—"

A knock on the door snapped our attention away. "Zane, your stylists are here," Lou called.

Bear kept his eyes on me as he called back. "He's ready. I'm going to need you to swap out with me, Lou." He lowered his voice so only I could hear as the door opened and Lou escorted the stylists in. "I'm going to make sure the royal family find their seats and have everything they need. I'll see you after the show."

I clenched my jaw and nodded. I was a professional, and I would remain professional. There was a show to put on, and I was going to rock the fuck out of it.

Bear's face softened as he reached out to brush my hand. "Break a leg. You got this. And Zane?"

"Huh?"

He leaned in and brushed my ear with his lips. "My happiness isn't in Ventdestine."

As he walked away, I turned in the chair to let the stylists have their way with me, my head spinning from his words. What had he meant, exactly?

Thankfully, all I had to do was sit in the chair and get worked on. I was already dressed, so all that was left was hair and makeup touch-ups.

Carlo moved around me in his typical silent but energized manner, applying bronzer to my neck, chest, and arms, while Kim chatted my ear off about the Bear Facts podcast she'd turned me on to as she turned my flat, tangled hair into something stage-worthy.

I let my mind drift off, wondering if I had the guts to sing the song I'd written for Bear. The song was light and fun—the melody still was —but the lyrics revealed way too much about my feelings for him.

I wanted Bear to know how I felt, to show him how much he meant to me, but I also didn't want to put him on the spot. Not that anyone in the audience would know the song was about him—though Landry might've guessed if he was here—but Bear would know.

I pressed a hand to my stomach, trying to summon my courage, to reach out and grab the fairy tale I wanted... but something about tonight felt off. I was too unsettled to risk that song.

Kim's pleasant chatter and Carlo's periodic giggle in response to it cheered me up. By the time I heard the crowd outside screaming for the opening artists, I was ready to hit the stage and give a great performance.

Lou and Boomer escorted me up to the backstage area, where I met with the opening band coming off the stage and thanked them for performing with us tonight. I quickly told the band we could debut my *other* new song, which I'd renamed "Mending Fairytales"... and then it was time to take the stage.

The only thing missing was my bodyguard.

TWENTY

RYAN

---

*Bears might seem like lumbering tough guys, but they've actu-
ally got some strong emotions going on! Scientists studying
bear behavior have noticed that bears show curiosity, playful-
ness, and affection toward each other. Beneath all that thick fur
and muscle, bears are a little like giant, furry softies with
serious heart.*
—Bear Facts for Insomniacs, Episode 6

I was angry at Kasper for monopolizing my time and implying I
should be prioritizing the royal family's security over Zane's. Ventdestinian royal protocol had been a pain in the ass when I was actually employed by the royal guards, but it was utterly intolerable when
I had a job to do and the man I loved might be in danger.

There'd been three new emails from the Stamper since the one
Zane had received in Norway, each creepier and more aggressive
than the last as the Stamper grew more frustrated by their inability
to get their hands on Zane. I was glad Zane had been spared the

turmoil of reading those emails, but replaying them in my mind had made my separation from him during the VIP meet extra torturous.

By the time I was able to extract myself from the king's box and make my way backstage to watch the concert from the wings, I'd mentally lectured the head of the royal guards about where he could shove his bullshit Ventdestinian traditions.

Thankfully, Zane was doing what he always did onstage—he was killing it.

The crowd had lost their minds when he'd walked onstage wearing the T-shirt he'd been photographed in last year while eating Rijsttafel in a place in Culver City. The shirt was heather gray with a stylized bicycle cartoon on the front with comically large tires and a tiny seat in front of a recognizable Amsterdam canal. He'd purchased it on a previous trip to the city, and the resulting social media posts had tagged him an Amsterfan.

It had been the perfect way to set the mood for the show, and now, his set list was knocking them dead.

Gerhard and Kasper's offers to lure me back to the royal guard had made me uncomfortable. Gerhard's entreaties had been personal, talking about how I'd been one of the family and his father had trusted him with his life. He'd mentioned the long-held belief that fate had brought me into their lives, and he truly felt it had happened for a reason.

"The winds put people where they're meant to be, Ryan," he'd said with such confidence. "Trust you were brought to us for a reason, and even if that reason was for my father's protection, it doesn't mean your time with us needs to end here."

It had been so long since I'd lived in a place with those superstitions and odd beliefs that it took me off guard. Kasper, on the other hand, had been more pragmatic. "We need your experience. We need people we can trust."

It hadn't been hard to politely decline. There wasn't a single part of me that wanted to go back, despite the ridiculous amount of money they'd offered. Not only was I happy being back in the States and closer to my family, I was also happiest with Zane.

I wasn't giving that up for any amount of money. And the next time Kasper emailed me a job offer, I might not be quite so polite about refusing.

I quickly typed several messages to Violet, letting her know what Boomer had said about Bodhi and also informing her that Noelle had been here. When I'd checked the VIP guest list, she hadn't been on it. I'd sent Dennis—one of our local guys—to interrogate the security personnel at the entrance to the event to find out how the hell she'd gotten admittance.

As I approached the backstage area, where Lou was waiting and watching Zane, I nudged her. "I'm here. Thanks for holding down the fort. How the fuck did Noelle get into that reception?"

"She said she's here with the Ventdestinian delegation. She's consulting with them on something." Lou shrugged. "I pulled Zane away as soon as I saw him with her, but Ryan... you should know Noelle was actually the one who brought him back to me when Gisella pulled him away to take a picture with her kids. We were separated by the crowd, and *Noelle* was the one who noticed. She could have taken that time to make her pitch to him about hiring her back or whatever the fuck she's been trying to contact him about, and she could have stamped him if she'd wanted to... but she didn't."

That seemed strange, but I didn't have time to figure it out right now. My eyes were riveted on my principal, and my goal was to make sure no one else touched him tonight but me.

"This next one's a new one," Zane began, reaching over to switch out guitars. The crowd went wild, and he laughed. "I thought you might appreciate that. It's... I dunno. Maybe you could say it's a coming-of-age song. I hope you like it. It's called 'Mending Fairytales.'"

As he began to move his fingers gracefully over the strings, I felt the familiar wash of awe and pleasure stream over me as his music filled the air. I'd never heard this one before—it wasn't the light, catchy tune he'd been humming—but I remembered him mentioning a second song, one that was more serious. And as the words unfurled, I realized this was about his mother.

> It wasn't a tower, and you didn't save me.
> The animals were feral, but you let them raise me.
> I needed more, but you didn't guide me.
> I reached for the stars, but you tried to
> Hold
> Me
> Down.
>
> And now you're gone,
> Left in a
> Blissed
> Out
> Haze.
> Left me alone and
> Afraid
> For
> Days.
>
> Some days, it seems kinder
> But then I remember
> The way
> You
> Sang.
>
> Oh, how
> I wish
> You'd
> Stayed.
>
> It wasn't a tower, and you didn't save me.

The animals were feral, but you let them raise me.
I needed more, but you didn't guide me.
You went away, and you fucking
Left
Me
Here.

I stared at him as he belted his anger and hurt into a crowd of fifty thousand people. Lou grabbed my sleeve while we stood there, transfixed.

The crowd was stupefied. The drummer hammered each short line with a bass kick drum as Zane wailed the words into the night air. His hair flowed out behind him as he tilted his head back and closed his eyes, singing to a woman who would never hear his words.

Tears sprang to my eyes, and I wondered how many people in that crowd of thousands saw themselves in his story.

And then the music shifted into the bridge, and his voice lightened.

Today, I see clearly
You only whispered your warnings
Out
Of
Fear.

It wasn't a tower, and you didn't save me.
The animals were feral, but you let them raise me.
I needed much more, but you didn't guide me.
A child with a child, you just
Did
Not
Know.

He smiled and opened his eyes, turning for just the briefest moment to find me in the wings before looking back at the crowd with a big smile still on his face.

And now, the sun glances
Off gingerbread houses
And I get to taste all the
Red candy apples
And confess all my dreams to
The welcoming grizzly
And laugh in the wind
While the fairytale happens
And spin in the wild
Broken dreams become mended
And breathe in the air
While my
Heart
Runs
Free.

I couldn't breathe. I watched as he patted his chest as he sang the final three words, and then he flung his arm out, thanking the crowd and turning to thank the band.

The crowd went wild. The noise was deafening, causing Zane to huff out a laugh and turn back to me with a giant grin.

He was so fucking happy. So proud of bringing joy to all of his fans. Of not fucking up. Of being his authentic self. Of living his dream.

I love you.

The words hammered in my throat, begging to come out.

I love you.

I'm so fucking proud of you.

I couldn't say them. Instead, I put my hand on my heart and mouthed, *You're amazing.*

"Holy shit," Lou said. "He's going to make a million dollars off that song."

I laughed. "More than a million."

The rest of the show seemed to pass in a blink. Zane was still high off the success of the new song, but I knew from experience that he would crash and crash hard. After the encores and his final good-nights, he came jogging off the stage, sweaty, smiley, and goddamned sexy as fuck.

I shuttled him through the backstage crew shouting kudos and down the corridors to his dressing room, where I stopped everyone else but the two of us.

As soon as I got him inside and closed the door, he was on me. "Fuck me, please," he said, grabbing at my clothes, my face, my hair. "All I could think about when I saw you in the wings was that I get to feel your cock inside me tonight. No one else gets that, just me. I get to know what it's like to—*hngh!*"

I turned him and pushed him face-first against the door, moving his hands up the smooth surface and growling at him to keep them there while arching my hardening dick against his ass and nipping at his earlobe. "Do not make a sound."

It was reckless and wrong, unprofessional and debauched, but I couldn't help it. Hearing that he was thinking of me, of *sex* with me, while he was performing in front of a crowd of tens of thousands of people was heady as fuck.

I fumbled for the front of his pants and shoved them down before wetting my fingers and reaching under the edge of his shirt to find his hole. He gasped and pressed back onto my hand. "Fuck, Bear. Fuck me. Want you to fuck me right here."

I was too far gone to let rational thought stop me. After opening my pants and pulling out my cock, I spit into my hand. "Don't have lube."

He spun around and dropped down in a squat before slathering my cock with his saliva and sucking it as far into his throat as possible. He gagged as he came off. Then, he grinned at me. "Okay?"

I spun him back toward the door and bent my knees before shoving the head of my wet cock against his entrance. It wasn't pretty, and it sure as hell wasn't slick, but it worked. Both of us were too riled up to care. I reached for his cock and jacked it as I used his hole to get off.

Our panting breaths mixed together under the sound of workers slamming doors down the corridor and people shouting instructions. The arena vibrated with the sound of tens of thousands of people all exiting at once. Thankfully, it was enough racket to drown out the sound of the two of us coming our brains out in the dressing room.

As soon as it was over, Zane said something about a shower.

"Showering at the hotel, remember?" I said, zipping my pants back up.

Zane looked up at me comically from where he was standing with my jizz dripping down his inner thighs. "What?"

I grabbed some tissues from the dressing table and handed them to him with a grin. "Do the best you can, honey. It's part of the security protocol. In and out of the venue as quickly as possible."

He narrowed his eyes at me while swiping ineffectually and then tugging his pants and underwear back up. "Just for that, my personal security detail is going to be personally responsible for cleaning this mess up when we get to the hotel."

I grasped the back of his head and leaned in to kiss him hard before whispering in his ear. "What the principal wants, the principal gets."

His little shiver was the cherry on top of a very unexpected sundae. After straightening up our clothes and grabbing Zane's few personal items from the dressing room, we headed out.

The crowds outside the arena were unbelievable. Zane stared through the limo window as we made our way through streets packed with fans singing and celebrating. The energy of the crowd was magnetic, and I knew it gave Zane a thrill to see it up close like this after a show.

We drove through the city in silence until pulling around the back of the hotel and meeting the security team waiting for us. Once we made it up to Zane's suite, I excused everyone to their rooms or duty stations and closed us up for the night with the security wedge.

Then, I shot Zane a predatory look, which sent him racing off to the bathroom with a squeal and a laugh.

I caught up to him and grabbed him around the waist, pulling him in for another kiss. "That song was amazing, Z," I finally said when I caught my breath. "So beautiful. Are you going to let Gran and Rinny hear it?"

He shrugged. "I mean, they won't be able to avoid it, but I'm not going to make a point of sending it to them or saying anything about it. Gran already knows how grateful I am she took me in, and they both know how bad it was before that. I hope if and when they hear it, they'll realize it's..." He shrugged as he yanked off his T-shirt. "It's part of the healing process. I'm proud of it. And I loved that the crowd loved it, too."

I grinned, loving that I got to be with him like this—just the two of us, relaxing and spending an enjoyable night together talking over the rest of the concert.

Then Zane turned around to drop his jeans...

Revealing a very clear, red-inked target stamp in the middle of his lower back.

And I lost my ever-loving mind.

TWENTY-ONE
ZANE

Bears don't take betrayal lightly. While they're usually calm and solitary, trust is huge for them, whether between mama bears and their cubs or during mating partnerships. If a bear feels threatened or deceived, their reaction is swift, and they'll avoid whoever caused the distress. For a bear, a second chance isn't given easily... so whenever possible, try not to piss them off.
—Bear Facts for Insomniacs, Episode 86

I was walking on air. The show had been a success, Bear had fucked me up against a wall at the arena, and now, we had the whole night ahead of us in the hotel suite.

"Baby."

"Hm?" I asked, reaching for the knob to turn the water on in the shower.

Bear hesitated, but I could see he wasn't playing or flirting anymore. He looked serious.

"Bear. What is it?"

His hands were so gentle on me. He reached for my hips and turned me back around, then traced his fingertips over my lower back.

It took me a moment to catch on, but when I did, my stomach plummeted. "No," I whispered.

I swiveled side to side as if I'd be able to somehow see my own lower back. Finally, Bear moved out of the way so I could see it in the mirror.

Last time it happened, I'd been scared.

This time for some reason, I was pissed as *fuck*.

"No!" I ground out. "No, they don't get to fucking touch me. They don't get to fucking toy with me! Who the fuck does this? Who the fuck comes into someone's personal space..." The reality of the situation slammed into me. "They got under my clothes this time," I breathed.

And then my breaths started coming too quickly. "I want them gone, Bear. I want them to stay away. I want to find out who's doing this. How could they do this? Who does this?" My voice sounded hysterical, which I hated.

I didn't want to sound hysterical. I was angry. Betrayed. Confused. And enraged.

Bear tried to reach for me, to pull me into his arms and comfort me, but I shoved him away and stepped in the shower. I was going to wash as much of it off as I could. And then I was going to figure out who the fuck had done this.

"Z."

"I'm not upset," I snapped. Bear furrowed his brows in confusion, so I corrected myself. "Okay, obviously I'm upset. But I don't need comfort right now. I'm pissed. How dare they? How fucking dare they."

I scrubbed my skin like it had betrayed me because I felt like it had. Did I not have enough situational awareness to notice when someone lifted up my shirt and inked my fucking bare *skin*?

Jesus fuck. Who was so oblivious that—

"Stop."

Bear's deep grumble was so calm it made tears smart in my eyes. I couldn't look at him, couldn't talk to him about this, really, because I knew he felt responsible. The worst part about all of this was the guilt he would feel for failing me.

"This isn't your fault, Bear," I said desperately. "You probably weren't even there." *Fuck!* That wasn't what I'd meant. "They're obviously slick. They obviously created chaos sufficient enough to do this without me noticing."

I could hear the panic in my voice, so I quickly closed my mouth and concentrated on scrubbing.

Bear yanked the soap out of my hand. It slipped from his grip and went shooting loudly across the tiles, banging like a tossed marble ball on its way toward the drain.

"Honey, take a breath."

I inhaled quickly, accidentally sucking in shower water. I coughed and snorted. I couldn't even breathe right.

Bear gathered me quickly into his arms and lifted me up to press my back against the frigid walls. I winced before sinking into him, curling around him and letting him hold me tightly.

I cried angry tears. For the asshole who had ruined my perfect night. For the motherfucker who had dared to violate me. For the actual mother whose abandonment all those years ago had finally begun to sleep peacefully in the grave I'd made for her in my mind.

"I had a song for you," I finally admitted in a small voice. "I'm sorry I didn't sing it."

Bear pulled back and cupped my face, keeping my back and ass pressed against the tile. "For me? I assumed I was the grizzly in your song."

I smiled through my snotty, swollen face. "You were. You are. But that one wasn't written for you. I wrote one for you."

"Yeah?" He asked, the edges of his lips quirking up. "Why didn't you sing it?"

"Chickened out."

He leaned in and kissed me, tender at first but then more hungrily. I let myself enjoy it. Let myself float away on the fantasy he offered. Let myself feel every caress and stroke of his big hands on my body.

Until I realized he was rubbing a hole into the skin of my lower back with his thumb.

"Let me go," I said, wriggling out of his grip.

"Sorry," he said. "I was trying to get it off."

"Fine, try to wash it off, but then you can Sharpie over it again. Draw me another angry saw blade or whatever. But then we're getting to work. I want the video footage and the time stamps from my watch. Not that many people managed to touch me, Bear. And I think they were all people we know."

I retrieved the soap and handed it to him while I washed and rinsed my hair. He scrubbed the stamp but gave up quickly. We both knew it wasn't coming off with soap.

By the time I hopped out and dried off, I was a man on a mission. "Call Violet. She should still be awake in LA."

Bear watched me cautiously as I moved to the other room to root out his laptop and hand it to him. "Pull up the footage. I'm going to get Lou in here."

"Do not open that door." His deep voice would have made my dick hard if I wasn't so distracted. "Text her."

I pulled out my phone. "Fine."

> Another stamp. Come to the suite for strategy sesh.

Then I went back to Bear's bag and pulled out the Sharpie before smacking it in his palm and turning around.

I hadn't put on a shirt yet, had only yanked on some baggy pajama pants, so he had full access to cover the mark.

The tip of the marker was cold, and it prickled my skin with goose bumps. This time, he took a little longer, and when I insisted he take a photo again, he looked a little sheepish.

"I told you. I suck at drawing."

I stared at the... "Mitten that's missing a thumb?" I asked. He narrowed his eyes and looked at the phone screen. "Santa's pack?" He made a little growly noise in his throat. "Upside-down chef's hat?"

"It's a honey pot! How can you not see it's..." He tilted his head and pointed at the black, shapeless blob. "It's a honey pot. Like in Winnie the Pooh."

I blinked at him. *Fuck*, he was adorable. Emotion welled up and filled my eyes. Had anyone ever cared for me like Bear did?

"It's a honey pot," he insisted again, firming his jaw.

I opened my mouth to tell him I loved him—that he was the kindest, sweetest, biggest-hearted man I knew—when the squealer alarm went off from the security wedge and Lou's muffled curses filled the space where she'd tried to open the door.

Bear quickly tossed his hoodie at me, and I yanked it on. He pulled the wedge out and turned it off, saving our ears from complete annihilation.

We spent the next hour scrolling through grainy surveillance video. Violet provided occasional updates from the speaker of Lou's phone, while members of the team in California moved in and out of the conference room she was in.

"How did you let people near him?" she kept asking. "There was a no-touching policy. Do you people need retraining?"

She'd already apologized profusely to me on behalf of the team and explained she would be notifying the label and letting them know every update. It was excruciating to watch Bear and Lou have to sit there and take the reprimands when I knew it hadn't been that easy in person. How did you tell the king of a country they weren't allowed to shake hands with a lowly guitar player?

According to the video, at least five people had touched my lower back. One of them had clearly done it over my clothes, but the rest were impossible to see because of the crowd.

Alana Vasa, the violinist, had hugged me around the waist when we'd greeted each other.

Little Carina had thrown herself at me.

Gisella, the queen, had steadied herself on my back when she'd teetered in her heels.

Bodhi had put his hand on my shoulder, neck, and back. But the one on my back was clearly seen as being over my clothes. After realizing just how many places Bodhi had touched me, I glanced at Bear.

His jaw was clenched, and his nostrils flared. Thankfully, I knew he'd examined the rest of my naked body in the shower to make sure the stamp we'd seen was the only one.

Noelle had put her hand on my lower back. I remembered that.

"That royal guard touched him," Lou said, nodding at the video while she scribbled a note.

"Kasper can't be our Stamper," Bear said, reaching to speed up the feed. "Besides, he was way too busy stressing about the king's security. Apparently, there've been some threats recently. Kasper didn't want them leaving Ventdestine at all."

"Lou touched me," I said, pointing to the screen. Lou's eyes widened in surprise before she realized I was joking.

"Yeah," she muttered. "All I need is for them to fire Ryan so I have to do double duty."

Her words took me by surprise. "Fire Ryan?" I glanced at Ryan, who was pretending to ignore our conversation. Thankfully, Violet was busy talking to someone in the conference room with her.

Lou shrugged. "What else could their motive be? All their emails seem to point out Ryan's inability to keep you protected."

I was confused. "*All* their emails? I thought there was only one?"

Bear glared at Lou, and her eyes went wide. Violet came back on, oblivious to what had just happened. "So, Alana Vasa was in Paris when the LA stamping happened. She's clear. But we need to talk about canceling Berlin. I'm not sure the label is going to be comfortable with the exposure, considering..."

I didn't listen to her words. All I could see was the truth in Bear's expression. There'd been more emails. Emails no one had bothered to tell me about. I turned away from Bear and focused on Lou's phone. "Violet, I want you to send me every email I've received, right fucking now."

There was a pause. "Uh... Zee, you're the one with the emails. They came to your account, and you and Ryan forwarded them to me. Remember?"

Embarrassment heated my face at the confirmation. I took a deep breath and tried to stay professional... something I was wildly unfamiliar with lately. "Yes, sorry. My bad. They must still be in my email account. Well, I'll leave you and the team to sort this out. I'm going to bed. Thank you for your help tonight."

And with that, I stood up, avoided Bear's face like the fucking plague, and escaped to my room.

Where I locked the door and spent the next half hour catching up on his many lies.

TWENTY-TWO

RYAN

Bears are actually brilliant problem-solvers. With their sharp memories and knack for figuring things out, they're known to use tools, crack puzzles, and even open car doors if they smell a snack inside. But even the brainiest bears sometimes get goofy when they're feeling the bear version of a crush. Imagine a smart bear who can remember every trail and scent suddenly stumbling around, distracted. Love makes even the cleverest bears a little clumsy!
—Bear Facts for Insomniacs, Episode 108

"Fuck," I hissed under my breath as soon as Violet ended the call twenty minutes later. "Fuck!"

Lou shot me a glare. "You didn't *tell* him about the other emails? What? Did you think he couldn't handle it?"

"Fuck!" I snapped at the ceiling.

Lou stood up, shaking her head. "For someone who cares about Zane, you sure do treat him like he's incapable of handling things."

I glared at her. "Are you fucking kidding me? I didn't keep those emails from him because I think he's incapable of handling things. I kept them from him to guard his peace! That's my fucking job, Lou, to guard him in every way possible. What good would it have done to let him see them? They would have either scared him or enraged him. Either way, that wouldn't have gotten us anywhere."

"You don't know that. Maybe there was something in those messages that would have seemed familiar to him."

"Bullshit. They were the same stupid message over and over again. And if he'd been busy worrying over those emails, he wouldn't have completed that new song he sang tonight. That man had a wonderful two weeks in Norway because he didn't have this shit crawling all over him every night."

Lou met my eyes with a knowing glare. "I could make a very tidy comment about something else crawling all over him every night, but I'm a lady."

Heat rushed to my face. "How did you know?"

Her face softened, and she reached out to squeeze my arm. "I saw it coming a million miles away. The two of you are so into each other it's disgusting. But it's also kind of wonderful. Go talk to him, Ryan. Help him understand you were trying to protect him, but don't—" She held up her hand to stop me from interrupting. "Don't make it sound like you were doing it because it's your job."

I sucked in a breath and nodded. She was right. "Thank you."

She leaned in and gave me a rare and quick hug. "And stop blaming yourself for this asshole. We'll figure out who it is. In the meantime, I'm going to give you a little bit of unsolicited advice."

I prickled at the idea she could know Zane more than I did, but then again, she'd been with him much longer. "What?"

"He's going to try and act like he doesn't need or want a protector. He hates being seen as weak, hates needing or accepting help from anyone. You know this. But what you may not realize is that he actually *does* need and want a protector. He *does* need help from someone, and that someone is you. Your job is to give him those things while also respecting that he's a man with dignity and agency. He wants to be part of the team. He wants to help find this asshole and take him down. Don't put that sweet man on a pedestal the way the rest of the world does, Ryan. He needs you to treat him like a regular person, not a trophy made of spun glass."

I opened my mouth to defend myself, to tell her that I would never treat him like the rest of the world did... but then I worried that might be exactly what Zane would think I'd done when I'd kept those emails from him. I hadn't kept it from him because I thought he was weak; I'd done it because he deserved peace. I'd done it because seeing him upset made *me* upset. I'd done it because I was in love with him... but Zane didn't know that.

"Thank you," I said softly.

She nodded and walked out, reminding me to replace the security wedge. Once I did that, I made my way to Zane's bedroom door and found it locked.

"Zane, can I come in? I owe you an apology. And an explanation."

I heard him moving toward the door. When it opened, he made his way back to the bed and threw himself under the duvet with only his face peeking out. He definitely looked angry. "I'm not skipping Berlin."

I moved carefully to the edge of the bed and sat down without touching him. "No. We're not canceling your Berlin appearance."

His eyes widened slightly in surprise. "Good. But I thought... I thought Violet was going to get pushback from the label. I thought you were going to insist on leaving."

"I told her you'd defy the label if they tried keeping you from this event, that it was way too important to you. And that it was better to accept you were going to do it anyway and go ahead and plan the security."

He moved to sit up, still keeping the duvet wrapped around himself like a protective cloud. "You told her that?"

"Was I wrong?" I challenged.

Zane shook his head. I could tell he had conflicting emotions, but I also knew he wouldn't miss the Berlin fundraiser for any reason. The opportunity to debut a new song with Jude Marian at the same time they'd brought a stellar cast of performers together to raise money for LGBTQ causes was way too enticing. He couldn't pass up the opportunity to do so much good.

It just meant I'd have to wrap the man in impermeable protection and ensure his safety no matter what.

I took a deep breath and let it out. "I'm sorry I didn't tell you about the emails."

"Are you? Or are you just saying that now because I'm angry?"

I thought about it. Was there still part of me that would be tempted to do the same again? *Yes.* I never wanted hate to touch him if I could prevent it.

"I'm sorry it hurt you," I said, meaning it. "Zane... I need you to know I didn't keep those emails from you because I didn't think you could handle them. It was because I didn't want you to feel the threat any more than you already did. I didn't want you to be scared or angry or... frustrated. It didn't seem productive. I wanted you to have a couple of weeks of peace—"

"I needed to know the continued threats were happening so I understood the danger," he said, eyes flashing. "By keeping me in the dark, I didn't realize just how bad it was. Maybe if I had, I would have agreed to cancel the VIP reception. Or maybe I would have demanded to have you with me instead of with the royal family today. Or maybe I would have agreed when you suggested I needed a minimum of two close personal security officers on me at all times."

"You said you didn't want to look like a diva," I said in frustration. "You refused to have guards on both sides of you because you thought that would look bad."

"I didn't realize there were four other emails, two of them within the last couple of days! That this guy was not going away. That he was frustrated he didn't know where I was when we were in Norway.

He said he would find me, Bear!" His voice shook with a mix of fear and rage. "And he did."

I wanted to touch Zane. Every cell in my body ached to reach out and pull him into my arms, but I didn't feel like I had the right to comfort him anymore.

And maybe he wasn't the one who needed comfort.

"I'm so fucking sorry," I said. The emotion was clear in my voice, too, and I hated it. "You're right. If you'd known, maybe you would have agreed to my recommendations. But by then, I didn't want to throw them out as evidence that there were good reasons for my suggestions. Ultimately, whether it was two emails or six, the threat was the same. And we should have had tighter security on today's event. We should have insisted on a guest list limit regardless of what the royal family wanted. Noelle should never have gotten in. Apparently, she was doing media consulting for someone there. And we should have pulled you out of that room once it got so crowded."

Zane met my eyes. "Do you think I need to be wrapped in bubble wrap, Bear? Is that what I have a personal security person for?"

I clenched my jaw to keep from snapping at him. *Yes, yes you need to be wrapped in bubble wrap. Because you're a precious fucking treasure. I'd do anything to keep you safe.*

"No. I believe you could handle just about anything, Z," I said hesitantly. "But I don't want you to have to." I clenched my jaw again. "I wasn't acting as your personal security officer when I made the decision to hide those emails from you," I admitted.

His eyebrows furrowed. "I don't understand."

"I was acting as the man who..." I swallowed as I stood toe-deep at the edge of a cliff. "Who *wanted* to protect you."

Zane's lips opened. I expected him to be angry, to tell me I wasn't making any sense, but instead, he surprised me with a soft smile.

"Why do you *want* to protect me, Bear?"

I looked everywhere but at him. The words were a bell that couldn't be un-rung. They would change things forever, for better or worse.

His smaller hand snuck out of the covers and slid into mine. "Why?" he repeated in a softer voice. "Is it not just because it's your job?"

I glared at him. "Protecting you isn't my job, Z. It's my fucking honor."

"Mm. Why is that?"

"You're impossible."

He opened the duvet and crawled over to straddle my lap, sliding his arms around my neck. His callused fingers stroked my neck, and he nuzzled my cheek with his nose before whispering the words into my skin. "Say the words, Bear. Please."

In the end, it wasn't a matter of making myself tell him but of allowing myself to stop holding back. Once I did, the words tumbled over themselves in their eagerness to be free. "I'm so in love with you I can't breathe. If something happens to you, my life will simply... stop. I can't... I can't let anything happen to you, Z. You're..."

His lips were wide with a smile, and his eyes were wet. "I'm your honey."

I rolled my eyes and kissed him, cupping the back of his head with both hands to keep him there. After drinking my fill, I pulled back just enough to agree. "You're my honey. And you're officially not allowed to listen to any more bear fact podcasts."

"I love you, too," he said, still grinning wide. "That's why I didn't play your song today."

I wrapped my arms around him and held him tight. "Make that make sense."

"It's too revealing. You would have known how I felt if I sang it. I didn't want to come offstage to find I'd scared you away."

That wasn't completely accurate. We hadn't been in a great place before the show, and I wondered now if I'd left him feeling unsure.

"Will you sing it for me now?" I asked.

He shook his head. "No. There are other things I'd rather do right now, but I'll sing it in Berlin. And you'll know it's about you."

I kissed him again, murmuring my apologies into his skin as I pushed him back on the bed and proceeded to take him apart, inch by inch.

TWENTY-THREE
ZANE

For the next two days, I carried around my newly confessed love like a locket nestled close to my heart. I knew it was there, Bear knew it was there, and that was all that mattered.

When I took the stage in Berlin, I felt like I was carrying a super-power. Not only was I getting ready to debut a brand-new song with Jude Marian on the world's stage, but I was also going to debut my secret song about Bear.

The show opened with a popular singing duo—and real-life couple—called Aria & Velvet. The women were like a mix of Lana

Del Rey and Stevie Nicks and had the crowd on their feet immediately. After they left, a solo artist named Kradle came out with a punchy two-song set featuring energetic choreography.

"You ready, kid?" Jude teased as we stood in the wings, listening to Kradle thanking the audience.

Jude Marian was the very definition of aging gracefully. He was a beautiful man, even in his fifties, and the silver threads in his brown hair only seemed to emphasize his good looks.

I still couldn't believe this was my life, that I was getting ready to take the stage with a music legend, an artist I'd idolized growing up. "Is this real?" I asked. "Because I've been trying to act cool since we got here, but I'm not feeling very cool on the inside."

Jude's giant of a husband stood behind him, massaging his shoulders. "Jude has that effect on people," he said calmly.

With the exception of reaching back to squeeze Derek's thigh, Jude ignored him and stayed focused on me. "You're the one used to performing. I never do shows this big anymore. What if I trip and fall?"

Derek scowled. "I'll owe your daughter twenty bucks. Don't do that."

Jude finally turned around to glare at his husband. "You bet I would *fall* on stage?"

"I bet you *wouldn't* fall. Complain to Rosie. She's the turncoat. She's convinced you're going to do something to embarrass her."

Jude closed his eyes and inhaled. "Zee, never have children. They're the worst. They look so sweet and innocent when they're tiny, but the next thing you know..."

"They're young adults," Derek said wryly. "With *opinions*."

Kradle began to introduce us onstage.

Derek winked at me over Jude's shoulder before leaning down and kissing his ear. "Break a leg, Bluebell. I love you. You're going to be amazing. You always are."

Jude turned to kiss him on the lips while I tried my hardest not to look at Bear, who was standing quietly next to me. I hated that he couldn't participate in this conversation as my partner, and I wondered how long it would take to convince him that was the role I wanted him in.

Watching Jude and Derek reminded me that this was exactly how the two of them had ended up together. Derek had been Jude's close protection specialist, and the two of them had fallen in love.

Jude and I moved forward toward the stage and away from our bodyguards. "Can I ask you something later?" I asked Jude quietly.

He turned to me with a look of concern on his face. "Of course. Anything. Anytime. I hope you know that."

I nodded and gave him a smile of thanks. He reached out for a fist bump. "Let's kill this. And don't let me fall, or I'll take you down with me to make it a bigger story."

We jogged out onstage laughing, took the mics, and began our performance. Jude started with a heartfelt thanks to the giant crowd.

"Thanks to you, we've raised over two million Euros tonight for LGBTQIA+ youth around the world," he said. "Thanks to you, fewer children will go without much-needed support of psychologists and therapists. Thanks to you, at-risk teens in our community will be more likely to hear a friendly voice on the other end of the line. Thanks to you, LGBTQIA+ kids who need food, shelter, clothing, medication, hormones, and any other essential needs will get it. And thanks to you, the youth in our community will know just how much we value every single one of them for being exactly who they are. This show is for them. Please help me welcome my friend Zee Barlo. Zee and I are going to sing a new song for you tonight if that's okay."

The crowd screamed and cheered their heads off while Jude grinned at me. My heart was so full, and my lungs felt like I could sing for days.

"Let's do this," I shouted, pulling the guitar around from where it had been hanging on my back.

It was a song we'd written especially for this event. Because both Jude's and my schedules had been so hectic this year, we'd had to collaborate over emails, texts, and Zoom, but we'd finally put it together. Jude had arranged for us to record it in a studio in LA next week so we could release it by Christmas.

His idea had been to record it with as many big-name performers as we could gather and then donate the proceeds to the same charity initiative the concert was benefitting. Between the two of us, we'd managed to pull in a powerhouse list of names for the recording, and I couldn't wait to meet them all in the studio.

As the chorus came around the second time, the crowd began to pick up on it and sing along. By the third time, thousands of voices joined ours.

You're my brave, my light, my truth.
The world shines brighter because of you.
Stand tall, let your colors show.
You're the brightest light, never let it go.

I sang with my whole heart. For men like Jude who'd waited a long time. For kids like Auden Salling who might never be able to come out. For women like Aria & Velvet who'd been out since the beginning but still struggled with prejudice and hate. For myself and all the times I'd felt like I wanted to help kids like me.

I was grateful to have a record label that supported me. An agent and manager who were on board with my goals. And now... now an actual boyfriend. Someone who was in love with me and who valued my career and my dreams as much as I did.

As the last chord echoed against the screams of the crowd, Jude and I shared a knowing look. This was good work. We were so fucking lucky to be able to live this life.

We went right into singing one of his songs together before I stepped offstage while he sang a solo about his husband called "Break Away." It wasn't a new song, but I still couldn't help but glance at Derek, who wore a lovesick expression on his face. Jude was so lucky to have him. Derek was famous for going all soft for his famous husband, and he was also famous for continuing to guard Jude Marian with his life, despite his middle age.

I was here for all of it. The two of them had the life I wanted, and I realized maybe Jude was the one who could help me figure out how to get it.

Once Jude's song ended, he introduced a popular German band and said we'd be back with more songs shortly. When he returned to the wings where I was standing with Derek and Bear, Jude walked into Derek's arms for a big hug.

"Good job not falling on your face, Bluebell," Derek teased. "I already texted Rosie, 'so far, so good.'"

Jude punched him lightly in the stomach before reaching out to fist-bump me. "They loved it. Great job."

"I didn't have the guts to tell you this when we first met," I confessed. "But you were an inspiration when I was growing up, not just for your music. Watching you thrive being out and proud in front of your fans encouraged me to be out from the beginning. I made sure I had an agent and a label who supported me because I knew it was possible from watching you."

Jude placed his hand over his heart. "You have no idea how much that means to me. I wish I could say I should have come out sooner, but I can't. If I'd been out sooner, I'm not sure I would have ended up with Derek the way I did."

I shrugged. "Maybe it happened that way for a reason." I wondered if the Ventdestinians had a point when they put their faith in the winds of fate.

"And now you can be that inspiration for the ones coming up," he said with a smile.

As we stood together watching the German performers, Derek and Ryan moved off a few paces to talk about something security related. I didn't realize I was watching Bear until Jude leaned over and spoke in a low voice.

"Does he know you're into him?"

I blinked and shook my head, looking anywhere but at Ryan Galloway. "What?"

Jude laughed softly. "It's like that, huh? Alright. Crush city, population one. I got it."

I scraped my upper lip with my bottom teeth while I tried to figure out how to ask his advice. "What if the city had a population of two? What would you do?"

Jude looked over at the two big, muscular guys standing together. Derek's hair was more salt than pepper, but he was still stacked with muscle and the same height as Bear. Jude turned back to me.

"I would grab onto it with both hands and let everything else fuck off. Life's too short, Zee."

I felt Jude's gaze on the side of my face as I turned back to the stage to wait for our cue to go back on for the next song.

After a moment, he reached out and squeezed my arm. "I'm here if you need me. Call or text anytime. In fact... why don't you come to Montana and see us over Christmas? I heard you were going to be in Wyoming for an event there. We're just over the border from Majestic."

"Ryan's from Montana," I said without thinking. "I didn't know you guys had a place there."

"My family bought up a bunch of land years ago when the kids were little so we could all have a place to spend our summers. It's grown into a bit of a family compound at this point. One of my nephews runs a ranch there at the heart of the place, and the rest of us either stay at the family lodge on the property or have built cabins or bring RVs. It's like a cult... only our religion is mostly pizza, alcohol, and dick jokes."

"And old-lady poker," Derek muttered, walking back over to us. "Don't turn your back on anyone during a poker game there, or you'll lose your shirt."

Jude snickered while Derek continued with a straight face. "And I mean your literal shirt."

Jude turned back to me. "Seriously, though. We'll be there for

Christmas, but then we have a big family wedding weekend. So check with me about dates."

The band onstage finished their song and called us back. Jude and I performed my song "Very Much Myself" together, and I found myself hoping that, wherever he was, young Auden Salling would hear about it.

When Jude left again so I could perform a solo, I took a deep breath and peered out at the huge crowd. "Here's a little-known fact about me, but don't tell anyone, okay? It'll be our little secret."

The crowd roared.

"When I come offstage after a show, it takes a while for me to calm down. So a little while back, I started listening to this podcast called *Bear Facts for Insomniacs*, and it's a miracle at putting people to sleep. I'd apologize to the podcasters, but this is actually the point of the podcast. Anyway, if you're at all like me, you might wanna give it a try. See if a bear changes your life like it did mine." I grinned wildly. "In fact, I have a new song about a bear. It's called 'Sanctuary.'"

The band began the intro as I tried to settle my nerves.

Jude's words swam in my head as my heart filled with thoughts of debuting this song in front of Bear.

I would grab onto it with both hands and let everything else fuck off. Life's too short, Zee.

He was right. I wanted a life with Ryan. I wanted the world to know he was mine and I was his. After tonight, I would need to find a way to talk to him about it, to figure out how we could be together without being quasi boss-employee.

Just as it was time for me to begin the lyrics, I turned to the wings and caught Bear's eyes.

And then I opened my mouth and sang.

TWENTY-FOUR

RYAN

It was eye-opening to see Derek Marian demonstrably in love with his celebrity husband. I'd spent so long in the closet in Ventdestine I hadn't been around openly gay couples much.

Honestly, I couldn't stop staring at them. Watching them be physically affectionate made me want to be able to do that with Zane. I wanted to be able to touch him when I wanted, press a kiss to the side of his face without worrying who would see, and express my concerns for his security as a loving partner, not a hired gun.

As Jude came off the stage, I stepped closer to the tape marking the edge of the wings and the beginning of the visible wing area.

I loved watching Zane like this. Even though I was still nervous as hell about him being exposed, at risk, I was secretly glad to be able to watch him in his element.

"Here's a little-known fact about me, but don't tell anyone, okay? It's our little secret."

The crowd went wild, screaming and cheering. Being the first to learn something new about Zee Barlo was an unexpected treat.

"When I come offstage after a show, it takes a while for me to calm down. So a little while back, I started listening to this podcast called *Bear Facts for Insomniacs*, and it's a miracle at putting people to sleep. I'd apologize to the podcasters, but it's actually the point of the podcast. Anyway, if you're at all like me, you might wanna give it a try. See if a bear changes your life like it did mine. In fact, I have a new song about a bear. It's called 'Sanctuary.'"

He turned toward me and locked eyes. My heart hammered.

I love you.

I wanted to mouth the words, make sure he knew he was loved in that exact moment, but I couldn't risk getting caught.

Instead, I sent out the love I had for him and hoped he felt even a fraction of it.

When he turned back to the audience, he began to sing. I immediately recognized the light, playful tune he'd been humming for weeks, ever since Barlo.

> I have a secret that no one knows.
> When the world feels heavy, there's a place I go,
> Where the salmon runs free and the honey flows,
>
> When the weight's hard to carry, and the road is long,
> When old voices scream loudly, and I yearn to
>   belong.

It's a crack in a mountain you can't see from the road,
Deep in the trees and fully covered with snow,
But if you look really close, you can just make out
Twin arrows pointing north, leading straight to
    the den.

When the night is long and lonely and the stars don't
    shine,
When new faces get too close, your honeyed words
    are like wine.

It's a crack in a mountain you can't see from the road,
A den filled with warmth, a cozy seat by the fire.

Hidden away from the world, no one knows where
    I go.
Quiet time with the bear, time away from the show.

When the world becomes too much and I need an
    escape,
When my heart gets cracked in two, or I get into a
    scrape.

I run to the mountain, and I step off the road,
Look for signs of the grizzly, and I listen for growls.
He always knows I'm coming, knows I can't stay
    away.
It's a den in a mountain, it's the bear at its heart.

When the world feels heavy, there's a place I go,
Where the salmon runs free and the honey flows.
And no one knows...
I'm at home with the bear.

His eyes danced as he plucked the tune out of the strings on his guitar and grinned into the microphone. He didn't dare turn to look at me, but I felt the same love I had for him coming back to me.

The meaning of the lyrics overwhelmed me.

I was his safe place. His sanctuary. There was no greater gift than hearing that he found peace and comfort with me.

The crowd roared as he thanked them and began to introduce the next artist. When he came off the stage, I wanted to grab him and squeeze him tight. Thank him. Kiss him. Tell the world that it was me. *I* was the bear who kept him warm at night.

But I didn't do any of those things. Instead, I waited for him to approach, and then I said in a low voice, "That was amazing."

He met my eyes and smiled, seemingly unperturbed at the strictures keeping us from being our authentic selves. The irony of not being able to express my love for this man at an LGBTQIA+ event wasn't lost on me.

I caught Jude Marian shooting me a look of extreme understanding and empathy.

He knew.

And, hell. Maybe you didn't have to be a rocket scientist to figure out that I was in love with my principal. I probably wasn't very good at hiding the way I felt about him.

Jude pulled Zane aside to congratulate him and talk about how his song had brought back memories of hearing Lyle Lovett play a bear song many years ago.

I took the opportunity to do a visual sweep of the area in preparation for the most challenging portion of the evening. The security protocols had done a good job so far of restricting the other performers to the far wing, but during the final farewell, all of the performers would be onstage at the same time, taking final bows and waving to the crowd.

There were rules against touching Zane, but I wasn't sure everyone would take them seriously.

"It's harder when you love them, isn't it?"

It took me a minute to register Derek's words, but then I blew out a breath. "Fuck. Is it that obvious?"

He let out a low chuckle. "Let's just say now I can see how easily people saw through me and Jude back then."

"How... how do we..." I tried to figure out how to ask what I wanted to ask.

He shrugged. "You just tell the world you're a thing. You let the chips fall."

I couldn't imagine that. There were way too many chips, and I felt like Zane would be the one to bear the brunt of the impact.

Derek continued. "It's not the end of the world. Sure, it'll make a splash, but shit like that comes out all the time and gets taken over by another salacious story soon enough. Hell, our daughter was just telling us earlier today about a rumor going around that some tennis player turned talk show host is dating her bodyguard. It's not like you invented falling for someone you work with, Ryan. It happens."

I continued to ruminate on his words as all of the night's performers went back onstage to thank the crowd, toss out T-shirts and other signed merch to the VIPs in the close rows, and then jog offstage. Finally, we were done.

"Thanks for everything," I said to Derek as we exchanged our goodbyes.

He nodded. "Don't be a stranger, okay? And if you ever need anything..."

"I appreciate it," I said, meaning it. I hadn't made many friends since moving back to the States, but I got the feeling Derek would be a good one to have.

Zane and I couldn't do more than exchange a secret smile as we made our way directly to the exit and into a waiting SUV with Lou right behind us. A prearranged escort helped us cut through the crowded streets toward the airport. Within an hour of leaving the backstage area at the arena, we were in the air... and heading home.

I couldn't fucking wait for the two of us to be in the relative safety of Zane's Santa Monica house, where we could hopefully have some privacy.

Unfortunately, we were on a chartered jet instead of Zane's own plane, and there was no private bedroom to sneak away to.

"I need to shower and change," he said, unbuckling his seat belt and moving to grab his backpack with toiletries and a clean change of clothes. I stood silently and followed him back to the bathroom, waiting outside as he moved into the small space by himself.

"You okay?" he asked before closing the door.

I met his eyes, warm brown pools I wanted to lose myself in. I *wasn't* okay. Not at all. I wanted to touch him, hold him, kiss his fucking face, and tell him over and over again how talented he was.

"I'm fine," I said instead.

Zane's eyes flared. "Fine?"

I clenched my jaw against the words that wanted to spill out. "Fine."

He hesitated before nodding and closing the door between us. We both knew I couldn't follow him into the bathroom as much as I might have wanted to. Instead, I sat down on the chair nearest the bathroom door and pulled out my phone.

There was a message from one of my brothers with an old photo of me taking second place in a youth biathlon competition. I held up the silver ribbon like it was an Olympic gold medal. Underneath was my attorney brother's favorite joke.

I don't understand biathlon...

I mean, how is it possible to have a rifle and still finish in second place?

I grinned and responded the way I always did when he sent this kind of message—by searching for the perfect meme making fun of defense attorneys from the OverheardCourthouse Instagram account.

Just as I heard the bathroom door click open, I caught a news alert in my Instagram feed.

Addison Canto sued by former bodyguard. Two-time Grand Slam tennis champion and host of Zero-Love talk show is accused of sexual harassment, fostering a hostile work environment, and other labor violations.

I stared at the headline graphic. This was the tennis star turned talk show host Derek had mentioned. This must've been what that his daughter had been talking about.

I clicked into the hashtags and saw hundreds of reposts and thousands of toxic comments. The ugliness was overwhelming, and it left me in no doubt about what people thought of celebrities hooking up with their security personnel.

My stomach churned with nausea. The salacious news would make it impossible for us to go public with our relationship, not only now but also in the future.

What the fuck were our options after this?

Zane stepped out of the bathroom and smiled up at me. His hair was damp and tangled, but his face was fresh and clean. His tattoos stood out on winter-pale skin. My heart lurched. I hated having to share this, but I'd promised I'd be honest. I'd promised I'd trust him to know what he could handle.

"All clear?" I asked. He knew what I meant. I'd tasked him with examining his bare body in the lavatory mirror to make sure there was no stamp. Even though I couldn't think of a time when anyone had had that kind of access to him tonight, I still needed to be sure.

"Yes. There are mirrors everywhere in there, and I didn't see any marks."

"Good." I took a breath. "Can we talk?"

I hadn't meant to phrase it so ominously, but his smile dropped immediately.

TWENTY-FIVE

ZANE

Bears are big on leaving their mark—literally! When bears rub up against trees, they're not just scratching an itch. By rubbing their backs, heads, and even paws against trunks and branches, they leave behind their scent, marking their territory and announcing, "This place is taken!" It's like their own woodland billboard, letting other bears know who's in the neighborhood.

—Bear Facts for Insomniacs, Episode 15

I hated not being able to touch Bear whenever I wanted to. We had a fourteen-hour flight ahead of us, and all I wanted was to curl up next to him and fall asleep against all that muscly warmth.

But when he asked if we could talk, enough adrenaline shot through my bloodstream to ensure sleep would be a long time coming.

"Okayyy." I gestured to the pair of captain's chairs closest to the bathroom because everyone else was sitting farther up toward the galley. "What's up?"

The night had gone well, and I'd seen the look on his face when I'd come offstage. I knew he'd appreciated my song. He'd said it was amazing.

But the look on his face now was totally different. I clasped my hands in my lap to keep from reaching out to grab his hand.

Instead of speaking, he handed me his phone. On the screen was an Instagram post with a large news headline about a famous talk show host.

My stomach dropped. "Oh shit." After reading the post, I clicked out of it to look for an article that might have more information. Instead, I found the world's reactions.

It was like a blast from an oven. Hot rage spewed from comments sections and gossip sites, accusing the powerful and wealthy celebrity of taking advantage of someone who worked for her, someone who wouldn't have been in a position to say no to her advances without losing his job.

My hands began to shake. I knew this wasn't the same situation as ours, and I knew Bear's feelings for me were genuine and not coerced. But I still needed to hear it from him.

"Ryan..."

"No," he growled, narrowing his eyes at me. "Do not *Ryan* me. And do not for one minute think—"

I reached out and clasped his forearm. "Okay," I said softly. "Okay."

He let out a breath and put his hand over mine for a brief moment, just long enough to squeeze it in reassurance. "I just don't know what to do now."

It was rare for my Bear to sound so uncertain. It made my chest squeeze with the need to protect him as fiercely as he protected me.

I scrambled to think of a fix. "What if we..." I dismissed several ideas without voicing them, options I knew Bear would never go for.

But there was another I knew he wouldn't go for that still needed to be put out there. "What if you asked to be reassigned? What if we lie low for a little while and then start dating publicly after the new year, after it's clear we're no longer connected as bodyguard and principal?"

Bear looked at me like I was obtuse. "And who would protect you in the meantime?"

I nodded toward the front of the plane. "Lou. Boomer. Whoever else Violet wants to assign."

He clenched his jaw. "Meanwhile, she assigns me to another principal, and I end up half a world away on some business trip while you have an active fucking target on your back? No way. No fucking way, Z."

"Bear..."

"Don't ask me to leave your protection detail, Zane. Not now. I can't. I won't."

I yanked my arms inside my hoodie and pulled my legs up in the seat, anything to keep from climbing into his lap and curling into his chest. "Then what's your plan?"

"My plan is to ask Violet whether we can proceed with some kind of legal action that allows for legal depositions or some way of asking our suspects questions under oath about their actions around you. If we can find and neutralize whoever's making these threats, maybe I'd..."

I couldn't help but grin at him. "You can't say it, can you? You'd hate it if someone else was my close protection officer."

He made a low grumbling noise under his breath.

I wrapped my arms around myself inside my shirt. "What if you..." I knew he would balk at this. "Hear me out, Bear. What if you quit? What if you traveled with me full-time as... *not* my close protection officer?"

"Well, one of the things that would happen is an eventual eviction from my apartment," he said. "My truck is paid off, but I wouldn't be able to keep it insured or gassed up for long. And then there's the matter of setting aside money for retirement. I know the super-wealthy don't have to think about these things, Zane, but the rest of us have to consider how our bills are going to get paid if we quit our jobs to spend all of our time with our boo-thang."

I could tell he was saying it with a teasing tone and the hint of a grin, but I still felt stung.

"Don't call me that," I muttered. "And I obviously wouldn't let any of those things happen. I'd—"

There was no teasing left in his voice when he cut me off. "Don't say it. Do not even think it."

I turned away and looked out the window into the pitch-black night. After a while, I felt him get up and move away. I closed my eyes and tried to sleep, if only to escape the stress involved in trying to solve this dilemma.

A few minutes later, I felt the familiar weight of my travel blanket settle over me. Bear's signature scent wafted through the air with it, and I opened my eyes to meet his. They were filled with love and affection, care and comfort, and I suddenly realized maybe this blanket could give us some cover.

The lights were low in the plane, and several people had leaned their chairs all the way back to sleep. The flight attendant would have easily offered to convert these back two chairs into a bed for me, but there was no way I was going to take a bed while everyone else sat around me in chairs.

I nodded for Bear to take the seat next to me again, and then I poked my arms back through my sleeves and reached for his hand, tossing the corner of the blanket between us to hide our twined fingers.

His voice was low when he spoke, even though the loud noise of the plane would have covered it at regular volume. "I can't take your money, Z. Not when we've only been together for five minutes. You have to understand that."

"We've been together longer than that," I said defiantly. "You've been my person for months, even though I didn't say it out loud."

His thumb ran across the back of my hand. "I understand. And I feel the same. But you know what I mean."

I nodded. He was right. I couldn't expect him to quit his job and become a professional boyfriend, even though that's all I wanted.

"We'll figure it out, Z," he said softly. "I promise. But not right now. Get some sleep."

I drifted off with the feel of my hand surrounded by his and the echoes of tonight's music in my head.

The rest of the flight was uneventful. I slept on and off for several hours until the flight attendant began brewing fresh coffee, and the scent was irresistible. I wasn't sure Bear had slept at all.

We moved up front to join Lou, Boomer, and the other support staff traveling with us as breakfast was served. After we ate, Bear jumped on his laptop and began going over more surveillance information from the concert and emails from Violet and the rest of the team.

After Amsterdam, Bear and I had examined the hidden emails together to see if there was anything in them that meant anything to me, but there hadn't been.

The only people in my circles who would know or use Latin were my college friends. Certainly no one back home would have used that kind of language, and it would have surprised me if many of my LA contacts would use that kind of language unless they were deliberately being dramatic.

I felt like we were at a dead end.

There was an email from Bodhi with more information about what he'd been trying to tell me before the Amsterdam show. A young woman named Keeva Temple played the mandolin better than anyone I'd ever heard—even Coot—and her voice was drugging like sweet, tipsy wine. I listened through my headphones as I clicked through her YouTube videos and saw all the supportive comments.

She was obviously queer in some way and had a few original songs about standing out while trying to fit in. Keeva was the kind of artist I dreamed about mentoring. She reminded me of myself when I was trying to figure out who I was as an artist in college. I let her voice carry me away as my brain noodled over my current situation.

I began to daydream about various scenarios while remembering something scratched above a urinal in the bar where I played my first gig. *"What's the point of any of this?"*

I remembered grinning at the line because it had been so incongruous with my experience. There I'd been, finally getting hired to play music in front of a crowd, and it made me feel high as a kite. The point? The point was the thrill of it. The utter joy in doing something I loved. Of living my dream.

I remembered thinking of a million answers to that provoking question.

What's the point of any of this?

Love. Joy. Helping others. Living a life of authenticity and happiness. Experiencing love and connection.

I looked over at Bear while Keeva Temple crooned in my ears about trying to find her place in the world, and I suddenly felt myself level up.

Zane Hendley was no longer a scared kid. I was no longer a questioning teen. And I was no longer a young adult unsure of my place in the world.

I knew exactly what the point was.

And I was determined to pursue it with everything I had.

When the plane finally touched down at Van Nuys Airport, I was surprised to see both Kenji and Micki waiting for us. Violet was there, too.

"Hey! What are you doing in LA?" I asked Kenji after giving him a hug. It felt good to see a familiar face that had nothing to do with my music career.

Micki spoke first. "The label's called a meeting first thing this morning. I thought we could go over some things before we get there."

I nodded but kept my eyes on Kenji. It made sense my manager was here, but why Kenji? He usually assisted me from his office in New York. "Is everyone okay?"

He nodded in his usual calm manner. "Fine. I figured you could use some help catching up after being gone so long, and there are some end-of-the-year financial decisions that we need to go over."

He made it sound like it was nothing out of the ordinary, but I knew better. This smacked of the brotherhood's meddling, but I waited until we got in the car before whispering, "Who sent you? Silas? Bash? It wouldn't have been Dev."

He gave me a dry look that spoke volumes. "Landry?" I hissed. "What the fuck?"

Bear stood outside the vehicle, speaking to Micki, Violet, and the rest of the security team while Kenji flicked his eyes to the ceiling. "He seemed to think you were getting in over your head. With *feelings*. You know how Landry feels about emotions. Doesn't like 'em. Doesn't know how to work 'em."

"My feelings are just fine," I snapped. "Yes, I have them. But I want them just the way they are. I don't need help with my feelings."

Kenji kept a straight face as usual. "Good. That doesn't happen to be my area of expertise anyway. I'm here to help with actions and tasks. Setting goals and achieving them. Give me a result, and I can help you get it."

It took a moment for the words to register, and then I gave him a Cheshire grin. "Excellent. That's exactly what I need from you. I know the result I want, Kenji. But I need help getting it."

He nodded and reached up to casually flick a shiny black strand of hair back into place. "I have some ideas."

"You don't know the result I want yet," I pointed out.

He opened his mouth on a long-suffering inhale. "Please."

I glanced over at Bear.

Kenji rolled his eyes and pulled out his tablet before handing it to me. "Step one, let's make a decision on the property you're purchasing in Majestic. Both of the places you looked at are still available. I'm just waiting for you to choose."

I looked down at the two spreads in Majestic. One was brand-new, modern, a little smaller but move-in ready, and wouldn't require much caretaking while I was on the road. The other was closer to Dev and Silas but had ten times the acreage, with room to develop cross-country ski trails, orienteering routes, and an outdoor shooting range. It also bordered both the Shoshone National Forest and Yellowstone, where there were miles and acres of outdoor playgrounds. It would be a massive investment of time and money, building a house there and keeping up with all those acres.

I'd thought I'd known which way I was leaning—which property would fit best with the life I led so nothing would have to change and no one else would be inconvenienced.

Now, though, I knew which property was right for the life I wanted, for the future I wanted, for the man I wanted. And I was ready to grab it with both hands unapologetically.

"This one," I said, tapping the image of the larger spread.

Kenji's mouth tipped into a lopsided grin. "Knew it. The architect is already booked to meet with us tomorrow to start the plans."

I grinned. I figured this was as close to Kenji giving my relationship his blessing as I was likely to get.

As I handed him back the tablet and he got to work tapping, I glanced out the window to see what was taking everyone else so long. Bear's nostrils were flared, and his jaw was tight. Violet was speaking to him emphatically. Lou and Boomer nodded obediently... but Bear didn't.

I started to get a bad feeling. Thankfully, Bear finally hopped in the SUV, taking the front passenger seat. "Let's go."

I waited for him to explain, but he didn't.

Of the others, only Micki joined us, sliding in next to me and politely asking Kenji to move back to the third row.

"Lou and Boomer aren't coming?" I asked Bear as Kenji slid his tablet into his bag and gathered his things.

"They're headed home for a break. Miguel and Paul are in the second vehicle with Ed, and they'll be taking over."

I had a million questions for him. "Did she tell you to go home, too?"

We both knew it was standard procedure for him to take a couple of days off after a long trip. Neither of us had mentioned it, but it had been a glaring elephant sitting between us on the plane.

Bear nodded once. "I... politely declined."

I could see the edges of Kenji's lips turn up as he passed me.

"And she was okay with that?" I asked.

"Dunno. Didn't ask."

I glanced at the back of Claudia's head. She and Ed Hilton took turns driving me when I was home in LA. I enjoyed the heck out of gossiping with her about celebrities in town, but her penchant for gossip was the reason I didn't dare say too much in front of her.

Bear must have known I was itching for more information because he added, "Miguel and Paul will take you home after the meeting at the label. I need to head home and get changed for my own meeting back at Violet's office."

I made a sound of acknowledgment like it was no big deal, but inside, it was a very big deal. Being back in LA with Bear's coworkers made me realize that ours wasn't the kind of relationship that could even exist secretly behind closed doors.

If he showed up at my house when he was off duty, everyone he worked with—including his boss—would know about it.

They would know if he stayed overnight.

They would know if he went into my bedroom with me.

They would know if I slipped and called him a nickname by accident.

I clamped my jaw tightly and vowed not to speak for fear of saying the wrong thing.

The nightmarish LA traffic made everything worse, dragging out the drive to the office in central LA longer than necessary. Thankfully, Micki filled the silence with chatter. She had updates on my recording schedule with Jude and the rest of the artists we'd gathered in a few days, feedback from the European shows, questions about whether I was willing to do the missed New York interviews virtually this coming week, updates to the final touches on the recording contract renewal I was due to sign soon, and finally information about what the label wanted to discuss so urgently that they'd called an impromptu meeting the minute I stepped off my flight.

"It's no big deal," Micki said with a little eye roll. "A tempest in a teapot. They're changing some of their policies and wanted to go over them with you. It involves signing paperwork, which is why it needs to be done in person."

I noticed Bear's jaw clench.

"Paperwork? This isn't the contract renewal, is it? Are my lawyers going to be present?"

"No, not the contract yet. This is their own internal policy stuff. They just need your agreement." Micki glanced at her phone and swiped through a few messages she'd received while we'd been talking. "It's my understanding the attorneys have already reviewed and approved everything. I wouldn't be surprised if Ellis wants to discuss the renewal, too, but that's not the point of the meeting, and we're certainly not signing that today."

I'd had a great experience with the label and had been happy with the contract negotiations. This time around, I was in the strongest negotiating position possible, and they'd acknowledged it by making a strong offer.

What's the point of any of this?

That question continued to rattle around in my head as we pulled up to the building that housed the record label's corporate offices. Miguel and Paul were already waiting to open the door of our vehicle, and Bear hopped out quickly to join them.

Heads turned as people realized there was someone of interest getting out of a vehicle. Before I could curse myself for forgetting to throw on a ball cap, one was plunked on my head by someone behind me, and my protective scrum hustled me through the crowd and into the lobby of the building.

We made our way up to the tenth floor, where we were quickly welcomed into a luxurious conference room overlooking downtown Los Angeles and offered refreshments. I declined, but Kenji took a small plate of food, and Micki accepted a cup of coffee.

Within moments, three executives entered the room and greeted me warmly. I'd been working with the same team for several years now, so it didn't take long before we were discussing how they'd spent their Thanksgiving vacations a couple of weeks earlier.

"I've lost track of time," I admitted with a laugh. "I usually hate missing Thanksgiving back home, but this year, I hardly realized it was happening. It's been a whirlwind. I have to admit to being happy I'm off the road for a bit. I could use some downtime."

Ellis Alberda gestured for me to take a seat. Everyone else filled in around me while Bear remained standing somewhere behind me. I hated not being able to see him, but it was nice to know he was there in the room. I could just make out his reflection in the window glass, enough to know he stood with his hands clasped casually in front of himself.

"Thanks for coming in, Zee," Ellis began. He flicked his eyes over my shoulder. "Your personal security isn't needed in the room, if you wouldn't mind having him wait outside."

Bear didn't move.

Micki shifted next to me. "Actually, Ellis, the current security protocol necessitates Zee's security team be in the room with him when in company. As we've discussed, there's an active security situation right now. I don't think it's a good idea to send Ryan out of the room."

She was right. There were at least three faces in here I didn't recognize, two assistants and an attorney. There was no way Bear would agree to leave me without a fight.

I was beginning to understand why he'd insisted on being the one to come here today.

"Understood," Ellis said easily. "I just thought it might be awkward for Zee, considering we're discussing his personal security."

I noticed every time Ellis didn't treat Bear like an actual human being in the room, and it set my teeth on edge. I didn't even think he realized he was doing it.

"What's the issue?" I asked, feeling the same nerves return from earlier.

"In light of recent news related to a high-profile celebrity and her close protection officer, we've taken the opportunity to reassess our policies in regard to securing high-value clients. The company has drafted new conduct agreements as part of this reassessment, and we need all of our clients to sign them for our records."

Suddenly, the purpose of the meeting became crystal clear. I must have had my head in the clouds all morning.

I tried not to jump to conclusions or panic. Instead, I took a slow, silent breath. "What is the revised policy, exactly?"

Ellis slid the paperwork toward me. "It's a standard no-fraternization policy between close protection officers and their principals. The purpose should be obvious. We want to make sure both sides are equally protected from the unfortunate situation others have found themselves in. If you wouldn't mind signing these three copies, we'll let you take one with you for your records."

I glanced at the window, catching Bear's reflection. His hands were no longer clasped in the middle. Instead, they were fisted by his sides.

This wasn't good.

"Don't worry," Ellis said. "All of the security companies we contract with will be required to sign the same policy agreement."

One of the attorneys passed down a pen while Ellis continued speaking. "But while you're here, I wanted to set up a time for our final contract signing. I mentioned to Micki that..."

His words drifted away as I looked down at the No Fraternization Agreement in front of me. Blood began to roar in my ears, and my palms began to sweat. If I refused to sign this today in a room full of people, they'd immediately suspect something was going on between Ryan Galloway and me.

I had no right to put Bear in that situation, regardless of my own feelings. But on the other hand, there was no way I could sign a paper saying I promised not to fraternize with him.

I wanted desperately to fraternize with him. In fact, I wanted him to fraternize me from behind as soon as I got home.

Micki leaned in and whispered, "The attorneys confirmed it's okay to sign."

I picked up the pen and unscrewed it, trying to buy some time. The cap jumped out of my hands and skittered across the table.

Kenji made a big production out of clearing his throat. His long fingers moved up to wrap around his slender neck as he did the worst acting job LA had ever seen.

"Excuse me. I'm allergic to *fish*. By any chance, was there salmon in the breakfast casserole?"

TWENTY-SIX

RYAN

Did you know that brown bears often part ways during winter? They hate the separation, though, and as soon as spring arrives, they'll roam miles to find each other again, sometimes even fighting off attackers to reunite with their nearest and dearest. You can't keep a bear separated from his friends or his honey for long.
—*Bear Facts for Insomniacs, Episode 47*

I stared at Zane's assistant for a nanosecond before muscle memory and habit spurred me into action upon hearing the word *fish*. "We need to get this man medical attention. Micki, can you step outside and find out if anyone has any antihistamine? Kenji, can you breathe?"

Zane frowned at me and opened his mouth as if to tell me that Kenji was obviously joking. Not only was he not allergic to fish, but his grandfather had been a commercial fisherman in Misawa, Japan, before coming to the US and marrying an American woman. Kenji had grown up on family fish recipes. His claim of being allergic was laughable, which was why I didn't understand Zane thinking I'd believed it for one minute.

"My throat feels a little…" Kenji made big eyes at Zane. "*Thick*," he added drily.

Finally, Zane got it. Unfortunately, he was worse at acting than Kenji was. "Oh no. We should get you to a hospital," he said robotically. He turned to the executives in the room. "I'm so sorry to cut our meeting short, but Kenji's been with me for over ten years. I need to make sure he's okay."

The people from the label nodded and expressed their concern, offering to have someone call an ambulance if necessary.

I assured them we would take good care of him. "Zee has a personal physician on call. She can meet us at the house. Thank you."

I ushered everyone out into the hall, where Paul and Miguel snapped to attention. "Fish," I said, moving us through the lobby to the elevator. They nodded and fell in line, calling down to Claudia to bring the car around. Thankfully, she and Ed were waiting for us. Unfortunately, Micki joined us, too.

Once we were en route to the house in Malibu, Zane threw himself back against the leather seat. "Kenji, fuck. You're the worst actor," he groaned.

Kenji tilted his head at Zane. "*You*—who knows I don't have any allergies except for pretty-boy supermodels—believed me. I'd say that makes me a great actor."

Micki looked between the two of them. "I'm confused. You aren't allergic to fish?"

Kenji speared her with an icy glare. When he spoke, his voice was cold enough to skate on. "I'm allergic to people who expect a high-level celebrity to sign papers practically the moment he steps off an international flight, without his attorney present."

While Micki stammered out an apology and tried explaining, I turned forward in my seat to hide my grin but caught Claudia's eye.

She lifted her eyebrow at me as if asking what the hell was going on. I didn't dare tell her.

"Drop me in Santa Monica?" I asked softly instead. She nodded.

We'd done this many times before, back before Zane had needed round-the-clock close personal protection and we would part ways at the end of a workday, letting our team's driver deposit him safely behind the monitored gates of his home.

Now, of course, he'd have Paul and Miguel with him for the next forty-eight hours, regardless of whether he was home alone or not.

As long as the threats continued and the Stamper was still at large, Zane's life was no longer his own.

Or mine.

I let out a frustrated breath.

"Is that what Violet was talking to you about this morning at the airport?" Zane asked. I didn't need to turn back around to know he was angry at me. "And you didn't bother to give me a heads-up?"

"She didn't say what it was, only that I needed to come into the office to sign some papers. She assumed I'd go with her immediately and knock it out before heading home." I didn't mention that Violet had also said she needed to talk to me about a temporary new assignment.

There was no point in mentioning that to Zane until I knew what the assignment was.

"This is ridiculous. Do they really think that piece of paper would have prevented what happened with... those other people?" He stopped himself from naming names in front of Claudia. "And what's next, huh? Does my pool guy have to sign one? My hairstylist? My attorney? Does my housekeeper have to sign one? That stupid agreement isn't going to stop someone from suing me, nor is it going to stop someone from being a dick boss. Come on! This is fucking ridiculous."

Kenji remained calm, as usual. "It's not going to go away just because you're upset about it."

Zane was on a roll. "Well, guess what? I won't sign it. And why should I? What are they going to do, fire me? Good. I'd like to see them try!"

Micki cut in carefully. "What's the problem exactly? It's not like this affects your current situation. Lou's a lesbian, and Ryan is straight. Why can't you just sign it?"

I closed my eyes and inhaled through my nose. This wasn't the time to come out to Zane's manager, but I also knew Zane would be uncomfortable letting the misunderstanding lie.

"It's the principle of the matter," Zane said stubbornly. I wanted to laugh. This wasn't the first time I'd heard him use the expression, or even the hundredth time. "Besides, why should I sign anything at all? What's the payoff for me?"

Micki sighed. "The payoff is that they sign it, too, and your personal security team doesn't target you the way Addison Canto's obviously did. No offense, Ryan."

I clenched my jaw against the desire to snap at her that saying "no offense" usually indicated big offense. The assumption that the close protection officer was a gold digger was annoying as fuck. But maybe it was a good reminder of the attitudes I'd be confronted with when our relationship went public.

Micki turned to Zane. "Violet's company is embracing the same policies. If they don't, the label will drop them. If the label's clients don't sign, then Violet's company will have to drop the label. Zee, everyone in town is doing this right now."

"It's reactionary," Zane snapped.

"Yes," Micki agreed patiently. "That's how this town works, and we all know it. No other label is going to accept you if you don't sign a no-frat policy after this."

They hadn't been paying attention to the drive because when Claudia finally pulled over at the end of my street, Zane made a squawking sound. "Why are we stopping?"

He'd obviously not recognized my neighborhood despite stopping here several times before to let me out. I chose to think it was because he was upset and distracted rather than take it as a disappointing reminder he knew very little about my life outside of the job.

I opened the door and nodded to Paul in the next vehicle to come up to this one. "I told you earlier, I have to get ready for a meeting. Claudia, thanks for the ride. Micki, thanks for going along with the lie. Kenji, if anyone crowdsources acting classes, you can count on me for a donation." I locked eyes with Zane and felt my heart tumble.

Warm brown eyes were wide with concern and a hint of betrayal. But they were still so fucking sweet.

Honey.

"Z. Text me later."

He didn't open his mouth. Didn't nod. Didn't react at all. Only stared at me while I grabbed my bag out of the back and began walking up the street to my place.

I heard the slam of the car door as Paul took my place in the SUV, and the two vehicles pulled away.

Before I reached my apartment, my phone buzzed with a text.

ZANE

I AM NOT FINE.

I closed my eyes and took in a shaky breath before texting him back.

No, honey. Neither am I.

And then I opened my eyes and walked home.
Alone.

———

The meeting with Violet came with a curveball.

"King Gerhard wants to hire us to provide supplemental security to the royal family for their holiday visit to the US. Isn't that amazing?"

I blinked at her in surprise. "That's great. Congratulations. They're very picky about the local companies they work with. They usually give their business to Alliance when they're here. At least that's how it was when I was in the royal guard."

"They originally hired Alliance and had it all set up, but then something happened, and someone dropped the ball. Since they trust you, and you trust us, they reached out. Only... they do have one condition," she said, pursing her lips and raising her eyebrows in a "pretty please" expression.

I gritted my teeth and forced myself to stay calm. "I already have a principal, Violet."

"Your assignment will only change temporarily. You will travel with the royal family for two weeks and be done in time for Christmas with your family in Montana."

I shook my head. "Zane is currently the target of a—"

She held up a hand. "I know. And we're obviously taking it very seriously. I doubled up Zee's coverage like we talked about, and I'm putting Joe Dudley as lead, starting tomorrow and for the whole time Zee's in Majestic. Bodhi Sorrentino's been eliminated as a suspect, and I'll be assigning Lou to shadow Noelle here in LA. If she gets any sudden urges to go to Wyoming, we'll know. Zee will be as safe as we can make him." She bit her lip. "I really need you to facilitate this royal visit for me, Ryan. You know what a big deal this would be for us in terms of getting other dignitaries to sign with us... and even the Ventdestinian royal family on future trips to the States. I really need your help on this."

She was right. Landing the royal family of any country would be a big deal for the company. And Violet had treated me incredibly well since hiring me. She'd paid me more than she was comfortable with and did her best to make sure I had schedule flexibility and first choice in shifts with Zane. Once she noticed how comfortable Zane was with me, she'd taken me out of any rotation that would remove me from working directly with him.

She must have seen my hesitation because she jumped in to reassure me. "Zee's going to be busy at the recording studio all week anyway. He's working on the Marian Foundation project, remember? And the studio will be locked down with so many high-value targets inside."

I wanted to say no immediately... but how could I? In light of the Addison Canto debacle and the no-frat policy Zane had refused to sign, would it seem suspicious if I refused to take a temporary assignment? Would it reflect back on Zane and force his hand to come out as a couple when he wasn't ready?

"What's their travel plan? What would the expectations be for me?"

As she described the royal family's trip to DC, New York, and the recent addition of Majestic, I hid a grin. Zane must have made an impression on the royal family for them to change their trip to accommodate a visit there.

Violet continued. "Apparently, they know someone with a hunting lodge near Majestic who's offered them accommodations. We've started researching the area, but since we're already familiar with that part of Wyoming because of Zee's visits, we're already one step ahead of any of our competitors."

"When would I have to meet them?"

"They land in DC tomorrow afternoon," she said with a wince when she saw my expression. "I know I'm asking a lot. You probably want nothing more than alone time and your own bed. I get it. But there's a bonus in here for you and my eternal gratitude. I can't make you do it, but I'm asking as nicely as I can."

I wasn't going to say no. Accepting it was the right thing to do. But I did make one condition of my own.

"Alright, I'll do it. But I'm heading home right now, and I don't want to hear from anyone for the rest of the day."

She grinned. "Done! I just need you to sign that paperwork before you go, and—"

I held up a hand and smiled back at her, friendly as could be.

"Nope. No paperwork. No work of any kind. I'm out of here. Catch me after the holidays for any admin stuff you need."

I made it sound like it had nothing to do with the paperwork itself, and she seemed to take it in stride. "Okay. I really appreciate this, Ryan. Go rest. I'll send you flight details in an email. Most likely a painfully early flight time in the morning. I apologize in advance."

I waved over my shoulder as I headed out the door. As soon as I got home, Zane buzzed me again.

ZANE

This is me waiting patiently for you to tell me how your meeting went.

I couldn't help but smile at his text. There was nothing patient about Zane Hendley when he was curious about something.

I kicked off my shoes, yanked off my clothes, and slid between cool sheets before video calling him.

"Did you sign it?" he asked as soon as he accepted the call. His face was crinkled in concern, but he was still the most beautiful man on the planet.

"No."

He relaxed back against his pillow. He was obviously lying in bed like I was. "You didn't?"

"I managed to put her off until after the holidays. But... I think you should sign it, Zane," I said, tackling the no-frat topic before breaking the bad news about my assignment.

He reacted the way I expected, squawking out an indignant response. "Why the fuck would you say that? I know it's not because you want there to be another obstacle keeping us apart. So are you saying I should just sign it and ignore it? In which case, it's ineffectual... which proves my fucking point. This is a performative piece of theater that has no teeth. What happens if someone breaks it? It means nothing."

I took a breath and tried to stay calm when inside, I was just as angry and afraid as he was. "Zane. You spent your entire career avoiding sexual and romantic relationships because you didn't want your reputation ruined by salacious rumors or a sex scandal. Think about that. If you don't sign this agreement, it's going to get out. Everyone's going to speculate on your reasons for refusing to sign it. After all this time avoiding scandal, you're going to be the one inviting it in."

"I'm not the one inviting it in!"

"I know, honey," I said gently. "And I'm so sorry you're—*we're*—being put in this situation. But I also understand why they want to cover their asses this way. People deserve to work in safe environments, free from harassment. And before you open your mouth, no. Of course I don't feel like you pressured or harassed me."

"Bear," he said, his voice sounding smaller suddenly. "I agree people should feel safe. I only disagree with the idea that a piece of paper is going to make a material difference in providing that environment."

He let out a breath. I heard the sound of his blankets as he shifted under the covers. I wished so badly I could be there with him, provide comfort and security with my own arms and lips.

"I'm tired of other people telling me how to run my business. I'm tired of feeling like I need to act a certain way or avoid acting a certain way. I'm tired of being told I should be a bad boy or a good boy. I just want to write and perform music. I want to help people. I want... I want to be myself. And I want to be with you."

I loved hearing those words, but I also knew how important his career was to him.

"Baby. Take some time to think about this. Think about what you want. What your dream is. You want to be a role model for kids. Maybe being a role model is making a public show of committing to this policy. Or at least not making a public show of opposing it."

"Is that what you think?" He sounded hurt.

I had to take a deep breath to calm my desire to burn the whole world before I could continue. "I think it's my job to protect you,

Zane, and I don't want to see your reputation negatively impacted by this, that's all."

"Your job," he said in a dull voice.

My heart filled with love for him. "My job as the person who loves you most in this world, Z," I said softly. "Yes. My job."

Thankfully, that made him smile. "You think you love me most? That's a high bar. Gran thinks very highly of me. So does Landry."

"Landry can fuck right off, and I'll even give Gran a run for her money. I've loved you for a long time, Zane. Longer than you know."

There was silence on the line for a beat.

"I introduced myself to you as Zane the day we met. I never do that in business. It's always Zee."

I thought back to his other interactions with people—other close protection officers, vendors, fellow artists. He almost always went by Zee in his professional life. It wasn't until the relationship became more personal that people called him Zane.

"Why?" I asked.

His eyelashes fluttered nervously. "I got flustered. Up walked this beautiful giant of a man, and suddenly, my tongue felt too big, and my skin didn't fit on my body anymore."

I loved imagining a flustered Zane in the recording studio. "So you spilled the beans. Gave me your legal name by accident? Should I have been calling you Zee all this time?"

"I want you in my bed." His words were soft and hot.

The man was less than fifteen miles up the coast from here in his sun-filled Malibu home. It wouldn't take me long to get there, half an hour this time of day.

But as soon as I arrived, I'd face Paul and Miguel.

"Will I see you tomorrow?" he asked hopefully.

My stomach dropped. This was the part of the conversation I'd been dreading the most. "Violet is pulling me off your detail temporarily."

His eyes bugged. "What? Why? Because I didn't sign the papers? I'll sign the papers, Bear. Jesus."

"No, honey. It's not about that. King Gerhard and the royal family are coming to the States. They've actually decided to come see you play in Majestic."

I could tell he didn't give a shit about that part. "So? What does that have to do with my protection detail?"

"They want me on their detail while they're in the US. They're willing to hire Violet's company to provide domestic coverage, but the catch is that it has to be me."

He stared at me in shock. "Are they for real? Do they not give a single shit about the fact you already have a job? You already have an assignment, and I don't say this often, but he's *kind of a big deal.*"

I bit my tongue against a laugh. "He is. But he's not royalty, despite the fact Pop-Rocks Daily once called him the King of Cool."

Zane's glare was comical despite being serious. It was rare to see him this annoyed. "Don't try to make me laugh right now. I'm extremely pissed off, Bear."

"I can see that, honey. You're not the only one. I wasn't happy about it, either."

"But you agreed to it."

"Yes, because I felt like I owed Violet a solid. She's taken good care of me since I came to work for her."

Zane propped the phone on a pillow and rubbed his face with both hands. "This is the opposite of how I wanted things to be when we got home. When the hell am I going to see you again?"

"Majestic," I said with a grin. "At least now I'll get to see you ring the bells or whatever the fuck."

His face softened into a reluctant smile. "Good. But then you'll go to Montana, right? To see your family? They're not keeping you from your visit home, are they?"

I wanted to tell him that I no longer wanted to go to my sister's place if it meant not being able to spend some time with him first, but I kept my mouth closed to keep from making promises we weren't ready for.

"The Ventdestinian designation is flying home after Majestic

Bells, I think. I'm not sure. But yes, Violet specifically said I'd be off for Christmas."

We spoke for a few more minutes before he was interrupted by a call from Micki. "I have to take this, Bear. I think it's about the recording schedule. Call me later?"

I nodded and blew a kiss at the screen. "Go easy, baby. Give yourself a chance to rest."

His smile made my heart too big for my chest. "You still looking out for me, Bear?"

"Always, honey. I love you. More than anything."

That night, we missed each other between catching up on work commitments, laundry and packing, and being carried away by jet lag. The following morning, I was two hours into my flight east by the time he woke up and texted me.

It was a video of him sitting out by the pool with the sunrise a warm peachy pink on his skin. He wore rumpled pajama pants and his Jude Marian hoodie. His hair was in an early morning tangle, and his first cup of coffee was still steaming by his side. He had his favorite acoustic guitar in his lap.

Damned if he didn't look right into the camera, grin and wink, and start right in playing "Sanctuary."

It was the last time I saw his face for ten days.

TWENTY-SEVEN
ZANE

Black bears are known for their independence and resourceful-ness. When it comes to nourishment, they don't just stick to one menu—these bears can eat a whopping 200 different types of foods! And if something doesn't suit their taste, they're not afraid to wander off and find something that does. They priori-tize their needs and desires because they know true bear happi-ness comes from following their own path.
—Bear Facts for Insomniacs, Episode 61

Keeping busy with the new project recording was a double-edged sword. On the one hand, it distracted me from the fact that Ryan wasn't there. On the other, it was pretty fucking unfair to suddenly find myself with a boyfriend and not be able to touch him or kiss him or feel his cock inside me or sleep in his arms.

I was bitter and resentful. I hated the king of Ventdestine. I didn't much like Violet right now. And I resented the fuck out of the fact I had hundreds of millions of dollars... yet my money couldn't solve this problem because my boyfriend had fucking principles.

"I hate principles," I muttered.

Kenji continued to tap on his iPad as the plane cut through the California sky on the way toward Wyoming. "Girl, same. Mrs. Rowland. She thought the jocks deserved precedence because they worked so hard to represent us. Meanwhile, those of us who were mathletes could suck eggs. Please tell me what a stinky junior varsity wrestler ever did to deserve second helpings in the lunch line? If you asked me—which no one did—it was the scrawny kids that needed the extra food."

I ignored him and continued grumbling under my breath.

"Please tell me you at least pleasure yourselves at night over Face-Time because you seem a little... frustrated." Kenji's voice was as dry as it would have been if he'd been explaining quarterly estimated tax payments.

"I would, but we're on completely different schedules! When I finish my workday, Bear's in the middle of all the royal family's evening commitments. It's been impossible. He tries calling me when he's done, but by then, I'm at dinner with the artists from the project this week. You know how it's been. I'm at my wit's end."

Kenji finally looked up and met my eye. "Maybe you should reconsider this relationship."

I glared at him. "I hope you're joking. I'm not reconsidering it! I'm just... sad. I miss the hell out of him. It's been ten days!"

"See, this is why I stay away from entanglements. The pining. I fucking hate pining. It's beneath my dignity, and quite frankly, it's beneath yours, too. You're better than this. I say you put the moves on hot Sheriff Foster this weekend." Kenji bounced his eyebrows. "He'd be up for it. Probably. And he's a big muscular guy, which is clearly your type."

I stared at him. "What the fuck are you doing right now?"

"You're like a baby bird. You took one step outside the eggshell and imprinted on the first thing you saw. It's common. Nobody blames you. But maybe this isn't the guy. Maybe you don't need one guy. Maybe you need lots of guys. I'd like to see you decide to sample all the... the forest... because there are plenty more animals out there, Zane."

I felt like he was trying to make a point, but I was too annoyed to see it.

"I'm in love with Ryan Galloway. It's not a whim, Kenji. And I'm not a fucking baby bird. I'm a man who knows what he wants. I'm a business owner, a billionaire, a motherfucking global rock star. And I want to be with the man I love."

"Mm," he said, going back to tapping on the tablet. "If only there was a way. But your hands are tied, really. I mean, between the label's strict rules and Violet's new policy." He pursed his lips and shook his head sadly. "Even billionaires have to play by the rules, I guess."

I finally saw through him. Saw through this ridiculous bullshit. He was provoking me into taking action.

"I fucking hate you. Why can't you just say what you mean?"

He shrugged. "Chaska Inira says the map to the answer is already drawn on your heart."

I had no patience for his Peruvian faith healer right now. "What the fuck does that mean?"

"It means maybe you need to be provoked before you realize you already know what you want to do. You already have the answers, Zane. I'm just trying to get you to drop your fear so you can get to it."

I opened my mouth to snap at him that it wasn't fear, but I stopped before the first word came out.

It *was* fear. Fear of fucking up. Fear of letting people down. Fear of upsetting people.

Fear of being abandoned.

"I'm worried it'll be too much. That he won't want to be with me," I admitted softly.

Kenji set his tablet aside and turned to me. "What else?"

"I'm worried the record label won't want to renew me?"

He shrugged. "Do you need them?"

Of course I needed them. Every big performer needed a big-name label behind them.

Didn't they?

I met Kenji's eyes. Whatever he saw in mine made him sigh and pull back out his tablet. "If only you could afford to start your own label," he muttered sarcastically.

Nervous butterflies began to riot in my gut. "Surely I can't just start my own label..."

"Check your email," he said mildly. "The business plan is already there, along with a list of ten artists who are up for contract renewal and would switch to you in a heartbeat. I also scheduled that call you mentioned with the Irish woman who plays the mandolin. You know she's unsigned, right?"

What's the point of any of this?

"Holy shit." I felt my chest rise and fall with excitement. "We're starting a record label, aren't we?"

"The attorneys are just waiting for you to choose a name before submitting the paperwork. I found a director-level executive I like for this, but I put together a short list of other options in case you don't like him. You'll like him, though. He's gay. I think it's important since you're going to focus on LGBTQ talent, but if you disagree, I'll allow it."

The edge of his lip quirked up as I shoved him. "I hate it when you know what we're all going to do before we do it. It's unnatural."

Kenji met my eyes. I could see he was as excited as I was. "You're going to be amazing at this, Zane. The brotherhood will be proud of you... and your Bear will, too."

Tears sprang to my eyes. After all these years of making money, making decisions, making moves in my multiple endeavors, this was the first time I felt the soul-deep certainty that I was on the right path. "Thank you for your support, Kenji. I don't know what any of us would do without you."

"I should have invested in a waterproof interior for this plane since it's seen so many tears," he muttered, patiently allowing me to kiss him on the cheek in thanks.

"I can't wait to tell everyone. Who all will be there when we arrive?"

He went back to tapping the tablet, probably initiating some of the business tasks that had been waiting for my approval. "Everyone. You're the last one in except for Landry, and god only knows when the prima donna will arrive. It's not like he keeps me informed of his movements."

I wanted to ask him why he was so bitter about Landry, but I honestly already knew.

Landry was everything Kenji hated. He was paid for being beautiful instead of smart and diligent. He didn't take things seriously. He got into trouble often—everything from missed flights to misdemeanors—and every time, he'd call Kenji to help sort him out. While Kenji was officially the personal assistant to all of us in the brotherhood—and ran a small army of under-assistants and various vendors to help, too—dealing with Landry alone could easily have taken all Kenji's attention if he let it.

I didn't think this was a coincidence. Landry was a brilliant strategist, and I was pretty sure he wanted as much of Kenji's time and focus as he could get... even if he had to get in trouble to do it. But for all that Kenji was insightful (and practically psychic) when it came to figuring out what the rest of the brotherhood needed and wanted, he seemed absolutely clueless when it came to Landry.

Or maybe when it came to *himself*.

My phone buzzed with a text from Bear.

BEAR

About to go wheels up. Heading to Mount Rushmore for the night, then on to Majestic. T-minus 24 hours until I see your beautiful face.

> I saw an ad on Instagram for a pop-up contraption soccer moms use to help their kids change clothes at practice when there's not a restroom nearby. It's like a tube-shaped tent. I keep fantasizing about whipping one of those things out when I see you and hopping into it so you and I can greet each other properly without anyone seeing us.

BEAR

> ... that's not what I fantasize you whipping out, Z.

I grinned at my phone like a fool.

> Will you be able to take a break and come to Dev and Tully's house?

BEAR

> Working on it. I'll see you at the Bells event, and then once I help get the family settled back at the lodge, I plan to come see you for a few hours. We need to talk about the future, and I need to feel your skin under my hands.

I shivered.

> Perfect. I vote twenty minutes talking, all the rest, hand-ing.

BEAR

> You think twenty minutes is enough to sort our whole future, huh?

> Honestly? I think twenty is excessive, but I want to be considerate of your needs. <laugh-cry emoji>

BEAR

> Zane...

> Nope. I know what I want, Bear. I know who I can't live without. And as some people have reminded me recently, it's okay for me to sometimes ENJOY the benefits of being a billionaire rock star, so that's what I'd like to do. But what you want matters more to me than anything. I know you love your job. So, we'll talk.

BEAR

> Yeah. We'll talk. But Z? There is nothing in this world I love more than you. So fuck the job. Fuck anything that keeps us apart. I know who I can't live without, too.

I sniffled a little, my need for him making my chest ache.

> You're not allowed to say nice things when you're so far away. Disallowed.

BEAR

> I'll keep that in mind. No more being far away.

Just as I prepared to type a response, an email alert flashed up. The words *Semper in scopum* grabbed my attention immediately.

To Zee,
He's back where he belongs.
See you in Majestic.
Semper in scopum.

My head felt like a helium balloon that had just been released into the sky. *He's back where he belongs?* What the fuck?

"Kenji," I breathed. "Kenji, fuck. Help. What does this mean? Does this mean what it looks like? *Is Ryan the target?*"

I handed him my phone so he could read the email. There was no point in panic-dialing Bear if I was off the mark.

"You need to send this to Ryan immediately."

I forwarded it to his email, copied Violet, and then dialed Bear with shaking hands.

There was no answer—he might have his phone in airplane mode —so I dialed Violet.

"Check your email," I said as soon as she picked up the call. "I think the Stamper's after Ryan. I think it's..." I hesitated before accusing someone in the royal family of a crime. "I think maybe Ryan is in trouble, Violet."

"Hang on." I heard sounds of her shuffling things as if getting to her laptop. "That makes no sense, Zee. Why would Ryan be the target?"

"I don't know. The royal family wants him back. They offered him a ton of money in Amsterdam, and he said no. Maybe... maybe they think getting to me somehow will make the record label lose faith in Ryan and replace him? Maybe then they think he'd go back to Ventdestine?"

"That's an awfully convoluted way to go about recruiting someone for a job, Zee," Violet said with excessive patience. "The stamp is the logo from your album. They got to you at your shows. You're one of the world's largest celebrities right now. How could it not be you? No offense to Ryan, but close protection officers aren't hard to find. They couldn't need Ryan that badly."

I shook my head in frustration. "You don't understand. They have this weird superstition. King Asger thought it was fate that Ryan saved him. That the *winds of fortune* had blown him to them at the exact right time. What if... what if King Gerhard thinks his father died because Ryan wasn't there? What if he thinks fate wants Ryan back?"

"I still think they would have made him a better offer," she said matter-of-factly. "If the king of Ventdestine wanted Ryan Galloway so much, he could make the offer tempting enough for Ryan to say yes, Zee. Everyone has a price."

I thought about the man I loved. About how I'd offered to support him so he could travel with me and we could be together.

About how living in Ventdestine meant Ryan had been forced to deny an important part of himself. "The price isn't always a financial one, Violet."

She hesitated. "You're right. Okay. I'll run this down, Zee. I promise. Hang tight. I'm also going to check with Lou and make sure Noelle is accounted for, too."

I had to admit, I hadn't even considered Noelle since Amsterdam. But I supposed she was doing PR liaison stuff for the royal family, wasn't she? It wouldn't hurt to run it down and see if she had any helpful insight.

"Do you have a way of tracking Ryan? He's not answering my call, and he's stopped texting." Why hadn't it occurred to me to ask him to share his location with me? What kind of boyfriend was I that I couldn't look out for him the way he looked out for me?

"His last location was Teterboro. They're probably in flight."

"I'm sure there's Wi-Fi on the plane. Why isn't he online?"

I could hear the sound of her typing. "Not sure. Let me go and see if I can contact someone else on their team. I'll be in touch. But Zee?"

"Yeah?"

"If Ryan's the target, that's good news for you."

My mouth dropped open as I tried to figure out how I was possibly misunderstanding her words. She couldn't mean that, could she?

"How so?"

"It would mean you're out of danger. If this is about Ryan, we can deal with that separately. But at least you'd be able to breathe a little freer."

I felt Kenji's hand slide into mine and squeeze it tightly. I turned to him with incredulity on my face as I tried to remain calm and keep from outing Bear without his permission or getting him fired on the spot.

"If you think I'll breathe freer knowing someone was using me to get to him, you don't know me very well. Please get in touch with him and keep me updated, Violet. I want to know as soon as you hear from him."

As she ended the call, the flight attendant notified us we were landing. Majestic's private airstrip had become a familiar landmark in the past couple of years. I looked out the window as we left the Rockies behind us and flew above the tumbling foothills. The Majestic River meandered out of the hills and onto the flats, curving around a tiny speck I knew was Way and Silas's tiny house on the Fletcher Ranch.

Something about Majestic anchored me. Even though I was terrified for Bear, I was relieved to finally be returning to the place where I felt loved and supported. The place where my family lived.

The brotherhood's roots here had been planted as tiny seeds when Silas had accidentally married the local mayor. Fresh shoots had sprouted up when Dev had followed him and settled here with Tully and their daughter, Lellie.

And now, I was buying up a fucking enormous piece of the land I'd come to love, in hopes Bear would want to build a life with me here and follow our dreams together. A winter sports camp. Apparently a freaking record label. A family. A *home*.

But in order for that to happen, we needed to take care of the threats to our happiness and security once and for all.

When the plane touched down, I told Kenji I wanted to refuel and immediately fly to Rapid City.

"We can intercept them," I explained. "It's not that far."

Kenji's eyes flicked ahead to where Paul and Miguel were placing bets on whether it would snow today or tomorrow.

"That's not happening, Zane," Kenji said softly. "He's not in actual danger. If the king wants him in the royal guard, they're not going to hurt him. And if you suddenly show up trailing the kind of lookie-loo media attention you always attract, it would turn a currently secret situation into a sensational story on a global scale. You need to let Violet's team handle it. I promise, if I thought there was something you could do right now, I'd make sure you were doing it."

I blew out a breath. Kenji was right. If it was the royal family behind the threats, that probably meant Bear wasn't in personal danger. But my mind spun wildly out of control.

"What if the king kidnaps him and flies him to Ventdestine? What if he won't take no for an answer? What if—"

"Then we will get him back. But for right now..." Kenji pointed across the tarmac to the waiting SUVs, where a familiar clutch of humans stood, and a bright-eyed little girl happily shook a little string of jingle bells in the air. "Take a breath, Zane. We're home."

I glanced over at him, surprised to hear him call Majestic home since he lived in New York. But then again, this little Wyoming town had charmed us all.

I made a beeline for Lellie and grabbed her out of Tully's arms to hold her tight. "Lellie-girl," I said, suddenly feeling tight-chested with affection and a true sense of family. She smelled like apples and peanut butter sandwiches.

"Zay!" she said happily, patting my face. "Zay sing me."

Dev stepped in behind her and hugged us both. Other than Shaky Knees in Atlanta, I hadn't seen them much in person, but Lellie knew me from the lullaby videos I'd sent them. She could play them on an iPad at night or whenever they needed to keep her entertained or distracted for a little while.

I loved being able to be a part of her life even when I wasn't there. "Thank you, guys, for coming to get me. I think my security team arranged for vehicles, but maybe they'll let me ride with you if you have enough room in the truck."

"Dev got me a minivan," Tully said with a shit-eating grin.

"It's not a minivan," Dev corrected with a sigh. "And it wasn't for you; it was for all of us. How many times are you going to give me hell for this? It's a luxury touring van. For when we want to drive through Yellowstone or go on a longer car ride as a family—"

"*Pfft.* Says *you.* I freakin' *love* my minivan. Someday, I'm gonna be driving that beast to soccer practices. I'm gonna be rockin' the school pickup line. Lellie's gonna say, 'Can you take me and twelve of my closest friends to the mall, but make sure you walk ten steps behind us so no one knows you're with us?' and I'm gonna say, 'Heck yeah, kids, pile in.' The minivan isn't a car, Devon. It's a way of life. And I'm here for it."

We made our way out to the parking lot, where, sure enough, a luxury Mercedes touring van shone like a beacon alongside the pair of dark SUVs my team had hired. Paul gave me a nod before accompanying me to the van with Dev, Tully, and Lellie, while Kenji went with Miguel so he could take a phone call in relative peace.

I checked my phone obsessively during the drive in hopes of getting a response from Bear or Violet, but there was nothing. My fingers itched to text both of them again, but I'd already texted Bear several times, and if I texted Violet again, my newfound obsession for my personal protection officer would set off alarm bells, especially given the current "no frat" situation.

By the time we got to Dev and Tully's place, I was starting to get very scared.

The rest of the brotherhood was waiting for us at Dev's house, but I'd barely gotten through a chaotic round of hugs and greetings before my phone rang with an incoming call from Lou. I immediately seized it and stalked into the kitchen, dimly aware that Kenji was hurriedly explaining the situation to the others in a low, urgent tone.

"Lou?" I demanded. "Is everything okay? Have you heard from Ryan? Is he—?"

"Zee?" Instead of Lou's rough cadence, I recognized the familiar voice of my former publicist.

"Noelle?" I blinked. "What's going on?"

"Lots of things, apparently," she said in a hurt voice. "I'm here with your bodyguard, answering her questions—which, seriously, am I actually being *investigated*, Zee? Because that is *incredibly* insulting. You and I wanted to take your career in different directions, I know, and I admit I made some mistakes, but I thought we were over that. In Amsterdam, I tried to thank you and explain how I'm actually way, way happier now. I'm a public relations liaison for visiting foreign dignitaries, and I freaking love it. I'm really good at it. And no offense, but like... you're gonna have a hot career for, what? Another ten years? Tops? Royalty lasts forever—"

There were the brief sounds of a tussle, and then Lou's voice clipped, "I'm gonna nutshell this for you since Chatty Cathy here will take all day."

"Harsh," Noelle muttered in the background. Lou ignored her.

"I asked if she could explain how she'd come to be in every single location where we've had an, um... incident," Lou said carefully, not revealing too much information. "Apparently, she was in San Diego meeting up with the head of the royal guard—"

"Kasper," Noelle called into the phone.

"Kasper. He was supposedly meeting her on behalf of the royal family to discuss publicist stuff for this holiday trip to the US. Noelle is working as a publicist for a company that provides domestic media support to visiting dignitaries."

Noelle tried to butt in again, but Lou spoke over her. "He met with her in San Diego and Los Angeles, both times at your shows there because he's supposedly a huge fan. Such a big fan Noelle ended up giving him a bunch of swag. You know, things like pens, temporary tattoos, a *novelty rubber stamp from your first album.*"

I couldn't believe what I was hearing. "Kasper? But... he couldn't have been at Shaky Knees."

I thought of where Bear was right now. On a plane in the air over god-knew-where with the royal family.

And Kasper.

My chest was tight, and it wasn't until I felt a hand on my shoulder and heard Kenji's low voice in my ear reminding me to breathe that I realized I was hyperventilating.

"Apparently, he was. He met up with Noelle there, too, and *someone* didn't seem to think that was an excessive amount of in-person meetings to arrange PR for a two-week trip, but whatever."

I heard Noelle complain in the background.

"Lou, did you tell Violet all this?" I demanded.

"She got the longer, Noelle-narrated version, but yes," Lou agreed. "She said she's checking on a few more things."

"Good. Please, *please* keep me posted. I need someone to notify me as soon as they contact Ryan. He needs to know to keep an eye on Kasper—"

"Kasper's not with Ryan. That's the other thing."

I let out a sigh of relief. "Couldn't you have led with that? Jesus, Lou. I was worried. Where is he?"

"According to a final logistics text from Ryan, Kasper is going with the advance team directly to Majestic. We're waiting for confirmation now, and Violet is contacting the sheriff in Majestic."

I sucked in a breath, suddenly panicked. He was coming here? What would Kasper do? How far would he go? Would he step up his fear campaign and actually try to hurt me? Oh, god, Bear would never forgive himself.

And all for what? Because Kasper thought if Bear stopped protecting me, he'd immediately run back to Ventdestine? Like there weren't a billion other jobs he could do instead?

Clearly, the man wasn't thinking logically. He'd believed in the winds of fortune too hard and had lost sight of reality. How could I make it clear that Bear was no longer coming back to Ventdestine under any conditions? How could I get Kasper to leave us the hell alone? How could I protect Bear from someone who couldn't see the truth when it was right in front of him?

How could I reveal the truth without spilling our secret?

I bit my lip as a memory of playing Secret Sauce tickled the back of my mind. "*...the best way to deal with multiple potential scandals was to let them all blow free at once...*"

Maybe I didn't want to divulge one truth but *five* truths.

"Noelle," I said slowly. "I need to write a few press releases." I bit my lip and gave Kenji a nervous smile. "Do you think you can help?"

TWENTY-EIGHT

RYAN

Black bears are sometimes more wary of each other than they are of other big predators like wolves or mountain lions. Turns out, the real threat can come from the least expected places— like another bear competing for food or territory. Despite this, bears rely on their families, their mates, and their close allies, especially when facing the unknown. They know they need to trust their instincts and lean on the people they love.
—Bear Facts for Insomniacs, Episode 101

I wasn't used to being so out of pocket, and I sure as shit wasn't used to being cut off from Zane.

The text exchange I'd had with him before boarding the plane went a long way toward reassuring me. I couldn't wait to see him. It had been too many days, and I was itching to hold him again.

After only ten days apart, I realized I was going to have to figure something else out for work. I couldn't be apart from him like this. We needed to make a change so we could be together.

"You're on edge," the king said, crossing his legs as he turned toward me in one of the leather seats on the sleek Gulfstream. "I told Kasper not to insist on you joining us for this trip. You probably wanted a break after the tour."

"Kasper?" I asked in surprise. "I assumed you were the one who insisted on having me be team lead."

He shook his head and rattled ice cubes in his glass. The flight attendant jumped to attention and refilled his glass with more water without being asked. Gerhard nodded his thanks. "I already have a team lead. *Kasper*. He's been with me a long time—you know that. I understand the need for hiring domestic security as well, but I certainly don't need our security liaison to be someone who already has an assignment. The entire situation made me uncomfortable. You know I don't like people making a fuss about me, Ryan."

It didn't make any sense. "Why would Kasper have told my boss that my involvement was required in order to give her the business? Do you think he was particularly worried? Is it those recent threats against you? Kasper mentioned something about it, back in Amsterdam."

He shook his head again. "There haven't been any threats that I'm aware of. Nothing over the usual amount of anti-royal malcontent. You know we found and tried the man who killed my father. He had mental health issues, which... I suppose anyone who shoots at another person has mental health issues, but I'm having trouble forgiving him. That's simply a bridge too far."

"I don't forgive him," I said bluntly. "Asger was a good man. No one had the right to take him from us."

We shared a quiet moment, each of us remembering Gerhard's father. Intrusive thoughts about Kasper broke through, though. "I'm surprised Kasper wanted to go to Majestic with the advance team," I said. "Doesn't he make a point of staying by you? He was superstitious to begin with, but I imagine Asger's death made him even more so."

"Yes." Gerhard frowned. "It's very unlike him. He almost never leaves my side when we're out of the country. The only other time I can think was when he went to Los Angeles last summer to see a friend while I was visiting the shipyards in San Diego."

His words were like pulling the plug on a bathtub, draining all the blood out of me at once. "You were in LA and San Diego last summer? When?" Those were the cities where the stampings had happened before Shaky Knees in October.

Gerhard's frown intensified. "I never went to Los Angeles. Only San Diego. Let me see when that was." He called over his personal assistant to ask. The older woman confirmed the dates, and my head began to spin.

Was it possible Kasper was the Stamper? No. He would have had to be in Atlanta in the fall. "Where was he in mid to late October? Did he come back to the States at all during that time?"

"Not that I can recall." He narrowed his eyes. "Why are you asking me questions about Kasper?"

Before I could begin to explain, he added, "He might have been in London in October. I recall him taking a week of holiday around that time."

Nerves made me restless. I had to remind myself not to jump to conclusions. Kasper, of all people, valued security. Surely he wouldn't put my principal in jeopardy to suit his own needs.

"I need to know exactly when he was gone."

Gerhard shifted in his seat. "First, you need to tell me what's going on, Ryan. You look very upset. Has Kasper done something to upset you?"

It didn't make any sense. But then again, Kasper held a strong belief in the Ventdestinian winds of fortune. "Someone has been threatening my principal," I explained carefully. "Zee has received threats, but the way they were written, it seemed to come from someone whose main motivation was getting me off his protection detail."

"Kasper has said many times you belong back in Ventdestine,"

Gerhard said hesitantly. "And he was very upset in Amsterdam when you refused our offer. I told him to let it go."

"Find out when he was on holiday. *Please.*" I pulled out my phone to text Zane.

> Zane, holy shit. I think I know who the Stamper is.
>
> Please tell me you're at the ranch.
>
> Stay away from Kasper! He's on the Ventdestinian advance team and he's in Majestic. Tell Miguel and Paul to lock you down somewhere safe, honey.

When I realized none of my texts were going through, I stood up and found the flight attendant, only to discover they were having problems with the router.

"Reset it, for fuck's sake," I growled. "Or tell the pilot I need to get a message to the private airport in Majestic, Wyoming."

Once they were able to get the Wi-Fi working, a string of texts came pouring in from Zane and Violet.

> ZANE
>
> Bear! Crap. You're still not getting these messages, are you?
>
> ZANE
>
> I think Kasper—Royal Guard Kasper!—is the Stamper.
>
> ZANE
>
> I know it sounds weird, but I promise it makes sense.
>
> ZANE
>
> I have to do something, Bear. Something big. Something that'll keep you protected. And I really wish I could talk to you about it first, but I need you to trust me. I love you.

VIOLET

> Ryan, Lou obtained credible information that the Stamper is Kasper. I'm locking Zane down now. Get in touch ASAP. We need to coordinate a response.

I stared at them in shock. It had only been two hours since I'd spoken to him. How the fuck had so much happened?

I returned to my seat next to Gerhard and updated him. His nostrils flared. "Someone get Kasper on the phone right now! If he has defied me, he will regret it."

His assistant scrambled to initiate a call over Wi-Fi, but there was no response.

"Fuck!" I hissed. "I need to be there. I can't believe this is happening."

"Keep trying," Gerhard commanded.

Gisella appeared from the back of the plane, where she'd been hanging out with the kids. "What's going on?"

Gerhard caught her up while I texted Zane. I didn't dare try to call him while the king's people were using what little internet we had.

> Whatever you're planning to do, STAY SAFE. Keep your protection officers with you at all times.

Then I texted the head of law enforcement in Majestic.

> Foster, BOLO: Ventdestinian foreign national named Kasper Beaulund.

I followed it with a physical description and short explanation of what was going on.

FOSTER

> Copy that.

A call tried coming in from Zane, but I had to decline it. I texted him instead.

> On plane, can't call. Give me update pls.

"Fuck, I need to be there," I said under my breath.

Gisella broke in. "Then we go there."

The king looked at her in disgruntled surprise. "But our plans—"

She reached for her husband's hand. "Your father owed Ryan his life, my love. He would have wanted you to help ensure his happiness. He's obviously worried about his..." She gave me a particular look, urging me to fill in the blank, even though she clearly knew.

"Partner," I said awkwardly. "He's my... he's everything. He's..." I let out a shaky breath. "Finding someone like him was the reason I left Ventdestine. And then the winds whispered fortune on me. Because three weeks after I got back to the States, I was assigned to protect him."

Gisella beamed. The king blushed and looked everywhere but at me. I didn't care.

"I want to go to him," I admitted, reaching out for what I wanted, the way I always urged Zane to do. "Please."

The king gave a nod, and Gisella grinned and turned to the flight attendant. "Tell the pilot to reroute us to Majestic, please. We need to get there as soon as possible."

What followed was a hectic and stressful hour, but soon, we were on the ground in Majestic, waiting for the steps to be lowered. There was certain security protocol that needed to be respected when the royal family landed anywhere, so I forced myself to focus on that process until the pilot had confirmed we were clear to deboard.

Thankfully, Foster Blake and several of his fellow officers were there with a fleet of official vehicles with flashing lights. A sleek Mercedes van was parked nearby, along with séveral dark-colored SUVs. Surely my people wouldn't have allowed Zane to come here until we found Kasper.

But as soon as I made my way down the jet's stairs, I saw Zane's familiar honey-brown hair being lifted by the cold wind coming off the mountains as he stepped out of the van. My heart lurched as I scanned the area for Kasper.

My rational brain didn't think Kasper was capable of physically harming Zane, but my heart didn't give a fuck what my rational brain thought.

Foster approached the jet stairs first. "We got him, Ryan. He's in custody, and we've confirmed he's your guy."

It was too good to be true. "For real? Just like that?"

He nodded. "It's not hard to find an outsider in Majestic, even when it's full up for the Bells. Your man registered at a hotel under his real name and was eating a sandwich in his room when we arrived. Easy peasy."

"That sounds too good to be true," I admitted.

"Well, fine. If you must know, your man took a little wind out of his sails first. So the perp was feeding his feelings."

I didn't understand what he meant, but that wasn't my priority at the moment.

Foster saw me staring at Zane as he approached the line of officers at the entrance to the tarmac. "Let him through," Foster called before turning to me. "I'll take over with the royals. You go reassure your principal."

Part of me felt like I needed to hold back on a big public display of affection at a Ventdestinian appearance, but then I remembered several things. This wasn't a Ventdestinian appearance, we were in the States, where I could publicly display just about anything I wanted to, and I loved Zane Hendley too much to hide my true feelings for him.

I didn't owe the Ventdestinian royal family anything. Not anymore.

Zane approached cautiously, but I threw caution to the wind and began running. Zane's face lit up, and he picked up the pace, too, throwing himself into my arms and hugging me tightly.

"They got him," Zane said. "He's in custody."

"Foster told me, honey. I'm just glad you're okay."

He pulled back so he could meet my eyes. "I did something, Bear. And I'm afraid you might be mad."

"Never," I insisted. I was too happy to see him, too relieved he was okay, to be upset at anything he might have done.

Then I remembered the one thing I wouldn't have forgiven him for. "Tell me you didn't put yourself in danger, Z."

He shook his head wildly. "No, not that. I promise."

"Then what?"

My phone buzzed with news alerts, one after the other. Zane's eyes flicked around, suddenly looking everywhere but at me. "Um, that's... that's probably part of it."

"What do you mean?"

I pulled out my phone to look, keeping one arm locked around him. A flood of headlines ran up my screen.

Rocker Reportedly Pledges $10M to Youth Winter Sports

Zee Barlo Admits to Being in Relationship with Bodyguard! "I'm In Love," He Says.

Rock star/Bodyguard Love Stories On the Rise... IRL and On Your Shelves!

Zee Barlo, Jude Marian, Gentry Kane, and others release single to raise money for LGBTQ youth

Rocker Zee Barlo Announces New Record Label: Fairytale Recording Studio

Zee Barlo Buys Sprawling Ranch in Wyoming

I waited for the string of headlines to end, but they simply... didn't.

I finally met his eyes. "Someone's been busy?"

"Don't be mad." Zane was suddenly white as a sheet. "Please. I felt more confident about your reaction when I did it, but now..."

I slid the phone back into my pocket and pulled him close again, leaning in to press a drugging kiss to his lips. "I love you. I'm on board with whatever our plan is. I just want to know what the hell the plan is because that... was a lot."

"I know, but when I found out Kasper was doing this because he wanted you back in Ventdestine, I realized... there was a way to make sure he wouldn't want you back there."

The realization came to me. "Tell the world I'm gay."

He nodded and swallowed. "And then I remembered your story about Secret Sauce and how the king took the teeth out of the scandal by flooding the media with lots of scandals at once."

I reached up to cup his beautiful face. "So you made up some stuff to distract them from the bodyguard affair?" I teased.

"None of it's made up."

I blinked at him. The headlines scrolled through my memory. "The winter sports pledge."

"I'm funding a winter sports program here in Majestic. And I hope my boyfriend will figure out how to run it."

My heart rate notched up. "On your Wyoming ranch?"

He rolled his eyes. "Now, that part they got wrong. It's not a ranch. Right now, it's a giant parcel of land without a house on it. But soon, it'll have a home on it, as well as a recording studio."

"Ahh," I said, starting to see his vision. "And that brings us to the record label."

My sweet Zane looked defiant. "It's time for me to do things my way, Bear."

"Because you believe in fairy tales again?" I wrapped my arms around his waist.

He nodded. "And I really hope..." He blinked, belatedly processing the giant grin on my face. "Wait. You're on board with it?"

I nodded and leaned in to kiss him softly. "Very on board. You're my principal, Zane. Where you go, I go. It's as simple as that."

EPILOGUE
ZANE

Bears may wander far and wide, but they always find their way to a home that feels just right. Black bears, for instance, are known to settle down in cozy dens for winter, often returning to the same spot year after year. Once they find a good place—a safe, warm, familiar haven—they stay. It's a little happily-ever-after of their own, where they can rest, feel safe, and simply be. And maybe that's the real bear dream: to find the place where they're fully accepted, totally at ease, and perfectly at home with their honey by their side.
—Bear Facts for Insomniacs, Episode 143

There was nothing like Christmas in Majestic.

"Waylon, so help me god, if you ask for me to pose for another picture, I'm going to withhold se..." Silas stopped as he remembered Lellie was in the room. "Celestial viewing opportunities."

Way, who hadn't been paying attention to Silas or Lellie, turned to him with furrowed eyebrows. "I don't need your permission to look at the night sky, *husband*. And you'll pose for whatever pictures I ask you to, or else you won't get oral…" He noticed Lellie playing with blocks on the rug. "Hygiene tips. Motherfucker. We suck at this."

Dev shot Way a glare. "I admit it takes some getting used to, but I'll remind you the f-word is also on the naughty list."

"Fuck that," Tully said, plopping a Santa hat on Dev's head before smacking his cheek with a kiss and going to sit by Lellie. "We talked about this, remember? I'm incapable of filtering out the f-word, so we agreed to teach her it was for adults only."

"That's not how toddlers work," Way said with a snicker. "Wait till you get that first letter home from Mrs. Hamrick in kindergarten. Fair warning, she doesn't hold back. Foster said the f-word one day after spending the weekend following a plumber around their house, and Aunt Blake never heard the end of it."

Tully's eyes nearly bugged out. "Kindergarten? That's not for years. We're not…" He put his arm around Lellie's little shoulders and looked at Dev. "We're not sending her there for years, right? Not for many, *many* years."

I felt the warm slide of a hand in mine as Bear took a seat next to me on one of the big sofas. The deep rumble of his laugh helped me release the last of the stress that was still gathered in my shoulders. Earlier this morning, Bear had received a formal apology from King Gerhard, along with an offer of an obscenely large amount of money as compensation for Bear's troubles after everything that had happened with Kasper. Bear had politely refused the money. "I'd like you to donate it to the 'Equality for Ventdestinians Now' campaign," he'd told the king without an ounce of hesitation.

"You know I can't do that officially, Ryan," the king had replied. After a pause, though, he'd added, "But I can promise you the donation will get there under a different name."

This hadn't been exactly what I wanted. I wanted things to change in Ventdestine, and I knew Bear did, too. Ultimately, though, I knew you couldn't force something to change simply because you willed it—just look at what Kasper had attempted to do—and it was more important for the money to get to the organization that needed it so that change could happen soon.

I'd given Bear a nod, and he'd told the king, "And you're okay with that?"

The king had sighed. "It's a small price to pay for what you've been through. I had no idea about Kasper, or I would have stopped him. As much as I've wanted you back on the royal guard, I never wanted you or anyone you care about to feel threatened."

Bear had let out a breath. "I appreciate that, Your Highness."

When the call had ended, I hadn't been able to help myself. "Why didn't you take the money? You could have quit your job!"

Bear had shot me an uncharacteristically large grin. "Who says I didn't already quit my job anyway? You may not know this, but I have a billionaire boyfriend."

And now, it was finally over. Kasper had given us both formal apologies and seemingly sincere ones. The king had revoked Kasper's passport for the foreseeable future and had assured us he wouldn't bother us again. Since Kasper's plan had centered around convincing Bear and Violet that Bear was ineffectual, and Kasper had never been motivated to physically harm Bear or me—he had no history of violence against anyone—I felt confident the threat was over.

And now, I had Bear all to myself.

"I'm torn," I said, moving closer to him to snuggle against his side. There was a large fire in the fireplace, and the lights on the giant Christmas tree twinkled, reflecting off the large wall of windows behind it. Christmas music played softly from hidden speakers while our friends and family chatted and celebrated around us.

"Torn how?" Bear asked.

"On the one hand, I'm happy for you to start the sports program, but on the other, I want you to still be my close protection officer."

Bear put his arm around me, pressing a kiss to the top of my head before moving me the way he wanted over his chest and shoulder.

"I'm still your close protection officer. I just don't work for Violet anymore."

It took me a moment to realize the point I was missing. "Once I'm not under contract with the label anymore, I'm in charge of my own security."

He kissed my hair again. When he spoke, I could hear the grin in his voice. "Exactly. And as the man in charge of security at Fairytale Recording Studio, I've assigned myself the premier role."

"How are you going to juggle the sports program with protecting me?" I asked, playing around with his fingers in the hand I held.

"Easy. You're not leaving my side."

Landry snorted from where he stood gazing out at the snow-covered landscape, nearly invisible under the cover of darkness. "Now you've got him, keep him barefoot and pregnant, Ryan. Atta boy."

Bear's chest rumbled with laughter. "Exactly." He leaned down to whisper in my ear. "I'm hiring help. And we're going to figure it out together, okay? That sound fine?"

I glanced up at him with a grin. "Fine. Super fine. In fact, way better than *fine*."

Bear leaned in to kiss me the way he always did when I said the provoking word.

Kenji spoke up from his spot at the kitchen table behind us, where he was working on his laptop, even though it was Christmas. "Don't listen to Landry. He wouldn't know anything about serious, committed relationships."

Landry glanced at him in surprise. "What the fuck?"

Kenji shrugged. "It's not a bad thing. You're very fun. The world needs fun-loving people."

"You can be fun-loving and committed at the same time," Landry pointed out.

"I'm just saying long-term doesn't seem to be your thing."

"And it's yours?" Landry snapped.

Kenji's nostrils flared, but he didn't respond. Meanwhile, the rest of us seemed to be watching the two of them like a particularly riveting tennis match.

Landry shifted, turning toward Kenji and crossing his long arms in front of his chest. "You talk a big game, but you seem to avoid serious relationships yourself."

Kenji finally looked up and met Landry's eyes. "I've yet to encounter someone worthy of me."

Tension crackled between them as the rest of us held our breath.

Kenji's eyes narrowed before he added, "But don't worry. When I get back from my trip to South America, I'm going to let my grandmother set me up."

Landry lowered his arms and stepped forward as if he was going to approach Kenji, but then he seemed to remember the rest of us were in the room. Instead, he meandered over to sit on a couch next to Rowe and Bash. "Well, good for you. I'm sure her pals in Boca are full up with wealthy, gay asshole grandsons they want to set you up with once you get back from your *cleaning retreat* with your pal *Chaska*."

"Not interested in wealthy, gay assholes," Kenji said, looking back down at his computer with a sniff. "I have enough of those in my life as it is. Why do you think I need this cleansing retreat in the first place?"

Landry sputtered. "Well! Well... *this* wealthy, gay asshole is going to go to Hawaii and fuck every guy there!"

Kenji didn't bother looking up. "You were going to do that anyway."

"Well, now I'm going to do it *harder*," he snapped.

Tully obviously felt the need to break the tension, so he said, "I've only been to Hawaii once on business, but I remember thinking it would be a beautiful place to get married one day."

Dev bolted up out of his seat, paused, and then sat back down again. We all turned to stare. Then he stood up again. "I..."

Tully was sitting on the floor, playing with Lellie. "Babe?"

Dev looked around at us before glancing back at Tully. "I wonder if..." He walked the few steps between the chair he'd been sitting in and the spot on the rug where Tully and Lellie sat.

Then he got down on one knee and pulled something out of his pocket.

A ring.

My sweet, shy friend had decided to finally pop the question to the man he loved, and the rest of us got to watch.

"I wonder if maybe you might want to plan that wedding sooner than later?" Dev asked. "I know that we already planned to spend our lives together, to raise Lellie together and be a family, but... well... I'd like to get married, too. Tully... I'm not great with words, but I know that my life got better the day you came into it, and it's only gotten better and better every day that you've stayed. Will you marry me?"

Tully lurched forward to kiss Dev, clasping his face and kissing him while Lellie giggled and tried to get between them so she could get kisses, too. Tully repeated the word *yes* so many times Lellie started saying it, too, thinking it was a game.

Silas helped himself to a bottle of champagne and had Way pass around champagne glasses for everyone. After offering toasts ranging from heartfelt and sentimental to bawdy and very wrong, Dev gave Tully a sheepish look.

"Now I can finally tell you about the money."

"What money?" Tully asked as the rest of us gasped in shock.

"You never told him about the money?" Silas asked.

"What the fuck?" Bash said.

"Even I know about the money," Bear said, looking a little smug. I'd already explained to him that we weren't technically allowed to tell people about the money until we knew they were our life partners but that I'd already known I could trust him with all my secrets.

Kenji muttered, "Wealthy, gay assholes." Everyone except Landry knew he was just saying those things to piss the hell out of Landry. But it worked.

Landry turned to snap at him. "Well, at least we're done with these fucking confessions now that everyone has a partner. You won't have to suffer through them anymore."

Silas shot a look at Landry. "Not true, Landry. We haven't told your person about the money yet."

Landry's gaze was laser focused on Kenji for a beat before he turned around and returned to looking out the window with his back to the room.

"He already knows."

————

Le gasp! Want Landry and Kenji's story? Click here to pre-order Finding Lord Landry → https://readerlinks.com/l/4426550

And if you want to see what happens when suspicious Boomer goes to Ireland to spy on Bodhi and discovers something completely unexpected, click here → https://readerlinks.com/l/4426525

LETTER FROM LUCY

Dear Reader,

Thank you for reading *Protecting Mr. Fine.*

Special thanks to Jacqueline on Patreon for helping me name Zane's new manager and to Aimee and Kari in my Facebook reader group (Lucy's Lair) for helping me come up with Zane's cousin's name. I love sharing this passion with readers, and getting help from all of you makes my job way more fun.

Up next is Kenji and Landry's story. I know everyone has been excited to see what's going on with these two, so check out *Finding Lord Landry* HERE → https://readerlinks.com/l/4426576

Be sure to follow me on your favorite retailer site to be notified of new releases, and look for me on Facebook for sneak peeks of upcoming stories. You can also join me on Patreon for exclusive content and behind-the-scenes glimpses.

Please take a moment to write a review of *Protecting Mr. Fine.* Reviews can make all the difference in helping a book show up in searches.

Feel free to stop by www.LucyLennox.com and drop me a line or visit me on social media. To see inspiration photographs for all my novels, visit my Pinterest boards. The Pinterest board for *Protecting Mr. Fine* can be found here → https://www.pinterest.com/lucy_len nox/protecting-mr-fine/

Finally, I have a fantastic reader group on Facebook. Join us for exclusive content, early cover reveals, hot pics, and a whole lotta fun. Lucy's Lair can be found here.

Happy reading!
Lucy

ABOUT LUCY LENNOX

Lucy Lennox is the USA Today bestselling author of over fifty gay romance titles including the GoodReads Hall of Fame winner Wilde Love. Born and raised in the southeast USA, she is finally putting good use to that English Lit degree she earned before the turn of the century.

Lucy enjoys naps, pizza, and procrastinating. She stays up way too late each night reading romance because it's simply the best.

For more information and to stay updated about future releases, sales and audio news and to grab some free and bonus reads, please sign up for Lucy's author <u>newsletter</u> on her website at <u>LucyLennox.com</u> or to stay in the know, join her exciting reader group, <u>Lucy's Lair</u> on Facebook.

facebook.com/lucylennoxmm

instagram.com/lucylennoxmm

amazon.com/Lucy-Lennox/e/B01N0IOYPT

bookbub.com/authors/lucy-lennox

patreon.com/lucylennox

pinterest.com/lucy_lennox

ALSO BY LUCY LENNOX

Find me online → https://linktr.ee/LucyLennox

Read my books:

Made Marian Series

Forever Wilde Series

Aster Valley Series

The Billionaire Brotherhood Series

After Oscar Series (with Molly Maddox)

Twist of Fate Series (with Sloane Kennedy)

Licking Thicket Series (with May Archer)

Champion Security Series (with May Archer)

Honeybridge Series (with May Archer)

Find a complete list of my stand alone romances and novellas at www.LucyLennox.com along with audio samples, freebies, suggested reading order, and more!